A LILITH NOVEL

HOLLYWOOD
MONSTERS

HOLLYWOOD MONSTERS

A LILITH NOVEL

DANA FREDSTI

TITAN BOOKS

HOLLYWOOD MONSTERS
Print edition ISBN: 9781785652646
Electronic edition ISBN: 9781785652653

Published by Titan Books
A division of Titan Publishing Group Ltd
144 Southwark Street, London SE1 0UP
www.titanbooks.com

First edition: October 2022
2 4 6 8 10 9 7 5 3 1

Printed and bound by CPI Group (UK) Ltd, Croydon, CR0 4YY.

To my husband, David, and my editor, Steve Saffel. I could not have finished this book without the two of you.

"Competition has been shown to be useful up to a certain point and no further, but cooperation, which is the thing we must strive for today, begins where competition leaves off."
—Franklin D. Roosevelt

"It's hard to beat a person who never gives up."
—Babe Ruth

PROLOGUE

Splashing and laughter emanated from the indoor pool through the archways across the spacious ballroom. French doors opened up onto a marble terrace, a perfect area to allow for spillover when things became too close inside. The doors were propped open by large planters filled with exotic plants, the scent of sage floating in on the night breeze.

Ned DuShane stood and surveyed his party with smug satisfaction, the three folds of his chin curving up into a multidimensional smirk as he watched the cream of Hollywood enjoy his generosity. Screen legends including Fairbanks, Barrymore, Shearer, and DuVal mingled with eager starlets, stuntmen, and struggling scenarioists.

Impossibly handsome bare-chested waiters in studded leather gladiator skirts and Roman sandals navigated the crush along with their female counterparts in flimsy silk togas, serving hors d'oeuvres and drinks.

The décor was a sultan's dream—cobalt blue, purple, and cream tiles with gold accents. Alcoves with silk curtains that could be drawn across the openings to give privacy—or left open if that was what the occupants preferred. Nothing was forbidden at one of Ned DuShane's parties.

Smiling, he popped a rich canape in his mouth, quickly following it with more. Some sort of buttery dough filled with savory mushrooms. Tasty as hell, but it would take platefuls to satisfy his appetite. The smile grew wider.

At first glance most people thought Ned's signature smile denoted warmth. His size—just over five feet, two-hundred-fifty pounds, all of it clothed in an expensive and impeccably tailored suit—worked in his favor, too. Fat men were all like Santa Claus, right? Ho ho ho, gonna bring you presents. *His smile, the comfortable stomach, even the steely twinkle in his eyes made people trust Ned DuShane, making it easy to get his films funded. And he* never *chiseled any of his butter-and-egg men. He reported the profits, made sure the accounting was clean, and gave everyone a good return on their investment.*

Even better, to his mind, Ned's amiable façade—combined with the chance to hobnob with stars of the silver screen, maybe even be in one of his pictures—convinced people to trust him in other ways. Once they found out how wrong they were about him, it was too late to extricate themselves, not without the kind of consequences that drove strong men to eat a bullet.

As a result, even though his studio, Silver Scream, wasn't one of the "Big Five"—or even one of the lesser three—Ned never lacked publicity or distribution for his pictures.

Letting his gaze travel freely around the crowd, Ned skipped over most of his guests to linger on those in whom he had a special interest. A curvy brunette with a heart-shaped face caught his attention. Bettina Gleason. Looked as innocent as a newborn, with huge brown eyes framed by impossibly thick, curly lashes. She was one of Silver Scream's most successful ingenues, exuding innocence and sex-appeal in equal measure. The innocence was an act—Betty wallowed in depravity. The filthier and more degrading the act, the more she begged for it.

She caught him looking at her and ran the tip of her tongue over lush lips painted a cherry red to match her silk dress. Ned nodded, just a slight movement of his chin, but it was enough to make those lips curve up in a smile that promised whatever he wanted. Whatever his friends and financiers wanted.

Bettina would do whatever it took to be a star.

"You throw one hell of a swanky bash, Ned."

A familiar voice, practically oozing with oily charm, sounded next to him. Rudy Angel. A good-looking man in his early thirties, dark hair slicked back as he did his best to emulate the screen-idol whose first name he'd co-opted. A low-rent version at best, with none of the pizazz.

"Rudy, how ya doin'?" Hiding his contempt, Ned clapped a hand on the actor's expensively clad shoulder.

"Hittin' on all eight, Ned," Rudy replied. Lifting his champagne coupe, he admired the sparkling liquid, the slur in his voice revealing that he'd already tipped a few. "This hits the spot. You ever gonna tell me who supplies your hooch?"

"Hey, that's real French champagne," Ned assured him, sidestepping the question.

Rudy laughed. "Sure, it is." He drained his glass and looked around for one of the bare-chested serving boys, his gaze sliding past a nubile blonde girl without interest before alighting on a handsome waiter with a tray of full coupes. "'Scuse me, Ned," he said even as he started across the room toward his target.

Ned was glad to see the back of the two-bit actor. He'd been sampling the rich food for the better part of two hours, and a low rumbling in his gut told him it was time to take a break from his guests. He began making his way through the crowd toward the main hall, where he could slip upstairs, disappear into his suite, and deal with things in privacy.

11

"Señor *DuShane.*" Manuel, one of the groundskeepers, stepped in front of him. He carried, of all things, a flashlight.

"What the hell is it?" Ned didn't bother trying to hide his irritation. Manuel had no business being inside during one of his parties.

"Señor, *there is something you must see. Flooding in the subbasement.*"

"Jesus." Ned shut his eyes, pressing a hand against his forehead. That was where he stored his highly illegal booze. "This can't wait until tomorrow?"

"No, Señor *DuShane. If we wait, the damage could be too much to fix.*"

"So go ahead and fix it."

Manuel shook his head. "It will not be cheap," he warned, "and I wish to have your approval before moving forward."

"Fair enough. Lead the way, José." He chuckled at his rhyme, and if Manuel's brow darkened briefly with a frown, well, he didn't give a shit. For what Ned paid these wetbacks, he could call them whatever he liked.

Heaving a beleaguered sigh, Ned followed Manuel through the throngs of guests—most either drunk on liver-rotting hooch or flying high on cocaine—and through the door leading downstairs to the wine cellar, then down another flight into the mansion's subbasement.

At the bottom of the second flight the gardener hit a switch and a single low-watt lightbulb flickered on above, illuminating a patch of bare cement corridor that stretched into darkness beyond. Construction on the subbasement had only begun in the last month or so, and most of it had yet to be wired for electricity. Manuel turned on his flashlight and shone the beam on the floor as they walked twenty feet or so down the corridor.

"Here, Señor *DuShane.*" Manuel stopped in front of a door leading to one of the rooms. He entered the room first, playing the light over the unfinished brick walls and hardpacked dirt. Water ran down the back wall where the smugglers' hatch was set into the bricks about four feet high, *and dripped from the ceiling to soak into the dirt.*

"How the hell did water leak down here?" Ned asked, as much to himself as his employee.

"This is below the pool, Señor," Manuel said in a deferential tone. "So far it is the only room it has reached, but as you can see, the damage here is very bad."

"Tell me something I don't know. Good thing we already moved the booze out, but still—"

Something smashed into the back of his head.

†

When Ned swam back up to consciousness, he was aware of two things— one, his head hurt like a sonofabitch, and two, his nostrils were filled with the smell of wet, moldy newspapers.

What the hell…?

He tried to move his arms, wriggle his fingers, but they wouldn't cooperate. His neck seemed to currently be the only part of him capable of movement, so he looked down. He was in some sort of barrel, with his arms, legs, and torso encased in some sort of sludge—

Wet cement. His body was submerged up to the neck in wet cement, slowly hardening around him.

He would have screamed if he'd been able. All that came out was a choked wheeze.

"Ah, Señor DuShane, you are awake." Manuel stood in front of him.

"What the…" Ned swallowed, his chest constricting with the effort.

"I know what you are thinking," Manuel said, his tone as neutral as his expression. "That this must be a bad joke. A joke that is not funny."

"Damn straight it's not," Ned snarled. Or tried to—fear and the cement squeezing the breath out of him made it more of a rasp.

"It is not meant to be, Señor. This is about Lupe."

"Lupe…?"

13

"*Your housekeeper.*"

"*Lupe went to Mexico to visit her parents,*" Ned choked out, *fighting to keep the panic out of his voice. Sweat broke out on his brow. Lupe, who'd been particularly beautiful—and uncooperative. She was buried on the property where it butted up against the mountains.*

"*That is impossible,* Señor."

"*How the hell would you know?*"

Manuel's expression didn't change. "*Our family, except for my niece and nephew, are dead.*" *A beat. Then he added,* "*Lupe was my sister.*"

The implications hit Ned hard and fast. The drops of sweat turned into a trickle, dripping steadily down his face, the salt stinging his eyes. Reflexively, he tried to wipe it away, but his arms remained where they were. He tried to think of something to say, some bluff that would buy him time. For the first time in his life, his vaunted silver tongue failed him.

Manuel held up a piece of cloth, and at first Ned thought the man was going to take pity on him. Wipe the sweat out of his eyes, and then pull him out before the cement finished hardening. The groundskeeper just wanted to scare him, that was all, and when he was free again? Well… Ned couldn't give the man back his sister, but he sure as hell could join her on the back acres.

Manuel shook his head. "*You,* Señor *DuShane, are full of shit, and you will remain so.*"

"*What the hell do you—*"

A dirty rag filled his mouth, cutting off his furious words. He could only watch as Manuel reached up for the light string, clicking it off.

Ned tried to scream, to plead, but only muffled grunts made it past the rag. Pausing at the door, Manuel was only a silhouette, framed by the dim lighting. "*Good night,* Señor."

The door shut, leaving the room—and Ned—in total darkness.

Ned felt the coiled knots of his intestines loosen as a stabbing pain knifed his gut. More sweat dripped down his face. Big greasy drops, the kind generated by fear and pain. He had to get out of there before his bowels exploded right then and—

Where would it go if the back door was blocked?

Ned found out, and screamed behind the rag stuffed between his lips.

CHAPTER ONE

VOODOO WARS

EXT. BAYAU – NIGHT

MARIE LAVEAU and PERRINE, both ethereal yet sexual in their
white cotton shifts, face off on opposite sides of the clearing, the
voodoo serviteurs cowering around the perimeter.

> MARIE
> For your treachery, Perrine, I will see you flayed before
> Erzulie and Baron Samedi.

> PERRINE
> (laughs cruelly)
> Like your lover was flayed by Louis?

She flashes a triumphant smile at LOUIS LALAURIE, standing
in the background. Imposing in black dress clothing. Pure evil.

> MARIE
> (quietly, to Louis)
> I will destroy you.

She suddenly whirls around, grabs a torch from the ground. Raises it and it turns into a sword, the blade rippling with blue flames. Louis's eyes widen with surprise and unaccustomed fear as he recognizes Marie's murderous intent.

Before Marie can launch the stroke, however, Perrine seizes a torch of her own and attacks, her torch undergoing the same transformation. Perrine parries Marie's sword just in time, flames crackling up and down the lengths of both blades.

A kickass fight ensues, both women utilizing their physical skills as well as their sorcerous powers. Shooting bolts of energy from their free hands. Invisible spirits raise winds, strike invisible blows. Snakes boil out of the earth.

Marie drops her sword and shoots bolt after bolt of power from her palms, Perrine finally falling to the ground, whimpering in pain and fear as Marie strides forward, standing over her.

PERRINE

Louis, my love, save me!

LOUIS

(lips curling in scorn)

You are neither worthy of my help nor my love. Marie is the only woman who is a true match for me. I have wanted no one else since I first saw her invoke Damballa... the sweat of worship glistening on her skin...

He stares at Marie with open lust.

LOUIS (cont.)

You are mine, voodoo queen.

CLOSE ON PERRINE...

Her expression a combination of betrayal, heartbreak... and the terrible fury of a woman scorned. She and Marie exchange one energy-charged look between them. They don't need words. They both know what needs to happen next.

Both women turn as one to face Louis, rising into the air in a united front. Marie once again wielding her flaming sword as Perrine sends bolts of energy from her hands.

Another kickass fight takes place.

BAYOU EF'TAGEUX
NEAR NEW ORLEANS, LOUISIANA
PRESENT DAY

Dressed in Marie's white chemise and full skirt, doing my best to look both sexy and ethereal—yeah, *you* try it—I picked up one of the "ensorcelled" broadswords that would ripple with flames during each take.

Real flames.

I'll admit I'd had major doubts about this when Cayden Doran, the film's co-producer, co-writer, stunt coordinator, and second unit director—Cayden wears a lot of hats—revealed his plans for *Voodoo Wars*' climatic battle. It had seemed like a bad idea, then and now, shooting in a clearing next to a bayou and waving flammable weapons around all the foliage.

Ideally, for an action sequence this complex and potentially dangerous, we would've been filming it on a studio lot. But no. Devon Manus, the film's director, wanted the authenticity of the bayou, complete with the dilapidated eighteenth-century house in the background. The very *flammable* eighteenth-century house, all weathered with warped gray boards and cobwebs.

Since the climactic fight took place in a torrential downpour, we had a local weather witch with mad skills that were augmented by all the ambient Louisiana humidity. Even so, CGI seemed a wiser choice. Any flames that might withstand the rain would be difficult to put out if anything ignited—like, say, the house… or an extra. Both Cayden and Devon were confident they could handle any mishap. I trusted Cayden more than Devon, but still… playing with fire wouldn't have been my call.

While we waited, the two of them held a quiet powwow behind the main camera setup on the far side of the clearing, near the side of the house. Devon was a well-built man who always looked pleased with himself. Sun-kissed blond hair. Like Cayden, he had the kind of tanned skin that only comes from outdoor activity. Copper-ringed brown eyes. He looked anywhere between thirty and fifty.

In his mid-thirties or thereabouts, Cayden outdid him. He topped the director by about half a foot. Pale blue eyes. Hair a shaggy mane, somewhere between red and auburn. Both men wore light khaki cargo pants tucked into sturdy leather lace-up hunting boots, Cayden in an off-white expedition shirt rolled up at the sleeves to show off muscular forearms, while Devon went with a short-sleeved bush shirt that screamed "crocodile hunter."

This allowed everyone to notice when he flexed his admittedly well-developed biceps.

The testosterone was as stifling as the humidity.

As the extras relaxed, Leandra Marcadet, the curvaceous actress playing Marie Laveau, sauntered off the set, deliberately choosing a path that took her past Cayden. She brushed against him with the casual drive-by attitude of the cat she was, and then headed for the craft service tables. Cayden managed to look smug and indifferent at the same time.

Taking a long pull from a bottle of ice-cold water, I looked around, a wave of sadness washing over me as I realized this was my last day working with the cast and crew of *Voodoo Wars*. I would especially miss Angelique, who played Perrine *and* did her own stunts.

I loved working with her. It's kind of like finding a good dance partner. Some stunt players are competent. Others match you move for move. With steady training, Angelique would someday be as good with weapons as I was—and, not to brag, I'm *damn* good. Her heritage as a feline shapeshifter gave her an athleticism and grace that would take her far. I hoped to get her out to the West Coast and into the Katz stunt crew.

"Are you sure this is safe?" Standing close by, Angelique directed her question to Cayden, a Cajun lilt to her voice.

He nodded. "The spell produces a fire specifically bonded to your weapons. If it touches your hair, clothing... anything that hasn't been spelled, it'll go out." We must have both looked dubious, because Devon walked over and put his arms around our shoulders.

"Ladies, you're *both* too valuable for us to be less than a hundred percent positive about this." Devon was half Irish *gancanagh*—

think sexed-up leprechaun—and half Australian manly man. He tended to favor whichever dialect got him what he wanted at any given moment. This time it was the Irish brogue.

I was surprised he didn't call us "lasses."

"Yeah, but this is the last day of filming," I pointed out.

"Ah, but there are sure to be reshoots," he replied with a grin, "so you can trust me."

I shrugged. "Fair enough."

Cayden muttered some arcane-sounding words and pointed at the swords. The flames licked their way up the blades, but no real heat came from the fire. Pretty damn cool—in addition to his other credits, Cayden also was a sorcerer.

I always preferred working on films where the cast and crew are aware of the weirder things in life. Some folks, when faced with the presence of creatures that have populated the nightmares of mankind for centuries, will shut down completely, end up in therapy for years, or utilize the age-old coping technique of compartmentalizing. It's a lot easier if everyone's reading from the same script.

We ran our choreography, marking it at half speed to make sure it was locked into our brains and bodies before going for a take, and then I asked for one more rehearsal. While I was confident of Angelique's skills, she'd been injured just a few weeks earlier. Thanks to her shifter blood, she'd healed quickly and was ready to rock and roll in less than two weeks.

Even though her injuries wouldn't factor into the stunts, I didn't want to take any chances. Sometimes she had to be dissuaded from overdoing it.

Like Leandra—and all the *serviteur* extras on set—Angelique was part of the Marcadet clan, a family of feline shifters. The

Marcadet lineage had started when a slaver brought a leopard shifter from Africa in the early 1700s, selling him to Antoine Marcadet, a French plantation owner with a reputation for abusing his slaves. After six months, Antoine, his family, and the overseer were found with their throats ripped out. The tracks of what looked to be a pair of large cats led off and vanished into the bayou.

Most of the plantation's slaves had run off, including a young woman from a tribe of indigenous werepanthers from Florida.

The two shifters managed to stay hidden during the subsequent hunt for the missing slaves. The search had ended when most of the slave hunters were found slaughtered at the edge of the swamp. Co-opting the surname of their former "master," the leopard shifter and his mate kept to themselves and raised children, occasionally finding other therianthropes to bring into their clan.

Angelique's clan were a thriving extended family, good-looking and impossibly graceful, with skin tones ranging from "I take my coffee black" to "a splash of coffee in my cream, please."

My skin veered toward the latter, depending on how much sun I got, but I was pretty much in perpetual stealth mode when it came to pinpointing my ethnic background. Thick, wavy, dark brown hair. Full lips, strong cheekbones, straight nose. Eyes so dark a blue, they looked almost black in some lights. I used to think I'd won some sort of genetic lotto, but then I found out my ancestress was Lilith, Mother of Demons, the first woman on earth. This explained how I managed to pass as pretty much any ethnicity—a very handy attribute when it came to stunt doubling.

That was the upside to the family heritage, which came with an obligation to kill the spawn of Lilith while she languished in a hell dimension. No 23andMe results had ever dropped a bombshell as messy.

"Lee, you ready?"

That knocked me out of my thoughts. Mike, one of the two Ginga brothers—aboriginal shifters from Australia—sidled up beside me, grinning and showing a few too many sharp, pearly whites. Dark, weathered skin and curly dark brown hair threaded with blond and bronze highlights from hours in the sun. Eyes an unusual shade of yellowish gold, with pupils that shifted between normal to a reptilian slit, like little eyes of Sauron.

Mike and his twin brother Ike were in charge of the rigging on *Voodoo Wars,* which meant—among other things—they'd been responsible for making me and Angelique rise into the air in a safe, controlled manner while making it look totally kickass. That sequence was in the can, and oh, was I glad. They were really good at their jobs, but it's just that some things really aren't comfortable, and a snug flying harness giving you a wedgie while you're being pulled around by wires is one of them.

CHAPTER TWO

FORD RIDING STABLES

LOS ANGELES, CA

PRESENT DAY

The Ford family was eating dinner when Banjo started barking. Gary Ford looked up in annoyance, a forkful of medium-rare steak halfway to his mouth as their two-year-old German shepherd mix scrabbled at the kitchen door.

"Dammit, dog, what the hell's gotten into you?"

Banjo whined and continued to scratch at the door.

"Probably has to do his business," Rose commented. She was nearest to the door, so she got up to let the dog out, wincing a little as her lower back seized up. She'd taken a fall off one of their friskier horses and the muscles were still unhappy. As soon as she opened the door, Banjo shot out into the backyard and raced toward the fenced-in field, where a dozen large shapes grazed in the darkening twilight.

"Horses are still in the field," she said, shooting a glance at their twin daughters. Deceptively angelic-looking with white-blond hair and long-lashed, cornflower-blue eyes, Claire and Molly were, to put it nicely, a handful.

Heckle and Jeckle were what he and Rose called them. "The Hellions" was the more widely—and less affectionately—known nickname given to Claire and Molly pretty much as soon as they'd figured out how to walk.

"They're just lively," Gary would say in response to any complaints about their behavior.

"So are hellspawn," their neighbor Connie had retorted after the twins had painted their chickens blue. They'd used water-based paint, so there'd been no real harm done, but pointing that out hadn't won Gary or the twins any points.

They were ten years old, strong and healthy and just as full of piss and vinegar as ever. While Rose sometimes wished they'd settle down, she loved her daughters dearly and never wanted them to lose their sense of self, even if she wished it could be less associated with doing mischief.

Oh well, least they weren't mean-spirited.

"Girls, I thought I told you two to bring the horses into their stalls before you came inside." Gary tried to look stern, but his much-vaunted authority stopped short when it came to the twins. They'd had him wrapped around their fingers since birth.

"We thought Luis was bringing them in," Molly replied. Claire nodded and both of them looked innocent as could be. Rose knew better.

"Luis was cleaning out the stalls and oiling the saddles," she said. "I heard your father tell you that, when he asked you to bring the horses in."

"But it's getting dark outside," Molly protested.

"Then you should've done what your father told you to in the first place, shouldn't you?"

The twins exchanged a look. Rose could tell they were trying to figure out how to spin this in their favor. She was half tempted to hear them out—their stories were always entertaining, part of the reason they got away with so damn much—but it was going to be dark soon. The horses needed to be put into their stalls, and the girls needed to learn a lesson.

Besides, they had motion-detector lights that would give them plenty of illumination. It wasn't like they had to go out with flashlights.

"Get a move on, girls," Rose said mildly.

"But, MO-om—" Claire began.

"Now."

Rose's mildness turned to steel in that one word, and the twins immediately got to their feet and headed out the back door. The light above the door clicked on.

Shaking her head, Rose looked at her husband and sighed. He glanced back at her, shamefaced. He started to speak, but she held up a hand.

"Don't bother," she said. "Until you actually lay down the law with those two, I don't want to hear it. But lord help me, one of these days I'd really like to be able to be the good cop."

Gary reached out, covering one of Rose's hands with his own. "I do not deserve a woman like you."

Rose smiled. "Proof that miracles happen."

Gary opened his mouth to reply but a pair of high-pitched screams from outside stopped him short. He listened intently, but there weren't any more cries.

"They're just crying wolf," he said, rolling his eyes in exasperation. "Getting back at us like they did when we made them clean their rooms before they could watch Netflix."

"No doubt," Rose agreed. It was one of their favorite tricks. She took a bite of steak, following it up with a sip of a very good cabernet.

"Mommy!"

The scream ripped through the air, punctuated by barking and the neighing of frightened horses, and was quickly followed by another.

"Daddeeee!"

Rose's heart skipped a beat. Another scream—this time it was Claire, Rose thought—filled with pain and terror. The girls weren't playacting.

"Oh my god."

Jumping to her feet, Rose shoved her chair back so hard that it slammed against the wall. Her back threatened to seize up but she refused to acknowledge the pain. She was out the door, Gary right behind her. Both were nearly knocked over by a stampede of horses thundering past the house, their eyes rolling in panic, hoofbeats thudding on the hard-packed dirt as if chased by the devil himself.

"What the hell!" Gary roared as their livelihood bolted down the driveway leading to the main road, shrill, frightened whinnies trailing behind them.

Another pair of screams sounded somewhere near the paddock gate, accompanied by Banjo's increasingly high-pitched and frantic barking. Then the screams cut off with terrifying abruptness and Banjo's barks reached a fever pitch before stopping, the cessation punctuated by a strangled cry.

"Girls!" Back pain and horses forgotten, Rose sprinted across the yard through the deepening gloom, out of range of the security light.

†

Gary shot one last conflicted glance at the horses vanishing down the driveway, cursed under his breath, and ran after his wife, who was already at the open paddock gate. Another motion-detector light mounted on the gate clicked on as she ran through. In its illumination he could see something moving in the field beyond. Something the size of a small pony, but it didn't look right. It wasn't a horse. Wasn't Banjo. And not the girls. Something… something wrong and out of place.

He stopped in his tracks. Something deep inside, some primordial instinct, told him that death was in that field.

"Rose, wait!"

But she was just another shadow in the gloom, and Gary couldn't bring himself to follow her, even though he knew his wife and daughters were in mortal danger. His legs were frozen in place, heartbeat too fast and too loud, the noise echoing inside his head until it drowned out all else. A pain ripped through his chest and left arm like molten lava.

With a loud grunt of pain, he crumpled to the ground, dead before he even realized he was having a heart attack.

†

Rose heard her husband. Knew something was deeply wrong even as she saw several odd shapes with far too many limbs moving in the middle of the field.

They were huddled over her girls. She saw those limbs handling them, rolling them up and around as swiftly as a sewing machine refilled a bobbin, wrapping something around them that looked like cotton candy threads until they were just vaguely human-shaped bundles.

"Claire! Molly!"

At the sound of her voice, the bundles wriggled and squirmed. One of the shapes paused in its movement and turned in Rose's direction, six ruby-red orbs reflecting in the light.

Oh god.

Rose's eyes widened and her nostrils flared, unconsciously mimicking the panicked horses, as she saw what had her daughters. She almost turned and ran, but her maternal instincts were too strong. Reaching out, she grabbed a rake that had been left leaning against the paddock fence.

Have to have a word with Luis about that, she thought in an absent-minded way. She hefted it like a stave and ran toward the monstrosities that dared to hurt her children.

"Let go of my babies!" she shrieked.

Then something wrapped around her ankles, yanked, and brought her toppling to the ground with no time to catch herself. She hit hard, rake flying off to one side, her chin smashing into the dirt with enough force to break teeth. Blood poured out of her mouth and nose, choking her.

Something stung her in the middle of her back, the pain making her convulse, body arching up and backward into a bow before a merciful numbness spread out from the site of the sting, working as swiftly as Novocain.

†

The security light blinked off as the last hint of sun vanished behind the mountains in back of the ranch.

CHAPTER THREE

True to Cayden's word, the fire didn't ignite anything it wasn't supposed to light.

After Angelique and I finished shooting the voodoo queen showdown, it was time to film the final duel between Laveau and Louis LeLaurie. This consisted of genuine sword-wielding badassery from Laveau, and lots of posturing with magic "jazz hands" on the part of LeLaurie.

Thankfully it didn't involve any more rigging.

Langdon Pinkton-Smythe, an actor for whose face the word "lugubrious" might have been coined, played Louis LeLaurie. He did his own stunts because, like most ghouls, he's extremely durable.

The final two shots of the day consisted first of Marie shoving her sword through Louis's heart, and then his entire body bursting into flames. We had to do the first shot from several different angles, and Langdon took having the ensorcelled flaming steel thrust into his body with remarkable aplomb. Certainly more than I showed every time he screamed and sent carrion-scented ghoul breath into my face. A nice enough fellow—even though his pretentious name unfortunately suited him—but there wasn't a mint strong enough, curiously or otherwise, to blunt his halitosis.

We had to get the shot that would show him actually bursting into flames, but instead of using Nomex and gel, Langdon's wardrobe would be spelled so only his clothing would catch fire. Cayden really did have some amazing skills.

"And... action!"

I drove the blade in, and Langdon's clothes lit up like a torch. He screamed, writhed, and otherwise overacted—exactly what *Voodoo Wars* called for.

"And cut!"

The crew and extras broke into an enthusiastic round of applause. Tikka, the youngest extra at four years of age, ran toward me on chubby legs, changing from human toddler to feline cub as she leapt through the air into my arms. I dropped my sword a millisecond before she hit my chest, needle-sharp claws finding purchase in my chemise and skin. I'm not much for kids, but this butterball was a charmer. Cuddling the fat little feline as she purred, nestling under my chin, I wondered if I could smuggle her home in my luggage.

"Great job!" Devon said with enthusiasm. His gaze fell on Langdon, now clad only in a pair of regrettable European thong underwear. Tall, skinny, and unnaturally pale, the ghoul's body reminded me of a graveyard worm. *So* not a visual I needed.

"Hey," Devon yelled, "someone get a blanket for our villain!"

"Oh, I'm fine," Langdon said. "Ghouls don't need much in the way of warmth." He giggled, his own particular brand of laughter that creeped me out every time I heard it.

We wrapped a little before sunrise. The various departments packed up camera equipment, set dressing, and props. After changing into jeans and a tank top and securing my waist-length mane into a single braid, I helped gather up the swords, a habit ingrained by years of working with the Katz Stunt Crew. Always make sure your weapons are stored away safely, no matter how exhausted you might be at the end of a shoot. Just one of the lessons that Sean Katz—founder of the KSC and the man who'd raised me after my parents' death—drilled into my head since the age of five.

"*Cher*, you were amazing." I turned in time to be enveloped in a heavily scented hug from Leandra. "Just magnificent," she continued with dramatic sincerity. "I am so lucky to have you as my stunt double."

This was quite a change from the reception she'd given me when we first met. Back then, she'd done everything but pee on Cayden to let me know that he was *her* property. Then I'd helped save her cousin, and ever since I'd been part of the family.

Leandra and Angelique, on the other hand, would always get into spats. They were cats. Fur was bound to fly.

"You will be at the wrap party tonight, yes?" She hugged me again, rubbing her face against mine in a show of affection. Her tropical flower perfume tickled my nose, but I fought the impulse to sneeze.

"I wouldn't miss it," I replied, returning the hug.

"See you then, *cher*." With that, Leandra sauntered up the deeply rutted drive that led to the main road. Most of the production vehicles were parked up there, including the town cars that ferried the principal cast to and from Hotel Monteleone in the New Orleans French Quarter.

The plan was to head back to the hotel and get some much-needed rest until the wrap party, which was being held in one of the larger hotel suites. I was all for partying, but even more enticing was the thought of a long soak in my room's large garden tub, followed by a few hours of sleep.

The back of my neck itched, and I gave it an absent-minded scratch. Mosquitoes were plentiful, and they were buzzing around me like I was a buffet. I slapped at one, wincing as it splatted against my shoulder, smearing blood on my bare skin.

Yuck.

"Tikka! Tikka, it's time to go!" Josie, Tikka's mother, looked around for her errant daughter. "Now where did you go?" She turned to an older man. "Jace, did you see where that cub of mine went off to?"

"Just saw her not a minute ago," he replied. "'Round the side of the house there, chasin' something." He pointed toward the side facing the bayou.

"She probably just got distracted by something, chased a mouse under the porch," Josie said. "I swear, that one is more trouble than all the rest of her litter put together." Her tone was indulgent, making it clear she didn't really mind. "Tikka," she called, "I'm gonna leave you here to spend the night by your lonesome if you don't get a move on." No reply, not even a rustle from the bushes. Josie shook her head. "Fine. I know some little kitten who's going to be unhappy when she's sent to bed while the rest of us go to a party tonight."

Turning to one of the other kids—a pretty girl in that awkward stage between childhood and teenage angst—she added, "Lally, go fetch your sister for me, will you?"

"But Mama—" Lally started to whine, but the look in her mother's eyes shut her up. She headed off around the side of the house, calling her sister's name in a put-upon tone perfected by preteens around the world. "Tikka! Tikka, get your tail out here now or I swear, I'm gonna jerk a knot in it!"

Grinning, I leaned against the side of a yellow Humvee—

Cayden's—the only vehicle currently parked near the set. After we'd lost Micah, our former production assistant and chauffeur, the stunt team had commandeered the Hummer as our choice of transportation. Another mosquito buzzed around my head. The back of my neck itched in sympathy.

Little fuckers.

"Lee!" Langdon breezed up to the Humvee. "Heading back to the hotel?"

"Mmmm…" I tried for noncommittal.

"Splendid," he enthused. "We can ride back together."

Stifling a groan, I scrambled to think of a reasonable excuse to take a different vehicle, but my brain wouldn't cooperate. Langdon loved to lecture, and I seemed to have become his chosen beneficiary. Maybe he thought being a stuntwoman meant my education was lacking. Whatever the reason, being stuck in a car with him for more than five minutes was a very special circle of hell.

Plus… ghoul breath.

"Lee!" Mike joined us by the Humvee, Ike following on his heels. "Langdon! You will be riding with us back to the hotel? Delightful! You can sit between me and my brother." Ike grinned, nodding like a bobblehead on coke.

I hid a smile. The Ginga brothers delighted in tormenting Langdon, usually by keeping up a running dialogue so he couldn't get a word in edgewise. The ghoul hastily shook his head.

"No, no, that's quite all right. I believe there's room in the town car. Wouldn't want the two of you to be uncomfortable. I'll just…" He trailed off and hurried up the drive.

"Thank you," I said simply.

"It is my pleasure," Mike replied.

"And mine, as well," Ike echoed. "No one should work as hard as you do and have to put up with that fetid, babbling brook."

What felt like an electrified needle jabbed the back of my neck. "Ow!" I exclaimed, slapping a hand over the spot.

"Mosquito?" Ike said with sympathy. "They are like sharks with wings out here."

"Momma!" Lally poked her head around the side of the house. "Tikka ain't back here."

"'*Isn't*' back there," Josie responded automatically, even as the first hint of worry shadowed her brow. "And I'm sure she is. You just didn't look hard enough."

"I swear I did, Momma!" Lally insisted.

"Go look again."

"But—"

"Now!"

Lally stomped back around the house, the sound clearly audible long after she was out of sight.

"So much for walking softly on little cat feet." Cayden had managed to approach without me noticing, Angelique and Devon behind him. If I hadn't been so tired, I would've jumped.

"*You* seem to have it down," I observed.

"Well-honed survival instincts."

"I see." A jaw-cracking yawn underscored my words.

He grinned. "Ready for a nap, I see."

"Oh, hell yeah."

"Well, you'll be happy to know—"

A bolt of electric fire shot through my neck.

A child's scream, rising to the wail of a frightened cat, ripped through the humid air.

"Lally!"

Josie took off like a shot around the side of the house, Cayden and I hot on her heels. The three of us rounded the corner and dashed into the clearing where we'd filmed. Crouched by the bayou's edge, Lally had shifted partway to her feline form. Skin covered with tawny fur. Slitted pupils in large amber eyes. Fingernails becoming sharp claws. Trembling, fur standing on end, she pointed across the murky water to the opposite shore, thickly lined with cypresses. Her mouth opened, but nothing came out.

"Baby, what is it?" Dropping to her knees, Josie grabbed her daughter by the shoulders. Lally whispered something, too quiet to hear. Josie shook her. "Lally, what did you see? Is it Tikka?" Lally whimpered, and Josie shook her again, harder this time.

"*What did you see?*"

"Nal. Ol' Nal," Lally finally choked out. She pointed across the bayou again. "I saw him. I saw him wadin' through the water. He had her."

"Tikka…?" Josie stared at her older daughter, indescribable horror etched on her features.

"He took her into the swamp! I saw him! Ol' Nal took Tikka!" Lally's rising wail of terror and anguish echoed through the trees.

DUSHANE MANSION

LOS ANGELES, CA

1925

Light streamed in, so bright that it seemed to pierce Ned's eyelids like needles.

"Ahhhh, Christ," he groaned, eyes still closed against the assault. "What the hell?"

As soon as he found out who thought it was a good idea to open the curtains the morning after one of his parties, someone was gonna be out on the street, his footprint on their ass. Last thing his skull-cracker of a headache needed was…

Huh. His head didn't hurt.

In fact, he was surprised at how good he felt. No dry mouth. No headache. No gut-churning nausea. If Ned hadn't known better, he'd have sworn he hadn't drunk anything stronger than water the night before.

Ned opened his eyes, then screamed.

He was face-to-face with a corpse.

His corpse.

Ned was in the subbasement chamber, the one where Manuel had bushwhacked him and left him to die. He stared at his own body, entombed in cement inside a very expensive planter. Mouth stuffed with a filthy rag. His skin was corpse gray. Eyes open.

Christ, he looked awful. What kind of sick bastard condemned a man to die with his own shit clogging up the pipes? Sure, he'd been responsible for more than a few people shuffling off this mortal coil, but those deaths had been quick. At least he thought so. He hadn't actually gotten his own hands dirty, but he'd never told his hired help to make anyone suffer. If they had, well, it was on them.

Taking another good look at his earthly remains, Ned walked around the planter slowly, drinking in the sights—and smells—of his own mortality. It didn't occur to him to question how he could see his corpse in the pitch blackness, or smell rotting flesh.

A sound from above caught his attention. Laughter. People laughing, maybe laughing at him. Drinking his hooch. Eating his food. And he sure hadn't invited them, because he was dead.

"Ain't gonna fly," he growled, striding to the door. Alive or dead, Ned DuShane was a man of action. When he tried to open the door,

however, his hand went through both the handle and the wood. Fine, he thought, and he tried to walk through the door to the corridor on the other side. Then he bounced off it like he was hitting a hard rubber wall. It didn't hurt—could he be hurt in this state?—but panic rose as he realized he was stuck in this cell with his own stinking, rotting corpse. Panic, then anger.

"No fucking way," he muttered. He'd figure this out, the same way he sorted through the tangled threads of film production. Sometimes you needed to coax out all the knots in a particular thread, so that it remained intact. Other times, the threads needed to be cut, ruthlessly, regardless of hurt feelings and burned bridges.

He was going to burn more than a fucking bridge when he got out of here. Casting a disgusted look at the contorted face of his corpse, he settled down to think.

CHAPTER FOUR

Nalusa Falaya. Ol' Nal. A flesh-eater from Choctaw legends. His favorite meal was children. First time I saw him was on the streets of the French Quarter, and he'd been wearing, at least nominally, a human—a tall, dark shape with a wide, hungry grin, but with limbs too long and something unholy lurking underneath, like maggots roiling beneath dead skin.

His aura had afforded me unwanted glimpses of dark appetites. Images of a dilapidated cabin, slimy, black-green moss growing on the floorboards, piles of heartbreakingly small bones in the corners, and other, gorier remnants of its meals lying in heaps on the floor. Flashes of children's faces, eyes round with a fear they should never have been forced to feel. Mouths opened in screams that would never be answered by their mothers. Toddlers and babies, mostly. Ol' Nal preferred his meat young and tender.

And now he had Tikka.

Josie collapsed, unable to process the fact her beloved Tikka had been taken by the bogeyman of the swamps. As far as the Marcadets were concerned, it was a horrific, agonizing death sentence, and there was nothing to be done about it.

Fuck that noise.

"I'm going to get her back." I stared at Cayden as if daring him to try and stop me.

"And I'm going with you," he replied coolly.

"Can we help?" Ike asked.

"We would very much like to help," Mike added.

"Take care of Josie and her family," Cayden said. "Lee and I are gonna need the Hummer, so you'll have to call for another ride to get them home." He shot a glance back at Devon, who, to his credit, had stuck around after this particular shit had hit the fan. "Dev, keep everyone calm, and keep your cell on in case we need you."

Devon nodded, for once devoid of the cockiness that usually defined his personality. Even he hadn't been immune to Tikka's charm. Turning to me, he said, "*Go n-éiri an t-ádh leat.*" Then he added, "Bring her back, *acushla.*"

"I will." And I meant it.

"Let's go," Cayden said.

We headed back to the Humvee, Cayden getting behind the wheel. "Do you have any idea where to find this thing?" he asked as he started the engine.

"No," I replied, "but I think I know someone who does."

†

Cayden drove from our bayou location to the French Quarter in what had to be record time, driving with a skilled disregard for the other vehicles on the road and getting us there in a half hour instead of the usual hour and change.

Automotive and pedestrian traffic was already heavy in the Quarter, but he managed to avoid hitting anything or anyone, although we did get honked at and drew obscene gestures more than once. At my directions he pulled into the red zone on

Toulouse Street, in front of what looked like a closed storefront, and hit the hazard lights.

"It's not even eight o'clock." Cayden raised an eyebrow. "Doesn't look very promising."

"We'll see about that." Hopping out of the Hummer, I went quickly to the front door of Loa Creations, lifted my fist in preparation to knock, and almost fell forward when the door opened before my knuckles made contact.

A slender black woman in her late thirties or thereabouts stood in the doorway. Hair twisted up in an elegant chignon. Fitted charcoal-gray skirt paired with a ruby-red blouse. Heels that made my feet hurt to look at them. Eugenie, the proprietor of Loa Creations.

"Come in, child," she said with a smile, her voice rich and musical. "I've been expecting you."

Why does this not surprise me?

With a little wave at Cayden, I went inside. Eugenie shut the door behind us.

The interior of Loa Creations was part art gallery, part store. The art—most of it related to voodoo and the loas—was displayed on the walls and in short open cabinets. Claret-colored brocade curtains were pulled shut over the windows. I'd hidden in here back when Ol' Nal had sensed my presence and come searching for me—the risk of major collateral damage to the tourists swarming the streets had been too high for me to confront him. A small, bitterly cold part of me wished I'd risked it anyway.

"Tell me how I can help," Eugenie said.

"Ol' Nal," I replied without preamble. "He stole a child this morning out at Bayou Ef'tageux. Took her right out from under her mother's nose."

Eugenie sighed, a deep exhalation that sounded like it hurt. "Now and again," she said in that rich, singsong voice, "Ol' Nal will kill himself a hunter what gets lost in the swamp, just because it's an easy meal. For the most part, though, he preys on the young and helpless. Families that live out there, they've learned to put up protection to keep him out. Too many babies, human and otherwise, have been lost to that devil, damn his black heart."

"I aim to carve it out and get Tikka back."

"There's many folks that'll thank you for it."

"Why hasn't anyone else tried to kill him?"

"Oh, plenty of brave souls have tried, but Nal, he's strong, smart, and fast. You'll have to know how to find his home, and how to get back out alive. He lives deep in the bayou, in his own special pocket of hell."

"Where should I look for him?"

"Bayou Malheur," she replied. "Your friend will know where it is."

"How—" I stopped, not knowing how she knew about Cayden, or how he would know where this bayou was, but I figured some things needed to be taken on faith.

"Once you're there," she continued, "keep an eye out for the Screaming Tree."

"Screaming Tree?" *Seriously?*

She nodded. "You'll know it when you see it. That marks the path to Ol' Nal's home."

"Is there any chance Tikka... the little one... could still be alive?" I stared at Eugenie, willing her to say yes, but she hesitated before answering.

"There's a small chance," she said finally. "Ol' Nal, he likes them seasoned, and fear is the best flavoring for a monster like him."

"That seems to be a staple in evil's diet."

"It is," she agreed. "Fear and pain and hopelessness. So you have to remember, you cling to whatever hope there is, no matter how small it might be. You hold on and follow it like a candleflame in the darkness, and it'll lead you to that child."

"Thank you." I started to leave, but Eugenie placed a hand on my shoulder. I stopped.

"Take these."

I turned back to see Eugenie holding out two gris-gris bags, a *déjà vu* to the first time I'd been in her shop.

"These won't hide you from his eyes, but it'll make it harder for him to sense you, and easier for you to find him. Let you get close before he knows you're there. But watch out for his sentries. Once you find the path to his little pocket of hell, they'll be everywhere."

"This pocket… is it behind the veil?"

"You're already familiar with these places." She gave me an approving smile. "That's good, child. You'll be able to handle the madness you find there—but be careful. If you succeed in killing Ol' Nal, that pocket is going to be mighty quick to collapse in on itself. Before that happens, you want to make sure you, and your friend, and—the loas willing—that little girl, are out."

She gave me a hug, the scents of herbs and spices washing over me, calming my soul and filling me with hope.

†

Cayden got us of the city and into the back country as quickly as he'd ferried us in, thankfully familiar with the back roads skirting the edges of the bayous outside New Orleans. Even though I hadn't had any sleep in almost twenty-four hours, I was wide awake, as wired as if I'd had three Depth Charges loaded with sugar. All I could think about was what would happen if we couldn't find Ol' Nal in time.

"Think we'll make it back in time for the party?" I asked, looking for something to distract myself. "Because if we're late, all the goodwill in the world won't stop Leandra from trying to claw my eyes out." I was only half joking.

Cayden gave a short bark of laughter. "I think she might give you a pass, all things considered." He kept his gaze on the road as he drove, something I appreciated. Nothing worse than someone who insists on meaningful eye contact while driving.

Despite everything, I drifted off for a little while into one of those fugue states between sleep and wakefulness. The images that danced through my head were dark and bloody, so it was with relief—and a sore neck—that I woke up as Cayden turned off onto an asphalt road that hadn't seen repairs in a long damn time. The suspension on the Humvee just laughed at the potholes.

"Bayou Malheur is a few miles off the beaten path," Cayden said as I rubbed my neck. "You feeling something?" He knew about the extra-special familial bond I had with my ancestor's demonic offspring, a bond that made the scar tissue on the back of my neck burn, itch, and otherwise flare up like a bad case of shingles whenever one was nearby.

"No, not like that," I replied. "It's just a stiff neck."

Abruptly, as if the universe was calling me a liar, I felt that all-too-familiar tingle. At the same time my mother's amulet—resting at the base of my throat—began burning my skin with an icy heat. The damaged tissue was like the world's most annoying GPS system.

"Spoke too soon," I said. "We're headed in the right direction."

"Good to know."

If anyone had told me before I came to New Orleans that

I'd be glad to have Cayden Doran along for the ride, I'd have laughed in their face. Our relationship hadn't exactly gotten off to an auspicious start. However, he wasn't the arrogant jerk I'd first met in Los Angeles. Oh, he had his arrogant moments, sure, but there was more to him than that. And if you had a monster to kill in a scary-ass swamp, you couldn't ask for better backup.

Since I'd found out about my... *interesting* ancestral lineage—as in, "may you live in interesting times"—I'd faced off against more than my share of monsters. A Janus demon who'd wanted to absorb me. Davea, shadow demons with the disposition of rabid pit bulls. A bloodthirsty seaweed dragon and, most recently, a sad, lonely, homicidal shambling horror from beyond the stars.

None of them had filled me with the repugnance I felt for Nalusa Falaya, because Ol' Nal preyed on innocent children. This was also the first time I'd set out to track one of the monsters to its lair. All the rest had either found me, or I'd pretty much tripped over them.

The road got narrower, the way turning darker, cypress trees and other swampy foliage hanging down and doing their best to block out the sun. Stray sunbeams broke through the gaps, giving an overall effect of driving through a strobe light. Beautiful but eerie. I rolled down my window and the loud primal grunt of an alligator echoed somewhere off in the distance.

We turned off the "paved" road onto a dirt one, and the sensation on the back of my neck increased to a low-level burn.

"We're definitely headed in the right direction," I said, then added, "Eugenie said to look for the Screaming Tree. Said we'd know it when we saw it."

"Like that?" Cayden nodded toward the right side of the road, up ahead a few dozen yards. I looked.

The tree was hideous, formed less by nature than some malevolent force, or the product of a nightmare. Maybe it had once been a weeping willow, the branches and swags of small, sickly colored leaves drooping as if the horrors they guarded drained all joy out of the world. The bark was somewhere between gray and green. Not the vibrant lush green of the bayous, but the color of something that had died and yet somehow managed to thrive.

It was the face in the trunk that gave the tree its name. Divots in the bark formed half-shut eyes, the hollow below opening in a perpetual scream. No matter how many times I blinked or tried to look at it from a slightly different angle, the face was still there. No way this was a whim of Mother Nature.

No, something else had created it.

The Screaming Tree guarded the way to what couldn't even be called a dirt track. No more than a yard wide, it disappeared into a dark, foreboding tunnel of hanging branches, like the Lover's Lane in so many of the Hook Man urban legends. We'd be walking from this point on.

As if reading my mind, Cayden pulled the SUV as far off the road as possible and shut off the engine.

"You got that big-ass knife of yours?" I asked, keeping my tone as light as I could manage. Maybe if I pretended not to be terrified by what lay at the end of that path, I'd start to believe my own bravery.

Cayden cut me a glance and nodded. "What are you bringing to the party? If it's another spork, I may have to marry you."

I snorted. I'd used a spork against the seaweed dragon. Not fun. "I hate eating with those things, let alone using 'em to fight monsters." Reaching in the back seat, I pulled out one of the hero swords from *Voodoo Wars*.

"You get permission from Props to borrow that?"

"Nope. You gonna report me?"

"Not this time." He reached out and ran a finger along the blade's edge. "It's dull."

"Better than a spork," I retorted. "And you saw what I could do with that."

"Point taken." Without another word, Cayden opened the door and stepped out. I started to follow suit, then paused. Unhooking the clasp holding the chain and amulet around my neck, I tucked the necklace into a neoprene pouch fastened securely around one calf. Only then did I exit the vehicle. I'd almost lost the necklace in a previous fight and wasn't willing to risk it again.

"Should I lock?" I asked.

Giving another of his signature barks of laughter, Cayden shook his head. "Unless gators or water moccasins have learned to drive, I'm not too worried. Besides," he added, brandishing the key, "this thing has a dead switch. You don't have it, you don't start the car." He tucked it into the back pocket of his khakis.

In an attempt to distract myself from the fear racing through my body, I deliberately checked out how well those pants fit his admirable ass. It almost worked, which is a testament to what a great butt Cayden possessed.

The air was thick and heavy. Rotting vegetation with an underlying sweet-sour fleshy decay underneath. No breeze, no sounds, not even the persistent buzz of mosquitoes. I heard something splashing in water a few yards away, but the vegetation was too thick to offer me a glance. It was also just… wrong. Decay. Colors and shapes that made no sense. The Spanish moss hung like cobwebs, and everything had an unhealthy sheen, as if coated with slime.

Yuck.

We set off along the path. My Converse high tops sunk into the mud, squelching with each step. And each step became increasingly difficult to pull out, as if the muck wanted to keep me there. To hold me in place until something could come and plant me permanently.

"Is it just me," I said carefully, "or does it feel like this crap is made of sentient Gorilla Glue?"

"You're not far off the mark."

"Somehow I'm not finding that comforting."

"You shouldn't." Cayden grinned. He had a weird sense of humor. "Just keep moving. You don't want to stand in one place for any length of time. It's not quite sentient enough to reach up and grab you, but if you stop and give it a chance to get your scent, that changes the game."

"Nal *would* live in a gross and skanky place, wouldn't he?" I muttered.

"What did you expect?"

"Just because you're evil, doesn't mean you have to be a slob."

"I'm sure he'll appreciate the housekeeping tips."

Our tepid banter fell flat in the unnaturally still atmosphere. Or maybe we just weren't that funny. Either way, the farther along the path we ventured, the more my hackles raised and the back of my neck burned. If I've been wearing the amulet, it would've been lit up like Frodo's blade.

We weren't in the real world anymore, or at least what most people think of as a real world. This was a strange bubble suspended inside reality, where Ol' Nal could live without fear of discovery. A place where he could retreat after venturing into *our* reality to steal the innocent for his meals.

The path grew narrower, as if trying to fool anyone stupid enough to wander this way that it was going to end any second, convincing them to turn back. The muck beneath our feet became bolder, hungrier. Tree branches snagged our clothing and hair, bringing to mind the forest in *Snow White* before she reached the safety of the Seven Dwarves' home.

An enterprising tangle of twigs dipped into my hair, snagging and snarling in my increasingly loose braid. It stalled me long enough for the ooze beneath my feet to establish a firm grip before I realized what it was doing. The carnivorous mud started nuzzling the exposed skin above my ankle socks, like a disgusting snot monster pretending to be a puppy.

I smacked at the twigs entwined in my hair, getting several puncture wounds in the palm of my hand. The branches seemed to twist so that they held on ever more firmly, stubbornly refusing to give way.

"Son of a bitch!" I swore. The mud moved farther up my shins, making it feel as if I was wearing rapidly drying cement shoes. I had no plans to swim with the fishes, though, or whatever otherworldly equivalent lay beneath the muck.

Holding the sword as if it were a fancy machete, I started whacking away at the underbrush. Arriving at the same idea, Caden used his knife to similar effect. I didn't think it was my imagination when the branches seem to recoil as others were lopped off.

Good. Let the evil Disney trees be afraid.

"Braid or bark?" Cayden inquired, his tone as relaxed as if asking if I preferred red or white wine.

"Bark, please," I replied, appreciating that he'd asked. I liked my hair.

Cayden obliged by grabbing the opportunistic branch and

chopping through it with two quick hacks. The branchlets entrapping me immediately stopped writhing, going all stiff and easy to pluck out of my hair. Grabbing me around my waist, Cayden gave a hard tug, pulling me out of the mud. Miraculously, my shoes stayed on my feet. A fetid smell swept upward from where I had been trapped, and I wasn't sure if I could ever get the stink out of the shoes or jeans. Or skin. I'd worry about that later.

A sense of urgency pressed down on me, as if an internal clock was ticking, speeding up with each passing moment. Time was of the essence if there was to be any hope of retrieving Tikka alive and unharmed. If that didn't happen, I swore inwardly, I was going to make Ol' Nal pay for what he'd done, past and present.

I'd make him suffer for every kill he'd ever made.

The path cinched in until it was no wider than a foot at best. Using our respective blades to hack our way through, Cayden and I finally reached what looked like a dead end. Refusing to give up, I pushed through the twisted foliage dripping with… well, I didn't want to know what, and the path abruptly widened, opening into a clearing with more threatening-looking trees.

It was a yard that looked like something out of *Better Homes and Gardens for Cthulhu*. Weeds grew in scattered clumps. There were flowers of sorts, but even that was too cheerful a description for the bloated, scabrous things that grew there. Meaty purple and red blooms that looked as if someone had sliced open bodies and planted the organs and viscera, which had improbably flourished. The smell that floated up from them was even worse than the odor left by the mud.

"No sane person should ever have to see this," I muttered. I glanced up at Cayden, and saw that unholy gleam in his eyes, the one that told me sanity wasn't an issue.

There was a building on the other side of the clearing, which made the dilapidated house we'd used in *Voodoo Wars* look like a palatial estate. The porch was warped so badly I doubted we could step on it without our feet going through rotted boards. Hellish cypress trees swayed in a half circle around the back and sides of the structure, and pools of murky water lapped gently against bubbling mud. Even as I watched, one of the bubbles rose up higher than the others and burst, releasing a smell that nearly made me vomit.

Moving closer, we saw slime the color of diseased mucus coating the shack, along with a blackish-green mold. Ribbons of sickly-looking moss intermingled with the fungus that clung to the wood. The whole structure looked almost organic, as if it had grown there rather than having been built.

Home sweet home for Nalusa Falaya.

"Is that shack going to try to eat us too?" I asked in an undertone.

"We won't know until we go inside."

"Great," I replied. "Thanks."

We walked through a patch of weeds and immediately I felt something trying to burrow into my leg through the denim of my jeans. Swearing, I grabbed what looked like a foxtail on steroids, yanked it out of the denim before it penetrated skin, and tossed it to the ground. I grabbed a few more that hadn't quite gotten purchase on the fabric, quickly pitching them away, and took care to avoid the clumps.

"I have been to some creepy places and seen some really disgusting things," I observed, "but this is the new number one on my 'never again' list." Then I froze, holding my breath. A sound carried from inside the shack

Something between a child's wail of terror and the scream of a cornered cat.

It cut off abruptly. Before I could leap forward, Cayden grabbed my arm.

"I have your back," he said.

He let go.

"I know," I replied, and I ran.

Almost immediately I felt something grab my shoulder from behind, and heard Cayden's berserker roar, followed by the sound of something that made a squelching, meaty sound as his blade cut into it. The grip loosened, and I sprang for the porch without looking back, not daring to let my feet rest in one place for more than a second at a time.

The rotting boards began to give way beneath me, so I hauled ass like Indiana Jones. My left ankle twisted slightly, nearly plunging that leg through the unforgiving splinters of wood. I felt them stab at me, and pulled my foot out before they could find purchase.

There wasn't a knob or handle on the shack's front door, but I wouldn't have used it anyway. Instead, I launched myself forward, putting all the power of my body into the heel of my right foot as I led with a side kick. The wood didn't so much shatter as collapse inward, the door popping off its frame. It hit the floor, sending clouds of dust and debris pluming into the air.

I stepped inside, my gaze sweeping the interior.

A small rust-stained cage squatted in one corner.

CHAPTER FIVE

Ol' Nal hunkered down by the cage, his impossibly long body folded up like a spider. Seeing it unfold, seeming to elongate even as I watched, was creepy as hell. Even worse was the oversized grin on his face, a grin that widened as it took me in.

Without the human disguise, his teeth, sharp and jagged, stretched out in an unholy, hungry smile. Something fell out of the side of that mouth, plopping onto the ground with a wet, bloody splat. Dark glee shone from his eyes, the whites the same sickly yellow as his nails. The irises were black, with dark drops of blood-red for pupils.

This creature was pure evil.

Oh, I am going to enjoy killing you, I thought.

I felt no ambivalence. No sadness for who or what it might have been. If this thing had ever been human, there was only darkness left.

The creature reached with a long, pus-yellow, talon-tipped finger and poked at the cage's unlucky occupant, giving a little gurgling laugh as if his mouth was filled with blood and saliva. A small figure whimpered, pressed against the back of the cage as far away from Ol' Nal as she could get.

Even in her current form, I recognized her—Tikka, stuck in

mid-transformation between human and feline form. Her legs and feet were the haunches and paws of a cat, bottle-brush tail wrapped around her body. Where her front paws should have been, however, were short, chubby arms and hands. Her eyes had the elliptical pupils of a cat, and fur was starting to sprout on her face, but the rest was human toddler.

Tikka saw me, those cat eyes widening with impossible hope. Her whimpers became cries—part kitten mews, part terrified little girl.

Please don't let me lose this one, I pleaded with any and all deities that might be listening. "It's okay, Tikka," I said aloud, even though I knew I might be lying. "I'm here to take you home."

Nal's smile widened. He looked from me to his prisoner, as if making a decision. Long bony fingers scrabbled at the lock, preparing to open the cage. I didn't have to read minds to know what he was planning. He was going to eat Tikka in front of me.

I didn't think. Picking up the nearest object, a broken wooden chair missing most of its back slats, I hurled it at his head with all my considerable strength. My aim was dead-on, the chair slamming into Nal's skull with a meaty *thunk*.

The noise that emanated from his now-cavernous mouth almost didn't register with the human ear. A wild, wet sound of fury, the kind of liquid growl you don't want to hear when you're standing in front of the creature making it. I had pissed him off, and his attention had turned entirely to me.

Good.

I planned on keeping it that way. Next thing I needed to do, though, was get that cage open, so that no matter what happened to me, Tikka had a chance to escape. Through the door I could still hear Cayden fighting his way across the yard, the sound of his battle rage immensely reassuring. If anyone could get Tikka out of this little piece of hell, it was Cayden.

Ol' Nal rose until he towered above me, his full height too tall for the ceiling, his physical body beginning to dissolve into a roiling black smoke that shrouded his human form. His head kinked to one side, almost as if his neck had a hinge that allowed it to fold like an ironing board. He bobbed grotesquely like a creepy-ass air-dancing Tube Man, and seemed to slip in and out of the shadows, reminding me of the Davea I'd fought.

I'd kicked their demon asses back to the hell that spawned them.

"I'm going to kick yours, too," I growled, squaring off as best I could against something out of an R-rated Tim Burton nightmare. "Let's do this."

Even as the cliché slipped out of my mouth, I gave a startled laugh, then gripped the handle of my sword. Not too tightly, but with deceptively casual confidence. I dropped down into a low *en garde*, knees bent but not overextended, one leg behind the other with both feet facing forward.

Ol' Nal strode toward me, those impossibly long legs eating up the space in an instant as it lifted its arms above its head—just like any good Red Shirt.

I smiled. Guess the hard part had been getting into Ol' Nal's shack.

Before I had a chance to congratulate myself, though, one of his arms reached over my head and down behind me. He smacked me in the back with enough force to send me stumbling forward, sword shooting out of my hand. Nal leaned in, mouth gaping wide, not averse to a more mature meal every now and again.

Instinctively I ducked and rolled, feeling the wind as he swiped at me, talons barely missing my back. Turning, he maneuvered in the tight space with unnatural ease. Roaring, he reached for me again as I made a running dive to the other side of the room. This time I landed right next to the cage, fumbled with the latch, and flung the door wide open.

Springing out of the cage as if propelled by a cannon, Tikka finished the transformation into her feline form, claws skittering on the wooden flooring as she bounded past. Nal saw her, mouth opening impossibly wider as he changed direction to intercept her. Giving another wail, she skidded to a halt and leapt into the air, this time landing against me, clinging to my chest and left shoulder with all four paws. Needle-sharp claws dug in.

Well, hell.

This was going to make things difficult, but I couldn't risk putting her down—Nal would scoop her up and swallow her whole. Breathing deeply, I centered myself, feeling Tikka's heartbeat jackrabbiting in her chest. She burrowed her head into my neck, and I didn't have to tell her to hold on. Nothing short of pliers could've pulled her off.

Nal edged toward us, slowly this time, knowing he had his prey backed into a corner. He raised those long arms and chuckled, the stench of fear and blood and rot carried on his breath. Suddenly, Langdon didn't seem so bad.

Waiting until the last possible second, I leapt sideways in a parkour-like maneuver, launching off the spongy wall with both feet and using my right arm to pave the way for an awkward yet serviceable shoulder roll. Doing my best to protect my little passenger, I hit the ground, rolled, and then threw myself the remaining distance, sliding on my right side as if going for home plate.

Instead of home base, however, the goal was my sword, and I reached it before that fucker could tag me out.

Sports metaphor for the win.

Still part flesh, part smoke, Nal snatched at me. As he did, my fingers wrapped around the handle, the blade thrumming in my hand as I half sat up and swung. Putting as much strength as I could into it despite the awkward angle.

It was enough.

The edge sliced through Nal's right wrist, a hideous hand dropping to the floor and twitching there like a dying spider. He roared again, this time in raw fury laced with pain.

"Hold onto my neck, baby," I said. Tikka did as I asked, which freed up my left hand to push off the floor so I could scramble to my feet. More importantly, I could use a two-handed grip on my sword.

Not one to waste an opportunity, Nal grabbed for Tikka with his left hand, even as black ichor dripped from the stump of his right wrist. He clawed at her, trying to peel her off me. She snarled and spat, but he managed to dislodge one of her paws. I needed distance to give me enough room to swing, but if I backed away, I might lose her.

So instead of stepping back and going for a double-handed cut, I ducked under Nal's arm and dragged the edge of the blade across his torso, feeling the flesh part like Jell-O. It might be dull, but my sword wanted this motherfucker dead, possibly as much as I did. Then I pivoted back around and cut down across his left arm, fueling my strength with a battle cry that came from deep inside me, tearing my throat raw as I let it out.

Nal's fingers lost their grip on Tikka, all four of her paws once again latching onto me so I could safely step back. I did so, then plunged the sword point through his black, flesh-eating heart.

The resulting shriek echoed off the walls of the shack, which seemed to shrink away from the sound. Not taking any chances, I sunk the blade in farther, twisting and turning it until I turned his innards into demon sashimi. Ol' Nal collapsed on the floor, the length of him shriveling up and then settling back into the husk of rank darkness that was his skin.

I stood there for a moment, clutching the sword with one hand, cradling Tikka with the other as she growled and hissed and spat at the thing on the floor. I rubbed my fingers through her fur, trying to let her know that things really *were* okay. Or at least they would be, once we got the hell out of there.

The walls of the shack started to sag, the floor buckling under my feet as whatever dark sorcery had been holding it up died with its tenant. I stumbled, then regained my footing and bolted for the doorway.

Which was now once again blocked by a closed door.

What the hell?

I'd kicked that door off its hinges, but it was back on the doorframe, blocking our way as if the place wanted to take us with it. Strange shapes, impossible to identify in the shadows, poked up through the floorboards. Writhing, grasping, accompanied by a bubbling, knocking noise like a clogged Jacuzzi. The floorboards started breaking apart, some of them lurching up as if shoved from beneath. Geysers of what looked—and smelled—like decades-worth of blood, rotted flesh, and bones shot up through the gaps. Looking down, I saw a large greasy-looking bubble rise, bursting to let out more of the now unbearable stench.

There was little more than six inches of floor left in front of the door. I'd somehow have to land there, not lose my balance with my little passenger, and open the door. Which swung in, not out.

I *so* didn't want to find out what was beneath the shack, although I thought I knew. So many victims, so many years of anguish and terror. Did they know I had killed the monster that had eaten them? Or would they try to drag me and Tikka down to join them, purely out of spite? The thought of even touching the bubbling goo made me want to vomit.

We had to get out.

Taking a deep breath, I prepared to jump.

The door burst open, flying off with what I swore was a scream of rage as it fell again with a muted clatter on the rapidly disintegrating floor. Dripping with even more foul-smelling liquid and viscera than me, Cayden stood there, holding the knife in one hand. He looked like he'd been gardening in hell, green strands clinging to the blade, handle, his hand and wrist.

We stared at each other for a fraction of a second. Then he held out his hand.

"Jump."

Without hesitation, I jumped. He grabbed my wrist, pulling us out of the shack and down off the porch. We rolled, but Tikka didn't let loose, her claws digging through cloth and into flesh. Gritting my teeth, I rose slowly and looked around.

Outside was a slaughterhouse, the meaty flowers and plants strewn about where they'd been ripped out of the ground. I started laughing, couldn't help it.

"It'll be a new reality show," I choked out between laughter. "Hell's Gardens. You'll be the landscaping version of Gordon Ramsey."

Cayden let out another bark of laughter, and then went serious. "This is going to go south damned fast," he said. As if to punctuate what he said, a branch broke off a tree with a *crack* like a gunshot. "We need to get the hell out of here before we lose our way back. You want me to take the kid?"

I shook my head. "No. I've got her." Besides, I thought, it would take more time than we had to unstick all the little claws.

If there was any fight left in the things that guarded Ol' Nal's lair, it wasn't apparent. Plants and trees wilted on all sides, some of the large ones leaning dangerously, and even the mud seemed to have lost its predatory hunger. The path out of the veil was visibly shrinking, and several times I thought we'd lost it. Finally, we emerged by the Screaming Tree with little time to spare. Foliage grew over the entrance to the path, obscuring it from sight.

Then the tree was a moss-covered oak like any other.

Inside the Hummer the air was close and hot, and we did our best to ignore the odors rising from our clothes. Switching on the engine, Cayden cranked up the air conditioner and handed me a bottle of water, which I opened and held in front of Tikka. She was still clinging to me like a clip-on koala.

"Have some of this," I said gently. "You're safe now. You and I kicked that monster's ass, and now it's dead."

Slowly, the cub's heart rate slowed down to something reasonably normal. Fur melted back into her skin, ears reshaping, paws becoming chubby hands, until I held a filthy little girl in rags that were all that remained of her white shift. She curled her fingers around the plastic bottle, tipped it back, and drank, then nestled up against me and purred.

I shut my eyes, tears burning paths through the muck on my cheeks. She was going to be okay.

Cayden reached out and ruffled Tikka's hair. He looked at me. "You okay?"

"What?" I sniffed. "I'm not crying. *You're* crying."

DUSHANE MANSION

LOS ANGELES, CA

1925

Ned wasn't sure how much time had passed. Maybe an hour or a week or a year. Maybe more than that—there was no way of knowing.

The party was over—the noises above had long since faded away. What he didn't understand was why no one had found his remains. When someone vanished, didn't the authorities search the property with the proverbial fine-toothed comb? So why the hell didn't the buttons and private dicks turn his house inside out?

Heaving a sigh of frustration with no actual respiration involved, Ned sat on the floor, back up against the planter, and stared at the door. The big wooden door with iron fittings that he'd loved because it looked like it belonged in a medieval dungeon. Sure, Manuel probably bolted it from the other side, but that shouldn't stop the intrepid boys in blue, right? He'd paid off enough of 'em to do their jobs, especially when the job was finding his body.

How much money had he spent to line the LAPD's chief of police's pocket? He'd always gotten a charge from wielding power over others. It energized him in ways that all the toot in the world couldn't accomplish.

Then something had shifted when he'd stepped foot onto the land where he built his mansion. Something had... intensified. He could feel power in the ground under his feet. His secretary had asked a stupid question and Ned remembered the anger. He had slapped her—nothing hard, just a quick flick across the cheek to remind her not to waste his time—and electricity had coursed through his veins, raising the hair on the back of his arms and neck. It had cycled through him and then back into the ground, almost as if the land was feeding off the charge that had jolted him.

He'd made the realtor an offer on the spot. Who gave a fuck if it was in Outer Mongolia? People would still come to his parties. He was Ned DuShane, after all.

And he'd been right.

His parties had been, if anything, more popular than before, when he'd lived off Sunset Boulevard. Friends and colleagues who shared his particular tastes appreciated a place that was off the beaten track and had the benefit of privacy. As a bonus, the amount of isolated acreage made it easy to dispose of indiscretions.

Frustration curdled in his nonexistent veins. If not for that wetback of a gardener, he'd still be laughing it up, drinking top-shelf whiskey, tossing back rich canapes, and continuing his climb up the ladder of Hollywood.

Now? The passage of time wasn't something he could calculate. No sunrise, no sunset. No appetite to let him know when it was mealtime. That was one of the things that bothered him the most, having the joys of food and drink taken away. He'd been a gourmand, for the love of Pete.

If he ever got his mitts on Manuel, he'd rip his head off and shit down his neck.

What mitts? Hell, he couldn't even open a damn door. The more he thought about it, the more steamed he got. What the hell could he do, even if he did run across that cocksucker again? Zilch.

The heat of his fury spiraled up from the ground. Caught up in his rage, he pictured the energy whirling around like some sort of tornado, spinning up through the soles of his feet and bursting out the top of his head.

A thumping noise caught his attention.

What the…?

Impossibly, the planter wobbled back and forth on its base. Even as he watched, the thing lurched a good foot across the hard-packed dirt, then stopped as suddenly as it'd started.

Huh. Ain't that a thing?

Ned settled back down, curiosity taking the place of rage as he examined the evidence before him. It would've taken a strong man to move it when it was empty, and filled as it was with cement and whatever was left of his considerable bulk, Ned estimated it would take at least three, maybe four to budge the damn thing.

So what had moved it?

The more he thought about it, the more he knew deep in his gut that he had done it. *That somehow, the force of his rage had caused the planter to move—and if he could make something that heavy wobble across the floor, what else could he do if properly motivated?*

He mulled over the possibilities.

"Okay then."

†

At first he'd had to whip himself up into a rage-filled frenzy. Not a problem—all he had to do was picture Manuel's face as he'd stuffed the dirty rag into Ned's mouth before leaving him in the dark to die.

But Ned didn't want to spend his afterlife in a lather. He'd always prided himself on staying calm under pressure—it was all about control, after all. So, he experimented, and soon discovered that whether it was Manuel's death or someone else's, it didn't really matter. It all had the same effect.

He tried dwelling on various cruelties he'd inflicted on others during his life. That did the trick. Strong emotions—especially those that came from wielding power over others—were the key. The more vivid the memory, the more he felt the twister. Before long he was storing the energy, stopping it before it could recede back into the ground.

So… what next?

Ned glanced at the planter containing his corpse. It had jittered and shifted over the room dozens of times, and his head, lolling side-to-side, rotting on the stem like a particularly ugly flower, started to bother him. And more than that.

Damn it, he wanted a glass of scotch. Single malt. He wasn't thirsty—or hungry, for that matter—but he still craved the things he'd loved while alive. If he could see and smell his own corpse, if he could feel the planter behind him, why couldn't he have—

The fuck?

There was a glint of ice in a crystal tumbler, surrounded by an amber-colored liquid. Sitting on the cement next to his rotting head.

He reached out, then stopped. If this was hell, his hand would go right through it.

The hell with it. Hesitating had never gotten him anything when he was alive, so he reached out and grabbed the glass. Felt the cool moisture on his fingers. Lifted it to his mouth and took a sip, reveling in the pleasant burn of the scotch, the peaty, smokey flavor as it coursed down his throat.

Definitely not hell.

And if he could taste the scotch, maybe he could open the door.

Fuck it. Nothing to lose, and everything to gain.

Facing the door, he focused. Remembering. Pictured the housekeeper Maria—Manuel's sister—and what he'd done to her before he'd decided it was time for her to disappear.

Ned approached the door... and went through it. There was a slight resistance, as if pushing through some sort of membrane, and then he was out the other side, standing in the corridor.

For the first time since he'd died, Ned DuShane smiled.

CHAPTER SIX

My 9:20 A.M. plane to LAX boarded on time. I'd no sooner settled into my comfy seat than a cute nerdy flight attendant brought me a glass of complementary champagne, assuring me in a rich southern accent that there was plenty more where that came from. Given half the chance, I could get used to flying first class.

After a seriously hot shower, I'd stayed up into the wee hours of the morning, partying with the cast and crew of *Voodoo Wars*. Dancing, drinking, and saying my goodbyes to everyone. A large portion of the festivities had been spent with Tikka in her feline form draped around my shoulders like a stole.

Cayden and I didn't dance with each other, partly because I wanted to leave on good terms with Leandra, and because finding and saving Tikka had been better—in a weird way, more intimate—than any dance could have been. Besides, he basically lived up the hill from me in Los Angeles, so we'd run into each other again.

I fell asleep pretty quickly into the flight. No doubt the two glasses of extremely good champagne helped the process. Unfortunately, the booze also woke me up a couple of hours later with an urgent need to pee.

Lurching out of my seat, still bleary-eyed and fuzz-brained from sleep and bubbly, I made my way to the restroom at the front of the plane. Just my luck, someone was already in there. I turned and looked across the aisle. Although I didn't remember there being two bathrooms, there was another one, and it was vacant. I opened the door…

…and found myself staring into dark nothingness, wind rushing around my hair, threatening to suck me out of the plane and hurl me into the void. Far below, so far I couldn't even imagine how many miles down it was, I saw a faint glow of red flickering against the darkness.

Shit.

"Lee."

That dark seductive voice. I knew if I turned around, he would be there, the faceless man who had been haunting my dreams for months. Hatred and lust ever present in equal parts. Always standing on the edge of some Peter-Jackson-esque death drop. Always faced with the choice of letting him have me or throwing myself over the edge.

A hand fell on my shoulder. Burning my flesh, the heat causing unbearable pain—and pleasure—through my body.

I screamed and hurled myself into the void.

†

"Miss? Miss, are you okay?"

My eyelids flew open and I found myself staring at one of the flight attendants, the same nice man who brought me my champagne.

"Yeah… Yeah, I'm fine," I managed to get out. "Just your run-of-the-mill nightmare." I also summoned up a smile, which must have been genuine enough to reassure him that he didn't have a crazy lady on his hands, because he smiled, looked relieved, and went about his business.

Dammit, I still had to pee. This time, though, when I opened the bathroom door—the *only* one in first class—all the walls were in place.

This better not *be another nightmare*, I thought darkly as I locked the door behind me.

†

After the relentless heat and humidity in Louisiana, the eighty-degree temperature when I stepped outside at LAX seemed downright temperate. Instead of moisture-laden clouds, a few cotton-candy wisps decorated the sky. As much as I'd miss New Orleans, it was good to be back home in Southern California.

I'd deliberately kept my arrival time to myself, deciding to spring for a Lyft instead of arranging for a pick-up, because I figured having some solitary time would help me reacclimate. I wasn't up to my Uncle Sean's concerned queries, his son Seth's interrogation about whether or not I'd slept with Cayden, or Randy's butt-hurt feelings about the way things had been when I'd taken the job. Like Seth and Sean, Randy was not a fan of Cayden.

All things considered, a nice anonymous Lyft driver who'd leave me to my thoughts seemed just the ticket.

A silver and suitably eco-friendly Prius pulled up to the curb, a Lyft sticker in the rear window and bearing the vanity plate "Britbond." I checked my phone. Yup, this was my ride.

The driver hopped out, a middle-aged man clad in a shiny fuchsia vest over an equally shiny black shirt and white pants that looked uncomfortably tight. He wore his dyed black hair long, under a pork-pie hat too small for a face as round as a pumpkin.

"Milo at your service, lass," he said in a pseudo-British accent.

"Shall we put your bag in the boot?"

"The…"

"The boot," he repeated with an annoyingly self-aware little laugh. "Oh, of course, most Yanks don't understand my British-isms."

I could've just given it to him, but I was tired and cranky.

"You're British?" I smiled sweetly. "I never would've guessed. And yes, please, in the trunk."

"Ah… oh… well then." He grabbed my monster suitcase's handle, hefting it with visible effort into the trunk as I got into the back and settled in for a quiet, peaceful ride home. Milo climbed back into the driver's seat with an audible huff.

"Traffic's a bit of a sticky wicket, but I'll have you home before you can say 'Bob's your uncle.'"

Did he really just say "sticky wicket" and "Bob's your uncle" in the same sentence?

Pulling out into the flow of airport traffic, he continued, "As I'm sure you may surmise, I am an actor." He beamed at me from the rearview mirror like a child expecting praise.

It was going to be a very long trip home.

†

The man would *not* shut up.

He regaled me with stories of auditions—"near misses, all"—and countless extras gigs where he *almost* was chosen to be a featured extra. Or missed out by *one camera frame* on standing behind the lead actor. The highlight—or lowlight, as it were—was the recitation of an audition he'd done earlier that day, reading, of all things, from *Winnie the Pooh*.

Please stop talking.

He didn't.

I shut my eyes and settled back against the seat—if my choices were listening to him or risking another nightmare, then bring on the bad dreams. At least they were sexy.

†

"Here you are, lass."

I opened my eyes as the Prius rolled to a gentle halt at the top of the Ranch's driveway in front of the sprawling Craftsman-style house. I'd taken a very satisfying catnap and considered suggesting to Milo that he start a podcast to help people with insomnia. Instead, I got out of the car while he got my suitcase from the trunk and set it on the ground. Shielding his eyes from the sun, he looked around as if searching for something.

"This is pretty far out," Milo said. "Isn't the old DuShane mansion somewhere in this neck of the woods?"

I nodded.

"Ah, capital! I've always wanted to take a look at it."

"If you turn right instead of left at the end of our drive and head up the hill, you'll pretty much run into it."

With a jaunty, "Thank you, lass," Milo got back into his Prius and drove away.

Sean's Xterra was nowhere to be seen, which meant he and his son Seth were probably on the set of *Spasm*—the sequel to *Twitch*, and one of the stupidest young adult series ever to achieve success in the wake of the vastly superior *Hunger Games*.

Part of me was still pissed-off that Sean hadn't seen fit to hire me for the films. Ever since my near-fatal accident taking a high fall, he'd been massively overprotective. So I was mainly relieved they weren't home. I needed a chance to decompress.

Pausing in the drive, I looked around. This was where I'd lived since I was six. Instead of swing-sets and jungle gyms, my playground had consisted of a Russian swing, trampolines, a sixty-foot-high fall tower, crash mats, and lots of space to swing swords and punches during fight training. Instead of growing up in Venice Beach—where my screenwriter parents had lived before they'd been murdered by a demon—I'd been raised around the ever-shifting pack of stuntmen that made up the Katz Stunt Team.

Human and supernatural. Male, female, and undeclared. Sean didn't care, as long as they possessed raw talent, had the commitment it took to hone it, and—most importantly—were team players. If you couldn't take criticism and play well with others, you had no place here.

As usual, the front door was unlocked. There were wards up, so if someone wasn't welcome at the Ranch, they became *very* uncomfortable when they stepped onto the property, and invariably turned tail before getting halfway up the drive. I'd asked Sean if he'd put up the wards and he just replied, *"I had some help."*

Walking inside, the sound of my suitcase wheels rolling on the chocolate-colored tiles in the entryway, I sighed in contentment.

It was good to be home.

A huge sunken living room with buttery-soft leather furniture, including an L-shaped couch that took up most of the space in front of the picture window. Huge stone fireplace on the wall opposite the entryway, framed photos on the mantel and hanging above it. Plush sheepskin throws scattered around. Growing up, I'd spent many hours in front of the fireplace, reading while stretched out on those cozy throws.

My gaze fell on a photo of me, Sean, and Seth taken a few years ago on a film set, the three of us wearing fantasy-type armor and standing in front of the façade of a castle. I smiled at the good memories.

My smile faded as my glance shifted to a photo of a tall, stern-looking man with a vague resemblance to Sean. Uncle Sam, Sean's older brother. He preferred to go by Samuel, but Sam was a lot easier for a five-year-old to say and I'd never bothered to change it. He'd treated me like an inconvenience when he visited, always trying to tell me what to do. The more he told me how I should behave, the less inclined I was to listen, and our relationship didn't improve with age.

Luckily, he didn't visit very often. The last time he'd graced us with his presence had been at least five years ago.

Everything was neat-as-a-pin orderly, which told me Seth had been home at some point recently, and long enough to clean. Inspired by the surroundings, I went right to my room, threw my suitcase on the bed, and unpacked. Then I took a long, hot shower in the front bathroom, the one with the nicest shower, secure in the knowledge that I wouldn't be interrupted. Drift, for example, one of the long-time regulars on the crew, knocking frantically and telling me he was gonna explode if he didn't get in there *right away*.

God forbid he used one of the other three bathrooms.

After my shower, I wrapped myself in a cozy flannel robe, shoved my feet into fleece-lined slippers, and decided to make some coffee. The kitchen was Seth's domain and he kept it particularly immaculate. Sparkling counters. Burnished copper pots hanging on hooks. Cast-iron pans so clean you'd swear they'd never been used. And *ooh*, it looked like Seth had gotten himself a new toy—some sort of "must take master classes before operating" espresso machine. It was a thing of beauty, taking up a third of the long counter next to the fridge.

I wasn't going to touch it.

Instead, I grabbed the smallest of three French presses, ground up some single-origin beans from Costa Rica that had been roasted two days prior. I knew this because Seth kept the coffee beans in individual canisters, all of them labeled with the date they were roasted. There was a hint of OCD in Katz the younger. Then I brewed myself a very fine batch of java, splashing in some cream even though Seth insisted that cream ruined the "integrity of the coffee."

Depending on our respective moods, Seth was the occasional bane of my existence. I preferred to think that I irritated him as much as he did me, but I'd done the metaphorical Jan Brady run up the stairs far more often than he had. It hadn't happened much since my teenage years, but every now and again a strategic retreat was preferable—and more mature—than thwacking him with whatever object happened to be handy.

Mug in hand, I went outside onto the wraparound porch, heading to the west side of the house where two rocking chairs and a little table stood. Setting my coffee on the rickety table, I settled into my chair—the one with an indentation in the cushion that was the exact shape of my butt. Looking out over the Santa Monica mountains, the perimeter of the Ranch's three acres marked by weathered gray fencing, I gave another happy sigh.

Growing up here, I hadn't had a lot of time to myself, and this was the one spot other than my bedroom where I was usually assured privacy. Now and again Sean would join me and the two of us would talk or enjoy a comfortable silence. There hadn't been much of the latter, though, since I learned the truth about my family history. It was hard to be comfortable, finding out that the person you'd loved and trusted most of your life had been lying for years. A lifetime of trust had taken a hefty kick in the teeth, and things weren't gonna go back to normal for a while.

If ever.

It's funny how emotions work. I mean, I understood why Sean waited to tell me. My family geas spanned centuries, and it was pretty fucked-up. If I put on my Mr. Spock cap, I had to agree with him. My inner Dr. McCoy, however, still thought it sucked. Still, I hoped that given enough time, the rift could be repaired.

At least he'd never lied to me about Santa Claus.

Seth, on the other hand... Back when I was still young and impressionable, he'd convinced me that Krampus was going to stuff me in his bag along with all the other bad kids and drag me off to be eaten. The rat bastard had waited until I'd gotten up in the middle of the night to use the bathroom and had ambushed me on my way back to bed, throwing a mildew-scented potato sack over my head. My screams woke Sean and earned Seth a major grounding.

Smiling at the memory, I took another sip of coffee. Seth could still be a rat bastard at times, but damn, he knew his coffee. He was wrong about the cream, though. It made the rich chocolatey caramel flavor even more decadent.

I rocked back and forth, perfectly content within the moment. There was a crisp coolness in the air that signaled autumn. The sun was still high enough over the mountains to afford plenty of light. The land around the ranch was lit by a soft rosy glow, with sage brush, anise, and eucalyptus casting their scents over the valley. A part of Los Angeles unappreciated by the countless hordes of people who thought LA began and ended with the Sunset Strip and Rodeo Drive.

Movement at the inner edge of the fence caught my eye. Two goats huddled up against a eucalyptus tree, nibbling on the sparse grass and weeds. And was that a jackrabbit? I squinted, shielding my eyes from the late afternoon glare. No, it was *five* jackrabbits. There were more birds in the trees than normal, a mix of crows, ravens, sparrows, blackbirds, robins, and ones I didn't recognize.

Huh. Maybe Sean or Seth had set up feeders during my absence. Whatever the reason, I kind of liked the Disneyesque vibe the animals gave the place. Although the birds would just as soon poop on me as sit on my shoulder and chirp.

My gaze fell on the DuShane mansion, hunkered against the base of the mountains about a mile away. Unoccupied for years, it looked like the love child of a Gothic castle and a Moroccan pleasure palace—extravagantly, awesomely tacky. Decades of Santa Ana winds and weather had long since taken the shine off the place, but it must have been quite the spectacle back in the day.

Built in the early 1920s by a maverick film producer, the mansion had seen some amazing parties, and was home to some of Hollywood's most gruesome legends. It was the kind of place that kids dared each other to sneak inside, bring back a souvenir, or spend the night. The kind of stupid dare that could get someone killed or traumatized for life.

It was also the perfect place for horny teenagers to hang out, get drunk, and flex their overactive hormones. There hadn't been a groundskeeper for more than a decade, and if one was willing to scale the foreboding ten-foot-tall wrought-iron entry gates and equally high cement wall topped with wicked iron spikes, the odds of being disturbed were slim to none.

Thick chains with an industrial strength padlock secured the double gates, but the chains weren't drawn tight, and there was a gap kids could squeeze through. Rumor had it there was a section of wall at the back of the property where the cement had crumbled away, the hole hidden by an overgrowth of ivy.

It wasn't the make-out spot it might have been, however, because people really *did* die there. After DuShane had vanished, or more likely split town just ahead of the law, subsequent owners had either vacated quickly or met gruesome ends.

Some pretty shady rumors had circulated back in the day, and they'd been embellished over the years. That DuShane had built his mansion this far out in the boonies lent credence to the rumors, at least in my opinion. Still, he'd been one of the power players in Hollywood, and the studio system had maintained a much tighter grip on the reputations of their stars. With the Internet and #metoo movement still decades away, a lot of unsavory things had remained hidden.

A shiver went through me, for no apparent reason. Not cold, just suddenly uneasy. Staring up at the mansion, I thought about its current owner—Cayden. He'd bought it just a few months ago, and was still very much alive. About the same time he'd purchased the place, I'd had a waking dream while sitting in this very spot—the first time Scary Sexy Dude had made an appearance. Cayden was kind of scary and sexy. Hell, there was no "kind of" about it.

Could he be…?

No. I shook my head at the absurdity of that thought. Yeah, Cayden wanted to sleep with me—that much was obvious. And what a nice, homogenized way of describing acts most likely so carnal that we'd have to change the rating system. I also suspected that Cayden and sanity were rarely on speaking terms.

But did he want to hurt me? My gut said no.

Yes, but is your gut reliable? an inner voice whispered.

That was the million-dollar question.

Sipping my coffee, I watched the sun complete its slow descent behind the mountains. The solar lights strung in the porch eaves came on and wrapped the Ranch in a comforting glow.

For now, it was enough.

CHAPTER SEVEN

"Hey, there they are!"

A low buzz of excitement ran through the crowd of reporters and photographers lining the curved cobblestone drive as a silver Rolls-Royce drove through the wrought-iron gates, the driver skillfully navigating through the throng. All were waiting for the chance to get a glimpse of the passengers, America's recently wed cinematic sweethearts Douglas Patton and Bettina Gleason.

The automobile pulled to a stop in front of the former DuShane mansion and the chauffeur hopped out, a strongly built man decked out in a gray uniform jacket and pants, a matching cap perched jauntily on his head. Ignoring the scribblers and shutterbugs, he circled around to the passenger side and opened the back door.

Bulbs flashed as a strong-jawed man in expensive wool trousers and brown leather aviator's jacket emerged, a white silk cravat tied around his neck. His sky-blue silk shirt matched his eyes. Everything about him screamed "matinee idol."

"Mr. Patton, was it love at first sight?"

"Maybe second sight," the man replied with a grin.

"I thought you said you'd never let a woman get the handcuff on you!"

"Sure, but that was before I met Bettina."

Flashing a white-toothed smile at the crowd, he turned back to the car and extended a hand. A beautiful woman emerged, well-manicured hands modestly smoothing a blood-red velvet coat over shapely silk-stockinged legs as she stood. She snuggled prettily into the coat's black mink collar and gazed up at her taller companion, eyes obscured behind dark sunglasses.

"Douglas! Bettina! Look this way!"

"Bettina, give us a glimpse of those beautiful peepers!"

"Hey, newlyweds, how about a kiss for your fans!"

The couple obliged before heading toward the front doors. A collective groan went up from the eager newshounds, but several refused to give up.

"Tell us about your honeymoon!"

"C'mon, we drove all the way out here!"

"Just a few more snaps!"

"Aww, give us a break, kids." Douglas gave a self-deprecating grin over his shoulder. "Betts and I've been on the road for hours."

His wife nodded. "I'm simply famished, boys."

"You heard her, gents," Douglas said. He turned to their chauffeur. "Earle, bring the bags in 'round the back, and see what's in the kitchen—my wife is famished." With that, Douglas scooped his blushing bride up in his arms, kicked the doors open, and exclaimed, "Welcome home, darling!"

Then Douglas carried Bettina inside, the sort of manly gesture his heroic characters were known for, that caused women of all ages to swoon in rapture. Bettina was no exception—at least not until they'd closed the huge wooden doors behind them.

Once the thick slabs of oak had slammed shut, Bettina slid out of her husband's strong arms.

"Oh, thank god," she said, heaving a sigh of relief. "I couldn't bear another minute."

Her husband shot her a wounded look. "You know, women around the world would pay to be in your shoes."

Bettina snorted. "Not if they really knew you."

"You know," Douglas continued as if she hadn't spoken, "you could stand to lose a few pounds." He grimaced, rubbing his lower back. "I think I pulled something."

"Screw you, Dougie," she shot back.

Douglas laughed. "Aww, Betty, you know you're not my type."

Pouting, she went over to the baroque mirror that hung above a mahogany console table, pulling out a diamond-encrusted lipstick case. Doing a quick touchup on already impeccable crimson lips, she cast a quick glance at the rest of her reflection.

Sure, she had gained a few pounds on their much-publicized honeymoon in Paris. Too many pain au chocolat, rich dishes with heavy cream sauce, and bottle after bottle of real French champagne. Who could resist? "Dougie's" waistline hadn't escaped the decadence either, but the studios went easier on their male stars.

Grinning, Douglas wandered across the entry hall toward an arched opening on the left. "If my memory serves me correctly, Neddie's wet bar is somewhere in here."

Bettina stopped admiring herself in the mirror, her momentary pique forgotten.

"What, it's still here?"

"You bet, Betts."

Dropping her beaded bag on the mahogany table, Bettina hurried after her husband, Cuban heels clicking on the tiles in a sharp staccato as she passed under the archway into the Great Room—where Ned DuShane had hosted his best soirees.

†

Noise from upstairs caught Ned's attention. Voices, one male, the other female. What the hell were they doing on his property?

It had taken him a few tries to leave the subbasement, but when Ned had finally reached the Great Room, he was delighted to find that nothing much had changed. Sure, a lot of the furniture had been draped with sheets, and dust coated anything that had not been covered, but his art collection—paintings and statues, Murano glass—all of it was still as he'd left it. Still, the place had an unlived air about it, devoid of the energy that had been there when he'd still been kicking.

That didn't mean he wanted anyone else to enjoy what was his.

†

Bettina walked into the Great Room and shivered. "Brrr, it's cold in this joint." Glancing around, she frowned. "Why's all the furniture still here?"

"Because the studio doesn't want people to know he's gone missing," Douglas replied. "As far as everyone else is concerned, Ned is in Europe and has kindly agreed to let us stay here, for the time being."

She pulled the sheet off a settee upholstered in royal blue velvet. "You think I wanna entertain our friends on the same couch where Ned and his pals took turns with me?"

Douglas shrugged with indifference. He'd been there, although he hadn't participated. "Stuff's all real quality. Expensive. Even with our salaries, we couldn't afford to redecorate this place, even if we had the cheddar to buy it."

She opened her mouth to argue, but he held up a hand. "Look, Betts, when Ned disappeared, most of Silver Scream's backers vanished, too. The first nibble either of us have gotten was because we got hitched, and agreed to live here. It's only for a year."

"I know, I know… but this place gives me the heebie-jeebies."

"Same, kid, but this publicity stunt might actually pay off."

"I guess," she agreed reluctantly. "Still, I hate this place. It's… it's gaudy."

"I'm not disagreeing, but…" He gave her a sideways glance. "Look, Ned still might come back, and if he does, we don't do ourselves any favors by redecorating. He'll raise hell."

"Fine," Bettina said, throwing herself into an overstuffed chair, its crimson silk an almost perfect match for her lipstick. "But as soon as the year's up, we're getting a place in town. Now, how 'bout you find us something to drink."

Sketching a mock bow, Douglas made a beeline for an ornately carved mahogany bar that took up nearly ten feet of wall space. As he ducked behind it, Bettina gave a derisive laugh.

"You really think there'll be any booze left?"

Ignoring her, Douglas reached up, grasped one of two brass wall sconces behind the bar, and pulled. A panel slid open, revealing row upon row of bottles. Some of them were brown glass, labeled plainly with the type of alcohol inside—gin, whiskey, vodka, and so on. Others had been imported from countries that hadn't suffered the indignity of prohibition.

Bettina's eyes widened with surprise. "How did you know that was there?"

Douglas shrugged. "When he had a few drinks in him, Ned liked to show off some of his toys." He grinned in satisfaction at the sight of all the bottles, and took a bottle of thirty-year-old brandy from the top shelf. "Want some?"

"You have to ask?" She licked her lips.

Grinning, Douglas poured a hefty measure into two crystal snifters and handed one to his blushing bride.

"Cheers," he said. "To Ned. May he rot in hell."

Bettina touched her glass to his. "I'll drink to that."

†

Reaching out, Ned could hear the conversation. Heard his name. Recognized the voices. Disrespecting him.

Heat bubbled up unbidden, incandescent white-hot spikes pounding into his head. Power borne by rage rushed through him, fueling his will. He moved swiftly through the subcellar's cement corridors, up the wooden stairs to the wine cellar, to the ground floor. Without even thinking, he grasped the door handle that led to the pantry and shoved hard, flinging the door open with a force that made the walls shake.

A big, dumb-looking gorilla of a man stood there, a bottle of milk in one hand.

"What the hell you doin' in my house, you ape?" Ned snarled.

The bottle fell to the tile floor and shattered.

†

A door slammed somewhere in the house. Bettina paused mid-gulp.

"What was that?"

"I didn't hear anything."

"You got wax in your ears? It was a door."

"Probably Earle," Douglas replied with an indifferent shrug.

Something clattered, like breaking crockery. "Did you hear that?"

Doug drained his glass. "Probably Earle again. Guy's a hick with two left feet."

"Or maybe someone thought this'd be a good place to squat. Or a newshound getting clever and hiding out to get snaps of us with our panties down."

"Don't be such a jitterbug, Betts."

"Go see, Dougie."

Doug opened his mouth to argue, but Bettina put a hand on his arm.

"Please?"

"Fine," he said with a put-upon sigh. "I'll go take a look." He strode out of the room, posture heroic even though there was no camera following his movements.

†

It took Douglas a few minutes to find his way to the kitchen. No sign of Earle, but the marble counters were laden with boxes of groceries and bottles of champagne they'd brought back from Paris. At least the hayseed had unpacked the car.

Douglas stepped into the pantry and slipped on something underfoot. He would have fallen but managed to reach out and catch himself on the counter, hand smacking hard into the corner. Swearing, Douglas looked down. Splinters of glass sparkled in a puddle of milk on the floor. Earle must have dropped a bottle, not bothering to clean it up.

"Hayseed," Douglas muttered. "Earle!" he called out. No answer. He turned to go back to his bride, then stopped as a cold blast of air rushed over him. "What…"

Pick up that knife on the counter.

"Huh?"

You heard me, Dougie, *the voice whispered in his ear.* That knife on the counter. Pick it up. Do *yourself.*

Douglas obliged by slicing his own throat. Dripping with gore, the hand that wielded the blade fell limp at the dying actor's side. A hot copper scent filled the pantry, mixed with the unpleasant odor of feces.

"Good job, kid." Ned relished the orgasmic rush of power that filled him.

†

Bettina sighed, relaxing back against the plush velvet of her chair, a snifter of brandy in one hand. She thought she'd like a cigarette, but that would mean fetching her bag from the entryway. Too much effort.

Shutting her eyes, she took a long pull of her drink. Smooth, *she thought. Neddie had been a shit of a human being, but he knew quality and where to find it. Like me, she thought complacently. She'd earned her place in Silver Scream's pantheon of stars, one hot dog at a time.*

Footsteps—Douglas returning.

"Did you find anything?" she asked, not bothering to open her eyes. He grunted in answer. She took that as a no.

"Be a dear and grab my purse, would ya? I'm dying for a smoke."

A hand caressed her hair. She smiled—Dougie normally saved the romantic gestures for the cameras. Opening her eyes, she looked up to see their chauffeur holding a braided cord. Before she could do more than gasp, he looped it around her neck and pulled it tight.

†

Ned watched in satisfaction as the chauffeur strangled his former star, the man's expression as blank as a tailor's dummy.

When he finally let the cord slip from his fingers, Bettina's eyes bulged from their sockets, tongue lolling out of those crimson lips that had more than once had Ned's cock between them.

"Good boy," Ned whispered, and he began to see the possibilities.

†

After killing Bettina, the chauffer gathered up all the cash he could locate—a substantial amount—and drove off in the limo. An hour or so later he was in a bar on Sunset Boulevard, a place Ned had often frequented.

After a short survey of the room, Earle chose a young woman who smiled his way. She had seen him drive up in the Rolls, and was especially impressed when she learned who his most recent passengers had been.

He took her up the hill to Griffith Park and strangled her.

Dumping the body in the trunk, he drove back down the hill to Hollywood Boulevard and headed east through Pomona, across the state line and into Arizona. In Peoria, just outside of Phoenix, he took a room in the Edward's Hotel. From there he traveled out and killed a half-dozen more women over the course of a week.

With each death, Ned's energies grew.

As fewer and fewer victims were available, Earle's value evaporated and Ned grew bored. He had Earle drive to the south rim of the Grand Canyon and send the Rolls hurtling off the edge.

CHAPTER EIGHT

Three days after I got back from New Orleans, the stars and planets aligned to give most of the Katz crew the day off, so we had a Saturday training session with most of the regulars.

First, a morning beginners' session for newbies and NSAs—non-supe-aware—during which I ran an intensive workshop on film-friendly hand-to-hand combat techniques and basic falls. Everyone had to warm up by doing repetitions of the now-infamous superhero three-point landing. They're as rigorous as burpees, and a useful skill as long as Marvel and DC kept churning out movies.

After that we had our invite-only advanced session with the crew and a few stuntpeople who aspired to join KSC, during which my hunky cousin Seth supervised what I call the American Ninja Tarzan drill. You had to leap off a platform twenty feet off the ground, grab a thick rope, and swing toward another platform twenty feet away. Ropes hung at regular intervals, so each person swung in a series of arcs until the goal was reached. *If* it was reached. There were foot-thick mats to cushion the fall for those who slipped.

During a beginner's session, this was an exercise in humility—very few made it across without hitting the mats multiple times.

Even in the advanced sessions, Sean believed in leveling the playing field, so he placed a spell on the ropes to ensure that supes—supernaturals—couldn't use their extranormal abilities to complete the drill.

The KSC had worked on dozens of films over the years. Actually, make that hundreds, since they've been around since the turn of the century when film first became a thing, transitioning from vaudeville to silent movies and into "talkies." Some of them were produced by people who were supes themselves, or at least supe-aware. In those cases, Sean could perform the amazing aerial stunts that he and Seth were known for—courtesy of their nephilim ancestry.

It was tougher with film crews who didn't know the score, because they'd freak out if they saw him leap off a building without airbags to cushion his fall, or glide through the air without the benefit of rigging. Times like that, Sean managed to find someone on the crew who could help with the subterfuge. A lot of second unit directors were aware of the supernatural underbelly of the business, and Sean was very good at creating smoke and mirrors.

For the day's festivities, a half-dozen regulars had joined us. Our fire gag expert, Dion, a ridiculously handsome phoenix with incandescent blue eyes and dark hair. Moira, half-harpy with short blond hair and a definite attitude. Drift, one of the best stunt drivers out there, with cave troll in his family tree. Jim "Tater" Tott, big and broad like his best friend Drift, and my partner in crime when it came to training newbies in sword work. Both were built like small mountains.

Tobias was one of the few non-supe members of the crew, yet talented enough to keep up with them. And Jada, with just enough air elemental in her DNA to be good at aerial and free-fall stunts. Sometimes I referred to her as "Wannabe Mini-Me." Was that nice?

No. But neither was Jada.

The stunt field, like most of the entertainment industry, is highly competitive. While some people treated the competition as enemies, ideally someone higher up the ladder would reach down and pull you up. Then you do the same for the next person. Pay it forward. Jada, though, was more likely to shove anyone off the ladder completely.

She'd always resented the fact that, even with what should've been her elemental advantage, I was naturally better at stuntwork than she was. Truth was, I'd taken my position in the crew for granted—not because of nepotism, but because I could take whatever was thrown at me. That changed for a while after my bad fall, when I'd developed a nasty fear of heights. Despite my recovery, it was Jada who got most of the jobs that once would've gone to me. And oh, she so loved to rub my face in it.

Conspicuous by his absence was Randy, who I'd been dating before I'd left for New Orleans. He'd been a young and irritatingly cocky newbie at the Ranch, and made the mistake of poking fun at me when I froze climbing the high fall tower. That fear-of-heights thing. Randy was under the misguided notion that the Ranch was a boys' club, and very nearly got his clock cleaned by me, Drift, and Tater.

It turned out that he could be taught. We'd worked on a film together and had settled into a low-key friends-with-benefits relationship. He took it more seriously than I did, though, and hadn't reacted well when I'd accepted the job on *Voodoo Wars*. He wasn't a fan of Cayden, either.

I'd left him a few voicemails since I'd gotten home, and the only response had been a brief text saying he was busy on set and would call when he could. Still, I'd been hoping he'd surprise me and show up for the training.

Ah, well.

Soon it would be time for beer, pizza, and a movie, a combination which made everything better. It also meant someone needed to go buy beer. We had some in the fridge, but not enough to satisfy this group.

"I'm gonna run up to Arlo's," I announced after we'd wrapped, as Tater and I carried one of the long mats back into the two-story barn where all the gear was stored.

"Want some company?" Tater offered.

"Sure," I replied. "But I'm driving."

Thankfully, Tater didn't argue. While he and Drift were excellent stunt drivers, they were kind of insane when they got behind the wheel, and my stomach wasn't quite up to the amusement park ride that I knew it would be—somewhere between Mister Toad's Wild Ride and Top Thrill Dragster.

We schlepped the mat to the back of the barn where they lived, tossing it on top of one of the piles. It landed with a *whump*, the resulting cloud of dust making me sneeze. Almost immediately there was a squeak from behind the stack.

"Did you hear that?" Tater asked, but I was already squeezing in between the stacks and peering around the corner.

Awwww…

Tucked into a little alcove created by the inner beams, and sheltered further by the mats, a fluffy black cat lay on her side, four tiny kittens nursing at her belly. Three were black, and the fourth smoke-gray. They couldn't have been more than two or three days old. My heart and brain melted.

"Hi there," I cooed softly.

Mama cat looked up at me, purring as her babies made biscuits and nursed. She looked as relaxed as could be, didn't even hiss. I must not have seemed like a threat. Still, I withdrew slowly and quietly so as to not alarm her. She and her babies weren't doing any harm where they were, and I didn't want her to feel like she had to relocate to keep them safe.

When I slipped out from between the stacks, Tater gave me a questioning look. Holding a finger up to my lips, I led him a few feet away before telling him the situation.

"We should have the crew put the rest of the mats away a little closer to the front of the barn, so we don't disturb the kittens," he suggested.

Big softie.

"Sounds like a plan," I agreed. "Why don't you give them the word, and I'll go grab the car keys." I made a mental note to pick up some cat food along with the beer. Mama cat had probably been living off rodents, and while that was all well and good, I could make it easier for her. I didn't think Sean or Seth would object.

Inside the house, I splashed some water on my face and ran a damp washcloth over the bits that needed it. Grabbing my purse and the keys to Sean's Xterra, I met Tater back outside.

Hopping into the driver's seat, I adjusted it to suit my shorter height, grateful that the Xterra had bucket seats instead of bench seating. If I'd had to accommodate for Tater's height, I'd have needed to tape boxes to my feet to reach the pedals. As usual, the SUV's interior smelled of stale burritos and sweat, and the back section looked like a college dorm room, all dirty clothes and fast-food wrappers. Seth's fastidiousness didn't extend to his father's car, especially when they were on a job.

Tater got into the passenger side. The vehicle groaned under his weight, tilting slightly before settling back in place. Without a word, he and I opened our windows, letting in the crisp autumn air to dissipate some of the funk.

"God, that breeze feels great," I sighed as I backed out of the carport.

"Had enough of that good old southern heat and humidity?"

I nodded. "Loved New Orleans, but man, there were days when it was like working in a sauna."

"Well, we're all glad to have you back," Tater said.

"Jada's not."

Tater gave a heavy sigh. "That girl needs to learn that it ain't all about competition, especially not with her own crew. She's this close"—he held up one oversized hand, making a gesture with thumb and forefinger—"to getting booted off the team."

"Really?" I was surprised. True, Jada had nearly gotten canned after an alcohol-fueled rant about nepotism. Since then, however, she'd toed the line. Sure, she slipped over it now and again, but nothing egregious enough to get her fired.

"Yeah, Sean's tired of it," Tater said. "The last few months, she's been way more worried about being better than you than she is about doing the best job she can, and being a team player. It's like she's always looking for the gold star, even if she hasn't earned it." He rolled his eyes. "And don't get me started on this whole schoolgirl crush she has on Seth."

I gave a snort of laughter. "Schoolgirl crush, huh? That sounds *so* weird, coming out of your mouth."

"Yeah, well," he said with a self-conscious shrug, "I don't know what else to call it, other than *really* uncomfortable to be around."

"Seth doesn't exactly discourage it," I pointed out. "I kinda feel sorry for her, because she's never gonna get anywhere with him, but he won't bother with a hard stop. Which kinda sucks on his part."

"Guess it might be easier for him to avoid confrontation, since she's part of the team."

I shook my head. "He needs to rip off the band-aid so she can spend a few weeks holed up crying and getting smashed on piña coladas, then move on."

"Like… maybe what you need to do with Randy?"

Ouch.

"That's different." I tried—and failed—not to sound defensive. "I actually care about him. We're friends. No way do I believe Seth gives a rat's ass about Jada."

"You see a future for you and Randy?"

I was a silent for a moment, focusing on the road in front of me. "I've been honest with him from the start," I said carefully, "and we both went into this knowing it wasn't permanent, or even exclusive. Not that I've been seeing anyone else," I added hastily.

"Yeah, but when someone thinks they're in love, they're gonna keep hoping unless things are pretty much chopped off at the neck, and a stake driven through the heart." He chuckled. "Well, in Randy's case, a silver bullet."

"Can we change the subject?" I burst out, nearly missing our turnoff. "I *so* do not have the bandwidth right now to figure out my love life."

"Sure," Tater replied, unphased. "What *did* you wanna talk about?"

I blew a puff of air out through my mouth. "Why does Jada have such a stick up her butt?" I asked. "About me?"

Tater sighed. "Lee, you could pull her out of a burning

building, and she'd find a reason to be pissed off at you."

"But why? I mean, she's getting the work these days, not me."

"Because you're better than her, and always will be," Tater said bluntly, "even though you're the one who bounced off the sidewalk and nearly died. Because she'll never be Sean's little girl. And because no matter how much you and Seth bicker and peck at each other like two grouchy crows, he'll never care about her the way he cares about you."

I chewed that over in silence for the rest of the drive.

†

We pulled into the parking lot for Arlo's, our local market that looked like a film set for every mom'n'pop store across America. Wood railing enclosing a wraparound porch. Vintage signs, none of them newer than the 1970s. An old-fashioned soda machine that still advertised bottles of Coke for a dime.

While you *could* get an ice-cold bottle of soda out of it, the price was actually a buck. A Post-it note informed customers of the inflation so they couldn't complain—and maybe sue—over false advertising. In this town, there was always a litigious asshat looking for something to piss them off.

The parking lot was empty except for a big-ass lime-green monster truck. One of those things with wheels twice the size they needed to be that practically required a hydraulic lift to get into the cab. It belonged to Marge and Hal, the couple that owned Arlo's.

"Did you bring any cash?" Tater asked, digging in his pockets and pulling out a ten-dollar bill.

"Nope, but my Visa actually has room for a beer run," I said proudly. It'd been a long time since I could buy more than a six-pack and not have my card rejected. In Hollywood there were few faster ways to earn a "loser" T-shirt than have a fifteen-dollar purchase declined.

We went inside, a bell above the door announcing our arrival with a happy jingle. Marge looked up from behind the register, her face lighting up when she saw me.

"Lee!" Coming out from around the counter, she enveloped me in a hug. "It's been too long since you've been in, that's for damn sure. Hell, girl, we were gonna have to shut up shop if you didn't come back soon!"

"I've been in New Orleans working on a film," I said, hugging her back. Below her capped-sleeve purple T-shirt, her arms felt rough, like scales. Marge and Hal were a mix of indigenous American and serpent. Pretty much the western equivalent of nagas. They both had raven-black hair, strong features, and lots of teeth. Several rows, in fact. Their two-year-old daughter Molly had chewed through a bunch of hardwood rattles during the teething phase.

"Had to be hard to leave New Orleans, though." She pronounced it, "N'awlins."

"It was," I agreed, "but it's awfully nice to be able to walk outside without sweating off ten pounds." Marge grinned, showing the row of teeth, which meant we were in her inner circle. She stepped back, looking me up and down.

"You look good."

"Yeah?"

"Yeah. Relaxed, fit. Metaphorically fat and sassy."

I laughed. "Well, I've been eating Louisiana cuisine for a month and a half, so that would account for the fat."

"I said, 'metaphorically,'" Marge said, swatting me on one arm. "Although you're always sassy."

Tater cleared his throat, the sound like a rusty motorbike.

"Good to see you too, Tater," Marge added. "In fact, as happy as I am to see Lee, I have to say I am twice as glad you walked in that door."

"Is that a fact?" Tater grinned.

"Oh, yeah. Hal ain't here, and we got a late order in, and the idiots dropped it off 'round the back and skedaddled instead of bringing it inside. Now I gotta take it in through the back stairs to the basement and get it into the cooler. I swear, some of these suppliers have their heads so far up their asses I don't know how they drive their damn trucks." She hooked an arm through his and tugged. "So how 'bout you use those muscles for something other than crashing cars and play-fighting, and give me a hand?"

"I would be happy to oblige, ma'am."

"Lee, anyone comes in, you tell 'em to cool their jets 'til I'm back." The two went out the door, leaving me to my own devices. I immediately pulled out my phone and hit Randy's number, fully prepared to leave a voicemail.

He picked up after three rings.

"Hey, Lee."

Okay... not the enthusiasm I'd hoped for.

"Hey, Squid." I tried to sound upbeat. "So, you didn't make it to the Ranch today."

A long beat.

"Hard day," Randy finally said. "I was gonna call, but I had a lot of stuff to do when I got home."

"No prob," I replied, hating the artificially chipper sound of my own voice. "Totally get it. I was just..." I paused, then forged ahead. "I was just hoping to see you at some point before, say, next year?"

Another almost painfully long pause.

"About that…"

Randy explained that he'd scored a stunt coordinator job on a television show for one of the streaming channels popping up to compete with Hulu, Netflix, and the like. A low-budget horror series being filmed in Romania. He was flying out tomorrow night on a red-eye, and had to pack for the trip, take care of last-minute details.

"Anyway," he finished, "I need to get packing."

"You got a ride to the airport?"

"Gonna take a Lyft."

This wasn't the Randy I knew, all eager-to-please puppy with an occasional flash of hot sexy wolf. This was more like one of those aloof dogs like a Shiba Inu that doesn't care if you have a bag of the best treats in the world, they're still gonna pretty much ignore you.

"Can I at least buy you a drink before you go?" Before he could say no, I pressed on. "How about we meet at the Ocean's End? Tomorrow, say, five. It'd… it'd really mean a lot to me."

Another one of those pauses. Then, "Yeah, okay. It'd be good to see you before I leave."

The Lee of a few months ago would have laughed at the wave of relief that washed over me. I still wasn't sure if there was any long-term future for Randy and me, as even a half-assed couple, but I wasn't quite ready to call it quits. Although maybe he was.

Well, I'd find out tomorrow. In the meantime, there was beer to buy. And cat food.

†

DUSHANE MANSION
DECEMBER 1925

He'd been a little hasty with Bettina and Douglas.

It'd angered him that they'd disrespected him in his own house. Still... he might have overreacted just a bit, and decided to let things play out longer the next time. He had nothing but time, after all. Might as well have some fun.

The next people to buy the mansion stayed a week and then left, putting the property on the market at a substantial loss.

"Something felt very wrong about the place." That was all the buyers, who did not want to be identified, said when asked why they sold so quickly. They said simply, "The place is just... wrong."

You bet it is, *Ned thought with a grin.*

CHAPTER NINE

One of the nice things about having money is that it makes choosing beer even more fun. I could get the guys plenty of their beloved Stella Artois *and* PBR—I try not to judge, but when would their taste buds evolve?—and I didn't have to choose between Stone Enjoy By *or* the Totalitarian stout. A six-pack of each, please. I even grabbed a couple of bombers of Arrogant Bastard for Seth, partly because he liked it, but mostly because my sense of humor can veer toward the childish.

Oooh, what's this?

At some point during my six-week absence, Arlo's had started carrying bombers of Dragon's Milk, an imperial stout aged in bourbon barrels. Dark bottles with adorable little white dragons and carrying a hefty eleven percent ABV. I pulled six out of the cooler, then remembered to grab a bag of kibble and a few cans of cat food. Nothing fancy, just Friskies for the time being, because that's what they stocked at Arlo's. I'd hit a pet supply store in the next day or two and get Mama Cat some high-quality stuff.

I heard a car corner into the parking lot, skidding to a halt with an unnecessary screech of brakes. My first thought was that Drift had decided to join us on the beer run, so I peeked out the window. A blood-red Spyder, top up, with black racing stripes, was parked vertically across three spaces. Definitely too sloppy to be Drift—even shitfaced, he drove and parked with a precision that was uncanny. Most likely it was teenagers who just got their license. If they came in and tried to buy booze with a fake ID, Madge would sort them out quickly enough.

As I started taking the six-packs, bags, boxes, and bombers to the front counter, the back of my neck started to itch. Just a tingle at first that quickly increased to a steady buzz.

Oh, come on, haven't I put in my time this month?

I reached up and touched my mother's amulet, suspended on a thick leather cord and currently resting below the hollow of my throat. The metal was warm, but that was all.

The passenger door on the sports car opened and a lanky, dark-haired man in jeans and black T-shirt got out. Small head set on a short neck between broad sloping shoulders. Limbs slightly too long for his torso. Missed being handsome by several fractions of an inch.

Great.

Skeet Silva, wannabe stuntman, *caminhante de aranha* or spider walker—a fancy name for arachnid shifter—and a real asshole. Which explained the itching, since his intentions toward me weren't good. He hadn't made the cut for the Katz crew, despite some major Peter Parker action. He had, in fact, been banned from training at the Ranch because he couldn't take direction or critique, and had basically pissed everyone off.

Then there was his creepy obsession with me. Last time I'd seen him had been at Arlo's a few months ago, when he'd gotten borderline rapey. I'd slapped him down hard and had been fortunate enough not to run into him since. Guess my luck had run out.

As I watched, the driver's door opened and a pair of muscular, denim-clad legs swung out, feet shod in well-worn brown leather cowboy boots. The rest followed in a quick graceful movement, revealing a man who bore an uncanny resemblance to the spider walker. But whereas everything about Skeet was just a little out of proportion, this dude definitely had the dark good looks of a *telenovelas* star. And unlike Skeet's slightly awkward physicality, he moved with a quick, almost aggressive assurance that was sexy as hell. Definitely tasty, but if I was gonna judge him by the company he kept, it was a nonstarter.

Before the two men had stepped away from the Spyder, another car pulled into the lot. Two teenage girls—one blonde, one auburn—jumped out of the pale blue Camry, both wearing tank tops and shorts showing off long, tanned legs despite the cool weather. Full of high spirits and that unconscious self-confidence that comes with being young and cellulite-free. I recognized them.

The blonde was Mary McDonnell, daughter of the owners of a local horse ranch, and the auburn-haired girl was her best friend Donna, the offspring of very minor Hollywood royalty. Too young to drink but old enough to drive, and definitely not mature enough to handle the trouble staring at them from across the parking lot.

Sucking in nonexistent stomachs, the girls tossed glossy manes of hair off smooth tan shoulders as they passed the two men on their way to the porch. Skeet and his buddy lounged against their car, making no effort to hide the fact that they were watching. Skeet reached up and ran a thumb over his red, wet lower lip, a gesture that made me want a gallon of antibacterial soap even though I wasn't his target.

His friend, on the other hand, wasn't so obvious. He looked at the girls, smiled, and said something that made them giggle. Then Skeet spoke and I saw their expressions change from coquettish flirtation to obvious discomfort, bordering on disgust. They quickened their pace, but Skeet didn't take the hint. Pushing off from the Spyder, he fell into step right behind the teenagers. The other man followed at a more leisurely pace.

Donna hurried onto the porch, but Skeet grabbed Mary by her wrist before she could follow. She jerked away and dashed up the stairs, saying something over her shoulder that made the handsome guy laugh. Skeet's expression darkened, however, and he started after her.

A-a-and that's my cue.

Putting down my haul, I gave the door an emphatic shove that made the bell jangle loudly, and stepped outside. Skeet reached the top stair and stopped in his tracks. I felt rather than saw his pal's attention switch over to me. The two teens might have been invisible, for all he cared.

Ignoring both men for the moment, I nodded at the girls.

"Hey, you two. Marge'll be back in a few minutes. Why don't you head on in?" I held the door for them. Mary nodded, relief and gratitude nakedly clear in her expression.

"Thanks!"

As soon as the girls were both inside, I let the door slam shut and leaned against it, arms folded. "Hey Skeet," I said casually. "You must have missed the 'sexual harassment' memo, huh?"

"Lee." Skeet smiled, not a pleasant sight. "Nice to see you."

Not everyone could give those words the sleazy snail trail Skeet managed to impart. If you were a woman, in his mind, "nice to see you" meant something a lot nastier, and I knew better than to ask him what was up. He'd tell me in pornographic detail. I suspected Skeet had a very rich inner life. When he'd hit on me hard during his short time at the Ranch, Drift and Tater had offered to rip his legs and arms off and use them to beat him to death.

They hadn't been kidding.

Mister Telenovela sauntered over, boot heels crunching on the gravel. "So, this is Lee Striga, eh, Skeet?" He had a low, gravelly voice that called to mind whiskey and cigarettes. A heavy accent that wasn't quite Spanish. Outwardly there was nothing threatening about his words or posture, but my scar and amulet told me otherwise.

"That puts you one up on me," I said. "You know who I am. How about an introduction, Skeet?"

"Yes," the man agreed. "Where are your manners, Skeet?"

"My cousin, Nigri," Skeet replied sullenly. "Nigri Barboza. He's here from Brazil. He's a stuntman, too."

"That so?" I replied. I sincerely hoped Skeet wasn't gonna ask about bringing him to the Ranch. "You in town for work, or just playing tourist?"

A slow smile spread across his lips, accenting their sensuality as he turned the smolder in his eyes up a few degrees. I'd bet he practiced the look in front of a mirror.

"I am here for work, *Senhorita*."

Skeet nodded. "Nigri worked on *Crocoboa* for Crazy Casa last month—"

Oh boy. "Wasn't someone injured during the shoot?"

"*Sim*." Nigri didn't take his eyes off me as he replied. "The stunt coordinator."

"That's right." Skeet sounded almost gleeful. "He did a high fall into the river and hit rocks instead of the deep water."

I winced. I couldn't help it. Way too close to home.

"Figured you could relate," Skeet said with a nasty grin. I ignored him.

Nigri continued. "It will be many months before he can work again, so Crazy Casa… they are looking for a new stunt coordinator. I hope to interview for the job."

Well, fuck me gently with a chainsaw.

This was news to me.

Okay, I really didn't want to work for Crazy Casa—they were known for crap movies based on higher budget crap movies, and original films like *Arachnapanther* and *Snow Yeti*. Their in-house stunt coordinator had gone through stunt crew like I went through bourbon barrel beer. Even so, it still stung that he'd turned me down for work when my agent had thrown my name into the ring.

"Nigri and I are starting our own crew," Skeet interjected, breaking into my gloomy "screw my career" retrospective. "Got about a half-dozen guys lined up."

"They all spider walkers?"

"Not all of 'em." Skeet's gaze shifted to one side as he replied, a sure sign he wasn't being straight with me.

"Any women on the crew?"

"Not yet."

No surprise there. No way Skeet would want a female spider walker on his crew—they were bigger and meaner than the males, and there was always the question of, "Is my girlfriend gonna eat me tonight?" Which is why most of the males tended to date outside their species.

"You interested?" he said. "You'd be working under me"—he actually *winked* at me— "but I can guarantee you'll enjoy it."

"Huh?" I was so used to Skeet hitting on me that it took me a moment to realize he was asking if I wanted to join his stunt crew. I almost laughed out loud, but managed to keep it to myself. "Thanks, Skeet, but I'm not looking to leave KSC anytime soon."

"Oh, get off your high horse," Skeet said with a sneer. "You ain't done a job with KSC for what, a year now?"

"I was healing."

"Maybe for the first six months, but from what I hear, Sean doesn't trust you enough to put you back into play."

I took a deep breath. Then another one. Anything to stop me from ripping Skeet's spinal cord out and beating him with it. "Sean's overprotective. If it were up to him, I wouldn't be doing anything for at least another year."

"Yeah, sure."

I stepped closer, got in Skeet's face. "You do know I've been working, right? Just got back from a shoot in New Orleans."

Skeet took a half step back. "Hadn't heard."

"Yeah, well, do your homework."

"That mean you're not interested?"

"What the hell do you think?"

"Hey, *menina*." Both Skeet and I turned toward his cousin. I'd actually forgotten he was there.

"Lee Striga," he continued, "I think you owe my cousin an apology."

"Really?" I replied, ignoring the crawling feeling running up and down my legs and spine, like dozens of little spider legs. "Why is that?"

"From what he tells me, you are the reason he is no longer working with this… this *Katz Stunt Crew*."

"Really?" I laughed. I didn't mean to—and probably shouldn't have—but it just kinda came out. "That's what he told you?" I shook my head. "Oh, Skeet, you just had to go there—the whole 'Eve ate the apple and got you kicked out of the Garden' story."

"Well, yeah, if it hadn't been for *you*, Sean and Seth wouldn't have—"

"Wouldn't have what?" I growled. "Wouldn't have booted your ass off the Ranch for being an arrogant asshat who can't work with a team?" I grew angrier as I remembered how Skeet hadn't been able to deal with any sort of criticism, even when his screw-ups could have caused injuries. "You were careless, sloppy, and arrogant. Trying to hit on me was the *least* of your mistakes, and it was still a pretty stupid one."

Skeet clenched his fists, face crimson with anger. "Y'know, Lee, forget I even asked you."

"*Cadela*." Nigri glared at me. "You do not judge my family."

"Dude, just fuck your honor culture bullshit, okay?" The words flew out of my mouth without thought. "Skeet acted like an asshat, and I'm thinking it runs in the family." My amulet lit up like a Fourth of July sparkler, leaving no doubt that they didn't have a good intention between them. Nigri reared up on the heels of his boots, a glimmer of red flaring up in the depths of his dark brown eyes as he swayed side-to-side.

"You should watch your words." He radiated menace, making Skeet seem as harmless as an extra in *Charlotte's Web*.

"You have no idea what I've faced down in the last month," I said, my voice soft and steady. "So, if you think I'm going to be intimidated by a couple of itsy-bitsy spiders…" I trailed off and looked pointedly at their crotches.

Yeah, I know, but see how *they* liked feeling like pieces of meat. They didn't like it.

Nigri swarmed up the stairs past Skeet, closing the distance between us with unnatural speed.

"Let's dance, little girl," he said softly, body swaying side to side almost hypnotically. All my muscles tensed.

"How 'bout we just fight?"

For a split second, I saw the spider under the human skin, ferocious and ugly, looking like the Predator without its helmet. Then the human mask slammed back down as he swung an open palm toward my face. I didn't stop to think, instinctively blocking the strike with the outside edge of my left hand while smashing him in the chin with the heel of my right palm. I didn't pull my momentum because he sure as hell wasn't pulling his—I could tell by the strength of the impact when I blocked his blow that he was going for some damage.

My strike rocked him back several paces, and the look of surprise on his handsome face was priceless. Before I could take advantage of the moment, though, Skeet, no doubt emboldened by his cousin's presence, grabbed my shoulder and spun me around to face him, throwing me off-balance into the porch railing. Still, I was able to avoid the sloppy punch he threw at me, turning sideways so it slipped past my face. I grabbed his wrist and gave a sharp tug, throwing Skeet past me into Nigri.

"Jeez, Skeet," I said, "with a punch like that, you couldn't even get a job at the old Universal Western stunt show."

He hissed and scuttled forward again, hands stretched out to grab me. Using the railing, I swung myself up and smashed Skeet in the stomach with both my feet, grateful for the rigorous daily training I'd gotten working on *Voodoo Wars*. My timing was perfect—Nigri sent out a fine mist of webbing that hit the railing where I'd been standing.

Goddamn spiders.

Nigri snapped something to Skeet in a language I didn't quite recognize—similar to Portuguese, but more sibilant, punctuated with clicks. I saw a shadow of doubt flicker over Skeet's face. Evidently common sense and second thoughts were starting to penetrate his rage-fueled stupidity.

His cousin, on the other hand, had clearly gone to eleven. Nigri hissed a single word. Skeet's face blanched, and they both started shooting webbing.

Spider walkers didn't spray out webbing from their wrists *à la* Spider-Man—it exuded from spinnerets in their hands, coming in strands and small sticky patches. Skeet had explained it to me back when he was still training at the ranch.

"When we're in human form, we can only spin webs enough to do things like climb walls, hang upside down, stuff like that. To do the serious web spinning, now that takes being in spider form. And naked." He'd leered at me, as if the thought of a Skeet-sized spider in the buff was a turn-on. It wasn't.

So there was only so much the two spider walkers could do with their webs, but it still made things difficult, and they kept throwing the sticky shit at me. Before I knew it, I found myself with my back against the storefront, sticking to the wood. My left hand was emmeshed in the webbing, several strands wrapped around my wrist.

Well, hell.

My right arm was still free, though. When Nigri tried to pull me toward him, I reached into my jeans pocket, pulling out the Xterra keys. They immediately heated up. Holding the fob in my clenched fist, keys sticking out between my fingers, I shredded the webbing around my left wrist. The stuff melted at the touch of the metal.

Seeing what I was doing, Nigri grabbed my wrist in a strong grip, fingers digging into my flesh as I tried to pull away. I heard Skeet coming up behind me, and donkey-kicked him where his spinnerets don't shine. He gasped for breath, a wheezing, squeaking noise that would've been funny under other circumstances. It was a good solid kick and it put him down.

There was no time to enjoy that little victory, because I still had to fend off his hot-tempered cousin. I cracked a closed fist against Nigri's nose. It was my left hand, so I didn't have quite as much strength or precision, but it was still enough to make him let go. Shoving hard against his chest with the heels of both palms, I put some distance between me and the reeling men.

Blood trickled from one flaring nostril as Nigri glared at me. He lunged, but jerked to a halt when Skeet grabbed him around an ankle.

"Nigri," Skeet said, voice reedy and thin as he clutched his manly bits with his free hand, "let it go."

"What the hell's going on out here?"

Marge rounded the corner of the building. Hot on her heels, Tater took in the scene, muscles expanding under his jeans and long-sleeved Henley. He only went "Hulk Smash" when he was *really* angry.

"These spiders bugging you, Lee?" His voice was deceptively mild.

Skeet had the good sense to flinch, but Nigri did that peculiar rearing up and swaying from side to side motion. He spat, the cords of his neck standing out with the force of it. A dark blob of sputum landed on the ground in front of Tater's feet, smoke rising from it. Nasty.

"Enough!" The single word pierced the night air, rising to a shriek and ending with a rattle in Marge's throat. Her body shifted and elongated as her legs flowed together into a sleek scaled body, muscles undulating beneath a black-and-red diamond pattern. Eyelids receded, green-gold bleeding into the whites, brown irises vanishing as the pupils expanded into horizontal ellipses. Her short, thick hair merged into her as she swayed back and forth in front of the men, a good three feet taller than she'd been just seconds before.

Wow.

Both spider walkers recoiled. Spiders and snakes are not friends, and Marge was damned scary in her current form.

"Skeet Silva," she hissed, "you've had your last chance. You are no longer welcome on our property, you or this *other* asshole spider." She glared at Nigri. "I'd make you clean up your damn mess, but I don't want you soiling the place any more than you already have."

Skeet scrambled backward. "Now don't be like that, Marge," he whined. "Nothing happened. Right, Lee?" He looked over at me, a sickly smile pasted on his face along with an emotion I couldn't quite read.

I stared at him silently.

"Awww, don't be like that," Skeet said. "You know we were just foolin'—"

Marge fixed her gaze on him, and he shut up.

"I'm only gonna say this one more time—*get off my property*. If you're still here when my husband gets back, there's gonna be two dead spiders. Your kind don't taste very good, but I imagine Hal would be happy to make an exception, on account he don't like to waste fresh meat."

Skeet did a scuttling crabwalk away from her. Nigri stood his ground a little longer, trying to save face, but we all knew it was bullshit. He finally spun on his heel, jerking his chin at his cousin as he stalked over to their car and got into the driver's seat. Skeet cast one last beseeching look at us before following his cousin, trying his best to look macho and failing miserably.

We watched the Spyder peel out of the parking lot and vanish over the rise in the road.

"Sonofabitch can drive," I observed. Tater growled in reply, which meant he agreed but didn't like it.

As soon as the car was out of sight, Marge's snake trunk divided into two legs again, clothing reappearing as if to say, *"Nothing to see here, folks."* Her eyes returned to their usual dark brown, only a shimmer of green-gold remaining as the pupils lost their elliptical shape.

The bell on the front door jingled as the screen door creaked.

All three of us turned. Mary stood peering out from behind the partially open door, Donna behind her.

"Um… Marge? Can we pay for our stuff?"

CHAPTER TEN

After Mary and Donna had left with their chips, candy, and diet cokes, Marge heaved a sigh, resting her elbows on the counter, chin cradled in her hands. I'd never seen her look so exhausted.

"You okay?" I asked.

She looked up at me and gave a weary smile. "I'm holding the line, Lee. Wish Hal would get back, though."

"I'm really sorry about riling up those spiders."

"Oh, hell, that wasn't on you," Marge said, waving a dismissive hand. "They've been here a few times over the last week or so, and I mean, Skeet is bad enough," she said, "but that cousin of his? Trouble on the hoof."

"Eight hooves," I agreed. "Or whatever spiders have on the ends of their legs."

"Claws," Tater supplied.

"Even worse," Marge continued, "they're just about the only customers we've seen today. I was only half joking about shutting up shop—it's been so slow this past week, we're thinking about shortening our hours until things pick up again."

"Arlo's is never slow," I replied. "You're the only market in the neighborhood that doesn't require a trek to the 101."

"And yet we've barely broken even this week. Things don't

pick up, we're gonna see our first month in the red in the last ten years."

Damn.

Unlike some of the other bedroom communities like Thousand Oaks, Camarillo, or Simi Valley, our neck of the woods didn't have subdivisions, condos, or apartment buildings. The people who chose to live here had small ranches, raised farm animals and livestock, or built extravagant homes like the DuShane place. People who valued privacy for any number of reasons, and almost everyone patronized Arlo's. It was a regional institution, and not even the advent of Instacart, GrubHub, or Amazon had impacted their business over the years.

"I'm here to tell you, Lee," Marge said, "something's up, and it's not good."

"What do you mean?" I glanced at Tater, who shrugged. He had no clue what she was talking about. Then again, he and the rest of the crew had been working long hours on *Spasm,* so it wasn't all that surprising.

"You know, people talk when they come in here," Marge replied. "Well, I've been hearing about animals going missing. Some of the birds at the ostrich farm, a few cattle, other farm animals. Lot of dogs and cats refusing to go outside their houses. Stuff like that. Then, a few weeks ago, a couple of tourists from Tucson went missing. And…" Her voice trailed off.

"And…?" I prompted gently.

"And the last place they were seen was Arlo's. Hal and I answered a shitload of questions about what that couple bought, how much time they spent in the store, whether or not they'd mentioned where they were headed—"

"And did they?"

"Point of fact, they were on their way to Solvang. Gonna do a self-guided *Sideways* winery tour. First they were stopping in Oxnard to stay overnight with her sister, and when they didn't arrive, the sister called the police. Last text they'd sent her included a picture of the storefront. Guess they thought it was quaint."

"There's a lot of miles between here and Oxnard," I mused. "Who's to say they didn't stop someplace else along the way?"

"Well, that may be so," Marge replied, "but their car was found abandoned a mile or so north up the 101 just a bit off the freeway."

"That's not good."

"No, it sure isn't," she agreed. "Over the last ten days, two more abandoned vehicles were found in the same general area. One was a Tesla. Owned by a techie from Silicon Valley on her way to the Google office in Santa Monica. She never showed up. The other belonged to an eighteen-year-old kid road-tripping with his friends to a concert. All of them are still missing."

"Jeez, Marge," I said, "I know we're kind of isolated, but it's not like we live in *The Hills Have Eyes* territory."

"Which is exactly why these disappearances have caused such an uproar." She sighed again. "This area has always had more than its share of weirdness, but not like this—and it gets worse. You know the Fords, right?"

I nodded. The Fords owned and operated riding stables up off Miller Trail, a couple of miles from the Ranch. Gary, his wife Rose, their son, his wife, and their kids—eleven-year-old twins who had rightfully earned the nickname, "the hellions." A photogenic family—Gary was in his seventies, looked like an aging Western star, all weathered skin, sky-blue eyes surrounded by crinkles, and a still thick mane of silver hair. Pretty sure he was part centaur.

"Sean used to take me and Seth riding up there. Nice family."

Well, except for the twins.

"Well, they're missing, too."

"What?"

"All of them?" Tater's expression made it clear this was news to him.

"All of 'em," Marge confirmed. "Including their housekeeper and one of their stable-hands. Even the dog is gone. The Stanton family across the road woke up Tuesday morning with their yard full of horses, all lathered up and spooked. Mark Stanton recognized a few of them, went up to check on things, and the stable doors were wide open, like it was deliberate."

"That's just weird," Tater said.

"Even worse, there was a smear of blood on the stable door. Mark said it looked like someone had been holding onto the door and been dragged away. Folks are scared to go out."

"Okay, this goes beyond weird," I said. "Has the Kolchak Division been brought in, or just the regular PD?"

"Far as I know, just your basic cops," Marge replied.

"Huh."

If these disappearances were supernatural in nature, I would've felt something when I came home. Then again, maybe the range of my monster GPS was limited to times when *I* was in danger. Or we could be looking at your basic human psychopath, no supernatural connection. There were plenty of people who got off on doing horrific shit.

"I wonder if we've got a serial killer," Marge said, as if reading my mind.

Tater frowned. "Well, whoever or *whatever* it is, you and Hal be careful." Glancing at me, he added, "We'd better get this stuff back to the ranch before Sean starts to worry."

†

Banjo hunkered down in the scrub brush at the base of the mountain. He'd been chosen by his family when he was a pup and had never known hunger or thirst. There was always a bowl of fresh water on the floor, biscuits and meaty snacks between meals.

There had been no food since he'd run away from his home. From his family. He had found some brackish water in a ditch.

His thick fur, always brushed and clean, was matted with burrs under his belly and on his tail. One of his front paws was raw and bleeding where he'd cut it on a tangle of fallen fence. His right haunch hurt, too, making him limp.

These were all bad things, but they weren't the worst. Those were the creatures that took his family away. Things that smelled wrong. Things that bit. Things that stung. Things that tore.

Things that killed.

When he'd heard his family screaming, Banjo had wanted to help. A good dog protected his people and his home. But the smell had been sharp, burning his eyes and the insides of his nostrils. The smell meant death, and instead of trying to bite the things that had invaded his home, Banjo had fled into the night, running in a blind panic up into the hills where he'd gone to ground under a rock ledge, trembling with fear and cold until the sun finally brought warmth.

Banjo had wanted to go back home then, but he'd run so far, he couldn't find his way back. He headed away from the mountains, approaching a house surrounded by a fence. When he'd poked his nose through a gap in the fence, however, he immediately backed away, hackles rising. Another bad smell, a place where bad things happened.

He kept going, heading farther away from the mountains, slinking down low until he'd passed the bad smell. Then he crept alongside a road, staying on the soft dirt shoulder. He finally reached another fence. There were more buildings. These, though…

These smelled safe.

CHAPTER ELEVEN

When we got back to the Ranch, Tater unloaded the beer while I made sure Mama cat had some food and water, leaving several bowls of both in between the stacks of mats. Then I hurried inside the house to make sure my Dragon's Milk was safely stowed away in the back of the fridge. It was, but I hid three bottles in the crisper drawer under bags of fresh greens, just to be on the safe side.

In a matter of just two hours, we consumed half a dozen large pizzas and an impressive amount of beer. Along with the rest of the crew, I was feeling no pain. Part of me wanted to bring up the disappearances, and see if anyone had heard anything about them, but I couldn't bring myself to dispel the overall good mood.

We were bingeing movies, and *Swashbuckler* was wrapping up. Not sure who chose that one. It's not a very good movie, but Peter Boyle's delightfully bad overacting combined with Robert Shaw in boots, tight red pants, and cavalier shirt—with the added joy of a young James Earl Jones in equally tasty pirate garb… well, what's not to love?

Jada sat cattycorner from me on the L-shaped couch, because Seth was there. I used to get a perverse pleasure from watching her chase my uncatchable "cousin," but at the moment I just

117

felt sorry for her. He was gorgeous, no doubt about it. I could recognize that, even though I generally wanted to smack him upside his head. Cheekbones that any supermodel would die for. Eyes the rich brown of bittersweet chocolate, framed with long lashes that used to make me bemoan the unfairness of the universe when we both were teenagers. Glossy dark hair that looked artfully tousled but was just how he looked when he woke up every morning.

No wonder I hated him.

Jada sat so close that I doubted there was room for a piece of tissue paper between their thighs. Seth made no effort to move away, but then again Tater sat on his other side, taking up what space was left on a couch that could easily fit eight people— provided one of those people wasn't built like Juggernaut.

I was squashed into the other corner of the L with Dion, Tobias, and Moira squeezed in next to me. Sean and Drift sat comfortably in their own chairs. Normally I opted for a chair, but after being away for so long it felt good to be surrounded by my dysfunctional family, even if it was hard to breathe.

"*Pull the curtain, the farce is ended!*" Peter Boyle—playing villain Lord Durant—yells as he plummets out of a second-story window. We all yelled the line with him, then raised our bottles and cans in a sloppy, foam-sloshing salute.

"So very bad," I said happily.

As the credits rolled, Seth vanished into the kitchen, returning with a pink bakery box from Desserts to Die For, one of the most expensive boutique bakeries in Los Angeles. He plunked it down on the coffee table in front of me, along with a stack of paper plates, forks, and a cake knife. Everyone except Jada stared expectantly as I opened the box, smiling widely when I saw, "Welcome home, Lee!" in elegant white chocolate cursive on top of dark chocolate fondant frosting.

"Welcome back, hon," Sean said with a grin. I smiled up at my godfather. Rugged good looks of an aging surfer. Blond hair kissed gold and silver by sun and age. Sky-blue eyes. He could have been anywhere from forty to sixty by human aging standards. I'm not sure how old Sean really was, since the nephilim have an entirely different biological clock than humans. I'd bet he'd be hunky until the day he died.

"We missed ya, Lee," Drift said, raising his can of beer.

Cutting into my present revealed five thin layers of dark chocolate cake with white chocolate mousse and raspberry in the middle, rich chocolate mousse in between the other layers, the fondant frosting covering the entire thing. I nobly handed slices all around before taking my first bite.

Sooooo good.

"If we hadn't been working, I would have made a better one," Seth grumbled. He could be an asshat without breaking a sweat, but was justifiably proud of his culinary skills. And the thought was sweet in its own Seth-like way.

"I'll gladly take a rain check," I offered.

"So, hey," Jada burst out, apparently unhappy with the Lee-a-centric turn in conversation, "I got the script for *Vampshee 3* today."

No, really?

I managed to refrain from saying it out loud.

"Wanna hear the opening?" Without waiting for a response, she jumped up and pulled a script bound in dark-red cardstock from her bag. Settling back down on the couch next to Seth, she flipped it open and began reading before anyone could object.

†

VAMPSHEE, CHILD OF CHAOS: THE UNDERWORLD CHRONICLES, PART 3

LELA, half-vampire, half-banshee, stands on the edge of a cliff overlooking an angry ocean, a lonely lighthouse behind her. Huge waves crash against the rocks and a storm brews in the sky above. Her hands cradle her stomach protectively—Lela is very pregnant.

CLOSE ON two strong, masculine arms as they encircle her waist. Lela stiffens, then relaxes against the well-built man standing behind her. CONNOR, Lela's husband. Half-werewolf and half-selkie.

The two stare out across the stormy sea, the various emotions playing over Lela's face at war with one another.

> LELA
>
> What if this is a mistake? What if by bringing a
> child into this world we are dooming him or her
> to live a life of never-ending conflict? What
> kind of life will this child have? Neither vampire or
> werewolf... banshee nor selkie...

> CONNOR
>
> We can't think that way. Only by bringing a child
> into this world... only by combining our different
> races can we ever hope for peace amongst our
> peoples.

LELA

But Connor...

CONNOR

You know that the prophecy says that only a child
who carries the four bloodlines can unite that which
have been at war for millennia.

Lela turns. Looks at him.

LELA

What if the prophecy is wrong? What if our child's four
different bloodlines tear him or her to pieces from the
inside?

CONNOR

Then we will guide our son or daughter as best we can.
As you and I, Lela, have learned to unite our conflicted
natures, so will we teach our son or daughter to combine
these different aspects in strength... in love... and not
in war.

LELA
(shaking her head sadly)
I don't think I can take that chance, my love...

Without warning, she HURTLES herself off the cliff's edge before
Connor can stop her. He stares after her, down into the foamy
depths of the water, and falls to his knees.

CONNOR

NOOOOOOOO!!

TIME CUT

EXT. LIGHTHOUSE – NIGHT

We HEAR SCREAMS as a storm rages outside the lighthouse.

INT. LIGHTHOUSE – SLEEPING QUARTERS – CONTINUOUS

Lela lies on the bed covered with a single quilt, sweat streaming from her brow as she clutches Connor's hand and screams, contractions wracking her frame.

CONNOR

Be brave, my love. It is almost time...

Lela SCREAMS in answer.

INT. LIGHTHOUSE – SLEEPING QUARTERS – LATER

Sitting up in the bed, a radiant Lela cradles a baby in her arms, Connor sitting next to her as he stares adoringly at the infant.

CONNOR

She's beautiful...

CLOSE ON THE BABY...

...Mournful, melting brown seal eyes. Pointed shaggy ears. Adorable, like something out of a fairy-tale painting.

Then the baby opens her mouth, exposing sharp fangs, and lets loose a wail that pierces the heavens. Connor and Lela both SCREAM, hands slapping over their ears even as blood pours out between their fingers.

CONNOR

NOOOOOOO!!!

†

For once, I was actually glad this *wasn't* where I'd step in—I had an aversion to putting my foot into big steaming piles of poo. I mean, I've worked on some craptastic movies, but this multi-million-dollar script was so bad not even MST3K—in any of its incarnations—could make the finished product bearable.

It wasn't helped by Jada's painfully over-the-top performance.

I had to admit to a small helping of sour grapes, because a year ago I was the stuntwoman doubling British import Haley Avondale—known for her intense and humorless portrayal of the perpetually leather-clad Lela in *Vampshee: Underworld Chronicles*. Because of that high fall gone wrong, Jada had taken over the job, and being replaced by her still stung.

After hearing the sampling of the script, though, those grapes tasted sweeter, helped by a side dish of *schadenfreude*.

Setting the script down on her lap, Jada stared around the room expectantly.

For thirty long seconds, no one spoke.

"Man," Drift finally said, "is it just me or are these Netherworld scripts just getting worse?"

"Definitely not just you," Tater replied.

"It… has some problems," Dion said with diplomacy.

"It sucks," Seth said bluntly.

"Well—" Jada looked uncertain "—I probably didn't read it the way I should've. I mean, I'm not an actor, and—"

"No, you're not," Seth agreed without mercy, "but that's not the point. How did Lela survive the dive off the cliff? Do they mention it at all later on in the script?"

"I… well, I haven't finished the script, so I'm not sure if—"

"It sucks ass," Drift cut in. "A saggy, eats-too-many Twinkies and fried-food type of ass."

"So, *your* ass then?" Tater grinned, easily dodging the nearly empty PBR can Drift chucked at him. A thin mist of cheap beer sprayed my face as it spiraled past, landing on the tiled living room floor. I wrinkled my nose—it smelled like the aftermath of a frat party.

Drift did have a sizeable backside, but in all fairness, he was a big guy. The overstuffed recliner he sat in sagged beneath his weight. It was his chair of choice, because so far it hadn't collapsed.

"I mean, even if she *is* a vampire," Moira pointed out, "it seems like falling onto rocks would at least require at least a *little* bit of healing. It's like the writers forgot something."

"Like writing," Tobias quipped.

"The first movie wasn't great," Seth continued without mercy, "and the second was worse, but since Avondale brought her husband in as screenwriter and director, everyone says this production is going to be crap."

Jada looked as though he had just slapped her. I opened my

mouth to agree with him, but what came out took me by surprise.

"Well, at least the stunts will be good."

Huh? Where did that *come from?* Even as my brain tried to rationalize why I'd stick up for her, after all the shit she'd given me, I added, "Hey, it's the Katz Stunt Crew. We're the best."

Jada looked confused, as though she wanted to argue with me, find fault with what I was saying, but couldn't. I didn't blame her—this qualified as the proverbial cold day in hell.

Maybe I was growing up.

Unfortunately, Jada wasn't. Without another word, she jumped up from the couch, grabbed her bag, and made a beeline for the entryway.

Well, hell.

"Jada, wait." I hauled myself to my feet, catching up just as she threw open the front door with enough force to bounce it off the wall. Following her out onto the porch, I put a hand on her shoulder. "Jada, come on."

Smacking my hand away, she whirled to face me. "Just leave me alone, okay?"

"I can do that," I said, "but seriously, do we have to fight all the damn time? We're on the same team. I mean, sure, I'd love to still be working on the *Netherworld* movies, but if I can't… at least it's still in the family. Right?"

For a brief moment—just a second, really—Jada looked as though she might want to bury the hatchet, too. A naked flash of something in her eyes that might have been the same exhaustion I felt at the constant rivalry. Maybe, just maybe, we could be, if not friends, at least not enemies.

Then her eyes shuttered over, the vulnerable look replaced by undiluted hostility. "Nice try, Lee," she spat. "You look good in front of everyone, while you make me look like a total bitch."

Oh, for fuck's sake…

"You managed that without my help." The words came out by reflex. They were true and she deserved them, but still… I wish I could've kept my mouth shut.

"Fuck you!" Jada stalked down the porch steps, down the drive to her car—a dark gray Xterra that was a match for Sean's—and climbed in. The engine growled and she roared out of the driveway with a speed and disregard for safety that both Drift and Tater would have admired.

Heaving an existentially exhausted sigh, I leaned against the doorframe. A comforting hand squeezed my shoulder. I didn't have to look to know it was Sean. There had been a time when just that small gesture would fix whatever was wrong in my world. His smile solved all problems, righted all wrongs. I hated the fact that my muscles now tensed up ever so slightly at his touch. If he noticed, though, he didn't show it.

"Don't let her get you down, hon," he said.

"Well, we gave her a pretty hard time about the script, and let's face it—she *should* be happy to have the job."

"Sure," Sean agreed, "but being happy about it and rubbing it in your face are two different things. None of this has been easy for you, and she needs to understand it."

I shrugged. He wasn't wrong. Jada hadn't tried to spare my feelings when I suddenly stopped getting jobs that would have been handed to me before my accident. But still…

"Maybe it wasn't so easy for her," I said softly, staring at the receding taillights. "Always losing out to me in the past."

"I'm proud of you, Lee."

I looked up at my *de facto* uncle.

"Not just because of the way you handled yourself in New Orleans," Sean continued, "but also the way you tried to be kind to Jada."

"Let's face it—I wasn't exactly the picture of empathy, back in the day."

A snort came from behind us. Seth.

"Back in the day? You mean, like, yesterday?"

I ignored that. "Seriously," I said. "We were pretty hard on her."

"No," Seth corrected, "we were hard on the script. It's not like she wrote it."

I looked at him warily. It almost sounded as if he was defending me. He shrugged.

"Jada needs to toughen up," he continued. "If she wants to be one of the guys, she can't act like a hormonal teenager."

"Being 'one of the guys' isn't the point here, right?" I said. "You get that, don't you? I mean, being professional on the job is one thing, but if you—or any of the guys, or me, for that matter—act like a jerk during off hours, is it wrong for her to get pissed-off?"

"No, but there are better ways to express it." Seth stared at me coolly. "She doesn't have to act like a drama queen on steroids."

"Maybe so, but—"

"More beer!" Drift bellowed from the living room.

"Ah, priorities," Sean sighed. Giving my shoulder another squeeze, he added, "Come on, hon. Just let it go for now and enjoy the rest of the evening."

CHAPTER TWELVE

Jada wiped angry tears from her eyes as she drove away from the Ranch. None of the Crew ever took her side against Lee. Never appreciated what she brought to the table.

No, it was always about Lee. About why everyone should be nice to her because of one stupid accident. An accident that was probably Lee's fault. No one wanted to admit that Sean's precious baby girl might have screwed up the stunt. That maybe Jada was a better choice for all the work that had been Lee's. That she was more qualified for the jobs that came her way, just because Lee had been injured.

Instead, everyone made fun of her, of the movie she was working on. Acted like it was crap. Even Seth. Especially Seth. And Lee pretending to be all nice about it, trying to look good in front of everyone else. It just made her want to puke.

No, Jada was done with the Katz Stunt Crew. She didn't need them anymore. She—

Something ran in front of the car, a flash in the Xterra's headlights.

Jada slammed on the brakes. The vehicle skidded, fishtailing wildly before coming to sudden halt on the road's shoulder. The jolt slammed Jada forward and back again, body brought to a halt by her seatbelt, air driven out of her lungs by the impact. Her heart pounded, adrenaline pumping through her veins. It wasn't a happy combination and her stomach rebelled. Shoving the door open, she barely managed to unclick her belt before tumbling out and vomiting up cake, pizza, and beer.

Head spinning, a bright glare in her eyes, Jada squatted, hands resting on her thighs, waiting to see if anything else was going to come back up. After a few minutes her vision returned to normal and her stomach stopped lurching. She stayed in that position for a few more minutes, though. God, she hated throwing up.

As she crouched there, Jada tried to figure out what had dashed in front of her vehicle. It hadn't moved like any human, animal, or supe she'd seen. All herky-jerky and disjointed. It...

It had skittered.

The memory of it made Jada feel suddenly vulnerable. Ignoring the tightness of her stomach, she got to her feet. Her gorge rose again, but she willed it down. Hell, she didn't care if she painted the interior of her car in vomit. She just didn't want to stay out on the side of the road any longer.

She was reaching for the door when something encircled her wrist, yanking her hand away from the handle. Her scream was cut off by something... something not quite a hand slapped over her mouth. What felt like steel bands wrapped around her body and jerked her backwards into the embrace of... of what?

"Lee..." something whispered in her ear. "We are going to have some fun."

Something stabbed into the back of her neck, and she lost consciousness.

†

When she woke up, Jada's head felt stuffed with cotton and poison. It hurt between her eyes, like nails were being driven into her forehead. Yet she couldn't feel the rest of her body. No sensation in any of her extremities. She remembered slamming on the brakes, but she thought... she hadn't hit her head or gone through the windshield. Or had she? Opening her eyes, she saw only blackness. Even so, her head spun.

Jada groaned as nausea coursed through her and hot liquid bubbled up like lava. She automatically reached for her hair—or tried to. She couldn't move. Vomit dribbled out of her mouth and down her chin. She choked, then coughed, turning her head to the side to expel it from her throat.

After she was sure she wouldn't choke to death on her own puke, Jada tried to get a sense of where she was. Her sinuses were clogged from throwing up, but a thick feral stench still made its way through.

Something shuffled in the dark and she whimpered. How far away from her, she couldn't tell. Maybe a few feet. Maybe more.

Maybe less.

Something touched her on the face. She whimpered again.

"You're not Lee," something whispered. Impossible to tell the gender.

"No, I'm… I'm not…"

"Too bad."

"So you can let me go… right?"

"Let you go…"

"Because I'm not Lee. You said—"

A rasping chuckle. "She's not here. But you are."

Jada tried not to scream because she knew if she started, she wouldn't be able to stop.

CHAPTER THIRTEEN

Waking up at 3:00 A.M. with a full bladder, I reluctantly left the warmth of my bed, padded down the hall, did my business, and returned to my bedroom. I slipped back under the covers and was just drifting off to sleep when a soft, insistent whimpering came from outside my bedroom window, and brought me to full wakefulness.

I lay still for a minute, letting my eyes adjust to the darkness as I waited to see if the back of my neck was going to start tingling. Thankfully, it did not, which meant I wasn't going to have to fight a demon before my first cup of coffee.

The whimper came again, a sad, lost sound that tugged at my heart.

Slipping on a pair of ancient Uggs held together by duct tape, I threw a fleece hoodie over my pajamas. Using the flashlight app on my iPhone, I crossed to the window and looked outside. Nothing. Then I looked down and saw two eyes glowing a lambent green, staring up at me. A dog, a good sized one, maybe even a coyote. Why was it outside my bedroom window, though?

Could Randy have changed his mind and decided to sneak onto the Ranch to see me? Kind of high school, but I could see him doing it. I cracked open the window.

"Randy, is that you?" I whispered. The animal startled and ran around the corner of the house. Even in the dark, I could see that it was limping.

Definitely not Randy.

Making my way to the kitchen, I stepped out the back door and onto the wraparound porch, as quietly as possible. Everything was still, other than the wailing of a cold wind blowing over the mountains, through the scrub brush and trees. A quarter moon played peekaboo with dark clouds scudding across the night sky. I stood for a moment, listening closely, trying to hear under the wind.

There.

Another faint whimper, almost a whine this time, coming from the far end of the porch to the right. I shone the flashlight and heard a low growl as whatever it was hunkered down on its belly. I couldn't make out much detail beyond its wolf-like shape, but as I drew closer, I could see the poor thing trembling. It growled again, but the sound had no real menace behind it.

"Okay now," I said quietly. "Not gonna hurt you." Stopping a few feet away, I knelt down as low as I could, going on hands and knees before cautiously extending a loosely closed fist, palm down. I stretched my arm out as far as I could without moving my body any further toward the animal. Hopefully it would get the hint that I wasn't there to hurt it, and not take a bite out of my hand. I didn't fancy getting a course of rabies vaccines—I'd heard those hurt like hell.

Just as cautiously, the canine lifted its long muzzle and gave my knuckles an exploratory sniff. Then, almost in surrender, it shoved its nose against my hand. I gave an inward sigh of relief and gently stroked a thick ruff of fur around its neck, rocking back on my haunches as a wet tongue did a hit-and-run swipe across my face. Oh well, a little dog drool never killed anyone, right?

"You wanna come inside with me?" I said softly. "Maybe have a snack?"

It whined, although whether that meant "yes," "no," or "I don't understand you, human," I couldn't tell.

The kitchen screen door creaked on its hinges. The dog and I both jumped.

"Lee, what the hell are you doing out here?"

Seth. Sounding cranky and put out, although I was pretty sure I hadn't woken him up, and sure as hell I hadn't asked him to check up on me. The dog gave a low warning growl, but it didn't move.

"We have a visitor," I said neutrally, pitching my voice low so as to not startle the animal. My eyes had mostly adjusted to the darkness and I could see some details of my new friend. Shaggy, thick fur in a mix of light and dark shades, long muzzle, ears that were pointed and upright, like a wolf or a German shepherd.

Seth approached us cautiously. The dog growled again, so he hunkered down a few feet away.

"I know," I said. "I feel the same way most of the time."

An impatient huff informed me that Seth had heard my comment, which had been the point. Something about my Hello Zombie Kitty pajamas encouraged childish behavior. When Seth cautiously scooted up next to me, however, the dog was quiet, sniffing his outstretched hand quicker than it had mine. It also didn't object when Seth scratched it gently on its head, rubbing its ears and working his hand around to its collar. He took a look at the dog's nametag.

"Banjo," he said. "Address is up on Miller Trail." He paused, then added, "This is the Fords' dog."

The Fords, who were now missing.

Oh, this is not good.

"You Banjo?" I asked softly. The dog whimpered in reply, pushing its dry nose against my hand. "Poor thing needs some water," I said.

Seth ran his hand over its ribs. "Food, too. Poor guy." This was a side of my cousin I didn't see too often. Probably just as well he was such a jerk most of the time, because the gentle compassion on his face underscored how handsome Seth really was. For a brief millisecond I understand why Jada had fallen for him.

"I could give him some of the cat kibble," I offered.

"I think we can do better than that," Seth replied as he got to his feet in one effortless motion. "I'll be back," he tossed over his shoulder as he opened the kitchen door and vanished inside.

I looked down at Banjo. He looked back up at me, pressing the top of his head into my hand with an audible sigh. I smiled even as my eyes burned with unshed tears. "Stupid mutt," I muttered without any conviction.

Seth reappeared with a bowl of water, and another filled with uncooked ground beef topped with a raw egg. He set both in front of the dog, who fell on the beef immediately, slurping up the bowl's contents in record time.

"Someone's hungry."

Seth nodded. "If he keeps this down, I'll get him some more in a few minutes."

"We're gonna have a regular petting zoo at this rate." I stroked the dog's neck as it dipped its muzzle into the water bowl. "Goats, cats, and now a dog."

"Something's out there." Seth stared out into the darkness, nostrils flaring as if scenting something in the night air.

"What is it?"

"I don't know, but it's not good."

I shivered, and not just from the cold wind blowing. It was true—something was wrong out there. I didn't know what, but my skin crawled with the sense that the night wasn't a friendly one.

"Come on," Seth said, holding out a hand to help me up. "Let's get him inside."

†

We set Banjo up in the laundry room, making an impromptu bed out of towels and an ancient comforter that Sean hadn't gotten around to throwing out or donating. While we fixed things up, I gave Seth a brief rundown on what Marge had told me. As I'd suspected, he and Sean had been too busy on the film to stay on top of the local news.

"We need to let the police know we have him," Seth said as he set down another bowl of food.

"But we won't take him to the shelter, right?"

"Hell, no." He looked at me as though he couldn't believe I'd even had to ask. "That's the last thing this pup needs." He scruffled Banjo's head. "He'll stay with us until the police find out what happened to his family."

"And if they don't?"

Seth shrugged. "Then I guess he can join the Crew."

†

The next morning it was obvious my comment about the petting zoo was less joke and more psychic prediction—several more goats had joined the ones I'd noticed when I'd first arrived back home, and when I went out to put food and water down for Mama cat,

135

a good half-dozen felines in varying conditions of weight and grooming meowed plaintively from the back of the barn.

One, a rotund orange tabby with thick, glossy fur, butted its head against my ankles.

"Okay," I said out loud. "Did someone schedule a convention here and forget to tell me?"

I brought out more bowls of water and filled several old cookie sheets with kibble and wet food. The cats swarmed around the food, with no hissing or fighting, as if some feline accord had been reached among them. Even weirder, a couple of mice wandered across the floor, paying no attention to the cats, who returned the favor by ignoring the rodents.

Stepping outside, I looked up. There were an unusual number of birds roosting in the trees and flying around. Ravens and their smaller cousins, the crows. Blackbirds, wrens, and robins. Sparrows and hummingbirds. Even several hawks. All of them sharing the branches without fuss.

Later that afternoon I drove my Saturn down the drive, and saw a squirrel dashing up one of the oak trees. A family of fat raccoons bustled across the yard near the front gate as I turned onto the road.

Hoping this wasn't a sign of an impending apocalypse, I kept driving.

†

DUSHANE MANSION

Over the years, Ned watched the parade of owners and tenants as they came and went. None lasted longer than a few weeks before hightailing it out of there. The sensitive types could always tell something was wrong, and for those who didn't, he gave them an extra nudge. If he couldn't influence them enough to make them his meat puppets, at the very least he could have some kicks by terrorizing them.

Some never left at all.

After a while, he discovered he wasn't the only revenant with a grudge.

A group of kids rode their bikes up and squeezed through a gap in the front gates. One had fallen partially off its hinges and the chain that was looped around the center was no longer pulled taut, leaving a gap just wide enough for an eleven-year-old boy. Ned had never been one to get all gooey over children, but his reaction was just mild annoyance. He'd let 'em run around for a little bit before spooking them.

Then one of the little shits threw a rock, smashing a crumbling statue on the terrace. The statue shattered.

Oh, you little punk, you are so dead.

The rage rose up. Rage at his property being violated. At these kids lacking respect. Still, Ned hadn't killed a kid before. Maybe he'd just give 'em a good scare.

"Hey, look at this!"

The same kid who'd pitched the rock had stumbled across one of the shallow graves Earle had dug for Bettina and Dougie, so many years ago. There'd been an unusual amount of rainfall the past year, and because the dipshit had dug the graves on the top of a slope in back of the mansion, the dirt had been washed away. Not quite exposing the corpses, but leaving only an inch or so of cover between them and fresh air.

Near one of the graves, now overgrown with foxtails, a gold bracelet glinted in the weeds. The kid reached down to pick it up. The second he touched it, skeletal fingertips, once impeccably manicured, burst out of the ground, wrapping around his wrist with bruising force.

He screamed, the sound exploding from his throat. His friends ran over to see what was going on.

"What the heck, Bobby?"

Bobby could only scream as he tried to pull away from whatever was tugging him toward the now churning earth. The screams went raspy as his throat went raw. When they saw what was happening, the two other boys stopped short. One turned to run away, but the other, a chubby ginger, grabbed Bobby by his free arm and tried to pull him to safety.

Good for you, kid, *Ned thought.*

The cowardly little shit got maybe two steps before what was left of Dougie thrust out of his grave and wrapped skeletal arms around him. The kid kicked and screamed until dirt clogged his throat.

Bettina still had Bobby by the wrist and had grabbed the ginger by his ankle. Ned thought briefly about intervening and letting the little hero get off with his life, but before he could make up his mind, Bettina had dragged both of them down for a dirt nap.

Huh. Ain't that a hell of a thing?

The bikes remained abandoned next to the wall for a good week or so until someone found them and reported the discovery to the police. The boys' bodies were never found.

CHAPTER FOURTEEN

I woke up to something panting in my face. Opening my eyes, I discovered Banjo at my bedside, tongue hanging out. I rolled over, not yet ready for the day. The stupid dog trotted around to the other side of the bed and licked my face, a big old stinky-dog-breath slurp.

"Hey, mutt," I murmured sleepily. "How'd you get in here? I thought we'd shut you in the laundry room." The door to my room was ajar. Seth must have let him out of there and into my room as his idea of a practical joke. "Is that what happened, Banjo?" I crooned. The dog gave me a doggie grin and another slurp across my face. "Blech."

Note to self. Buy breath mints for this canine.

What a night. On the upside, no freaky nightmares about sexy, faceless men and falling. Just dog drool.

Moving as quietly as I could, I let Banjo into Seth's bedroom and shut the door. Padding down the hallway, I slipped into the bathroom and took a long soak under a hot shower, then dressed in a violet broomstick skirt and black camisole. Gladiator sandals and a lightweight denim jacket completed the outfit.

I had a meeting with my agent in the early afternoon before meeting Randy for drinks, and even though I was already

Faustina's client, I still liked to try and make more than a token effort to look nice when we had a face-to-face. She was, after all, a former goddess of the harvest—Dacian, to be precise—and used to a certain amount of respect.

Her office was in Beverly Grove, a slightly less prestigious zip code than Beverly Hills, but Mana Talent Agency was no less sought-after. Out of half a dozen agencies, MTA was the premiere choice for supes in the entertainment business. Faustina was honest, at least with her clients. I'd heard her shade the truth on her clients' behalf a few times, but if anyone could get you a good deal, it was her.

I was, as far as I knew, her only non-supernatural client, although being a descendent of Lilith might qualify to some degree. Lilith was one of the First People, and according to Sean, I was among her non-demonic offspring who'd survived multiple cataclysms over the centuries.

Yay me.

Faustina was one of the few who knew my family history. It seemed as if being one of the First People should get me some street cred, but since Faustina was determined to keep my secret, jobs had been scarce since the debacle that had been *Pale Dreamer*. Killing a producer was a no-no. I'd have gotten more work if I'd been Francis Ford Coppola's second cousin's niece, twice removed.

Sigh.

Normally I didn't have to wait to see Faustina, but with unusually light traffic on the 101, 405, and 10 freeways, I'd arrived a half hour early. After a quick pit stop, I cooled my heels in the agency's waiting room, a copy of *Under the Stage* open on my lap as I tried to ignore the unblinking stare of a… well, I wasn't sure what. He, she, or it had large amber eyes, almost all iris, a flat nose, and glossy black hair that vanished into its collar.

As a rule I was pretty good at identifying supes, but there were so many out there I was occasionally stymied. There may have had some snake in the DNA, but I didn't like to assume. Regardless, I didn't like the way it was staring at me, but wasn't in the mood for confrontation. Besides, for all I knew it didn't have any working eyelids.

So, I buried myself in the magazine, the equivalent of *Backstage* for supernaturals, flipping through and finally settling on an article about a new firm called Leivithra Creative Consulting. *"Your muse gone missing?"* the tagline said. *"Call us and we'll hook you up!"* There were nine consultants, the Sarasvati sisters, and each one specialized in different areas. According to the piece, they covered everything from fiction, non-fiction, poetry, and script writing, to music and dance.

The article was short, and before long I closed the magazine. The unblinking critter was still—maybe—staring at me, so I took out my cell phone and shot Eden a message. *Meeting with Randy at OE at 5,* I typed. *Coming clean re: demon hunting and stuff. Can I come cry on your shoulder when I'm done?*

I hit "send," shut my eyes, and settled back in the shabby but comfy chair in a lobby that smelled of desperation and decades of stale cigarettes. I was tired after the weird-ass night I'd had.

†

"Lee?"

A gentle hand touched my shoulder. My eyes flew open.

"I'm awake."

Faustina's assistant Tracy. Mid-twenties. Big long-lashed brown eyes and mass of curly brown hair held back in a barrette. A black pin-striped pencil skirt and white blouse that didn't quite look businesslike on her curvaceous figure, but worked nonetheless.

"Hey, Tracy," I said, trying and failing to hide a yawn with one hand.

"Faustina is ready to see you." Her tone held a note of worship that spoke of her boss's past as a deity. I followed her through the door that led down a hallway to Faustina's office. Both hall and office ditched the whole shabby has-been feel of the lobby, giving way to plush hunter-green carpeting, cream-colored walls, and dark wood and leather furniture that would have been at home in a hunting lodge.

"Lee, so nice to see you!" Faustina rose from her chair, rounded her huge desk, and enveloped me in a hug, the scents of pine forests and exotic flowers wafting over me. Her glossy dark brown hair was pulled back in an elegant chignon, huge brown eyes framed with long lashes, and a few tasteful wrinkles that somehow made her look ageless. Her cream wool skirt and jacket came across as both incredibly chic and comfortable.

How the hell did she do that?

"Thank you for coming in, hon," Faustina said, breaking the hug. "You want a cappuccino?"

"Oh god, yes." I'd had nearly half a pot of coffee before I'd left the Ranch, but more caffeine was never a bad thing. Letting Tracy know that two cappuccinos would be needed, Faustina sat back down and gazed at me from across her desk. "How was New Orleans?"

"It was amazing," I replied. "Anytime you wanna send me back for a job, I'm there."

"Oh, I'm so glad, hon." She steepled her fingers. "You didn't have any issues with Cayden Doran?"

I shook my head. "He can be an asshat, but he was surprisingly professional to work with. Not to mention invaluable when it came to fighting swamp demons and elder gods from beyond the stars."

"Oh dear." She shook her head. "I was hoping there wasn't any truth to what I'd heard."

"What did you hear?"

"Word coming back from New Orleans says the production went well, but someone leaked a rumor of some trouble on set, and your name came up."

"Oh, for fuck's sake," I burst out. "Stuff *did* happen, but it wasn't related to the production. And just for the record, no producers died during the making of this movie. We lost a production assistant, but he was a jerk and was helping a sorcerer summon the elder god, so he deserved what he got."

"Well, that's good to know," Faustina said without batting an eye. "If we could get some sort of statement from Doran to mitigate any of the rumors floating around, it might be helpful."

"He'll be happy to help me with damage control," I said firmly. I was sure of it, and if not, I'd kill him. Quietly.

"Excellent." Faustina beamed at me.

"And in the meantime…?"

"Well, things are still a little hinky when it comes to your reputation."

"Hinky." I laughed, the sound short and bitter. "A nice way of saying, 'no one will touch you with a ten-foot-pole dipped in a bucket of hand-sanitizer.' Right?"

Faustina looked at me with genuine sympathy. "Oh hon, you know how things are in this town, what with the #metoo movement and everything that's been going on."

I did indeed. I also suspected that some of the pushback

against me was because so many men in the film industry were being called on their shit and taken down. A woman who'd been responsible for such a death—albeit unavoidably—couldn't be a power player in the boys' club. It was witch-hunt time.

I said as much to Faustina, and she didn't deny it.

"Just hang in there, Lee. Eventually the Industry will either forgive or forget."

"Hopefully before I'm too old to work."

"In the meantime," she continued as if I hadn't spoken, "I'll keep putting your name out there. Don't worry," she added kindly. "These things never last. You just have to be patient."

Easy to say when you've been around for centuries, I thought.

Faustina chuckled. "Don't worry, hon," she replied. "It won't take that long."

†

Ocean's End is my favorite pub in Los Angeles.

In a city full of bars, nightclubs, and gastropubs, it stood out both for the beers they had on tap and the clientele, most of whom were supes or at least supe-friendly. If you were a supe you could let your hair, tentacles, or fangs down, and let your freak flag fly without worry of exposing the supernatural underworld to the straights.

Tucked between a bike rental place and a brewpub on Oceanfront Avenue at the north end of the Venice Beach boardwalk, it was at the end of a dimly lit alley that only exists if you can see it. Most people can't, kind of like Diagon Alley, and it's nearly impossible to find the place unless you're with someone who's been there before.

If you managed to get in and Manny—the owner—didn't like you, you could forget a repeat visit. For a long time I'd been

144

paranoid that one day I wouldn't be able to find the alley, and thus be forced to drink at the nearby brewpub with all the hipsters and tech bros from Google. My idea of hell.

The front door to Ocean's End looked like it belonged on an Elizabethan pub, all wooden slats with a genuine ship's wheel plunked directly in the middle. No matter the time of day or night, a brass lantern hung on a hook above the door, casting just enough illumination to prevent customers from tripping on the cobblestones.

Yup, cobblestones. It was that kind of place.

Pushing open the heavy door and stepping inside, I scanned the dark interior. The place was still fairly quiet, about a third full. There were plenty of empty tables and booths to choose from. The regulars were there—two nereids who I'd swear spent all their time draped over the long, polished redwood plank of a bar, dripping water from their skirts onto the floor while throwing back countless drinks. I wondered if I could get paid to do that. Stunt drinking. Falls optional.

Manny, however, was MIA, his usual place behind the bar taken by a slender girl with a fall of silvery blonde hair that skimmed her perfectly shaped jeans-clad butt. Huge lavender eyes framed with dark lashes. Impossibly graceful, even while drawing a pint from one of the many taps lining the back of the bar.

Paging Lothlorien—one of your elves is missing.

"Hey, Eirian." I gave a little wave, doing my best to ignore the tasteful painting of a giant Cthulhuesque sea monster pulling a sailing ship down to its doom. The terror on the faces of the sailors was captured with amazing—and disturbing—detail, their expressions clearly visible in the light cast by two fat pillar candles on either side of the painting. I used to think it was kind of funny until I actually had to fight something that looked a lot like the monster. Now it just depressed me.

"Manny not in?"

Shaking her head, Eirian deftly removed the pint glass from the tap just before the head rose beyond the lip.

"He's taking a break," she replied in a voice that rippled as melodiously as harp strings. "A group of twenty sea nymphs were in earlier for a wedding shower, and got more than a little tipsy. They started shouting for Manny to take his shirt off."

I gave a shout of laughter. "Bet that went over well."

Eirian gave a rueful smile. "If the bride-to-be hadn't been Manny's great-grandniece, I'm not sure what would have happened."

"Wow. Even with you here to calm him down, huh?"

She shook her head. "Not even close."

Eirian was kind of like walking, breathing valium—she kept Manny's volatile temperament on an even keel during peak hours. If he'd come close to losing it with her in the house, it must have been something.

"I miss all the fun stuff," I said wistfully.

Eirian shot me a small grin. "Oh, it was a sight. As it was, he stomped out the back about two hours ago."

"Where does the back door go?"

"Wherever Manny wants it to," she replied.

I refrained from asking if she was being literal, or politely telling me it was none of my business. Fae were notorious for not giving straight answers, and honestly, I could see it going either way.

Ordering two pints of Triple Threat—Ocean's End is the only bar I know that serves high-octane beer by the pint—I took up residence in a corner booth on the other side of the two plank-style tables that ran the length of the room. I imagined a couple dozen tipsy sea nymphs seated on the benches, thumping their glasses on the wood and chanting, "Take it off!" at Manny.

I really *did* miss all the good stuff.

Ten minutes passed with no sign of Randy. I checked email, played on Facebook for a while. Then it was 5:30. Half hour late, which wasn't normal for him, at least not without letting me know. Traffic in LA is notoriously shitty, but unless he'd had his fingers chopped off and mysteriously lost his voice since yesterday, he could text or call.

Maybe he wasn't gonna show.

My glass was half empty—*so* not in a half-full kind of mood—and the pint I'd bought for Randy was gonna go flat. Okay, I'd drink it before I let that happen. Some beer is too good to waste, y'know?

The front door opened, and I looked up expectantly.

Ugh.

Not Randy. It was Marty, Scaenicus demon and bottom feeder agent. Dark-gold skin, blood-red corneas surrounded by ebony instead of the normal whites of the eyes. Pug nose that made a Persian cat look stately. Potbelly protruding in between narrow slumped shoulders and bandy legs. An expensive suit couldn't help the situation, and the entire unattractive package was topped by sparse gray hair worn in a man-bun.

If he wasn't such a sleaze, Marty might have almost gotten away with being ugly-cute, but he was the stuff of which cautionary tales are created. This particular demon was determined to get my best friend Eden away from her current agent to join his stable, and he'd cast feelers out in my direction, too. Luckily, he was too preoccupied with his current companion—your standard Hollywood starlet, all legs, boobs, and glossy mane of auburn hair—to cast a bloodshot cornea in my direction.

The starlet, hanging on his arm and onto every word, looked genuinely pleased to be with him. Either her taste was way different than mine—I was trying not to be judgy here—or she was a *really* good actress. In which case, maybe Marty would actually submit her for jobs as opposed to just trying to get into her size-two pants.

They took a seat at a booth on the opposite side of the bar. I sank back into the cushioned booth and checked my email again. Saw one from CDoran@BeserkProd.com.

Cayden.

Ah me. I felt the usual cocktail of mixed emotions I associated with Cayden Doran. Things really had been simpler back when I'd thought he was just an arrogant creep. The subject header served to further complicate things. Just two words.

Another Job

Ooh, boy. I opened the email.

Lee. Got another project I think you'll be interested in. I'll be in touch soon.

Way to not tell me anything, dude.

"Hey."

Startled, I looked up to see Randy standing in front of me. Snug jeans and an equally form-fitting athletic cut thermal showed off a well-toned physique, the shirt the same dark green as his eyes. His brown hair had been cut since the last time I'd seen him. He looked good.

Trying not to feel guilty as I closed Cayden's email, I slid out of the booth to greet him and we exchanged an awkward embrace, like our bodies weren't quite sure how they wanted to fit together. This hadn't previously been a problem. We sat down on opposite sides of the table.

I gestured at the still-full pint glass. "That's yours."

"Thanks." He nodded, not quite meeting my eyes. "You didn't have to—"

"Said I was going to buy you a farewell drink," I said firmly. When he started to protest, I added, "Hey, don't ruin the fun of my actually being able to treat, okay?"

That got a flicker of a smile. "Thanks." He took a tentative sip, then an enthusiastic swallow. "Oh man, this is good." He looked up briefly, then back down at his beer. "Sorry I'm late. Traffic down the 405 was pretty much what you'd expect and my phone's dead. I should've given myself more time to get here."

He pulled his phone and a little portable charger out of a well-used khaki messenger bag, plugged the phone into the charger, then set both on the table. I cast a surreptitious glance at the battery level. Red and dead. He hadn't lied. One of the knots in my chest unclenched.

We made some small talk, me asking about *Deadly Emancipation*, the low-budget *Deliverance* rip-off Randy had been stunt-coordinating when I'd left. He in turn relaxed a bit, relaying a couple of all-too-typical cautionary tales about testosterone-filled actors who wanted to do their own stunts without any experience.

"'Yeah, like, I took judo in high school,'" Randy said, mimicking one of the actors, "'so you bet I can take a forty-foot fall off a cliff into a river, no prob.'"

"And you said...?"

"I said, 'Be my guest.' Then I took him to the edge of the cliff in question and had him look down." Randy grinned. "After he finished puking, the subject didn't come up again."

I laughed, drank some more beer. "So, tell me about the new job. Sounds like quite a score."

"Well, it's still low-budget," Randy said, looking both pleased and embarrassed. "But definitely a step up. It's for a Netflix original television series called *Paroxysms of Terror*, with hour-long episodes all dealing with different types of monsters based on the main character's nightmares."

"Sounds pretty cool," I said neutrally. It *did* sound cool, even if the title kind of sucked, and I'd be lying if I said I wasn't envious.

"Yeah. Faustina has connections with the production company in Romania. I think one of the executive producers is an old friend. Like, *really* old." Considering how far back Faustina went, 'really old' could mean centuries.

I didn't begrudge Randy the work, but why hadn't he told me about it sooner? Sure, we hadn't talked a lot while I was in New Orleans, but we'd been in sporadic contact, and it stung that he hadn't shared the news with me until now. I had worked with Randy on his first stunt coordinator gig—a truly horrible low-budget film called *Steel Legions*, about underground gladiatorial games. He'd hired me because I had years of sword training to his month or so, and we'd pretended that I was his assistant to satisfy the machismo of the director and one of the actors. We'd worked well together and had both expressed the desire to repeat the experience. Circumstances just hadn't cooperated up to this point, what with me killing a producer, and *Deadly Emancipation* having no female action roles to speak of.

It was a bitch how these things work out.

"You bringing anyone on board?" I asked, striving for casual but only succeeding in stilted. So much for my acting talent. His gaze once again skittered away from mine.

"I'll be hiring local when I get there, at least to start. We'll see how that goes." He looked everywhere but into my eyes.

I sighed. "Look, Squid, if you don't want to work with me, I get it."

"It's not that." Randy looked trapped. "I really do want to work with you again, Lee. It's just…"

Ah hah. Here we go.

He shook his head. "Look, when you were gone, all I could think about was you and Doran. Drove me crazy. And I know that we've never made this exclusive, but I guess it never really bothered me until I thought something was going to happen with him."

I opened my mouth, but he held up a hand.

"No, let me finish." He downed half his remaining beer in one gulp. At this rate, he was gonna be a loopy lycanthrope on that flight to Romania. "I know it wasn't fair of me. I acted like an asshole when you left, but I really do get how important the work is to you. Doesn't matter if I like who you're working with. Doesn't matter if I think the production company is crap. The choice is up to you."

"Nothing happened between me and Cayden," I said quietly.

"Did you want it to?"

Ouch.

How to be honest without hurting his feelings? I chose my words carefully. "Under different circumstances, maybe. But he was kind of sort of involved with someone else, and so was I."

We both noticed my use of the past tense.

"So," he said finally, "how would you feel if I got involved with someone while I'm in Romania?"

"Look, I don't know how to answer that." I was a little angry and a lot defensive and didn't try to hide it. "Not because I don't really like you, because I do. And not even because I'm all happy at the thought of you boinking your way around the forests of Europe." He smiled at that. "But there's just… well, I've got a lot of stuff going on right now, and it makes everything else that much harder to figure out."

"What kind of stuff?" He looked at me expectantly.

This was it. Time to come clean.

I took a deep draft of my beer. "Have you ever heard of Lilith, Mother of Demons?" Off his nod, I continued, "Well, turns out, well… she's my ancestress. And all those demons she supposedly gave birth to? Also true, and it's my job to kill them. Go figure."

Randy stared at me in silence for a few beats.

Looked at our near-empty glasses, then back at me.

"How 'bout I get us another round?"

"Good idea."

CHAPTER FIFTEEN

Randy took things a lot better than he might have. The only rough moment was when I let slip that I'd already told Cayden about my ancestral *geas*. Given the context, though—Cayden and I had fought a demon together before the job on *Voodoo Wars*, and there was no guarantee it wouldn't happen again—Randy agreed that it would've been wrong for me to keep it a secret.

"I still wish you'd told me," he said, hurt seeping through his attempts to hide it.

"I wish I had, too." And I really did. "But let's be real here. Before I left, last time we talked… Well, it wasn't exactly conducive to sharing, and this wasn't something I could talk about on Zoom or email, y'know?"

"Yeah."

We sat in silence for a few minutes.

"So," Randy finally said, "where does that leave us?"

"All I know," I replied slowly, "is if me taking a job that you don't like makes you that insecure, then maybe this—" I waved a hand back and forth between us "—isn't a good idea."

Randy's hand tightened around his glass. "And all *I* know is that if I felt a little more secure about us, then you working with Doran wouldn't bother me so much."

153

"Great." I laughed, a short, bitter sound. "One of those catch-22 type situations. So, what the hell do we do about it?" He looked down at the table for a minute, then finally met my gaze, a hint of feral gold in those hazel eyes.

"I really thought I was okay with the way things were, but I guess I want more."

"And I'm not quite ready for that," I said with complete honesty.

"Do you think you ever might be?"

And that's where complete honesty left the building. My gut said no, but my heart and the small part of me that hoped maybe this could work out down the line weren't ready to call it quits.

"I can't answer that right now," I said carefully. "I'm still trying to unwrap what happened in New Orleans, and you should take some time to think about who I am. What it means to be with someone who might have to hunt down a nasty drooling demon at a moment's notice."

Randy heaved a sigh that sounded like it hurt.

"Okay. Here's what I think. I'm gonna be gone for a few months, and you'll be working another job soon. So why don't we just table this for the time being, so we can both do some thinking?"

I smiled even as tears welled up. "Sounds good." My voice was husky. *Stupid emotions.* "Dammit, when did you get all adult and shit?"

Reaching across the table, Randy covered my hands with his. They were warm and strong, and felt damned good. He was one of the good guys. Really. I wished I could believe in my heart of hearts that it was what I wanted.

†

Randy left for LAX a half hour later. I stayed in Ocean's End, both of us agreeing it was better to say our goodbyes inside. Neither of us liked that whole movie cliché of waving goodbye while a car drove out of sight.

Watching him walk out the door was hard, but at least we'd cleared the air before he left for Romania. No final decisions, and I had some breathing room before I had to start thinking about what the future might hold. What I *wanted* it to hold.

I glanced at my phone. It was 6:30. I'd made plans to stop by Eden's around 7:00 and fill her in on how it had gone with Randy. I metabolized alcohol more quickly than most non-supes, but I still needed a little bit of time before I got behind the wheel of a car.

There was no kitchen at Ocean's End, but you could order food from a couple of eateries that were approved by Manny, which meant they could find their way to the front door. I hadn't tried them, but delivery was supposedly speedy and the food tasty. Three laminated one-page menus sat at the center of the table, and my choices were Supe Kitchen, Hell's Kitchen, or Fee Fie Fo Food.

Alrighty then.

I went up the bar and placed my order with Eirian—loaded fries from Fee Fie Fo Food—then glanced around the room as I walked back to the booth. In the last half hour, the bar had filled up. Naiads, dryads, vamps, shifters of various sorts, succubae, demons, and more. Some still wore their human faces, while others dropped their disguises. Most of the available seating was full, including the long tables and every stool at the bar.

Manny still hadn't returned, although there were two more servers behind the bar, one male and one female, both of whom looked like they were related to Eirian. Maybe she had her own version of the Horn of Rohan to summon help in times of dire need.

My food arrived in under ten minutes, so I nursed the last of my beer and drank some water while nibbling on what were possibly the best loaded fries I'd ever had. Covered in ground venison, crumbled white cheese, and some sort of smoky sauce, they were still crisp.

I also became aware of envious glances—and a few outright resentful ones—being cast my way. The place had officially hit crazy crowded and I was taking up a whole booth on my own, admittedly kind of a dick move. Popping the last of the fries into my mouth, I started to slide out of the booth, only to be waylaid by none other than Marty.

"Lee Striga," he said with his idea of a pleasant smile, showing way too many yellow teeth. He stood right in front of the bench, blocking my escape route, potbelly at eye level as it strained the buttons of his shirt. I added it to the list of things I could go without seeing again for the rest of my life.

"Hey Marty." I flashed what I call an auto-smile. Brief, not entirely genuine, but good enough to avoid being outright rude. "If you'll excuse me, I was just—"

Ignoring my none-too-subtle hint, Marty slid into the seat next to me and I was in engulfed in a cloud of sweaty demon.

Well, hell.

Have you ever smelled a Scaenius demon? All smoke and sulfur with a whiff of dead things buried in the earth. Mix that with cheap-ass cologne and you had the odor that wafted off of Marty.

He leaned in even closer. "Have you thought any more about jumping ship on MTA and coming where the real action is?"

Sean had taught me the value of not burning bridges, even ones you hope you never had to cross, so my eye roll was purely mental. "Happy where I am now," I replied as nicely as possible.

"But I'll be sure to keep you posted."

Marty's smile brightened. I really wished he wouldn't do that. It was the kind of smile that gave little kids nightmares.

"Really? If even half the rumors I've been hearing are true, old Faustina hasn't gotten much work for you since *Pale Dreamer*. Doesn't sound like she's really doing her job."

"If you've been paying attention," I said between gritted teeth, "you would've heard about that little incident on *Pale Dreamer*, and know that it wasn't Faustina's fault. *Or* mine. You'd also know that I've been out of town for the last couple of months working on a film for Berserker Productions."

"So you had a little trouble with a producer." Marty waved a hand in dismissal. "A *really* good agent can get you work no matter what the hell you do. Except for sexual harassment. That's a big no-no these days."

"Yeah, I'll try to keep my hands off those poor studio heads."

"Oh well," he said, as my irony blew right past him, "the pendulum will swing in the other direction, sooner or later."

"I sure as hell hope not," I muttered.

"Anyway, sweetie," Marty continued, oblivious to the fact that I was just about ready to burn this particular bridge, and shove him out of the booth, "you think about what I said. There's a lot of work out there, and not just with psychos like Cayden Doran."

Yet before Cayden had hired me for *Voodoo Wars*, I couldn't get a job on a student film. But I didn't say so. "Don't let me keep you from your… business," I said, hoping Marty would take the hint and bugger off.

No such luck.

"You mean the arm candy? Business done. Signed, sealed, and delivered."

Ugh. Could he sound any grosser?

"Tasty little piece," he added, licking his lips.

Yes, he could. I was glad I had finished the fries before he'd ruined my appetite.

"Well, I'm sure you've got other things to do."

"Yeah, meeting another prospective client here. In fact—" lifting one horny-nail-tipped hand, Marty waved enthusiastically toward the front door "—there he is now. Looks like someone snagged my table. You don't mind if we share your booth, do you?"

"Look, Marty." I didn't bother to hide my irritation anymore. "You're welcome to this booth, but you'll need to move so I can leave." He didn't budge. "*Now.*" My voice cracked like a whip. Marty flinched, standing up as quickly as he could, what with his stomach. I slid out, restraining an urge to kick Marty's hefty hindquarters as I got to my feet.

Before I could escape, however, the crowd seem to part as an unwelcomely familiar figure strode toward us, oozing enough dangerous sexuality to catch the attention of more than one bar patron.

Skeet's cousin Nigri.

We locked eyes and he smiled. It was not a nice smile.

Of all the weird bars in all the weird towns in all the world, he had to come spider-walking into this one.

"Nigri, baby!" Marty's greeting more than made up for my lack of enthusiasm, reaching forward to envelop the spider walker in an avuncular embrace. Nigri tolerated it, nose wrinkling as if smelling… well, Marty.

"Lee Striga." The words were practically a caress, even as his eyes flashed a promise of payback. Marty looked from Nigri to me and back again.

"You two know each other?"

"We've met," I said flatly.

"We have indeed," Nigri said smoothly. I saw the spider flicker under those deceptively handsome features. "And I hope to see much more of you in the future."

Missing the double innuendo, Marty threw an arm around Nigri's shoulder. "My boy Nigri here's got an interview with Crazy Casa Productions."

"Well, good luck with your interview." I flashed a totally fake smile. "You're a good fit for Crazy... Casa."

One corner of his mouth twisted up. "You are too kind." His thought balloon said, "*Bitch*."

Not wanting to waste any more breath *or* thought balloons, I just nodded and walked away. Squeezing through the crowd, I bellied up to the bar to settle my tab with Eirian, muscling past two imps and a very voluptuous succubus who turned and winked at me as I inadvertently brushed against her butt. Reaching my destination, I found myself face-to-face with Manny.

"Lee, girl!" he bellowed in a thick Gaelic accent so low and sexy that it almost made up for his overabundance of facial fur. Manny's hair was long and fiery red, falling well past his shoulders and down his back. The front was tied in narrow braids, with bits of seashells, multicolored glass, and silver beads woven into his beard. His mustache flowed into the beard, with just enough space between the two to leave a gap for eating. A non-consumptive Jack Sparrow.

Manny's eyes changed color according to his mood—very seventies, like a mood ring—and at the moment his irises were a lovely calm shade of blue, like the sea of a tropical paradise. Which, judging by the almost visible cloud of rum wafting from his mouth, might be where the back door led.

"What can I do you for, *acushla*?" he asked. "Some Triple Threat? Dragon's Milk?" He grinned, showing a flash of very white teeth. "No, wait, we have a new imperial stout on tap that ye must try, lass. Not bourbon barrel, but so rich and flavorful you'd swear it's made of angel's tears."

"That's okay, Manny." I held out my credit card. "I'm closing out my tab."

Ignoring me, Manny grabbed a four-ounce taster, filled it from one of the taps, and set the glass in front of me with an emphatic thump, yet somehow managing not to spill a drop.

"Drink!" He glared at me, calm blue irises darkening to an ominous gray, storm clouds scudding across a turbulent sea. I knew better than to argue with Manny when he was sober, let alone however many sheets to the wind he was at the moment. I'd never seen him drunk before, so I had no basis for comparison. Besides, who was I to turn down free beer?

I took a sip.

"Oh man…" Manny had not lied. Nodding my approval, I slapped my credit card down on the bar top. "That is seriously good, Manny," I said. "If I hadn't already had two pints of Triple Threat, I'd be all over it."

Looking disappointed, Manny nodded. "If ye're certain I can't tempt ye."

"Next time for sure."

Muttering to himself, Manny closed out my tab, handed me back my card and the charge slip. I added a hefty tip to the amount, handed it back to him, and—

Manny grabbed my wrist, eyes whirling like ever-expanding and contracting pinwheels, irises changing color with each gyration.

Oh hell.

Along with his mad bartender skills, Manny had an oracular streak. I knew what was coming when his eyes started spinning like a spirograph. Kind of like that old arcade fortune-teller Zoltar the Great, but in Manny's case you didn't have to stick a quarter in, and you never knew when it was going to happen.

He never remembered what he said during one of these spells, but whenever he'd gone all Delphi on my ass, he'd been pretty accurate. He started speaking, voice low and spooky.

Above the hill
Beneath the earth
In the manse so still
The grave gives birth.

When four becomes three
and three becomes none
Then shall all see
what has now begun.

For the room
turned tomb
begins to bloom
bringing doom…

Silent as midnight,
Silver as moonlight
A shape unconcealed
In a flickering field
All of black and white.

What the what? This was the third oracular message Manny had given me, and the other two had been short, sweet, and... okay, not really clear, but did I mention short and sweet?

They hadn't made sense to me until well after the fact, but this one was what I'd expect if the Sphinx decided to combine riddles with a lengthy poetry reading at a coffee house.

And... Holy Moses, he wasn't finished yet.

Vortices in spiral urge
forces in a tidal surge.
Like a fever, like a fire
burns the ever-widening gyre.

Rage and madness hold in thrall
until the nothing devours the all—
unless the balance is restored
good and evil must be moored.

Then the pinwheels in Manny's eyes stopped spinning, slowly spiraling backward until his irises settled on a silvery blue. He shook his head as if to clear it. "And watch out for spiders," he muttered.

"You okay, Manny?" I asked.

"Just fine, girl," he replied. His face clouded over briefly. "Did I—"

"Manny!" someone bellowed from the other end of the bar. "Get down here, you old mariner, you!"

"Excuse me then, Lee." Manny shook his head again and wandered down the bar.

Watch out for spiders. I couldn't resist a quick glance over at

Nigri, who appeared deep in conversation with Marty. Then he looked up at me and smiled, and I knew he'd been watching me the entire time.

With a quick farewell to Eirian, I made my way to the front door and left Ocean's End.

CHAPTER SIXTEEN

Glancing at his car's clock, Floyd Bush frowned. He had a little over two hours to get to Fig and Olive in West Hollywood, and while he'd given himself an extra hour for unexpected traffic, he didn't like cutting things this close.

"Should I—?"

"No," Floyd snapped, cutting his assistant Bebe's sentence off at the knees. "Tell Mrs. Wilson it would not be a prudent decision to give her current tenants another break in rent. There's a reason she and her family aren't doing better financially, and it's choices like this. Remind her it's business, not charity. Not her problem if they end up on the street."

Just as he punched the "end call" button, a streak of silver cut in front of him and he hit the brakes. A loud explosion sounded from the rear passenger side of his BMW and the car went into a messy skid across four lanes of the 101 freeway, Floyd yelling all the way until he managed to bring it to a stop on the shoulder, heart thudding so hard he thought he might be having a heart attack.

Holy shit.

Floyd sat there for a few moments until his heartbeat slowed to a semi-normal rate. He checked to make sure the front of his pants wasn't wet. Still dry but damn, it had been a close call. Too close. That fucking silver Porsche had nearly slammed into him. If he hadn't had to slam on his brakes, the tire wouldn't have blown. Sure, he'd missed a couple of basic maintenance appointments, but when you were a good driver, you didn't need 'em, right?

Finally, he opened his door and got out, pissed to find his legs were wobbly as he rounded the car to check out the damage.

"Shit."

The rear passenger-side tire was shredded, rubber no doubt scattered across the freeway. The hubcap was gone, and the rim had buckled under the weight of the car.

"Shit," Floyd repeated, more heartfelt this time around. He'd nearly died, no way around it. He glanced at his watch. Even worse, he was going to be late to his meeting. Time was money, and this particular client didn't have any trouble with Floyd's "it's just business" mindset.

Maybe he could get a rideshare. Lyfts and Ubers were everywhere these days, and even if it took someone half an hour or so to reach him, it'd still be faster than waiting for Triple-A. First, though, he'd have to get off the freeway so the driver could stop safely to pick him up. He'd have Bebe call for a tow and just leave the key under the front seat. Not like anyone could steal his BMW without a tow truck.

Hitting Bebe's number, he started walking along the shoulder of the freeway back the way he'd come from. He was certain there had been an exit not too far back, although it was a part of the San Fernando Valley he wasn't familiar with, some little armpit sandwiched between Agoura Hills and Calabasas. Sure, there was money out here, but who wanted to live anywhere north of the Sepulveda Pass?

The call went to voicemail. Black mark, Bebe, he thought. If she wanted to keep her job, she'd better answer no matter what time he called.

Clutching his phone, he tried to ignore the wind of the cars speeding past him, hugging the shoulder as close to the guardrails as possible.

Ending up splatted like roadkill by a day laborer in a pickup was not how he wanted to go.

"No fucking way," he muttered as an eighteen-wheeler roared past. He nearly jumped out of his skin when the asshole driver laid on the horn, coming as close to dousing his trousers as he had during the blowout. "Motherfucker!"

Good thing he didn't have a weak heart.

"Not too far back" turned out to be almost a mile of backtracking before he reached the exit, although it was technically an on-ramp. Should've checked a map. *Luckily there weren't any vehicles currently looking to merge onto the 101, so he trudged up the ramp to a single-lane asphalt road without further incident, looking around for some sort of signage to tell him what road he was on. No luck. Just a lonely asphalt road crossing the freeway to the west. No gas stations, no restaurants, no sign of life other than some lights up in the hills.*

No big deal, *he thought. All he had to do was use "current location" on Uber or Lyft and they'd find him via the wonders of GPS. He looked at his phone, only to discover the "no service" message where bars should be. Shit, how was this even possible? This was Los Angeles County, not the fucking Ozarks. There had to be cell service.*

Should he retrace his steps to the car? The bone-rattling roar of another eighteen-wheeler jamming down the 101 answered that question. He'd keep walking, head toward the lights. Maybe with a little extra elevation, his phone company would give him a fucking signal.

Using the distant lights as his compass, cursing the lack of streetlights and the increasing cold as the wind kicked up, Floyd kept walking, a frigid gust piercing his expensive linen jacket and silk shirt beneath. He was dressed for success, not warmth. His shoes weren't made for walking, either—he could feel blisters forming on both heels.

After nearly biting his tongue when he tripped over random debris,

Floyd switched on his phone's flashlight app. He focused on the splash of illumination in front of him, wondering when the last time a road crew had been out. His path was littered with debris and potholes.

"Fucking disgrace," he muttered.

Another ten minutes of trudging up the increasingly windy road brought him close enough to see the source of the light—a small mom'n'pop market that made his upper lip curl. All it lacked was a couple of geezers in rocking chairs on the porch. Made him want to puke. Fuck it. This looked like the only game in this shithole. He checked his phone's readout—still no bars, and worse, the battery was in the red, with only seven percent remaining.

"Shit!" Floyd quickly switched to low-power mode, shut off the flashlight, and pocketed his phone, stopping to consider his options. There was a large field to his right, a wooden fence separating it from the road, and the store was on the other side of it, about a football field's distance away. Cutting across would save him a good ten minutes.

He'd take it.

Ducking down, Floyd shimmied between the fence boards, swearing yet again when his jacket snagged on a splinter. The ripping sound was like a fart, which both embarrassed and pissed him off at the same time, even though there was no one there to hear it. As if his own body was in on the joke, he let loose an involuntary fart loud enough to make him blush.

A soft laugh floated across the field. Low, almost like a hiss.

What the fuck?

Had to be his imagination.

Shaking his head, Floyd set off across the field, shoes sinking with every step into god knows what muck. Probably cow shit, from the smell. Everything he was wearing was pretty much a write-off at this point.

Sploosh. *His left foot sank ankle deep in what was* definitely a cow patty. He wondered briefly why there were no cows, but a repeat of that sibilant laugh distracted him.

"Hey, anyone there?" he said loudly.

Nothing.

"Seriously, if there's someone there and you have a working phone, I'm more than happy to slip you a G-note to help me get an Uber out of here." Only the wind answered. Fuck. He kept walking. The lights beckoned to him, and he picked up his pace as if he could outdistance his own fear.

Something snagged his ankle and he fell on one knee, hard enough to bring tears to his eyes. Before he could get to his feet, something tightened around his ankle, yanked, and dragged him across the rough ground and down into darkness. Floyd's scream was swallowed by the earth as he fell into the ditch, hole, whatever it was, limbs flailing and scraping against unseen walls until he hit bottom, bouncing slightly against a spongy surface.

Stunned, Floyd lay on his back in pitch blackness, for how long he couldn't say, heart pounding erratically like badly played bongo drums. When the initial shock receded, he took stock. No injuries as far as he could tell, other than a few scrapes and bruises. He sat up, cautiously lifting his hand to make sure he didn't bash his head.

He must have gotten disoriented in the dark, gotten tangled in wiring or something, and tripped. Stepped in a ditch, or maybe a sinkhole. He wondered if he could sue the landowner. Sure, he'd ducked the fence, but there'd been crazier lawsuits that never should have seen the light of day.

As comforting thoughts of litigation calmed him down, Floyd became aware of a faint sweet-sour smell. He didn't recognize it, but it creeped him out, hairs rising on the back of his neck. Time to get the hell out of there. Fumbling in the dark, he pulled out his phone, hit the "home" button, nearly crying with relief at the faint glow.

The battery was down to four percent. He'd have to be quick.

Using the flashlight app, Floyd lit the space around him. A rounded chamber dug in the earth, the ceiling about five feet above with enough room to stretch out his arms on the sides. Directing the flashlight beam upward, he saw that the walls narrowed to create a tube-like tunnel that went up another ten feet or so. Maybe a well…? The darkness at the top was lighter than below and he could hear the wind blowing. That had to be where he'd fallen in. Floyd thought he could climb out, using the spongy stuff for hand- and footholds.

All surfaces, including the one below him, were lined with what looked like cotton batting. He touched it—soft and springy. The indentations his fingers made quickly bounced back, like memory foam. He didn't know what had created this burrow and—

Burrow?

Now where did that come from? He didn't like it.

Something rustled behind him, the sound furtive and somehow… threatening. He shivered. Right about now he didn't care if he ever got another client. Didn't care if the Wilsons never charged their deadbeat tenants another month's rent. Didn't care if he had to huddle in cow shit all night to keep warm. He just wanted to get the fuck out.

Another soft rustle, like layers of silk rubbing together.

Don't look, *he thought.* Just focus on getting your ass out of here. Just. Don't. Look.

Turning slowly, Floyd looked.

A round opening where one hadn't been moments before. The carrion stench was no longer faint, a draft pushing the smell out of the opening into his chamber. He couldn't see anything in the blackness beyond, but he knew something was there. Watching. Waiting.

Then it moved.

"Fuck it."

Shoving his phone into his jacket pocket, Floyd scrambled off his hands and knees, launching himself up the narrow tube toward fresh air. Clawing with his fingers, he dug into the sides and hoisted himself up, thanking Christ he'd stayed in shape, scooting himself upward with elbows and ass. Wriggling like a well-dressed inchworm.

Just a couple more feet.

He could smell fresh air, right above him. Sweat poured down his forehead, stinging his eyes, dripping down the back of his neck. Muscles in his back and shoulders strained.

Then his fingers gripped the edge of the hole. Felt hard-packed dirt and rocks. Floyd nearly wept with relief as he hoisted himself up the last foot, forearms trembling with the strain as his head emerged into the fresh air. A powerful gust of wind blew dirt into his open, panting mouth. He could have eaten it in gratitude, just at the sight of the stars peeking out from between the clouds scudding across the sky. He rested his forehead on the dirt, then tensed his muscles for one last heave to pull himself out of the hole.

Something whipped around his ankle again and yanked hard, pulling him back underground. The last thing Floyd saw before he was dragged back into the foul-smelling darkness was the disk of the night sky shut out by darkness.

CHAPTER SEVENTEEN

In the half-dozen or so months since we'd met, Eden and I got together at Ocean's End whenever her schedule allowed. Unlike me, her acting career was on an upward trajectory, so that limited things a bit. However, I'd crashed at her place more than once after sampling the many wonderful craft beers Manny had to offer.

I walked down the boardwalk, which was shutting down as twilight gave way to night. The rollerbladers, skateboarders, and tourists thinned out as the sun went down, and most of the vendors had already closed their tables and booths. There were still people out walking, mostly hipsters and techies heading down to the brewpub on the other side of Ocean's End.

They'd wish they were cool enough for Ocean's End, I thought. *If they knew it existed.*

Shaking my head, I made my way to Paloma Avenue and turned left. Eden's brick building was originally built in the thirties. Five stories rose on three sides of a central courtyard, an iron fence and gate keeping out anyone who didn't belong. Eden had an apartment on the ground floor, although it could almost be called a basement apartment as the view from her windows started slightly below ground level.

Punching the code "EDEN" into the keypad at the front gate, I pushed it open. She'd shared it with me shortly after we'd become friends, and that kind of trust wasn't something you shrugged off. I'd always been so busy working with KSC that outside friendships had never come easily. Eden had been a welcome surprise.

We'd worked together on *Steel Legions*, a horrible movie—the same one that had convinced me that Randy wasn't just another douche bro wannabe—and then she'd ended up on *Pale Dreamer,* a film that should have been my foot in the door of acting. It had almost tanked my career, but had given me a great friend.

Going down the stairs, I'd barely lifted my hand to knock when the door was flung open and she grabbed me in a hug. Eden Carmel—"Car-MEL" like the seaside town—was the epitome of the girl next door. Beautiful, sexy, and wholesome all in one package. A tall, curvaceous blonde who wore shell-pink kimonos with silver embroidered butterflies on them. As usual, she looked happy to be alive. She woke up like that, too. I am not a morning person by choice, but I manage. Whereas Eden is like a sunflower. She blossoms as soon as dawn breaks over the horizon.

I also suspect she farts rose petals, but cannot confirm that.

"Come *in*," she said, practically dragging me inside. "I've missed you!" The interior of her apartment looked like a classy version of the bottle in *I Dream of Jeannie*. Rose-colored silk draped across the ceiling. An antique-looking light fixture illuminated the room in flattering rose-gold shades, like being filmed through gauze and Vaseline. Eden called it her Cybill Shepherd lighting. The living room was all silks and velvets in various shades of pink thrown over an overstuffed couch and two matching chairs. Lots of flowing drapes and pleasantly scented candles.

Taking a deep inhale, I collapsed onto the couch and sighed happily.

"Want something to drink? I'm drinking chardonnay, but I've got some good zin if you want it."

"I really shouldn't," I demurred. "I had beer at Ocean's End."

"And…?"

"Lots of beer." I amended. "I have to drive home at some point, so it's probably not a good idea."

"Megan's at Tandy's so… if you wanna crash here, totally not a problem."

Megan was Eden's roommate. She'd been the makeup artist on *Steel Legions* and I think I'd seen her maybe twice since then. Tandy was her girlfriend, a costume designer for a lot of artsy student productions at UCLA, and Megan spent most of her time there. Which was convenient, since I didn't feel like I was putting her out if I stayed over. And tonight, hanging out with Eden was the perfect antidote to the funk I'd felt since Randy had left.

"Lemme just shoot Sean a text so he doesn't freak if I'm not home before midnight and yeah, I'll take a glass of wine."

"Excellent!" Eden headed off into the kitchen while I kicked off my shoes and texted. At twenty-nine it felt kinda silly to be checking in like a teenager with a curfew, but Sean worried… Given my family history, I guess his concern was understandable.

Eden returned with a big glass of red wine in one hand and a bottle of Rombauer zin in the other, handing them both to me. She topped her own glass off with some chardonnay from the same vintner and plopped down next to me on the couch.

"Cheers!" she said brightly. We clinked glasses and sipped our wine. I sighed in contentment.

"This is good shit," I said.

"I got some good news today and wanted to treat myself."

"Tell all."

"Well, okay then." Eden pulled her legs underneath her and leaned toward me. "I just got booked for a show that mixes reality and historical recreation. I'm playing an up-and-coming actress from the twenties. Evidently I'm a dead ringer for her."

"What was her name?"

"Dawn Jardine."

"Very cool!" I'd never heard of her, but that didn't stop me from being happy for my friend. We clinked glasses again. "Have you done reality TV before?"

"Back when I started out, I did a season of *The Stag*."

"I'm sorry," I said with total sincerity. *The Stag* had been a sleazy knock-off of the much more successful *The Bachelor*. The females vying for the stag's attention had been called "does," as in female deer, and they were vying for the ultimate prize known as "Rutting Season." *Oy*.

"I know, right?" Wrinkling her nose, she continued, "Most of the other does were kinda horrible. Just trashy and always getting drunk and screaming at each other. And the stag…" She gave a delicate shudder. "I think he missed the turnoff to *Duck Dynasty*."

"So you're doing this show why, exactly?"

"Because it's *True Horrors of Hollywood*."

"No way! Totally one of my guilty pleasures." While not as cheesy as, say, *Ghost Detectives* or any of those other "real life" ghost-hunting shows involving shaky cams and lots of *"Oh my god, do you hear that?"* fake narrative, it was still pretty bad.

"I know, right? I mean, it's totally over the top, but it's so much fun, and I've been hired for the recreation portion of the show, not the ghost-busting."

Sitting up straight, I gasped. "I think I heard something," I said in an over-the-top tremolo. "Did you hear it? Oh my god, I'm so scared!" Wine sloshed in my glass as Eden smacked my shoulder.

"*Very* funny. What about you? Anything in the pipeline?"

I heaved a sigh.

"Have you checked in with Faustina?" she pressed.

I nodded glumly. "Guess I'm still *persona non grata* around town. I should be grateful she hasn't dumped me as a client. Although she did get her fifteen percent of my salary on *Voodoo Wars*."

Eden nodded in commiseration—it was standard practice to pay one's agent a percentage, whether or not they actually sent you out for a job. I'd gotten *Voodoo Wars* on my own, but Faustina had handled all the contract negotiations. Professionalism is a form of paying it forward. Even so, I decided to change the subject before I got depressed.

"So, what horror of Hollywood is this episode about?"

"Ned DuShane and all the crazy stuff that's happened on his property over the years. They're going to be filming at his old mansion."

Oh boy.

My expression must have given me away

"What?" Eden raised an eyebrow.

I ripped the Band-Aid right off. "Cayden bought DuShane's place a few months ago."

Eden's jaw dropped. "Wait. Doran is living in DuShane's horror castle?"

"Yup."

Eden sat with that for a minute. "Huh."

"So… are you ever going to tell me what the deal is?"

Eden opened her mouth, hesitated, then shut it again. Drank some wine. "Not a lot to tell," she finally replied. "Just some stuff in the past that makes being in the same room as him kinda uncomfortable." She waved a hand, dismissing the topic. "How did the talk with Randy go?"

That was as much as I was gonna get for the time being, so I dropped the subject and answered her question.

"Pretty good. I mean, we weren't in a great place anyway, but it didn't seem to make it any worse."

"You mean the fact you told Cayden—and me—before you told him?"

"I think he understood." I hesitated. "Mostly. At least he tried. I'm pretty sure part of him is still hurt by it, even if it's not rational."

"Since when are relationships based on rationality?"

"Too true."

"Where did you leave it?"

I sighed. "He's off to Romania, and I'm probably gonna be doing another job." I looked down at my glass. "Who knows where things will stand when we see each other again."

"You sound relieved." I glanced up at that, sharply, but there was no judgment in Eden's expression. If I'd heard anything in her tone, it was my own guilty feelings that put it there. We drank our wine in silence for a moment, Eden topping off both our glasses without asking.

She knew me well.

"So, I think Megan is moving in with Tandy, sooner rather than later," she said as she poured.

"Really?" The eagerness in my voice made me wince.

"Yup. She's been talking about it for months, and I've noticed more of her stuff's been vanishing every time she goes over there."

"Will you stay here if she moves out?" I asked, trying my best to sound casual.

"Hell yeah," Eden said. "Having a roommate is great as far as saving some money, but not really necessary. I could handle the rent on this place on my own without hurting too much."

I nodded, trying not to let my disappointment show. Why would Eden want to have someone like me as a roomie? Sure, I'd earned some good bank during *Voodoo Wars*, but that wouldn't last forever, and until I started getting work on even a semi-regular basis again, she'd be better off going with one of the many waitress-slash-model-slash-actresses out there. At least they'd be guaranteed to pay their share of the bills.

"I don't suppose…" Eden stopped.

"What?"

"Well, not sure if or when this is gonna happen, and I know you have a sweet situation where you live now, but… would you maybe wanna move in with me?"

"Really?"

"Really."

"Oh my god, yes!" I practically shouted it. "You have no idea how much I'd love that. But… my financial situation isn't exactly stable. And while I'd like to think I'll be back in the job market on a regular basis, given demons and dead producers, there's no way to predict the future."

Eden shrugged. "Like I said, I can swing this place on my own if I have to. And I'd so much rather have someone live here who won't sneer at me for binge-watching *The Witcher*."

"I'd watch it with you," I declared loyally.

"I know you would, sweetie." Eden smiled, a big bliss-filled smile. "So you wanna have more wine and watch *The Witcher*?"

"Yes please."

†

DUSHANE MANSION

1945

"This is amazing," Dr. Hodel murmured as he wandered through the mansion, admiring the art nouveau furnishings. He touched a hand-carved teak side table. "It's like a museum." The real estate agent, a self-effacing man in his thirties, nodded.

"These are the original furnishings."

"Absolutely magnificent," Hodel replied.

He was sorely tempted by the property. The price was inarguably a bargain. If only the estate was closer to Los Angeles proper... Beverly Hills, Los Feliz, Hollywood. Even Encino or Burbank, but this was a good forty-five minutes out on the 101, not counting the drive once he left the freeway.

Plus, he'd fallen in love with the Sowden House in Los Feliz. Lloyd Wright's Mayan revival seemed somehow more dignified than the mishmash of styles presented here.

Still, the price of the DuShane property was tempting, but would it present the sort of appearance he wanted to convey?

Doubtful.

Hodel had already made up his mind, but he still wanted to tour the rest of the estate. Something about its energy appealed to him. Sparked ideas. Gave him confidence that he could do far more to follow his desires than he'd even considered.

†

Ned watched the prissy sap wander through his house. Thought about popping out of a mirror or manifesting at the top of a staircase so that the intruder would tumble back down, hopefully breaking his neck along the way.

For no real reason, however, Ned let him reach the top of the stairs unhindered, to meander down the hallway. He stopped in front of one of Ned's favorite pieces of art—a reproduction of Michelangelo's David *that he'd bought in Florence.*

The man sniffed in disdain. "Tacky."

"Cocksucker," Ned snarled.

The man paused and looked down the hallway, where Ned stood in front of his old bedroom.

Huh. Can he hear me?

"Can you hear me?"

Cocking his head to one side, the man made his way over to where Ned stood. Reached out a hand, put it right through Ned's chest and touched the wall behind him.

Hodel. His name is Hodel.

Ned immediately saw into the man's soul—black, depraved, utterly selfish—and decided not to kill him. He felt a surge of energy from the man's dark thoughts and knew he could use him.

The guy left and didn't return. Ned was disappointed, but some of the seemingly random jolts of power he felt over the next few years had the… well, the flavor of Hodel. He decided to push a little harder, make more meat puppets out of the people who came through the doors of his mansion. A few more revenants wouldn't hurt, either—he liked the idea of an army at his command, even if they were rotting on the hoof.

Ned wasn't sure, but every now and again, when he tapped into the power of the land, he sensed the presence of Something Else.

Something even nastier than him.

†

Having fallen asleep in the middle of the third *Witcher* episode, I woke up a little before five. Eden had left a pot of coffee ready to brew and a to-go cup in the kitchen.

I love that woman.

Thanks to Eden's most excellent—and very strong—coffee, I was wide awake for the drive home. It was a pleasure navigating the freeways when traffic was light. Singing loudly along with a Billy Idol CD, I made it to my exit off the 101 in a little over half an hour—going only slightly over the speed limit—turning off onto the dirt road leading up to the Ranch at a more sedate pace.

Good thing, because if I'd been speeding, I would have hit the coyote trotting across the road, several pups trailing along behind it. Slamming on the brakes, I stopped the Saturn with a lurch that made me grateful for my seatbelt. The little parade continued until the last pup crossed the road, joining its siblings and mother as they headed into the sage and chaparral, moving in the direction of the Ranch.

Curiouser and curiouser.

Giving in to an impulse, I shut off the Saturn's engine, cutting Billy off in mid-rebel yell. Unrolled the driver's side window for a moment and listened. Nothing. I got out and walked a few steps away.

Normally the sound of crickets and other critters could be heard before dawn, especially on a morning as still as this one. No wind, really not even a breeze, but there was something in the air, something that smelled and *felt* wrong, like when Banjo had turned up at the Ranch. Underneath the familiar scent of sage and the licorice fragrance of anise was the smell of something bitter and overripe at the same time.

As I turned back to the Saturn, the rising sun glinted off something hugging the foothills at the base of the mountain. It was as if someone was trying to send a signal with a mirror.

I stared, and it didn't stop.

What if someone up there needed help?

Following my gut—my stupid, gonna–get–me–killed–someday gut—I got back in my car and drove up the road. Both my amulet and my scar were quiet, though, so it seemed worth the risk. I drove up the road until it dead–ended against the foothills.

The DuShane property backed up against the mountain a few hundred yards to the south, the wrought–iron fence that surrounded it scarcely visible in dawn's early light. Pulling a Maglite out of the glove compartment and a crowbar from the trunk, I pocketed my keys and left the road, using the light in my left hand to avoid gopher and snake holes, and hefting the crowbar in my right. Just in case.

The east took on a rosy glow that blended with the indigo of the night sky. I wished I was sitting on the porch at the Ranch, coffee in hand, watching the sun rise so I could fully appreciate the beauty. As it was, the muted blues, grays, and pinks were haunting as dawn began to break. Almost creepy.

As I walked across the hard–packed dirt, boot heels crunching softly on rocks and weeds, a rattlesnake slithered past me, not bothering to shake its rattle. I stopped, but might as well have been a stump for all it cared. And surprise–surprise, it was headed in the direction of the Ranch. I started walking again, nearing a gulch lined with scrub oak. Probably a remnant from earthquakes past that changed the face of the terrain with crevices and hillocks.

Glancing up, I noticed a dark patch against the dirt, rocks, and scrub oak clinging to the base of the foothill. A rectangular slit, like one of those skinny windows at the top of castles that archers used to fire arrows. Then the light glinted in my eyes again, and I turned my attention back to the gulch.

As I drew closer, I saw that it was really more of a glorified ditch. Maybe ten feet across and six feet deep at its lowest, hugging the curve of the hill. Sage, scrub oak, alder, and laurel grew all along its length, but whatever the light was reflecting off, there was an overabundance of brush and branches as if—

As if someone had tried to cover up the vehicle that lay on its side in the ditch.

A black Xterra, just like Sean's.

Oh god.

Jumping down next to the car, I clambered up on the side so I could get to the driver's door, tossing aside tree branches that had been spread over it. Opening the door was no problem, but it wanted to slam shut on me. Gravity was not my friend. Finally, I managed to slither inside, letting the door shut and unrolling the window. The passenger window was closed, but cracks spiderwebbed through it, so I braced my feet on the more solid door below it and looked around.

No keys in the ignition. No fast-food wrappers either, and instead of stale burritos it smelled like the air freshener hanging from the rearview mirror, which made me heave a sigh of relief. Sean's Xterra never quite lost the funk left over from the days he and Seth lived on fast food.

Leaning my crowbar against the now vertical back of the seat, I opened the glovebox and reached inside, pulling out some papers. Dawn was still a few minutes away, so I shone the Maglite beam on them. Some maps of Los Angeles and the surrounding counties. A movie schedule for a pretentious northern Hollywood art theater. A photocopy of a car registration under the name of Jada Zephyr.

Shit.

Scrambling out through the Xterra's window, I pulled my cell phone from my jeans pocket and dialed the number for Maggie Fitzgerald, head of LAPD's Kolchak Division.

CHAPTER EIGHTEEN

The Kolchak Squad was a division of LAPD that dealt with the weirder side of life—in other words, anything to do with supernaturals. Every major city has one, although only the Los Angeles division was named after Carl Kolchak of *Nightstalker* fame.

I've heard the department compared to *The X-Files*, except there are no skeptics on the Kolchak Squad. Their members are either supes themselves or well aware of their existence. A prerequisite for the latter is not being freaked out by the thought that it was entirely possible the ordinary-looking couple next table at your favorite restaurant might not be human.

Detective Maggie Fitzgerald had her notebook open, pen in hand, while she asked questions and recorded my answers. Tall and broad-shouldered, Det. Fitzgerald was a quintessential example of Black Irish. Glossy dark hair in an impeccable French braid. Blue eyes the color of gentian. A slight lilt to her voice that spoke of her Gaelic ancestry.

After she and another member of the Kolchak Squad—a tall, skinny man, so thin that the phrase "stick insect" came to mind—had met me by Jada's vehicle and poked around for a bit, we'd gone to the Ranch. Sean and Seth were there, and the five of us were sitting in the kitchen, drinking coffee courtesy of Seth.

Much to his annoyance, Maggie took hers with cream and honey.

Her sidekick had a small plastic case dangling from a nylon cord around his neck, the word *Bose* stamped on it. *Earplugs*, I thought. Probably noise-canceling to keep his eardrums from imploding should his boss lose her temper. If I worked with Maggie Fitzgerald, I'd want those too, because being yelled at by a banshee is potentially lethal and never pleasant.

"When was the last time any of you saw Ms. Zephyr?"

"Saturday, two nights ago," I replied.

She nodded, then turned to Seth and Sean. "What about you two?"

"Same," Sean said. Seth nodded silently.

Back to me. "Anything weird or abnormal about her behavior?"

"She'd left the Ranch in… well, in kind of a huff."

"Which isn't necessarily abnormal for Jada," Sean added.

"What d'ya mean by that?" Det. Fitzgerald shot him a sharp glance.

"She and I had words," I interjected. "She got her feelings hurt, I tried to talk to her, and it didn't go over well. We don't get along that well and—"

"And Jada tends to overreact," Sean said. Neither he nor his son looked the least bit perturbed at being questioned by the police. Not entirely surprising. Nephilim don't have a lot of guilt in their genetics.

"Hmm." She scribbled something in her notepad.

Meanwhile, I stared into my mug as if it held the secret to Jada's disappearance. Maybe—just maybe—someone had stolen her car and crashed it. If this were the case, her being out of contact with any of us wasn't a big deal. But had she shown up for work this morning on *Vampshee 3: Child of Chaos*?

I asked the question out loud, finishing with, "Because if she didn't, that's a reason to worry." Det. Fitzgerald nodded, scribbled down some more notes. Turning to her subordinate.

"Check and see if she checked in with the production," she said brusquely.

He nodded and left the room to make the call. I hoped Jada was there on set. That her vehicle had been stolen, taken for a joyride that hadn't ended well, and that the thieves had limped away from the scene of the accident.

"Do you have anything to add, Ms. Striga?"

"Huh?" I looked up, startled out of my thoughts. "No, not really. I just hope she turns up on set."

"Why didn't the two of you get along?" she asked.

Oh lord, I thought. How did I even begin to unpack the baggage that Jada had where I was concerned? Before I could even try, help came from an unexpected source.

"Sibling rivalry without the benefit of being related," Seth said bluntly. "Jada has always been resentful of Lee's talent and place in our crew, and even though she took over Lee's stunt-doubling of Kaley Avondale on *The Netherworld Chronicles*, it didn't do anything to make Jada more secure, because she just wasn't as good."

I stared at Seth, trying to pick my jaw up off the ground. I could count on one hand the times he'd complimented me to my face, most of them in the last few months, and I didn't think I'd ever get used to it.

Det. Stick Insect came back into the kitchen. He shook his head.

"She didn't show up on set, and hasn't called in."

Sean and I exchanged worried looks. Seth's face was expressionless, but his jaw tightened a little bit as he topped off our coffee without being asked. Det. Fitzgerald added more cream, stirring it in with a thoughtful look.

"Jada's not the first to go missing in this neck of the woods over the last month or so, is she?" I asked.

"Sadly, she is not," the detective confirmed. "Nor, indeed, over the last eighty or so years."

My eyebrows shot up. "Seriously?"

"As a heart attack," she replied. "This area—" she gave a vague wave with one hand "—has always been known for assorted weird happenings. Not all bad, mind you, but enough in the files to ensure the Squad pays attention when we get a report out here." From her tone, it sounded as if Maggie Fitzgerald had passion for this topic. "People began disappearing in a roughly ten-square-mile patch around here back when Ventura Boulevard was the main thoroughfare in the Valley."

"Kind of a landlocked Bermuda Triangle," I offered.

She gave a humorless smile. "You're not the first to describe it as such." She drained her coffee mug. "At any rate, if you hear anything from Ms. Zephyr, let us know. In the meantime… be careful."

CHAPTER NINETEEN

After the Kolchaks drove away, I poured myself yet another cup of coffee, watching the cream pinwheel with the rich brown java in my mug.

"You okay, hon?" Sean put a comforting hand on my shoulder.

I looked up at him. "Honestly, I don't know how to answer that."

He gave a rueful smile. "Guess I understand that. Just let me know if there's anything I can do, okay?"

"Will do." Standing, I gave him a quick kiss on his cheek, took my coffee, and wandered outside onto the porch, making my way around the side to sit in my rocking chair. There I stared up at the Santa Monica mountains… and the DuShane mansion.

I'd barely settled my butt into the cushion when my phone rang. Heaving an aggrieved sigh, I pulled it out of my jeans pocket.

Cayden.

Briefly thinking about letting it go to voicemail, I instead hit "answer" and took the call. It would take my mind off Jada's disappearance.

"What's up?"

"Enjoying the view of my house?"

I sat up straight in my chair. "How do you know where I am?"

"Uh… sorcerer, remember?"

I raised an eyebrow. "Now *that's* not stalkery."

"Hmmm… well, would it make you feel better if I promise only to use my powers for good, and not for evil?"

I laughed. "Do you really expect me to believe that?"

"The one thing you *can* trust is that I will not lie to you." Oddly enough, I believed him.

"Asshat," I said without malice. He gave a low chuckle. Did he know how sexy that was? I bet he did. I drank some more coffee.

"So what's the job?" I asked.

"*True Hollywood Horrors.*"

I almost did a spit take. *Oh, Universe,* I thought. *You and your whacky synchronicity.*

"Would this by any chance be the segment on Ned DuShane?" I knew the answer even as I asked the question.

"Good guess." He didn't sound surprised. Which didn't surprise me.

"And they want to film at the mansion," I continued, "because they want to do a recreation of one of DuShane's infamous parties."

"On the nose. The production company also wants to film a few 'what if' scenarios, different theories that have surfaced over the years. Speculations about DuShane's disappearance, for instance, and—"

"Wait, I thought he went all hermit in the late twenties, and then some relatives found his body a few years later."

"Nope. That was just one of the many rumors that was spread. He actually vanished in the middle of what had evidently been quite the hedonistic orgy-fest. The studio didn't like the optics."

"Seriously?"

"Yeah. The police searched for him for weeks, in the mansion and on the surrounding grounds. Popular theory was that he'd done a runner because his more unsavory activities had come to light. Back in the day, the studio system did what they could to protect their money makers, but there were some things that couldn't be swept under the rug."

A breeze wafted across the porch, bringing the scents of eucalyptus, sage, and anise. I watched a jackrabbit hop across the dusty ground, unphased by the proximity of what looked like a bobcat—make that a bobcat and two bob-kittens—at the far western edge of the fence.

"What exactly do you want me to do?"

Oh, for a chance to rephrase that.

He chuckled but, surprisingly, let me off the hook. "I'm not going to be around for a chunk of the filming, so I need someone on hand to oversee the stunts and make sure they're safe. We are, after all, talking about Crazy Casa."

I blew out a huff of air that was part exhalation, part sigh. "Their stunt coordinator is concentrated ego and testosterone on two legs."

"Right now," he replied calmly, "one of those legs is badly broken."

Oh, that's right. With the current situation, I'd managed to forget that little tidbit. "You should know that they've turned me down for jobs ever since *Pale Dreamer*. Plus, I know for a fact they're interviewing for a new stunt coordinator."

"They can hire one, but whoever it is will have to give you final say. Given the reputation the mansion already has, the potential for lawsuits is staggering—even with the stack of liability waivers and insurance riders I'm making them sign. So

I'm damn well going to have someone I trust on hand, even for something as simple as a right cross. So, if they want to film on my property—and trust me, they do—they'll have to suck it up and give me what I want.

"And I want you," he concluded.

Oh my.

"What's the pay?" I asked, determined not to read anything into those last four words.

He told me.

"Hell yeah, I'm in," I said. The amount he was offering would enable me to pay rent at Eden's place for a good six months.

"Good. Meet me at the mansion tomorrow at three." A beat. "There will be coffee."

"Deal."

†

DUSHANE MANSION
SIX MONTHS EARLIER

It'd been a while since anyone had come to the estate. Ned was growing bored, even as his children—as he thought of them—spread out over the greater Los Angeles area. Sure, their actions provided some sustenance, but the distance diluted it. It was like trying to live on cotton candy when he craved red meat.

So when the front doors opened and a big redheaded man entered with yet another real estate agent, Ned smiled in anticipation. Either the customer or the real estate agent would die today. Whichever way it played out, it would provide him with some entertainment, and more importantly, much-needed nourishment.

He decided to eavesdrop and went to the Great Room where they were standing.

"What do you think, Mr. Doran?" The real estate agent's voice was sickly sweet, with the kind of simper Ned despised.

Sure, she was attractive in a fake sort of way. Hair dyed blonde. Small blue eyes with impossibly long lashes. Tiny nose that didn't fit with the rest of her features, especially the oversized lips. Breasts larger than nature intended. The entire package wrapped in an obviously expensive skirt and jacket ensemble in charcoal gray, uncomfortably high heels finishing the outfit. She didn't look comfortable or confident, despite the time and money she'd put into her appearance.

"This is exactly what I've been looking for." The prospective buyer, on the other hand, looked relaxed and at home in a suit that fit his strong frame like an expensive glove.

"Oh!" The bimbo looked surprised. "And you're okay with the property's history?"

"Every place has history," he said with a dismissive wave of a hand. "Doesn't bother me at all."

"Why, that's... that's wonderful." Her face brightened, probably calculating her commission on the sale.

"Put my offer in immediately, please."

"Right away, Mr. Doran." She walked over to the French doors leading out onto the terrace and went outside, pulling a small silver rectangle out of her purse as she did so. A goddamn telephone.

Ned had seen some weird stuff over the decades thanks to the parade of meat puppets who'd come to the mansion, but this kind of stuff took the cake. He pushed aside the thought. It was time to decide how he wanted to play it with these two. Definitely be easier for the man to ice the woman—the guy could be a gladiator with those muscles.

The man looked up, ice-blue eyes staring right at the place where Ned stood. And damned if the son-of-a-bitch didn't grin, as if he knew what Ned was thinking, and found it a real belly-tickler.

Ned frowned, and decided to see how it played out.

†

A month later the guy moved in.

Just the redhead gladiator at first. No staff. Just the cocky son-of-a-bitch himself, walking into the mansion. Striding into the Great Room and looking around as if... well, as if he owned the place.

As if he knew there was more going on than met the eye.

He would have to go, Ned decided.

That night, all of the revenants on the property were on the move. Ned watched in smug satisfaction as they rose from their graves all over the property, lurching and crawling toward the jerk who had dared to move in.

Ned grinned. He loved introducing new owners to the current occupants. Seeing their faces when rotting corpses staggered inside to say hello. Stay for a snack. Some people made it out of the mansion and off the property. More than a few autos and their occupants had been totaled trying to outrun madness.

The son-of-a-bitch just smiled.

"This the best you can do?" The man gestured at the half-dozen corpses that had lurched into the room. "Not impressed." He tossed back his drink and muttered a few phrases of a language Ned didn't recognize, although he felt the power that ran through them.

The revenants paused, then turned away. Before they went more than a few feet, however, their flesh dissolve into the floor.

What the fuck...?

This wasn't how things were supposed to go.

"And now," the man said softly, "it's your turn, Mr. DuShane."

Before Ned could do more than snarl, more words were muttered—dark, arcane language that cut off Ned's energy supply with the suddenness of a guillotine. His "body" went limp, his mind fogging over until things went dark.

†

When Ned woke up—funny thing for a dead man to do, but there it was—he was back in the shithole room he'd died in. When he tried to get to the corridor, it was like walking into a brick wall.

Son-of-a-bitch.

He was stuck there again, with no access to his meat puppets or the source of his energy.

Ned roared in frustrated fury.

Upstairs, he knew, the new owner was smiling.

CHAPTER TWENTY

Shaina opened her eyes, lashes sticking together with sleep goo. Her pores oozed with the smell of stale tequila and sweat. She really needed to drink more water after one of Dad's parties.

"Ugh." Groaning, she rolled out of bed, staggered to the bathroom, and slid on a wet spot on the tiled floor. Grabbing onto a towel rack, she saved herself from a potentially nasty fall, frowning in disgust when she realized she'd stepped in a puddle of urine that led to the toilet. Guess she hadn't made it quite in time.

The room was decorated like a mermaid's wet dream, all blues and greens and faux beach glass and shells. The shower was huge, the size of her housekeeper's bedroom. Some days she thought she should feel guilty about this inequality, but most of the time it seemed fitting. After all, wasn't she heir to the Crazy Casa kingdom?

Lucky me.

It was impossible not to be aware of the contempt serious filmmakers had for the dreck Crazy Casa churned out. Which was why Shaina totally approved expanding the company's scope with different programming. True Horrors of Hollywood *had been her brainchild, and she hoped that the* Silver Scream *segment would succeed in elevating it to the next level.*

She wanted to be taken seriously. To create something more than mutated monster mashups eating the Barbies and Kens of the acting world. Wanted to work with A-listers, instead of aging has-been television actors and pop stars past their prime. Wanted her father to be proud of her.

Shaina might get lucky and achieve the first item on her "Dream the Impossible Dream" bucket list. Possibly the second. The third? Not likely. Shana could win an Oscar for Best Picture, and Harry Gilchrest would still think it was "less than" because she wasn't the male heir he'd always wanted. What the hell was it with some men and their need to have a little mini-me with a little mini-me penis to carry on the family name?

Love was hard when the object of your affection had no redeeming features. Dad loved the power players in the industry, even the fallen ones—he'd smuggle Harvey Weinstein a cake with a file in it if he knew how to bake. Yet Shana loved Harry Gilchrist, even though he couldn't be bothered to return her affections. Chasing that impossible dream on a hamster wheel.

That was enough self-introspection for one hungover morning, she decided. Time to pull her act together.

Shaina had a meeting in the afternoon. Not one she particularly wanted to take, but she didn't have much of a choice if she wanted to secure permission to film on the DuShane property.

†

Driving up the gently winding road, I reflected that in twenty-some odd years since I moved to the Ranch, this would be the first time I'd seen the inside of the DuShane mansion. Like most local kids, I'd been warned to stay away from the property and—like most of my contemporaries—I'd gone up there.

Seriously, if you tell a kid a place is haunted, the first chance they get, they'll check it out to see if it's true.

I reached the front gates, seven-plus feet of wrought iron.

There had been thick chains and an industrial-strength

padlock back in high school, when Dan—one in a long line of Bad Boy crushes—took me there to make out. We'd arrived shortly before sunset, but before we'd had a chance to do more than peer in between the bars, I'd gotten a text from Sean making it clear he knew where I was, and he expected me at home in the next fifteen minutes. Later I realized that anyone sitting out on the porch at the Ranch had a clear view of cars heading up the road to the DuShane property, but at the time I was sure that Sean had some sort of supernatural tracking system where I was concerned.

The gates were wide open, but other than that they looked the same, straddling a line between picturesque and utilitarian. They hid a fortress-like practicality behind lots of decorative loops and swirls, with very sharp fleur-de-lis topping each bar. I could picture all too well what would happen if someone landed on top of one of those things.

From what I'd heard, it had happened at least once. What puzzled me, however, was how someone could actually fall on top of the fence. It was well away from the mansion and there weren't any trees that would make it viable. Maybe they'd been cut down to prevent any more "accidents."

What I saw during my aborted high school escapade had left the impression of a forgotten graveyard. Weathered marble statues standing sentry on either side of the drive. Dead grass and weeds growing up between cracked paving stones. Foliage so overgrown it looked like a jungle. The once opulent building covered with ivy, bougainvillea bushes climbing columns and meandering over balconies, dangling down in places like colorful serpents.

While the statuary was still weathered, the weeds had been pulled and the paving stones replaced. The grass was green and well-kept, and beds of colorful drought-resistant flowers and succulents were scattered about the grounds. There were still vines and bougainvillea, but they were trimmed back and flowered on trellises in shades of fuchsia and pale orange, framing the doors, windows, and balconies instead of obscuring them. Roses blossomed in beds nestled against the walls. Less Haunted Mansion and more *Home Beautiful*.

I parked my Saturn behind Cayden's silver Porsche 911 Turbo, which was parked in the driveway directly in front of wooden double doors twice my height. There were brass knockers in the shape of lion heads in the center of each door. There was a doorbell, too, so I pressed it and was greeted with a low, irritating *ding-dong*. Disappointing. I'd expected something more along the lines of Bach's *Toccata and Fugue in D Minor*.

The door opened, revealing a slender Japanese woman who could have been anywhere between thirty to fifty years old. Smooth skin with only a tracery of wrinkling around serene brown eyes. Small straight nose above a perfect rosebud of a mouth. Glossy black hair pulled back into a tight chignon flanked by two red-jeweled combs. She wore black leggings below a crimson top that reminded me of a kimono. Flat black slippers. Casual yet elegant, the type of woman who'd be equally at home at a Starbucks or a black-tie dinner.

"May I help you?" Her voice was soft and melodious.

"I'm Lee Striga," I replied, feeling like a large ox next to her. "Cayden is expecting me."

Neither scar nor amulet were acting up, but I was on edge. Maybe it was a combination of Jada's disappearance and being on Cayden's home turf. Or maybe it was the triple-shot cappuccino I'd made myself earlier.

The woman smiled, a lovely and genuine smile. "Yes, Doran-san mentioned you would be here. My name is Kana, and I manage Doran-san's household affairs." She offered her hand, dainty fingers tipped with red lacquered nails, and I took it. Cool flesh. Strong grip. I met her gaze as we shook hands. She inspired instant trust and I felt my nervous energy drain away, as if I'd just mainlined Valium. She ushered me through the doorway.

"I will get Doran-san for you," she continued. "If you'll just wait here…"

"Of course."

Kana vanished through the archway on the right, leaving me to gawk at my surroundings. There was a lot to gawk at. Gold leaf on dark polished wood. Gemstone-encrusted finials. Ornamental lamps with jewel-colored glass, mounted on the wall. Art-deco-style molding along the ceiling and floors. Rich cobalt blue-and-cream colored tiling on the floor. And all this just in the entryway.

I couldn't resist peeking into a large central hall—not a hallway, but a hall, like in a medieval castle. Lofted ceilings three stories high. A central staircase running up the middle and branching off to either side—I expected Von Trapp children to come down and start singing. On either side, railings of polished dark wood lent a modicum of safety to slender walkways running the length of the room. The walkways vanished into hallways at the far end, doors at an interval of ten feet or so.

The walls alternated strips of the same dark wood as the balustrades with a lustrous hunter-green wallpaper. Tacky and beautiful at the same time, as if the architect and interior designer had both been equally influenced by *Arabian Nights* and *Hammer House of Horror*.

I couldn't decide if I loved it or hated it.

"What do you think?"

I almost jumped when Cayden's voice came from behind me. Almost.

"Trying to catch me by surprise?" I said, trying to disguise the fact that my heart was beating double time. From the little smile playing around the edges of his mouth, I thought he'd been counting on it.

"Maybe, but I'd have been disappointed if I'd managed," he admitted. "I'm hiring you for your ability to keep a cool head under pressure. That, and your fine taste in beer."

"No PBR on set, then?"

Cayden gave a delicate shudder, an incongruous gesture on a man of his size. Not for the first time, I reflected that he wouldn't have looked out of place on the cover of a thirties pulp novel, wrestling alligators all bare-chested and sweaty…

Okay, put that image right out of your head, I told myself.

What was it about this man? I'd almost been more comfortable when I thought he was just another Hollywood asshole, all arrogance and money. Not that he couldn't play that part when he felt like it, but there was so much more to him than that. Was he undeniably hunky? Oh yes, but not for me.

"Come on," he said. "I'll give you a mini-tour."

"Mini?" I tried not to sound disappointed.

"The director is going to be here around three-thirty, and I want to go over a few things before she arrives. Trust me," he added, shooting me a sideways glance, "I'll be more than happy to give you a full tour in the near future."

Cayden led me through an ornately tiled arched entrance into a huge space that was large enough for an epic party central. Positively opulent, with plush couches and chairs upholstered in rich silks and satins in rich jewel tones. A magnificent art deco bar took up most of one wall, weathered mirror glass showing a flattering reflection of both of us in between bottles of liquor and wine. The surface of the front bar was a rosy-white marble while the backbar was a highly polished cherry wood.

Directly across from the bar were French doors leading out to what looked like a terrace. The place was an absolute mishmash of architectural and decorating styles.

"Holy moly," I murmured.

"This is where Ned DuShane held most of his infamous Hollywood parties," Cayden said, confirming my first impression. "He called it his Great Room." On the far side of the space, another arched opening beckoned.

"What's through there?" I asked.

"Ah," Cayden said with a toothy grin, "you could call that the spillover room. Indoor pillows, multiple cabanas, lots of silk and cushions. I'll show you later." He moved so that he was facing me, just slightly closer than I found comfortable… or safe. I countered by stepping to one side on the pretense of looking at an obviously expensive antique desk.

"In answer to your original question," I said, trying to sound casual, "this place is impressive, if not what I expected."

"And what did you expect? Collinwood?"

"More of a bachelor pad," I replied. "More stainless steel and black leather. Less velvet and fussy antiques. Maybe a few Nagel prints."

Cayden laughed, that sharp, explosive sound that meant he was highly amused. "This place would not take kindly to Nagel prints," he said, still chuckling. "It has a definite aesthetic and I've found it best to leave it alone."

"So, the place really is haunted?"

"It was."

"Was?"

"No spirits on my watch. They don't like me."

"Can't imagine why."

"I suspect it's related to knowing that the person you're trying to spook could send you into a hell of your own making."

"You gonna add that to your resume? Because I don't think you could fit that on a business card, even with an acronym."

"Sounded kinda full of myself, huh?"

I spread my hands and shrugged. "What can I say?"

"Doran-san, would you like your coffee here or on the terrace?" Kana had unobtrusively entered the room, carrying a tray with two thick white mugs—classic fifties diner style—a coffee pot, cream and sugar, several plates, and a platter of chocolate almond lace cookies. A couple of croissants with dark chocolate peeking out. Cayden looked at me, raising an eyebrow.

"Preference?"

A gust of wind keened outside, rattling the French doors.

"Definitely inside, please." I smiled at Kana, who nodded and set the tray down on a prissy little table before slipping away again. I watched her leave, intrigued. "So how long has she worked for you?"

"I met her in Japan about six months ago," Cayden replied. He sat down on an overstuffed couch upholstered in claret-colored velvet. "She was looking to find a new home, so when I bought this place, I offered her a job as… well, housekeeper doesn't begin to encompass what Kana does here."

Hmmm. I tried not to let my mind wander down the path of what her duties *might* encompass. She was, after all, quite beautiful. I poured myself some coffee to distract myself, eying the platter of cookies. Grinning, Cayden reached out and set two on my plate, along with a croissant, handing it to me.

"Your mind is an open book."

Oh god, I hope not.

"Are there firm dates for the shooting schedule here?" I asked quickly.

"Next week, if they're still on schedule."

"That soon, huh?" I said. "Not a lot of time to prep. What kind of stunts are we talking?"

"Well, if the script follows real-life events—"

"You haven't read it yet?"

"That's what I'm paying you for."

I stopped myself mid-eyeroll, because he wasn't wrong. He pulled out a piece of paper and handed it to me.

"I took the liberty of printing out the show's opening monologue for you. The producer will give you the entire script."

"Hmm." Taking the paper, I started reading.

†

The DuShane mansion. Once a Xanadu of decadence for the royalty and bottom-feeders of Hollywood. Ned DuShane welcomed them all into his mansion. Built in the 1920s as what DuShane called his "retreat from the stress of the film industry," the mansion is part Moroccan palace and part Gothic castle, a testament to DuShane's extravagant lifestyle.

That lifestyle included opulent parties to which the crème de la crème of Hollywood was invited. It was during one such party that Ned DuShane disappeared, leaving his famous guests and household staff equally baffled as to what had happened to the producer of such movies as Frankenstein's Nightmare, Voodoo Orgy, and Death Vampires of Transylvania.

The mystery of Ned DuShane's disappearance was never solved. The equally mysterious—and sometimes gruesome—deaths of subsequent owners of the mansion also remain a mystery.

†

"Wow," I finally said. "The only mystery I can see is why the scriptwriter didn't get canned."

"Oh, it's not *that* bad." Cayden grinned. "At least not compared to her first film. The writer is also the director who is also the producer, who happens to be the daughter of Hal Gilchrist, the executive producer of Crazy Casa."

"*Aaaand* the mystery is solved. I hope she's a better director than she is a writer."

"Ah. This would be her second directing gig. The first was *Pandademic.*"

I winced. A truly awful Crazy Casa film, bad even by their standards. Think pandas catching a virus from mutated bamboo that turns them into crazed—but adorable—flesh eaters.

"She wrote that too, by the way."

Great.

"How much are you paying me again?"

"Hopefully enough to ease the pain of the bad writing," Cayden replied. "And by the way, Crazy Casa is also going to be paying you for this."

My eyebrows shot up. "Really?"

"Oh, yes. Shaina's not happy with the extra expense, but she wants to film here badly enough to put you on the payroll." No doubt Cayden enjoyed making the production company jump through hoops, just because he could. Whatever the reason, I'd take the money.

"On the upside," Cayden went on, "when you meet Shaina,

you're going to think she's like every other spoiled brat born into Hollywood royalty, but she's a lot smarter than most of them. She'll piss the hell out of you at first. Get under your skin like... well, like some of the weeds in Ol' Nal's neck of the woods."

"This is not incentive for taking the job, y'know."

"Ah, but I'm not finished."

"Ah, then please continue."

"Once you get past the prickly and admittedly irritating first impression, there's a lot more to Shaina that's worth your time. I think she's got talent, but she hasn't found her niche yet. She's also not great with people."

"I'm still waiting to hear about the part that's worth my time."

"She's got some good ideas as far as where she wants to take this series, but she needs to forget about directing and writing dialogue. Focus on broad stroke outlines and research. She's really good at that."

"Have you told her this?"

"Hell no." Cayden laughed. "One does not tell Shaina Gilchrist how to live her life. She'll figure it out on her own, or she won't."

"So how does she feel about you bringing me in to oversee the stunts?"

"I didn't ask her," Cayden said coolly. "Most likely she's not particularly happy about it. Not that I give a cold shit about her feelings. My house, my rules. Besides, she's already spent money on promoting the fact they'll be filming here. The reveal is airing at the end of tonight's episode." He grinned. "You should watch. I figure prominently."

"Does Shaina Gilchrist know about supes?" Industry buzz said Crazy Casa was an NSA production house, with supes keeping their backgrounds under wraps while working on the company's films.

"She's fascinated by the paranormal and supernatural, but I don't know if she has any experience with either. *True Horrors of Hollywood* is her brainchild, though, and she takes it very seriously."

The doorbell went off, the sound loud and irritating as it reverberated through the mansion. Cayden grimaced. I didn't blame him.

"Is that the original doorbell?"

"Not entirely sure. I haven't gotten around to replacing it yet with something more subtle."

"How about one that plays the opening of *Night on Bald Mountain*?" I suggested. "Or the *Addams Family* gong? That'd be subtle."

Kana entered the room. "Ms. Gilchrist, Doran-san." She glided out of the way to make room for a petite blonde in skinny jeans, a plain black T-shirt that probably cost a few hundred dollars, and calf-high black leather boots. I didn't want to speculate how much those had set her back.

Thin lips, a Jennifer Gray nose before plastic surgery, and large, rather beautiful, brown eyes. The expression in those eyes, while not openly hostile, wasn't friendly. There was a wariness about her, like a semi-feral cat that couldn't decide if it wanted to be pet or claw the shit out of you.

I'd keep my hand out of reach until she decided.

Cayden got smoothly to his feet, remarkably graceful for such a large man. "Shaina," he said in welcoming tones. "So nice to see you."

"Hello, Cayden." Shaina Gilchrist's tone was somewhere between friendly and indifferent, her attitude purely professional.

Wow.

This made her one of the few women I'd seen in proximity to Cayden who didn't drool all over him—metaphorically or otherwise. It was a refreshing change.

"Lee, this is Shaina Gilchrist, writer, producer, and director of *Silver Scream: True Horrors of Hollywood*. Shaina, this is Lee Striga."

I stood, held out a hand. "Pleased to meet you." Shaina looked at my hand as though it had been dipped in snot. Then she touched the tips of my fingers for the briefest of seconds and gave me a nod so cool I almost got frostbite.

This is gonna be fun.

"Would you like some coffee, Ms. Gilchrist?" Kana reappeared next to Shaina's chair, moving as quietly as a ghost.

Shaina nodded. "Decaf. I don't do caffeine after noon."

More and more, I wasn't looking forward to spending any one-on-one time with this woman. As if reading my mind, Cayden looked at his watch.

"I need to take another call," he said. "I should be finished in about a half hour or so. I expect you two have plenty to discuss in the meantime."

Rat bastard, I thought.

With that he left the room, Kana following unobtrusively on his heels, leaving me alone with Shaina Gilchrist.

CHAPTER TWENTY-ONE

Shaina and I looked at each other. I could tell she was waiting for me to speak first, so I didn't. I could play passive-aggressive power games, too.

I busied myself with my coffee, taking a long, satisfying sip. It was good coffee, just the right ratio of cream and honey. Then I nibbled on the chocolate croissant. It was delicious, the dark chocolate rich, just on the right side of bittersweet, and a perfect contrast to the buttery croissant.

Shaina, on the other hand, didn't have her coffee yet, so had no props.

She broke first.

"I don't see the need for you on this set." She threw the words as if slapping down a gauntlet in challenge.

"Oh?" I raised an inquiring eyebrow and drank more coffee.

"No." she snapped. "I just hired a perfectly respectable stunt coordinator, and he's not happy at the thought of taking orders from someone who doesn't know the stunt business."

I nearly did a spit take at that. "What on earth gave you the idea I don't have experience?"

She sniffed. "Cayden didn't mention any when he informed me that he was hiring someone to oversee the production."

"Tell me, Miss Gilchrist, have you ever heard of the Katz Stunt Crew?"

"Of course I have. Everyone has, but what—"

"I started training with them when I was seven and worked my first stunt job when I was twelve."

That made her pause. Cocking her head, she took a good look at me. "What did you say your name was?"

"Lee Striga." My tone was flat. Either Cayden hadn't mentioned my name, or she hadn't bothered to remember it. Either way, I was getting pissed-off.

"I've heard of you. No one wanted to hire you after what happened on *Pale Dreamer*."

I swear, you kill one lousy producer...

"And yet," I said, "here I am. I also worked on Cayden's film *Voodoo Wars* for the last two months. Do you really think he'd hire me again if there'd been any problems?"

Shaina chewed that one over for a minute or two. "I suppose not." She gave me a sharp glance. "You didn't sexually harass anyone, did you?"

I looked at her for a moment, tempted to be pissed-off that she would even ask me that question. Stared long enough for her to start getting nervous. Good. I wondered how many times in her life Shaina had actually felt intimidated. Not often, I imagined. Brought up in the rarified atmosphere of low-budget royalty, she'd probably gotten what she'd wanted most of her life.

Then I felt ashamed of myself—Miss Judgy McJudgerson. I didn't know who Shaina was, what her life was like. I'd met her father a few years back, at a premiere for *Gatorcane II*, part of an improbably successful franchise. Hurricanes in Florida that carried alligators on the storm surges. The series had relaunched the careers of several actors whose careers had tanked back in the nineties.

Regardless of my opinion, the movies performed well on the various streaming platforms, and Walter Gilchrist's ego expanded like the Blob after eating a small town. At the premiere I'd made the mistake of offering him my hand, which he'd clasped between damp palms while staring at my cleavage. He'd made the mistake of asking me what I thought of the movie. I'd made the mistake of being honest—I blame the champagne—and my cleavage hadn't been enough to take away the sting of honesty. Or the sharp smack I'd delivered to his wandering hand.

It might well explain why I'd never been hired at Crazy Casa, even though I was way out of their league.

"Hey!" I was brought back to the present by fingers snapping loudly under my nose. "If you're not going to pay attention when I speak, why are you here?"

Well, hell. I should have known better than to lose focus. Having made that mistake, though…

"You ever do that again, I'll break your fingers." I smiled as I spoke, but I meant every word. "I'm not a dog and I'm not your employee, even if you are paying part of my salary. I work for Cayden Doran, who has hired me to oversee the stunts on this production because he doesn't want anyone hurt while filming in his home. Crazy Casa does *not* have a good record for safety."

Shaina opened her mouth to blast me, but I raised a finger—just one—and continued.

"If you want to film here, you will cooperate with me. You will treat me—and anyone I bring onto this production—with respect. I will do the same for your stunt coordinator and the rest of your crew. Are we clear?"

Most likely Shaina understood the power dynamic all too well, and bitterly resented it. I'd cry a few tears for her in my next life.

"So, are we going to be able to work together?"

"I don't see that I've got much choice."

I shrugged. "Guess you don't, if you want to film here. But just so you know, I'll try and make it as easy as possible. I've got nothing to prove." I paused, and Shaina stared at me without blinking, like a blue-eyed snake. I counted a good thirty seconds before she finally replied.

"Good."

Guess we won't be BFFs anytime soon.

Ooh boy, this was gonna be fun. Good thing I was getting double pay for it. But I was still gonna make Cayden buy a shit-ton of beer to make up for the aggravation.

The doorbell *ding-dong*ed again.

"Ah, that should be my stunt coordinator," she said. The emphasis on "my" was deliberate. The click of boot heels heralded the newcomer as he followed Kana into the room. My scar tingled slightly.

Ah crap, I thought.

I rose to my feet, putting on my best professional demeanor for none other than Nigri Barboza.

CHAPTER TWENTY-TWO

Nigri and I stared at each other, no love lost on either side. Even Shaina, self-absorbed though she appeared to be, could see the tension between us.

"You've met?"

"We have." I did my best to keep my tone neutral, but my expression wouldn't have won me any poker games. My only consolation was that Nigri wouldn't have done any better. I decided to cut right to the chase. "Mr. Barboza, has Ms. Gilchrist had a chance to explain to you what my job will be on this production?"

A tight smile crossed Nigri's face. "She has."

Buzzz went my scar.

"Will you be able to work under those conditions?" I was pushing it, hoping that Nigri would pack up his toys and go home. Preferably back to Brazil. Sadly, I was doomed to disappointment.

"*Si, Senhorita.*" A subtle tightening of his jaw was the only sign that Nigri wasn't on board with the situation, but at least he had the common sense to try and hide it. And at least my amulet wasn't flaring up like it did at Arlo's. Who knew? Maybe he could play well with others when he was being paid to do so.

"Good," I said. "We should find some time to go over the script, so you can fill me in on your plans."

"Of course," he said neutrally. The muscle in his jaw twitched again.

"If you need any help mapping out costs, finding reliable equipment rentals, or anything else, just let me know."

"Thank you, *Senhorita* Striga. I appreciate your willingness to help. Although I am certain Skeet has ideas, and many of the necessary connections."

I was certain Skeet had *lots* of ideas, most of them X-rated. As far as useful connections, I wasn't so sure, but that was up to Nigri to discover for himself. I'd only step in if it looked like cast, crew, or set were in danger.

Shaina interrupted my gloomy thoughts.

"Did Cayden give you a copy of the script?"

"He said you'd have one for me."

Opening her briefcase, she pulled out two thin scripts bound in black card stock, silver letters embossed on the front.

Horrors of Hollywood:
Silver Scream

Crazy Casa Productions

She handed one to me and one to Nigri.

"Fancy," I murmured.

"I want everyone to take this production seriously," she said seriously. "I know the reputation Crazy Casa has, and want to elevate it."

I limited my response to a nod. On one hand, I admired her desire to do more than the usual crock of shit that Crazy Casa brewed up. On the other hand, it was hard to take her seriously when she used an expression better suited to one of Seth's beloved cooking shows.

"Originally we were going to film the party scene first," Shaina continued, "but the actor playing DuShane isn't available until Monday, so we're going ahead with the other segments." She sounded put out at the change of plans, but her expression was resigned. "So I'm hoping to get re-enactments done, along with any stunts, over the weekend." It was already Thursday.

I started to ask what she needed, but caught myself and settled back down, determined to remain professional. It wasn't my job, it was Nigri's, and even if I didn't like him—oh, the understatement!—I wasn't going to interfere unless he presented a danger to personnel or property.

"What would you like to film first?" he asked respectfully, without a hint of arrogance. Maybe he'd have a career as an actor, too.

Shaina leafed through the script. "Let's go for the segment where Tommy Chaffron falls off the third story," she replied. "No one else was present when that happened, so we just need the stuntman." She paused. "If whoever you have in mind for the stunt isn't a total piece of wood, I can save some money here."

Nigri nodded. "This we can do." He glanced over at me. "Do you agree?" His tone was respectful but his expression… not so much. I chose to acknowledge the tone.

"Yup, sure thing."

Nigri gave me stink-eye. *Go ahead*, I thought. If he made one false move, he'd be off this production and blacklisted anywhere that the Katz name meant anything. If Crazy Casa wanted to keep him on the payroll after they finished filming here, that was their problem. Until then, however, he was mine.

Lucky me.

✝

Every day since that smug bastard had trapped him back in his tomb, Ned reached out with the power he'd collected over the years. He could still feel it coursing through his non-corporeal veins, but he couldn't do anything with it. Couldn't reach any of his puppets on the grounds.

He tried summoning the same rage that had busted him out before, but even though the fury he felt was epic, all he could do was make the planter dance around. Which made him even angrier. Still, he kept trying. After all, he had nothing better to do with his time other than plot out what, precisely, he'd do to the trespasser in his mansion once he did get out.

Truth be told, he might have admired the bastard, if he didn't hate his guts so intensely.

The most frustrating part was that Ned could sense someone close by. Not on the grounds, but near enough. Someone or something whose mind and soul he'd touched before his current interment. Someone with the reek of petty evil on their soul. It hadn't taken much to push them over the edge, but whatever the rat bastard had done to contain Ned down here, it stopped him from being able to reach outside the four walls.

It was like dying for a drink with a bottle of scotch just out of reach.

So, Ned occupied his time with a particularly pleasant fantasy of watching the man's skin being peeled off his skull, inch by inch. It didn't get him anywhere, but it made him feel a lot better, his spirits buoyed and his energies spiking. Pure malice did that for him.

He almost didn't notice when a wolf spider crawled through a crack in the far wall at the edge of the smuggler's hatch. When he spotted it, Ned thought about sending one of the loose bricks to smash it, but then something else occurred to him.

He reached out to the spider, the same way he had with Dougie and so many others after him. The spider essence was alien, but there still was a connection.

Go on, *he instructed.* Go find someone who can get me out of here. *He tried to convey the essence of individual he had in mind. After a moment or two, the spider scuttled back into the crack, vanishing from sight.*

Well, fuck.

All Ned could do was settle back and wait, so that's what he did, mentally disemboweling his jailer with a very dull knife.

†

He had no idea how much time had passed when he heard a scratching at the hatch as something poked through the crack, enlarging it. Ned felt a rush of triumph.

Now he was getting somewhere.

CHAPTER TWENTY-THREE

I stayed at the mansion another hour or so. By the time I left, Nigri and I had a meeting set up for the next morning, to go over the stunts. I wasn't looking forward to it, but was determined to see this job through as professionally as I could manage.

Sometimes I hated being an adult.

When I left the mansion, the sun was thinking about setting and the nervous energy I'd felt when I'd arrived flooded back almost immediately. It got even worse when I turned out of the front gates onto the road, with a clear view of the mountains. I pulled to a stop, the Saturn idling as I stared at the area where I'd found Jada's car.

What the hell had happened to her?

The drive home didn't help me to relax at all—I kept having to brake for animals and reptiles crossing the road. And when I got back to the Ranch, it was apparent most of them were headed here to join the abundant wildlife already hanging out on the grounds. A few cows, a horse, and a half-dozen goats wandered the backlot near the fencing, feasting on weeds and shrubs. I love goats, but I hoped they'd stay up that way since every goat feast turned into goat poop and I'd rather not be wiping it off the bottom of my shoes every time I went outside.

I parked the Saturn and stepped out of the car, nearly tripping over a garter snake as it slithered away. The bobcat and her kittens were sitting next to the barn. Just sitting there, as calm as you please, next to a coyote, more rabbits, some chickens, and what looked like a mountain lion. Yup, definitely a mountain lion, without any apparent interest in the goats or any other possible easy prey.

Holy shit.

I glanced around, half-expecting to see Radagast the Brown, or some other St. Francis of Assisi-type animal magnet. The last time we'd had even half this many creatures hanging out was right before the Woolsey Fire. They seemed to know where they were safe.

I wondered if Jada would still be safe, if she hadn't left early the other night.

Seth was in the middle of dinner prep while Sean lounged at the kitchen table, a glass of iced tea in front of him. The aromas wafting from the oven and stovetop made my stomach growl. The normalcy of the scene was comforting, and I felt my jittery nerves calm down.

"You know, Seth," I said conversationally as I wandered over to see what was cooking, "if you ever get tired of stunt work, you could always open your own restaurant."

Seth gave a non-committal grunt, but didn't smack my hand when I cracked open the oven and peered inside. Roast chicken, just reaching golden-brown crackly-skinned perfection. A loaf of bread sat next to it, covered in foil, and when I peered over Seth's shoulder I saw that he was making balsamic-glazed Brussels sprouts in one of his cast-iron skillets. A pile of crumbled bacon sat on a plate, paper towels soaking up the grease.

One of my favorite meals and he knew it.

Getting to his feet, Sean gave me a kiss on the cheek. "How's your day going, hon?"

"Okay, I guess," I said with a shrug. "Demon-free thus far, so that's a win."

Sean resumed his seat. "So," he said, his tone casual, "how are things with you and Randy? You haven't mentioned him lately, and he hasn't been by the Ranch at all." Seth didn't turn away from his cooking, but I could tell he was waiting for my answer.

"We're taking a break," I said shortly. "He's going to Europe for a few months."

"Where's he headed?" This was Seth.

"Romania. He's stunt-coordinating on a horror anthology show filming over there."

Seth gave a derisive snort. "Just what the world needs. I mean, *Supernatural*'s only just ended after fifteen seasons, and if there's such a thing as a supernatural kitchen sink, they've already thrown it into that show."

"Very true," I agreed. Back when I was recovering from my near-death experience, I binge-watched a lot. Sean spent time watching them with me, and once in a while Seth would join us. *Supernatural* was one that the three of us had torn through. We'd been simultaneously horrified at what they'd gotten wrong and charmed in spite of ourselves.

I opened the fridge to see what was inside. There was beer left over from the previous night's debauch, along with a bottle of Rombauer chardonnay lying on its side. I reached for a Stone Delicious IPA, only to have Seth smack my hand before I could grab it.

"Dinner's gonna be on in just a few minutes, and we're going to crack the wine."

"What if I'd rather have beer instead of wine?"

"The wine pairs with the chicken," he informed me between clenched teeth.

"I know," I said, pouring myself some sparkling water instead. "I just like seeing that stick go a little further up your butt."

"So, you and Randy are taking a break, huh?" Sean interjected before Seth could fire a retaliatory shot back across my metaphorical bow.

"He's going to be gone for a few months, and we both just need to do some thinking."

"About…?"

I sighed, not wanting to go into detail but knowing Sean would keep fishing until he caught something.

"He wants to take things to the next level. I'm not ready."

"Big shock," Seth muttered.

"Then it sounds like the two of you made a good decision," Sean said, all warmly supportive. It was time to change the subject.

"Hey, can you check with Trey and see if we're due for anything major, like a big quake or something? It's looking like Noah's Ark outside." Trey was a local weather-witch who sometimes did a little weather manipulation on productions.

"Way ahead of you—I checked in with him earlier," Seth commented as he cooked. "Nothing big in the works as far as he can tell. We're due for some heavy rain, so no wildfires."

"Then why all the wildlife?" I directed the question to Sean.

"I'm not sure, hon. Maybe something to do with the disappearances."

Like Jada, I thought. I waited until Seth served up the food and poured us all a glass of golden-hued wine before saying, "Looks like I got another job, so that's another good thing."

219

"That's great, hon!" Sean enthused. "Guess we need to toast." He picked up his wine glass. Seth and I followed suit. We clinked glasses and sipped.

Yum, I thought. Very tasty.

"What's the gig?" Sean asked.

"*True Horrors of Hollywood*."

"Seriously?" Seth shook his head in undisguised disgust. "That show combines everything bad about documentaries and reality shows. It makes *Ripley's Believe it or Not* seem credible."

"I cannot disagree," I replied calmly, slicing into the chicken and taking a bite. Melt-in-your-mouth yummy. Seth was a damn fine cook. "And yet, it's a job. Pay's good, too."

"What's the horror of Hollywood this time?" Sean speared another piece of chicken with his fork.

"The mysterious disappearance of movie producer Ned DuShane and the subsequent spooky-ass shi—" Sean shot me a reproachful look "—stuff that's happened on his property since then. The episode is called *Silver Scream*."

"So," Seth said, "you're working with Doran again." He didn't bother to hide his disapproval. He looked as if he was going to say more, but a sharp glance from Sean shut him up.

I nodded. "Yup, and they're filming most of it at the DuShane mansion, so I'll be right up the hill. If you feel the need to check up on me and make sure I'm not knocking boots with Cayden, I'm sure he wouldn't mind you dropping by." I smiled sweetly, slathering gourmet butter—imported from France, no less—on a slice of warm bread as Seth grasped for a response. It wasn't often that I succeeded in rendering him even temporarily speechless, so I enjoyed the moment.

As I reached for the napkin on my lap, something cold and wet nudged my hand. I looked down to see Banjo staring hopefully up at me with liquid brown eyes. I slipped him a piece of chicken, which he took from my fingers in one swift chomp.

"Lee, are you feeding that dog at the table?" Sean shot me a stern look.

"Nope, not me," I said, trying and failing for an innocent look as Seth, grinning, quickly tossed a piece to the dog while Sean's attention was on me. That didn't work, either. His father gave a long-suffering sigh.

"If we're going to keep the dog, there'll have to be some ground rules. One of which is absolutely *no* feeding him at the table while we're eating."

Banjo snuffled against my hand again, ever hopeful. "Sorry, boy," I said, patting his head. "Mean old Sean says no."

The dog gave a little harrumph and lay down on top of my feet. I smiled, but then remembered why he was here.

An entire family, missing.

Just like Jada.

†

After we'd finished dinner, the three of us settled in the living room with more wine—a Rombauer zinfandel this time—to watch *Horrors of Hollywood*. Seth might sneer at bad TV, calling it junk food for the brain, but he enjoyed it the same way he did when he and his dad porked out on Taco Bell.

The show had two hosts. Kyle, a sensitively handsome guy with thinly drawn features and a shock of black hair. He did most of the narration. Marnie, a sexy blonde woman who favored four-inch heels and tight dresses, handled the in-person interviews and was irrepressibly cheerful, no matter what the topic.

The episode was about ghosts in Hollywood Forever

Cemetery. There are ghosts in most cemeteries worldwide, which "ghost hunters" claimed to contact. The shows were rife with, "*Did you hear that?*" or, "*Oh my god, something touched me!*" or, "*Whoa, dude—the temperature dropped by ten degrees when I walked over Virginia Rappe's grave!*"

I yawned.

I've been to Hollywood Forever. Met a few of the ghosts who hang out there—Virginia Rappe was not one of them—including Jonathan, an Edwardian gentleman who liked to take visitors on tours of the grounds. He was charming and eloquent, and it was only at the very end, when he vanished into his crypt in one of the mausoleums, that he gave the tourists their first inkling that their guide had come from beyond the grave. Even then… it was Hollywood, so it had to be a special effect, right?

Not so much.

Finally, the show wrapped up and they ran the promo for the *Silver Scream* episode.

†

Close-up of Kyle staring intently into the camera, mansion in the background.

Kyle

Once the home of infamous Hollywood producer Ned DuShane, the allegedly haunted house has since been owned by over two dozen people. Over half of these individuals met untimely and gruesome deaths within the ten-foot-high walls surrounding the property. The current resident—film producer and screenwriter Cayden Doran—told our interviewer that he hasn't seen or felt anything out of the ordinary during his tenancy so far.

Cut to a two-shot of Cayden and Marnie in the *Horrors of Hollywood* studio, all dark walls and scary artifacts, like a Halloween haunted house with a budget.

> Marnie
>
> So, Mr. Doran, you haven't seen anything since you bought the place?

> Cayden
>
> I didn't say I hadn't seen anything, but certainly nothing I would consider out of the ordinary.

Cut back to Kyle.

> Kyle
>
> Hollywood, and indeed Los Angeles County, is home to many legends, both on the silver screen and off. But amidst all of the designer labels and expensive champagne are darker tales, legends of death caused by suicide and murder.
>
> Some of the deaths appeared to be from natural causes. Others, however, were rumored to be caused by forces outside of this world. Supernatural forces. Evil forces.

†

Seth snorted. "Could the writing be any more over-the-top?"

"Yes, it could," I said.

We continued watching.

†

Kyle

The fate met by some of these poor souls was gruesome beyond belief. Others evidently just vanished, one victim's purse laying on top of the ground... which was disturbed as if something had dug its way out.

†

"Lying," Seth growled. "Not laying. Doesn't anyone learn proper English anymore?

I shrugged. "What do you expect from someone who used to work for Vixen News?"

Our attention returned to the television.

†

Kyle

Producer, director, and writer Shaina Gilchrist of Horrors of Hollywood Productions has this to say.

Cut to a close-up of Shaina somewhere outside.

Shaina

After the first groundskeeper had vanished in the thirties, two others were found dead—one of a heart-attack and the other ripped apart by what the authorities had deemed probably an attack by a pack of rabid coyotes. Several others had quit shortly after taking the position and yet another ended up drooling in a psych ward after less than a month. That was over twenty years ago, and the position has remained vacant—as had the mansion—until Cayden Doran moved in a few months ago. We are delighted he's given us permission to film there.

Cut back to Kyle.

Kyle

Will Cayden Doran survive what is arguably Hollywood's most lethal haunted house? Only time will tell.

†

I held out my glass for more zinfandel. Seth obliged, topping off his own glass. His father declined, shaking his head.

"You kids are gonna regret this in the morning," he said.

"Only time will tell," Seth and I said at the same time, in a rare moment of accord. Grinning at one another, we clinked glasses and settled in for a viewing of *Pandademic*.

CHAPTER TWENTY-FOUR

I arrived at the mansion bright and early—what Drift eloquently referred to as "the butt-crack of dawn"—a travel mug of coffee in one hand, a large canvas tote in the other. Opening the door, I walked in, only to be stopped by a twenty-something in jeans, dark green T-shirt under a many-pocketed khaki vest with a picture of Boba Fett and the words "Han totally shot first" visible. He carried a radio in one hand and a clipboard in the other.

"Can I help you?" He did not sound helpful.

"Hi!" I said brightly. "I'm here to see—"

The radio squawked. "Hang on," he said brusquely and pressed a button on the radio. "Yeah?" He listened to the reply, an unintelligible string of words as far as I could tell, but he seemed to understand it. "Yeah, no. Tell Oscar no drilling in the walls… uh-huh. Yeah, no… Uh-huh… Not downstairs. The basement's off-limits." A loud squawk indicated the displeasure of the person on the other end of this conversation.

I sighed audibly enough to get the attention of the crewmember. He glanced up blankly, as if he'd forgotten my presence.

"Yeah?"

Great.

I wiggled my fingers in a little wave. "Here to see Cayden Doran."

"Who?"

Oh, come on.

"The owner of—" I gestured around "—all this."

"Look, we're shooting a television show here," he said with the exaggerated patience usually reserved for small children and actors. "I don't know this Cayden Doran guy. I don't think he's on my list." He barely glanced at his clipboard.

You're on my list, I thought. *My shit list.*

Luckily for him, Kana appeared, seemingly out of nowhere. "Ah, Lee!" She sounded genuinely pleased to see me. "Doran-san had to leave on his trip a day early. He said to tell you that whatever you need, you are to ask me. I will make sure it happens." She turned to Han Shot First. "Please remember that I will greet people as they arrive. It is not your job."

The twenty-something didn't look happy, but he backed down. Resisting the impulse to stick my tongue out at him, I followed Kana into the Great Room where Shaina, dressed in another pair of designer jeans and expensive T-shirt, darted around like a hummingbird on crack, talking to this crewmember, staring over someone else's shoulder as they worked, basically being everywhere at once. Her nervous energy vibrated across the room.

My boot heels clicked softly on the tiled flooring as I stepped over cables. She looked up and saw me. Didn't smile, but she waved and came over to greet me, nodding to Kana as well. It was at that moment I began to like her, just a little bit.

"Lee, good to see you. Did you have a chance to meet with Nigri yesterday?"

"I did indeed," I replied.

"How did it go?"

I could have lied, but I didn't. "We have a few things to work out, but I think it'll be fine." Okay, I lied a little. I wasn't entirely sure it would be fine, but I was tentatively optimistic that it would be kinda okay. No need to stress out Shaina any more than she already was.

I'd met with the spider walker at the mansion the day before, so he could go over his plans.

It had not started well.

†

"I will be doing the fall from the third story."

"No, you will not."

The words had popped out of my mouth before the politic part of my brain could stop them. I meant what I said, mind you, but as Sean likes to say, there was a nicer way to say it.

"Let me rephrase that," I added quickly before Nigri could get all up on his wandering spider heels. "It's not that I don't think you can do the stunt. It's that you *shouldn't* do it, because that's not your job on this production."

"Where I come from, stuntmen can do both." He already was as angry as a bag of snakes.

"Not stuntmen—stunt coordinators." I tried to choose my words carefully, but I suspected it wouldn't make a difference. "You need to focus on coordinating, not on performing. If there wasn't anyone else on set who could do the stunt, that would be different. But—" and oh, it pained me to say this "—Skeet is more than capable of doing a high fall."

"You do not tell me how to do my job." Nigri's tone was soft, almost sibilant. More snake than spider.

Ahh hell, sometimes I hate being right. I refused to give ground.

"Normally I'd agree with you, but the owner of this house hired me to make sure no one gets hurt, and no damage is done to his property. He empowered me to use my best judgment, and that includes final say on any stunt performed here. If I feel someone is not the best choice to perform any given stunt…" I shrugged. "That's how it's gonna go."

"And if *Senhorita* Gilchrist does not agree?"

"Then she's welcome to find another shooting location."

We'd glared at each other, a grown-up version of a kid's staring contest where whoever blinks first is the loser. I could see Nigri struggling with his temper, the spider under the skin wanting to have a smackdown. My scar itched and I prepared myself for trouble. Instead, he drew a long, deep breath, exhaled, and nodded.

"I do not like this, but it will be as you say."

†

Shaina Gilchrist didn't need to know any of this.

"Good, good." She glanced across the room toward the terrace doors, where a man and a woman sat at opposite ends of an antique table, both typing frantically on iPads. "Oh! I'd like to introduce you to my advisors for this episode." I followed her over. "This is Donald Dickson and Gil Hartley, president and vice-president of the Silver Screamers."

Oh boy.

The Silver Screamers had sprung up in the early 2000s after DuShane's movies had been pulled out of a vault somewhere and made available on a rare movie website. The first copies were grainy pirated versions, but once whoever held the rights got wind of what was going on, they released high quality—and legal—copies for sale. They were now all available exclusively on Shiver, a streaming service that specialized in horror and exploitation films. Lots of foreign zombie and cannibal movies, and obscure horror titles dating back to the twenties.

The fan club had a podcast, a YouTube channel, and a blog, and had done in-depth reviews of all of Silver Scream's films. Probably more in-depth than the writers or directors had ever dreamed, and definitely with more subtext than intended. And here were the president and VP on set as Shaina's advisors, making sure that a simple day's shoot would be more complicated than it should be.

Le sigh.

Donald Dickson. Mid-thirties, medium height, brown hair, brown eyes, brown skin. Jeans a little too large and a black T-shirt bearing the Silver Scream logo, a silver skull, mouth open wide in a—you guessed it—scream. He wasn't bad looking, but a lifetime of sugar and preservatives hadn't done him any favors.

Gil Hartley. A petite woman in her early forties. Hair dyed a rainbow of purple, blue, and pink. Large blue eyes framed with dark lashes. Jeans and the same T-shirt sported by Donald. They also shared a certain fanatical gleam in their eyes common to mega-fans of any stripe.

"Hi," I said, going for a spot between friendly and neutral. "Guess you guys are the experts here."

"We've studied Ned DuShane's films extensively," Donald replied without acknowledging my greeting. "If we don't know it, it doesn't exist."

Wow. Okay then.

"We're totally happy to finally visit the mansion," Gil said. "This is just… it's such an honor, and thank you so much, Ms. Gilchrist, for letting us film our vlog here. It's an amazing opportunity."

Shaina gave a stiff smile. "I very much appreciate the knowledge and research your group has brought to my project, and am happy to reciprocate."

Could she be any more stilted? Oh well, the Silver Screamers didn't seem to notice. They both beamed as if they'd been offered the keys to the kingdom. Maybe, by their standards, they had. After all, getting to roam inside their idol's supposedly haunted stronghold was awfully damn cool. They also might be able satisfy some of my own curiosity about the place.

"Can you tell me anything about the accidents that happened here? Whether they're fact or fiction?"

"Oh, pretty much everything that's been rumored to happen on this property is based in facts," Donald replied.

Gil nodded. "When the Screamers first started our research, the common opinion was that the majority of the stories were just rumors, blown up into urban legends." She smiled, a truly creepy expression on that almost elvish face. "Turned out they weren't. Some truly horrific things have happened on this property—and off it, too."

"Off it? What do you—"

"Ms. Gilchrist, craft service is here." My question was cut off by the arrival of Han Shot First, looking harried. It was the natural state of most production assistants. "Where do you want them to set up?"

Shaina darted off across the room to deal with the latest issue. When I turned back to Donald and Gil to resume the discussion, they'd both sunk back into their work, and I could tell our conversation was over for the moment.

†

The more I observed Shaina in action, the more I decided she wasn't half bad. Once I'd got past the initial "Respect mah authoritay!" she had a quiet sense of humor buried under the seriousness, and despite a brusque impatience that seemed to be a part of her personality, she treated both cast and crew with respect. She'd make a good producer if she'd just focus and stop trying to go the Orson Welles route.

All in all, there was a lot more intelligence and thoughtfulness in Shaina than I'd have expected from the daughter of Hal Gilchrist. I was determined to help make this production run smoothly.

Nigri and I stood in the main hall, looking up at the third story, where an unfortunate film director had fallen over the railing and smashed onto the tiled floor below. His wife, who'd been standing on ground level in the main hall, said he hadn't jumped. There'd been no one else up there who might have helped him over the balustrade that ran the length of the open hall. So how had he ended up smashed like a pumpkin on the floor below?

We were about to go over the stunt with the DP when Skeet and another of Nigri's arachnid stunt-spiders showed up. The back of my neck gave a low-level warning and I resigned myself to an itchy scar for the duration.

"Hey, Lee," Skeet said, the usual sleaze crawling out of his mouth when he said my name.

Ugh.

"This is Eduardo," Nigri said, ignoring his cousin. "He will be doing the fall." Skeet opened his mouth to protest, clearly having expected the gig to go to him. Then he thought better of it, mouth snapping shut. He saw that I'd caught the moment, though, and his look of mortified anger wasn't lost as he scuttled from the room.

"Not Skeet, huh?"

"He is not as qualified as Eduardo," Nigri replied absently.

If it had been anyone but Skeet, I would have felt a lot sorrier for him. It was hard, however, to conjure up any sympathy for his sleazy behavior. Plus any expression of sympathy on my part would be met with anger, since I'd witnessed his shame.

Shortly, Nigri and I watched as Eduardo prepared to take a tumble over the third-story railing, an airbag positioned on the ground floor.

"He does not need an airbag," Nigri argued. "He has taken higher falls without trouble. He can throw webbing well enough to catch himself."

"I thought spider walkers could only really throw webbing in their spider form? At least, that's what Skeet told me."

"Skeet." Nigri said his cousin's name with dismissive contempt. "Eduardo has much more skill than he does. Eduardo, he does not need an airbag."

"Look." I tried very hard to keep the impatience from my voice. "Does it really matter? It's a good safety measure, in case something goes wrong. Besides, most of the cast and crew here don't know about supes, so you're gonna need airbags for cover, even if your team can do somersaults in the air, okay?" It was not an option.

A muscle in Nigri's jaw twitched. Just a little bit.

"*Sim*. You are right."

It cost him to say those words, so I left it alone.

Nigri and I would never be buddies, but we were both trying. I'd googled the Brazilian wandering spider, Nigri's alter-ego, and it was a nasty beast. Videos of the spider showed it getting all up in the face of threats, and I could see where the stuntman's weird rocking back and forth came from. I also realized how hard it was for Nigri to overcome nature's hardwiring, so I vowed to try and summon a little more patience.

"Eduardo!" Nigri called to his stuntman. "You are ready?"

"*Sim*!" Eduardo's voice echoed in the spacious hall from three stories up.

Nigri turned to John, the director of photography, and nodded.

"Scene twenty-three, take one!" A grip slapped the clapboard together and the camera rolled, or whatever the video equivalent would be.

We watched on a screen as Eduardo stumbled along the hallway three stories up, feigning drunkenness with a verisimilitude that spoke of real-life experience. It was video only—most of the scenes would have music and narration laid over the action. A good thing, 'cause Eduardo was singing in Portuguese. He stopped a few feet away from his mark. Frowned. Glanced around as if looking for someone. Stumbled forward again to the spot where he'd tumble forward over the banister.

Instead, Eduardo jerked upright, staring around in all directions before hitting the rail with his back and tumbling over in an uncontrolled fall. Nigri gave an indrawn hiss as the stuntman plummeted to the ground floor… right into the airbag I'd set up. Just in case.

†

"*Credo!*" Nigri declared. We stood in front of one of the monitors watching the playback of the stunt Eduardo had almost died performing. "This is impossible."

Eduardo had been by himself on the second floor, yet in the playback we clearly saw a shadowy figure grab him by the shoulders and shove him over the banister.

"You saw it," I said. "So did I."

The spider walker sat with what he'd just seen for a few minutes. "*Sim*," he finally said. He did not, however, acknowledge the usefulness of the airbag. "I saw it, but it is hard to accept."

Seriously?

"You don't believe in ghosts?"

"*Aff,* of course I do." Nigri waved a hand at me. "I have seen many *fantasmas* in my years, but never have I seen one try to kill before. Only the *mortos-vivos* do that."

Mortos-vivos. I parsed out the words in English.

Undead.

This could not be good. I called Cayden on his cell and got voicemail.

"Weird shit going on here," I said. "Potentially deadly shit. Call me back."

He didn't, which pissed me off, but there wasn't much I could do about it. In the meantime, I had to deal with the Silver Screamers.

Gil and Donald were creeping around the mansion in places they weren't supposed to be. Kana had caught them more than once in the pantry, as well as down the hall where Cayden's study was—areas that were strictly off-limits to the production. As a result, I grew to dislike the Screamers. They poked their noses where they weren't supposed to be, and when caught, acted as if they had every right to be there. Shaina made excuses for them because of the research they'd brought to the table, but I knew that wouldn't cut any mustard with Cayden.

"You *do* realize," I said to her after catching Donald for the third time, "that Cayden doesn't give a shit *what* they know about DuShane. So, if you don't want them tossed off the property, you need to keep them reined in."

"Look," Shaina said with a sigh. "I know they're a little out of control, but that's just because they're excited about being here. This is like a dream come true to them. They're actually on DuShane's property."

"Yeah, except it's not DuShane's property anymore, is it? It's

235

Cayden's. So, keep them on a short leash, *please*. This means no going upstairs unless they ask first. No going into the basement at all, because it's completely off-limits."

"I know, I know…"

"Seriously, Shaina, if they can't respect those simple rules, they're gone."

"I get it."

"Then talk to them, okay?"

"I'll try."

"Good. Because I will seriously punch the next person I find prowling around where they're not supposed to."

CHAPTER TWENTY-FIVE

The next stunt, if it could even be called that, was a simple one. The strangling of Bettina Patton by Earle, their chauffeur. Nothing complicated. As long as Dennis, the actor playing Earle, didn't get too enthusiastic with the curtain tie, it would be a piece of cake.

No big deal, right?

Cherry, the actress playing Bettina, lounged on a purple velvet sofa in the Great Room, glass of liquor in hand as the faux chauffeur crept up silently behind her. Suddenly the actor dropped as if pole-axed, falling face-first onto the floor. There was a loud clatter as something bounced off the floor next to him. Cherry screamed.

I ran over to the prone man, Nigri on my heels. A heavy crystal ashtray smeared with blood lay near his head, while a nasty gash in his scalp glistened under the lights. A puddle of blood was already forming.

"Call an ambulance," I barked, "and get the on-set medic here now!"

Nigri approached me while we were waiting for the ambulance. "Lee," he said, calling me by my first name for the first time. "Where did that ashtray come from?"

"I don't know," I admitted. "Maybe someone thought it would be funny to throw it and hit Dennis by mistake."

"One of those Silver Screeners, perhaps."

I didn't bother correcting him, just shrugged. "Maybe. They really want this place to be haunted. It would make better fodder for their YouTube channel." But I wasn't entirely convinced this was the case.

A half hour later, Dennis was loaded up into an ambulance. He'd lost a lot of blood and most likely had a concussion, but odds were good he'd be okay. That didn't leave me any less worried about what was going on, but in the meantime, we had another crisis to deal with, so I compartmentalized. We had to find another actor who could play Earle. According to the uber-fans, the man had had an unusually large build. Not quite Andre the Giant large, but bigger than your average man.

Shaina paced up and down the length of the dining room, currently doubling as the production office.

"Oh my god, how are we going to find someone on such short notice?"

"Maybe someone from WWE...?" Gare, the first AD, suggested.

"Maybe," Shaina replied tersely, "but we need someone today, or it'll put us behind schedule." I thought her head was gonna explode, and not because of the flying ashtray. Crazy Casa may have been a cheap-ass production company, but it had a reputation of finishing under budget and ahead of schedule. To be behind, even a day, wasn't a small thing.

I left the room to make a phone call.

When I came back, I was smiling. "Good news," I said without preamble. "I know someone who's perfect for Earle and, lucky for us, he's available." Which was how, an hour later, we were treated to the unlikely sight of Drift in a 1920s chauffeur's uniform. The jacket was tight across the shoulders and back, but otherwise it fit surprisingly well.

"Just try not to move too much when you get out of the Rolls-Royce," the wardrobe mistress cautioned him. She looked nervously at the costume.

"Maybe just don't move at all," I offered.

"Thanks, kid," he growled at me.

"You can take the jacket off for the scenes inside." Shaina, who was over-the-moon with the last-minute casting replacement, gave Drift a radiant smile. It changed her face from mousy seriousness to a fragile beauty which didn't go unnoticed by the object of her approval.

Mindful of his wardrobe, Drift moved with a careful stiffness that worked well for the role of a chauffeur back in the twenties, and he made for a really creepy killer, making his eyes go all blank and staring when it came time to strangle Cherry.

Nigri took his presence surprisingly well, most likely because none of his team had the physique to play Earle. Drift refrained from doing any of the posturing I've seen when two different stunt crews collided—not quite the Jets and the Sharks, but it could get ugly. And Skeet? Well, he showed a surprising amount of self-preservation by staying out of sight. I'd lost track of the number of times Drift had threatened to rip Skeet's legs off during the short time he'd trained at the Ranch.

"Drift is really good," Shaina told me happily during the third take. "Thanks again for recommending him. He's cute, too."

Really?

"Is he dating anyone?"

Was he? I didn't remember the last time I'd discussed Drift's love life. Maybe never? *Could this get any more disturbing?*

Shaina stared at me expectantly.

"Well, he—"

"Shaina?" John, the DP, stood behind the main camera setup. The strain in his voice caught both our attention. "Are you seeing this?" At the same time the two gaffers manning the other two video cams looked up from their posts, identical expressions of disbelief on their faces.

Frowning, Shaina turned back to the monitor and froze. I looked over her shoulder, Nigri and the Silver Screamers crowding behind me. We all watched in the monitor as Drift moved slowly and almost mechanically across the Great Room, a length of drapery cord dangling from his hands. Cherry, meanwhile, lounged unaware on a purple velvet couch, a drink in one hand. Behind her, however, were two other figures that hadn't been in the scene.

A man and a woman dressed in clothing very similar to what Cherry and Drift were wearing. The woman's face was purpled, tongue protruding from rouged lips. The man's handsome face was greenish-gray, blood splattering his white shirt, a gash in his throat speaking of his end. They both stared first at Cherry, then back at Drift… and then looked directly into the camera with eyes that were pools of malevolent darkness.

Holy shit! I thought.

"Holy shit!" Donald stared at the monitor in excitement. "That's Dougie and Bettina! That's the Pattons! That's really them!" The two ghosts jerked at Donald's yell and faded away, leaving only Drift and Cherry visible in the monitor.

I texted Cayden this time, instead of calling.

Weird shit still happening here. Really weird. You appear to
have an infestation of pissed-off ghosts. Maybe worse. Pretty
sure this can't be good. Please text, email, or call. Better yet,
get your ass back here.

By the time I went to bed that night, he still hadn't contacted
me. Had Cayden lied to me about the place being spirit-free?
And if so, did they have anything to do with what happened to
Jada? For that matter… did Cayden?

It was a long time before I fell asleep.

CHAPTER TWENTY-SIX

"Hey, Lee!"

Looking up, I saw Eden wafting across the drive. She wore a fifties-style dress, pink and yellow roses scattered across the fabric. Matching pink sandals and a yellow clutch purse completed the outfit. She also carried two venti-sized coffee cups from Starbucks.

"Eden!"

"Hi, sweetie!" Eden enveloped me in a hug redolent of roses, coffee, and chocolate. Then she handed me one of the cups. "Thought you might be in need of some sugar and caffeine about now."

"Always." I took a sip. *Nom…* one of Starbucks' extra dark mochas. "You *do* love me, Chandler Bing," I crooned.

Eden giggled. "Any idea where I'm supposed to go for costume and makeup?"

"I do indeed." Hooking an arm through hers, I led her inside, through the entry hall, into the Great Room and beyond into the indoor pool area where racks of twenties-style clothing were set up. DuShane's sex cabanas had been repurposed for wardrobe and makeup stations. She didn't seem as dazzled by the entire tackily gorgeous decorating as most of the other cast and crew members. In fact, Eden seemed very comfortable in her surroundings, as if…

"Have you been here before?"

"What?" Eden shot me a glance. "No, but I've seen residences just as tacky, if not more so, and I've read a lot about Ned DuShane. He was all about the whole Arabian Nights craze, and he loved the idea of owning his own castle. That's where the mishmash of styles comes from."

"You sound like one of the Silver Screamers."

"Oh, good god, I hope not." Eden rolled her eyes. "I can't imagine anything sadder than dedicating my life to a dead man. No, I just like to research projects I'm involved with, and I have to admit, DuShane was a fascinating—if hideous—character."

"Hideous?"

We both turned to find Donald standing there, a plate piled with assorted snacks in one hand, a soda in the other. He looked horrified.

Eden gave him a smile. "Well, he wasn't exactly known for his altruism, was he?"

"How would you know?"

"You're not the only one who does your reading," Eden said gently. "See you later, Lee, 'kay?"

"You bet."

With a little wave in my direction, she continued on to Wardrobe. The rest of the cast and crew didn't exactly stop in their tracks when she walked by, but more than a few heads swiveled to watch her progress.

"Who the hell is that?" Donald wasn't one of Eden's appreciative audience. He glared after her, piqued that someone had insulted his hero. Before I could answer, however, Nigri came up next to me, staring after Eden as if she was the last cold drink in the desert. His voice lacked its usual hostility, instead sounding as if he'd been sniffing glue or something equally soporific.

"Who is that?"

"Eden Carmel," I replied neutrally. "Why?"

"She's beautiful."

"Yup, she is. She's my best friend." I dropped that last bit casually.

"Perhaps you could... perhaps you would introduce me to her later?"

It was all I could do not to snort. I started to say, "*On a cold day in hell, Spider Boy,*" but managed to restrain myself. Instead, I said something noncommittal, and went about my business.

The mansion seethed with activity, so much that it was hard to remember the skin-crawling creepiness when the ghostly figures had shown up on the monitor. Most people who'd witnessed it managed to tuck it away at the back of their minds, the same place where dreams lived. Or nightmares.

The Great Room was being prepared for the big party scene. There were going to be upwards of sixty extras on set the next morning, most arriving at the ungodly hour of 5:00 A.M. so they could get into wardrobe and makeup in time to start filming by 10:00. Very little set dressing was necessary, but with three cameras being used to catch the action from different angles, gaffer and grips had a lot of work to do setting up the lighting. I had to hand it to Shaina, she was really trying to do justice to this project without the usual lowball budget that was synonymous with Crazy Casa.

Since there weren't any stunts involved, I could just kick back, watching the fun and keeping an eye on Gil and Donald.

"Hey Lee." Speak of the devil, there was Gil in her usual Screamers T-shirt and jeans. She had a necklace on—a disk of hammered copper with gemstones set in it, hanging from a silver chain.

"That's different," I said, nodding at it.

Putting a hand almost protectively over the disk, Gil gave me a vague smile. "Family heirloom,' she said, then drifted off toward Donald.

Had I mentioned that I didn't like them?

Out of the corner of my eye I spotted Donald making a beeline for the kitchen, which was off-limits. Heaving a martyred sigh, I followed, catching him just as he slipped into the pantry. Clearing my throat, I glared as he spun around, a guilty look on his face.

"What are you doing?" I didn't bother softening my tone. "You know damn well you're not supposed to be in here."

"Uh… well, I was hungry."

"That would be a decent excuse if there wasn't a bunch of food at the craft service table. Try again."

"Look, there are so many rumors about this place," he said, his tone pleading. "This is our chance to find out what's true—don't you *get* it?" He glanced almost desperately over his shoulder at the pantry wall. I had no idea what he was looking at and didn't much care.

"Kana and I have told you and Gil more than once to stay out of here. Just because Shaina gave permission for you to look around, doesn't mean the owner of this place doesn't have his own ideas. That's the bottom line."

He looked at me sullenly. "There'll never be another owner besides Ned DuShane," he muttered.

That was it. I'd had enough.

"Yeah, well, I'll be sure to mention that to Cayden Doran when I tell him why he should toss you out on your ass."

Donald huffed in indignation and stomped out of the pantry, brushing past me hard enough to knock me into the counter. I would deal with him later. Now, I just wanted to get through the next scene and then relax until the following morning, preferably without killing anyone.

†

I emailed Cayden again, this time going into detail about what had happened with Eduardo, the flying ashtray, the creepy images on the monitor, and finally asking if he had any idea what the Silver Screamers might be searching for. He actually emailed me back this time, and within the hour—the first time I'd heard from him since he'd left.

A few thoughts.
Nothing that won't wait until I'm back.

"Oh, for fuck's sake," I muttered.

And when's that gonna be?

I stopped myself from adding, "asshat."

Sometime tonight.

I was still annoyed, not to mention worried, but breathed a little easier after that.

†

Most of the crew and cast—except for the crowd of extras who'd show up the next morning—spent the night in the mansion so we could start filming bright and early. Kana and I were in the study, sharing a bottle of very good red wine.

We'd invited Shaina to join us, but she wanted to spend the

evening doing yet more research with Donald and Gil, just in case there was anything they'd collectively missed. I admired her dedication, but not enough to emulate it. I'd wanted to ask Eden as well, but she'd gone up to her room after dinner, pleading a headache. So it was just Kana and me.

I liked Kana. She was good company. I found myself relaxed in her presence, as if I'd just had an hour-long massage. Sipping the wine, I shut my eyes in appreciation.

"Ooh, nice."

Kana smiled. "Doran-san has many good bottles in his cellar."

I looked at the label. A Rafanelli Terrace Select, 2016. A far cry from the Apothic Red he'd bought at Arlo's the first time we'd met. Kana poured out the rest of the bottle between our two glasses.

"Hello, ladies."

We looked up to see Cayden standing in the doorway, as tired as I'd ever seen him look. Walking over, he picked up the wine bottle, frowning when he realized it was empty.

"What, none for me?" Cayden raised an eyebrow at his housekeeper.

"I would be more than happy to fetch another bottle, Doran-san."

"Please do."

Standing, she slipped out of the study.

"She's something," I commented, taking another swallow of wine. "This is really good."

Cayden sat across from me. "It should be. Their wine club has a waiting list to get on the mailing list."

"And this is why I hang out with you."

He smiled. "So how are things going?"

"You mean aside from the weird-ass shit I wrote you about, that you never answered?" I shrugged, enjoying the glow of superlative wine spreading through my body. "Okay, I guess. Nigri—the stunt coordinator—isn't as aggro since he almost lost one of his stuntmen. Shaina isn't half bad either—I'd like to work with her again, and I think she and Drift are kinda crushing on each other, which is weird, but oh well." I took another sip of wine and stared at him. "And I still can't explain what we saw on the monitors when the Patton stuff was being filmed." My tone sharpened. "But... maybe you can."

"The place is haunted," Cayden said bluntly.

"I thought you said hadn't had any disturbances since you moved in."

"I hadn't," he replied. "I put up wards to make sure I'd have peace and quiet."

"Wards against what?" I sat up straight. "And more importantly, why didn't you tell me about them?"

"I was hoping it wouldn't be an issue." Kana came into the study, bearing another bottle of Terrace Select and a clean wine glass. "Ah, Kana, thank you." Taking them both from her, Cayden set the glass down, picked up the waiter's helper Kana had used on the first bottle, and deftly uncorked the new one. I tried not to stare at the contrast between his large, almost brutal hands, and the agility with which he moved them.

I didn't want to admire anything about him right now, after he'd as much as admitted he'd kept secrets from me about things that could have dangerous—possibly fatal—consequences.

"Unless you need anything else, Doran-san...?"

"Thank you, Kana, we're good."

I don't think so, I thought as Kana nodded and left the study.

Cayden cradled his now-full wine glass between his hands. Stared into it.

"Tell me more about these wards," I said, holding my temper. "Like, what kind of wards are we talking about?"

He sighed. "The kind that keep homicidal revenants locked up. While I can deal with angry ghosts, I prefer peace and quiet. Unfortunately, some of them have been removed during my absence."

"What the actual fuck?" So much for keeping my cool. "You're saying they're not in place anymore?" My voice rose in outrage. "And homicidal revenants? Why the *hell* didn't you think to tell me about this?"

"I had no reason to believe they'd be tampered with. As soon as I felt the first one go down, I changed my flight and headed home."

"First one?" My head hurt. "How many are there?"

"Four inside, four on the grounds outside."

"And they're all down?"

"If they were all down," he said with a patience that just made me want to punch him, "you'd know it. Three of the ones I placed inside the mansion are definitely gone, but the most important one is still in place."

"You're sure about that?" When he didn't reply, I stared. "How about we go check. *Now.*"

Cayden's jaw clenched. Without a word, he stood up and strode out of the study, down the hall to the kitchen. Following closely, I didn't bother asking any more questions—there were too many people still roaming about, prepping for tomorrow's shoot.

Once in the kitchen Cayden went into the pantry, shutting the door behind us. Then he went to the back wall, where Donald had been nosing around earlier. With a few muttered words and a wave of one hand, Cayden knocked sharply on the wall and a door suddenly appeared, the outline and knob hazy at first, like heat lines in the desert. Then it solidified.

"Clever," I said.

"I'm not stupid," he said as he opened the door, revealing a wooden staircase going down into darkness. I gave a noncommittal grunt in response.

The flick of a switch turned on a succession of bare lightbulbs set into the ceiling along a hallway that stretched off into shadows. At the bottom of those stairs was another staircase descending even further.

"Here." Cayden stopped in front of what looked to be to be just another rough section of wall made from crumbing concrete blocks. The difference from the rest of the dank corridor was how it jutted from the rest of the wall by a few inches. There was a nail driven into mortar about five feet above the floor, and something hung there on a silver chain—a bronze or copper disk with what looked like gemstones. It looked somehow familiar.

Curious, I touched it and almost immediately felt energy running into my fingertips, like a low-level electrical current. It didn't hurt, but it was weird. I took my hand away and turned to Cayden, who observed me with a small smile playing about his lips. By this point I wanted to belt it off his face.

"You can feel it, can't you?"

I nodded. "What is it, exactly?"

His smile widened. "Aside from—"

"Let me rephrase that," I cut in before he could finish. "What is *this*?" I tapped the disk of bejeweled metal.

"A ward of containment," he said simply.

"What's it trying to contain?" I asked, even though I damned well knew the answer.

"Ned DuShane."

Give this girl a prize.

†

The mansion's "owner" and the bitchy woman vanished into the pantry. Gil and Donald waited just as he instructed.

After what seemed like enough time, they looked inside the pantry to see that there was a door, cracked open ever so slightly. Gil used her phone to take a picture so they could find it again later. They didn't want to get caught—the man, Cayden Doran, was scary, and they had no doubt that he'd kick them off the property.

"What if it's gone when we come back?" Donald said in an undertone.

"Then we'll get an axe."

CHAPTER TWENTY-SEVEN

Cayden and I had exited the subbasement, and we hardly said another word. He didn't seem to want to disclose anything more, and I was too angry to trust myself to speak. I was torn between curiosity and the increasingly familiar urge to belt him.

I went up to my room but wasn't about to fall asleep. There was so much to untangle, knowing there was a homicidal revenant imprisoned several floors below me. Was all the weirdness connected—the missing people, Jada's disappearance, the flying ashtray, the apocalyptic-level flood of animals at the Ranch?

If it *was* all connected, then how?

I couldn't stop thinking about the Silver Screamers, and how they were obviously hunting for something in the mansion. I'd lay odds they had removed the first three wards. How they knew about them was another matter altogether.

Then there was the matter of Cayden. While there was an undeniable attraction between us, more than ever I had no idea if I could or should trust him. At the moment it seemed like a very bad idea.

I finally fell asleep around 2:30 A.M., waking up three hours later to roll out of bed and stumble downstairs for some much-needed coffee. Call time was 6:00 A.M., and there were extras trickling in for makeup and wardrobe. It was going to be a very full house.

Eden emerged from wardrobe and makeup looking resplendent in a clingy floor-length gown of silver satin, blonde hair curled lightly against her face. Nigri, along with half the crew, couldn't take his eyes off her.

Crazy Casa had spared no expense for this scene. There were at least fifty or sixty extras milling about in twenties garb—flappers in fringe and feathers, jeweled bands around bobbed hair, crystal beads hanging down to the drop waists of their dresses. Sophisticated women in long gowns of silk and velvet. Men in suits, looking like they'd stepped out of a speakeasy.

One particularly large, broad-shouldered fellow stood out above the crowd, looking like a hired thug—Drift, who at Shaina's urging had agreed to come back and play a partygoer. Which was kinda weird, but it felt good to have him there should anything else happen. His curly brown hair was slicked back, and makeup had given him a pencil mustache. He saw me and waved, grinning from ear to ear.

The servers, on the other hand, could have been refugees from the set of *Spartacus,* dressed as Roman servants with knee-high gladiator sandals and short tunics for the women. Each man wore leather strips attached to a waistband via metal studs, their oiled bodies glistening in the lights.

Authentic 1920s music played softly in the background.

I turned to Eden, who was carefully sipping water through a straw to avoid smudging her carefully applied lipstick. Followed her line of sight directly to a well-muscled if somewhat hairy male extra in leather war skirt and sandals, talking to two darkly good-looking men in suits—Eduardo and Skeet. There were no stunts, but Shaina had drafted everyone she could for the scene.

Sidling up to Eden, I said, "Say, Jimmy, do you like gladiator movies?"

She choked, nearly spitting the straw out. Grinning, I headed off to do one last check around the mansion before filming started, and make sure all was as it should be. At least to the best of my ability.

Cayden hadn't appeared yet, which was fine by me.

Donald passed me in the hallway, gave me a nasty look, and kept going toward the Great Room. Gil, on the other hand, was nowhere in sight. I took a quick peek in the pantry, but there was no sign of her. Heaving a sigh of relief, I went back to get another cup of coffee, and watch the party scene being filmed.

When I got back to the Great Room, Cayden was standing in the back with Kana, near Shaina and her bank of monitors. I drank my coffee and stood next to Shaina, stubbornly ignoring him even though I could feel his gaze burning into me.

Why couldn't I feel this way about Randy?

Life would be so much less complicated.

They did several takes of general party atmosphere, the "guests" laughing, drinking, eating, and in some cases getting PG-13 frisky. Toby Hissong owned the room as Ned DuShane, clapping men on the shoulders, putting a more-than-avuncular arm around the women, pinching a cheek here, a derriere there, and all in all doing a great job playing the larger-than-life producer of Silver Scream.

When Eden made her entrance as Dawn Jardine with her escort, "DuShane" descended on them, wrapping a proprietary arm around her waist and leading her off to get a flute of champagne, leaving her escort standing by himself. I couldn't help but notice that the server looked more put out than Eden's escort.

Then I saw his face—fer chrissake, it was Nigri.

"Pretty tame for one of DuShane's orgy-fests," Cayden whispered in my ear. "Most of the racier action happened in the spillover area next door. And upstairs, of course."

"It *is* a little mild," I said. "I mean, given their audience they can't exactly go all Caligula, but still…"

"Disappointed?"

I elbowed him in the ribs without turning around and heard his low, rumbling chuckle.

"Asshat," I muttered.

After a few takes with sound to catch the ambiance of the crowd, the music, and a few lines of dialogue from the actors with lines, Shaina called a ten-minute bathroom break and conferred with John, the DP. I moved to talk to Eden, but Nigri got there first and I didn't think he'd thank me for interrupting their conversation. I didn't like it, but Eden was a grownup and could handle herself.

Glancing around, I scanned for the Silver Screamers. They were over by the craft service tables against the back wall of the Great Room, Gil nibbling on a cookie while Donald stuffed handfuls of tortilla chips into his mouth. They caught me looking their way and gave me synchronized death-ray stares. That helped my mood—I hid a grin.

"Okay, Dax, time for places," Shaina called. Dax, otherwise known as Han Shot First, didn't answer. "Where the hell did he go off to?" Shaina sounded understandably irritated.

"Maybe he's in the bathroom…?" a crewmember suggested.

"Oh, for chrissake. How long does it take?" Shaina waited another thirty seconds, then yelled, "Places, people!"

The actors and extras slowly returned to their marks. Picked up small plates of food, champagne flutes filled with sparkling cider, whatever props they'd been given to work with. Nigri reluctantly left Eden's side to retrieve his serving tray. I was surprised he'd agreed to play one of the waiters until I saw him subtly but deliberately flex his arm and back muscles. He knew he looked good and wanted to make sure Eden saw it.

"Party scene, take six!" The sharp clack of the clapperboard echoed through the room, followed by a muffled pounding.

Cayden glanced up sharply.

The scar on the back of my neck itched and my amulet began to heat up against my chest.

Uh-oh.

Once again guests circulated, had vivacious conversations that most likely had nothing to do with the characters or time period they were supposed to be portraying.

"I swear, this is the last extra gig I'm going to take," one toga-clad server said as she handed glasses of "champagne" to a group of suit-clad men. "I spend enough time as a waitress—I don't need to play one on TV."

"Can I offer you some champagne?" a voice said almost immediately. The extra looked around, the movement so sudden she sloshed some of the sparkling cider onto the floor. As I watched, another toga-clad woman, looking like an art nouveau nymph, superimposed herself over the extra.

Blinking to clear my eyes, I looked around. The same thing was happening all over the Great Room, which had suddenly become twice as crowded as it had been seconds before. It was like watching shadows take form, loosely attached to the actors and extras. The shadows looked more authentic, even though they were transparent.

Holy shit.

My amulet was full-on burning. The muffled pounding sound reached my ears again. Instead of stopping this time, though, it repeated itself. Once. Twice. Then again in a rapid frenzy of what sounded like blows. I turned, looking for Cayden, who was rapidly moving through the Great Room toward the main hall. Before I could follow him, a muffled explosion shook the house.

Someone screamed.

The specters gained substance. They weren't all DuShane's guests from parties past—there were people in clothing that spanned a hundred years, and some of them had died badly. Bettina and Dougie Patton were there, dressed in the clothes they'd died in. Skin rotted. Nothing of the glamor remained. Many of the other new party guests were much the same—and they all looked pissed off.

As I watched, Bettina drifted over to Cherry, put her spectral hands over the actress's face…

…and ripped it off.

Things went quickly south after that.

More screams, a lot of them in pain, many of them abruptly cut off.

Threading my way through the panicking cast and crew members, I dashed down the hall to the kitchen. The door was flung wide, as was the entrance to the pantry. Someone had smashed open the door Cayden had concealed with his magic. The lights were on in the hallway below. Bolting down two flights of stairs, I ran to where Cayden had taken me the night before. I found him standing in front of that section of wall, Kana next to him.

The ward was gone. Concrete and wood lay shattered on the

floor, leaving a hole in the wall. Something had burst through from the chamber beyond.

"Well, this is bad," Cayden said.

"No shit."

We dashed back the way we had come, and when we got back upstairs, the truth of his words became horribly evident. The screaming was louder with every step. Revenants were caught up in the party, attacking the people unlucky enough to be within their grasp. Cast and crew members were doing the screaming, but some of it was delight as they snatched up lighting fixtures, knives, bottles, whatever was close at hand… and started butchering those who were trying to get away.

I looked around for Eden—she was nowhere in sight. I hoped to god she'd found a safe place to hide.

Shaina was huddled in a corner by the terrace, Drift standing guard over her, deflecting would-be attackers with massive fists. He was bleeding from several cuts on his arms and face, but still looked okay.

"We need to get out of here," Cayden said.

"Where?" I asked.

"The Ranch. It's safe there."

"Drift!" I hollered. He looked up at the sound of my voice. "Get Shaina to the front gate! We need to get back to the Ranch!"

Giving a thumbs-up, Drift scooped Shaina into his arms and dashed out through the terrace doors.

"Let's go," Cayden said as people boiled around the arched entrance between the Great Room and the main hall. Without waiting, I nodded and dashed forward, right arm outstretched to knock people and revenants aside. Half the time I was hitting rotten flesh. Cayden did the same, Kana ghosting behind us as a swarm of crazy people turned to follow.

The three of us reached the terrace and leapt over the balustrade. Shaina and Drift were waiting for us underneath the cover of the terrace, Drift panting like he'd run a marathon.

"You okay?" I asked, putting a hand on his massive shoulder.

"I…" He dipped his head down, chin resting on his chest. Could he be having a heart attack? "I'm fine," he muttered. Then he lifted his head up. "I'm… I'm… I'm…" I looked into his eyes—they were veined with red. "Get me to the Ranch, Lee." Drift's voice was desperate. He dropped his head again, hyperventilating.

All the production vehicles were parked in the grass and side areas. "Hang on," I said, and ran over to a grip truck, hoping the driver hadn't thought it necessary to take the keys out in a place as isolated as this. They hadn't.

Thank you, I thought to no one in particular.

Waving at Cayden, I pointed at the truck. Then I opened the tailgate as Drift staggered up with Cayden's help. He looked into the back, clear of lighting equipment.

"Yeah, okay," he muttered. "Just get me there fast. I can feel things changing inside."

As soon as Drift was settled, I slammed shut the back gate, latching it in place before jumping into the cab next to Shaina. Kana was squished into the space in back of the seat, looking as comfortable and content as if she were riding in a limo.

Cayden put pedal to the metal and ripped down the drive, not bothering to avoid any of the crazies trying to stop us. One of them, a PA, bounced off the truck's front bumper as Cayden careened through the front gates. A look in the passenger-side mirror showed the unwelcome sight of least a dozen shrieking cast and crew members pelting after us. Every shred of sanity had left the building.

"Shit," I muttered. *Eden...*

"What?" Cayden glanced at me.

"Just drive as fast as you can."

He shot a look into the rearview mirror and hit the gas, taking the turn onto the dirt road at a speed that would have made a sane Drift proud. A dust cloud rose behind us.

"Holy fuck," I muttered, hanging on to the handle.

"Is there such a thing?" Cayden grinned at me and kept driving.

The distance from the mansion to the Ranch was maybe a mile as the crow flies, but we weren't crows and had to take the road, so it was at least two and change. The grip truck wasn't meant to be driven much above 50mph, but Cayden drove like it was headed to NASCAR. This was both good and bad, because the road was strewn with some truly nasty potholes, and if the truck bottomed out and we lost a strut or blew a tire, we were seriously screwed.

"Slow down," I cautioned. "If we lose the truck, we lose Drift and maybe more. You and I can run, but what about Shaina and Kana?"

"Oh, I will be fine," Kana spoke up. "I can move very quickly when necessary."

"I've never jogged a day in my life," Shaina's voice was raspy and strained, as if her throat was tightening around her larynx. "I'd rather not start now."

Jerking his chin toward the rearview mirror, Cayden snapped, "There's a good chance they'll catch up with us if I go any slower." Still, he decelerated to a reasonable speed.

"So... why the Ranch?" I asked.

"Have you heard of vortices?"

I stared at him, confused. "Well, yeah, but what's that got to do with anything?"

"One of the largest—and least-known—vortices lies between the Ranch and the mansion. Both were built directly on ley lines intersecting this vortex. Which means there's a tremendous amount of power, if someone has the wherewithal to access it."

"Still not getting it," I admitted.

"The mansion has always had a reputation as an evil place," he said. "Whereas the Ranch…"

"Whereas the Ranch has always been a safe place." I thought of the way animals flocked onto the property at times, and nodded slowly. How no one could come there if they had ill-intentions toward any of the residents.

"Exactly. It's soaked up as much psychic energy as the mansion over the years, but it's always been, for lack of a better term, used for good. If we can get Drift there, it might—"

"Might flip the switch from evil back to good?"

Cayden nodded, then swerved to avoid a pothole. I braced my left arm against the dashboard to steady myself and Shaina sunk her teeth into my forearm. Screaming in pain and surprise, I gave an involuntary jerk and she sunk her teeth in even harder. It hurt like hell and I saw red.

"Get off me!" I yelled. Making a fist with my free hand, I popped her in the side of her head. She didn't seem to feel it.

Cayden looked over and swore. "I need both my hands," he said tersely.

"I can handle it." My voice was laced with pain, the reply squeezed out between gritted teeth as Shaina started worrying at my arm and snarling like a rabid honey badger, blood welling up around her mouth and trickling warmly down my wrist.

Instead of pulling away and risk losing a chunk of flesh, I jammed my forearm into Shaina's mouth hard enough to split her lips and pinched her nose shut with my other hand. She immediately began kicking and clawing, her carefully manicured nails raking furrows across my face and neck. I jerked my head back as she went for my eyes.

Kana reached over the seat and looped an arm around Shaina's neck, trying to pull her off me. Meanwhile, Cayden did his best to keep the truck on the road as Shaina's thrashing body slammed against his side, causing him to jerk the steering wheel to the left. He fought to control the truck as it whipsawed back and forth, almost skidding off the road before he managed to bring the vehicle back on course.

BOOM.

Something hit the inside of the truck bed with a force that shook the entire vehicle. Then a loud irregular thumping commenced, like a really bad drummer more interested in volume than keeping consistent rhythm. Another *BOOM* followed by a blood-curdling roar confirmed that Drift had also lost his grip on sanity. I didn't know how long the integrity of the truck would last against the full-on fury of a psycho troll, but I didn't think it would be very long.

Meanwhile, Shaina kept ripping at me with her nails, and all I could do was take it while continuing to shove my forearm against her mouth and keep her nostrils pinched shut. She had to breathe sooner rather than later. At least so I hoped.

After what seemed an eternity, she unlocked her teeth to take a breath. I immediately jerked my arm out of her mouth and grabbed the back of her head.

"Let go of her!" I screamed. Kana immediately released her

grip and I slammed Shaina's head against the dashboard. She slid down against me, unconscious. Blood streamed from her rapidly swelling nose, a bruise already rising on her forehead.

"You okay?" Cayden kept his eyes on the road.

"Peachy." I looked at my forearm. Blood streamed from deep, ragged bite marks. Her teeth had broken the skin and the bites were at least a quarter-inch deep, if not more. They hurt like a motherfucker.

"If this was a zombie movie, you'd be screwed."

I started to laugh, but grimaced with pain instead. "Hell with zombies," I replied. "Do you know how many germs the human mouth carries? I just hope the whole insanity virus can't be transmitted that way."

The truck hit another pothole, throwing Shaina's inert body into me. She smacked against the bite wound, pain making my vision blur around the edges. I concentrated on breathing so I wouldn't throw up or pass out. Both were distinct possibilities, and I couldn't afford to do either. The pain throbbed in time to my heartbeat.

Holy crap, it hurt.

Then I felt a hand on the back of my neck, cool and soothing. "Breathe," Kana said softly. I didn't know what kind of being she was, but her touch dulled the pain, almost seeming to draw it out, like a poultice pulling poison out of a wound. I no longer felt like I was gonna hurl or join Shaina for an unwilling nap. I didn't question it or try to figure it out, just accepted the gift.

"Thank you."

"I can do more when we are somewhere safe," she said, "but this should help a little for now."

I sagged back against the seat, trying to ignore the sting of blood dripping from the bite wounds and nail gouges. Kana's mojo helped, but the shock from Shaina's attack still cycled through me.

"Are we there yet?"

A loud *BOOM* from the back answered me. The screech of tearing metal reverberated through the truck—Drift was getting antsy.

BOOM.

BOOM.

BOOM.

The entire truck shook with the force of Drift's blows.

"If we don't get there soon," I said, "he's gonna trash the damn truck."

"Just about there," Cayden replied calmly.

He was right. We were a scant few hundred yards from the entrance to the drive that led up to the Ranch. Some of the crazies were still in hot pursuit, but we had a decent lead on them. No reason we couldn't make it there before they reached us.

BOOM.

Unless Drift punched through into the cab and crushed our skulls.

The Ranch's open gates beckoned like a signal fire. Drift hammered on the metal between the bed and cab, this time breaching the rear panel and smashing against the back of the cab. The impact sent Kana lurching forward. Another smash. The rear of the cab began to bulge inward. I wondered how much longer it would take Drift to pound his way through.

As if reading my mind, Cayden pushed down harder on the accelerator, the entire vehicle vibrating unhappily with the extra effort. The pounding paused. Cayden took the left turn at a speed that threw Shaina's limp form across his lap, and I nearly followed. A bone-breaking thump from the back told me Drift had hit the interior side-panel. For an instant I wondered if he'd be knocked unconscious by the impact, but the hope was crushed by an inarticulate roar of rage. He renewed his assault on the partition.

Shaina stirred, groaning a little. "You are not waking up yet," I told her, steeling myself to punch her again if necessary.

The gates were less than twenty feet away. We closed the distance, and for the first time since we left the mansion, I believed we were actually going to make it.

The truck slammed to a halt right in front of the gates, as if it had hit an invisible brick wall.

CHAPTER TWENTY-EIGHT

Cayden and I rebounded off the dashboard, hard. No airbags, which meant nothing cushioned the impact. Shaina flopped around like rag doll, head smacking against the dash, but thankfully held in place by her seatbelt so she didn't go through the windshield.

"You okay back there?" I shot a look back at Kana, who wiped a thin streamer of blood from her nose.

"I'm fine."

"Why did you stop?" I practically shouted the words.

"I didn't," Cayden replied with a grimace. "The wards on the property won't let us pass."

"What? That's impossible! They only way that would happen is if someone in the car meant harm to anyone on—*oh*."

"Yeah, 'oh.'" Cayden jerked his chin at the back of the truck. "I don't think either Drift or Shaina have good intentions toward anyone but DuShane about now."

Or it might be you. The thought popped into my head without volition. Cayden must have seen something in my face.

"Really, Lee? You still think I've got something to do with this mess?"

"I don't—" I stopped. Thought about it. I owed him an honest answer. Except I didn't have time to parse this out. "I'll call Sean." I reached for my bag, then realized I'd left it back at the mansion, cell phone inside. "Shit. I'll go get him."

Cayden looked in the driver's-side mirror. "Run fast."

Throwing the door open, I leapt out of the cab and took off at a dead run the minute I hit the ground. I didn't look back to see how close the crazies were—I could hear them, the noise of their howls punctuated by Drift's roars and the sound of his fists hitting the interior of the truck, followed by a shriek of metal being torn.

I ran faster.

Please let Sean and Seth be home.

When I saw the Xterra in the carport, I nearly sank to my knees in gratitude, but instead pelted across the driveway to the front door, flinging it open so hard it bounced off the inner wall of the entryway with a loud crack. Both Sean and Seth came out of the kitchen, speaking at the same time.

"Lee, is everything okay?"

"What the hell, Lee?"

"We've got a truck stuck at the gates," I got out between breaths, "and Drift is in the back, turning into a full-on evil troll, and we need to get onto the Ranch *now*."

To give them credit, they were out the door before me, parsing the implications of Drift turning evil and the spells keeping the truck from driving onto the property. I caught up with the two of them at the gates, just in time to see both their faces when they saw who was driving the truck.

"He's not coming in." Seth's expression was uncompromising.

Oh, for fuck's sake.

"Take another look, Seth—" I pointed to the road where, not a hundred yards away, it looked like a scene out of *Train to Busan*

"—and tell me we can discuss this later. Because we don't have time for this bullshit."

Seth opened his mouth to argue with me.

"She's right," Sean said.

Seth closed his mouth without a word as his father muttered a few unintelligible words and raise his hands. For a moment, phantom wings appeared behind him, shimmering in the late afternoon light. He looked downright angelic.

I could feel it the instant the ward at the gate went down. I could also see it in the reactions from a few goats grazing near the gate. They went from relaxed to alert in seconds, and instantly there was a new, raw tension in the air.

Boom!

The hole in the side of the truck grew larger, and another metallic shriek filled the air as fingers the size of salamis peeled away another swath, creating a hole large enough for Drift to stick his big troll head out.

I'm here to tell you, trolls do not look like Shrek. Sure, they're green, but they're not cute. His teeth were the size of Pop Tarts, all yellowed and jagged, viscous bile-colored liquid dribbling down his chin. His eyes yellow, all veined with red. He made the Hulk look like a Care Bear.

"Move it!" I yelled, waving my arms at Cayden. He gunned the engine and hit the gas.

The instant the truck drove over the Ranch's property line, Drift shrunk back to… well… Drift. No jagged teeth, and the look in his soft brown eyes was confused, not homicidal.

The crazies, however, were still pounding up the road toward the now unprotected gates.

"Sean, can you put the ward back up?"

Seth shot me a look. "What the hell do you think he's doing?"

"How the hell would I know?" I shot back.

"Try having a little faith."

The truck roared up to the carport. Sean, Seth, and I stayed behind. My amulet was burning like a solar flare.

I looked around for anything to use as a weapon, but I didn't even have car keys on me—they were back at the mansion in my bag. I wondered how many of the oncoming psychos I could take on before I died.

"Seriously," I whispered to Seth. "How long does this take? He took it down in seconds."

"It's always easier to destroy something than it is to create it," Seth replied, managing to sound accurate and self-righteous at the same time.

Whatever.

Fuck.

Still, I tried to cool my jets and just be there to defend our home. The crazies closed in, fifty yards maybe. Close enough for me to recognize some of them. Jake, the irritating PA. Toby Hissong, the actor playing DuShane. So many other cast and crew members from the production.

Eden... She wasn't with them. Was that a good thing?

I didn't think I had it in me to hurt any of these people.

Sean, please.

I felt power increase around us as Sean continued in the same powerful and unrecognizable language, voice rising until it was painful to my ears. Suddenly something locked into place, like a gate slamming shut. The crazies slowed down, then stopped as they reached the open gates, frustration on their faces as they realized they couldn't follow us.

The goats went back to their grazing.

Okay then.

I tried to take a step, up toward the house. My knees buckled and I crumpled to the ground, trying to ignore the throbbing from the wounds in my forearm and face.

"Lee?"

I looked up to see Sean and Seth staring at me in concern. I wiggled my fingers at them.

"Hiya."

"Come on, hon."

Reaching down, the two men pulled me gently to my feet, supporting me all the way up to safety.

†

Cayden got everyone out of the truck. Drift was sprawled out on the floor of the living room and Shaina lay unconscious on one of the couches. Kana sat across from her, looking impossibly pristine even with a wad of Kleenex held up against her nose.

Cayden looked like he always did—full of confidence.

Half of us looked like we'd survived a war. Me with my arm bandaged, bruises, and bloody furrows on my face and arms. Shaina with blood drying around her nose, which might be broken, a lump on her forehead, bruising already developing around both eyes. She was going to hate me when she woke up. Drift was groggy as hell, his clothing ripped to shreds, but he sat up, and Seth handed him a cold PBR. Which meant he was back to normal.

I turned to Sean. "So it's the energy in this… this *vortex* causing all of this, right?"

"The energy comes from the vortex," Sean said, "but the question is why the balance has shifted so radically. The vortex is, by its nature, neutral."

"It's DuShane."

Shaina's eyes were open, just narrow slits between the bruised and swollen tissue, but her gaze was sane. I crouched down next to her, handing her the icepack I'd been holding up to my cheek.

"How you doing?"

She shook her head. "Don't ask."

"Do you remember what happened?" A rueful smile crossed her lips. She pointed at the bandaged bite marks on my arm, wincing when she saw my face.

"Yeah. I'm sorry."

"I think it's safe to say you weren't yourself, so we're good. Unless I have to go to the ER, and then you're paying the bill."

"Fair enough."

"For what it's worth, I'm sorry, too." I sat down on the ottoman in front of the couch. "You remember *everything* that happened?"

"Yeah." Nodding, she gingerly held the icepack up to the bridge of her nose. "I could feel something... something pushing at my mind, trying to burrow its way in. Wanting me to do things. Things I'd never thought of doing before. But—" She swallowed. It looked as if it hurt. "Part of me wanted to do them, and the worst of it is, I know that part has always been there. I just... I never knew it, and now I can never forget it."

"She's right," Drift said. "I mean, I've always known what I am, and it can take some work to keep my temper under control, but I've never gone full-on troll in my life. And yeah, I could feel some sort of goddamn puppet master crawling around inside my head, but still..." He looked up at me. At Sean. "It's always been inside me."

"How do you know it was DuShane?" I put the question to

both of them, but it was Shaina who answered.

"I could see him," she said. Her face looked haunted. "See his thoughts and see through his eyes at the same time." She shook her head as if to clear it, then put a hand up to her temple. "He's... somehow he tapped into the power of... of whatever you called it—"

"Vortex," Seth interjected.

"Yeah. He can soak up its energy like a battery, and then use it to... to make people do things."

"He didn't seem that strong when I met him."

We all looked at Cayden.

"What do you mean, 'when you met him'?" It sounded like an accusation. I didn't care.

"When I first bought the place, DuShane tried to get into my head. When his Jedi mind tricks didn't work, he sent some of his rotting puppets after me. That's when I trapped him back in his tomb and warded the property."

"You knew he could do this shit, and didn't bother mentioning it to me when you hired me?" Rage and hurt duked it out inside me. The urge to punch him was getting harder to resist.

"Easy, hon." Sean put a calming hand on my shoulder. Seth just looked murderous.

"He wasn't that strong." Cayden gave an infuriatingly nonchalant shrug. "I didn't think it worth mentioning."

"But you *knew* he was capable of manipulating others, didn't you?" I wasn't ready to let this go.

"Not if he couldn't get out of his tomb. Hence the wards."

I made an inarticulate noise of disgust and frustration.

"He's been doing it for decades," Shaina said. "Scaring some of the people that came to the mansion. Killing others. His favorite was—is—when he can *use* them, though. He calls them his 'meat puppets.'"

"I guess it works on supes, too." Drift looked ashamed. I suspected he thought he should have somehow been stronger, able to resist DuShane's influence. I wasn't sure why Kana, Cayden, and I hadn't been affected, but I didn't think it was because we were any better than Drift. I'd bet good money Cayden had committed more questionable acts than Drift ever had.

"That's not the worst of it," Shaina continued. "When one of his puppets does something violent… something horrible, like rape, murder, arson…" She swallowed again, looking sick to her stomach. "…it *feeds* DuShane somehow. Makes him stronger. And it's… it's like a virus. I'm not sure if it's transmitted by touch or just proximity, but some of the people who've left here passed it on to others.

"This explains so many of the accounts. Even in the research, I didn't believe it. *Couldn't* believe it. This place is a focal point, a 'locus,' they call it. The energy, it's been building over the years… and when you locked him back up, all it did was make it worse when the wards were removed. Because we thought it was safe to film there—and it wasn't."

Cayden's face was expressionless.

"Jesus," Drift muttered.

"It gets worse," she said.

Color me unsurprised.

"Every person who's susceptible along the way is going to take this crazy shit and spread it further, and the more it spreads, the stronger he'll become and the more it'll keep spreading. It… it won't stop."

I turned to Cayden. "Can you lock DuShane up again? Put the wards back up?"

He hesitated. Then sat down on the floor, cross-legged, and shut his eyes.

"What—"

"Shhhh." Sean held up his hand and I shut up.

Cayden sat there for a minute or so, motionless, hands resting lightly on his knees. Then he opened his eyes, shook his head.

"No. He's too strong. The only way to stop this is to restore the balance of the vortex."

"What exactly does that mean?" I glared at Cayden. "How do we do that?"

"We need to reboot it," he replied. "Take the power from DuShane, neutralize it, and then put it back into the vortex."

"And again I ask—what... exactly... do we need to do?" I growled.

"We need to take down all the wards at the mansion," Cayden said. "And the protective sigils here, as well."

"Here?" I cut a glance at Sean, who looked decidedly uncomfortable. It was Seth, however, who replied.

"The power of the vortex needs to cycle freely in order to take it away from DuShane. The wards at the mansion and the protections put up here at the Ranch have maintained a neutral balance for decades." Seth glared at Cayden. "But shit went sideways when this jackass didn't pay attention to what was happening right under his nose."

Cayden didn't spare a glance for Seth.

"I'll do whatever needs to be done to fix this."

"You'll need to shut it down first," Sean said quietly. "Which means temporarily taking its power into yourself and drawing it away from DuShane." He paused, then added, "It could burn your power away permanently. Or kill you."

"Or he might step in and take up where DuShane left off." Seth glared at Cayden. "You created this mess, you sonofabitch, so you fix it."

"It's too late for that," Cayden replied. "We have to work together. Are you willing to risk the end of the world just to spite me?"

Seth turned to his father, practically vibrating with outrage.

"You're not actually going to help him do this, are you?"

"No," Sean replied. "*We* are." Turning to the rest of us, he added, "Please excuse us. My son and I need to call in some reinforcements." With that, he and Seth went into the kitchen and shut the door.

†

Okay, I'm not proud. I eavesdropped. But Sean and Seth had kept yet another secret from me all these years, so I managed to live with the guilt.

Why hadn't they told me about the vortex? Or that the protective wards or sigils were not just here to protect the Ranch, but in reality had a much greater purpose? The more I thought about it, the angrier it made me.

"I don't understand why you agreed to this," Seth said. "Undo the protection of the Ranch, to turn the power of the vortex over to him? Even if we could release the seals—"

What seals?

"You and I can't release them."

"Then what are we even talking about—"

"But three of us could."

"You don't mean…"

"Of course I do."

Seth was silent for a moment. "He won't like it," he said finally.

He. Who he?

"When have you ever know him to like anything?" Sean said. "Besides, he knows what our job requires of us, of him. Time to bring him into the ring. You and I have been handling this situation on our own long enough, goddamn him."

"God *might*, you know," Seth said after a pause. "He might damn all three of us."

"He certainly will if we fail. Come on, we're wasting time we don't have."

"Do we even know where he is now?"

"Beersheab maybe. No, some Nabatean ruins in the central Negev, I think. Not that it matters. He'll come."

There was another pause, and then...

"*Sammu-El, ha'ăzînāh,'āḥînū*," Sean intoned.

Okay, this was new. Something else they'd been keeping from me.

"Samuel, our brother, hear us now," Seth echoed.

Oh jeez, not him.

"*Wə'āḥ ləṣārāh, yiwwālêḏ, wəyāḇōw lānū...*"

"For adversity, is a brother born—he will come to us..."

"*Sammu-El, tāḇōw lānū...*"

"Samuel, will you come?"

"*Sammu-El, tāḇōw lānū.*"

"Samuel, will you come?"

"*Sammu-El, tāḇōw lānū.*"

"Samuel, get your ass over here!"

"Peace, you two." It was a new voice. "I'm here."

I recognized that voice.

Well, hell.

The kitchen door opened, almost smacking me in the face. I scrambled backward as Seth and Sean came out, followed by a third man, one with the look and muscular build of a mountain man, with long hair and salt-and-pepper beard. He was dressed for desert hiking, in weathered boots, drab brown jeans and shirt.

"Lee."

"Uncle Sam," I said flatly.

We stared at each other without love.

†

"Okay," I said, doing my best to ignore Sam's disapproving stare. "Just to be clear. We have to get back onto DuShane's property without being noticed by whatever crazies are still up there." No one said anything. I glared around the room. "Am I getting this right, folks?"

Seth and Cayden nodded at the same time, both looking irritated by their synchronicity.

"That's about the size of it," Cayden said.

"So we can't drive back up the way we came. DuShane will probably have his crazies all over the front gates. We need to find a back entrance."

Kana cleared her throat. "I believe I can help you with that."

Cayden looked over at her. "Are you thinking…"

She nodded.

I rolled my eyes, trying to ignore a wave of irrational emotion at the private "we share a secret" look that passed between her and Cayden. I didn't want to feel anything toward Cayden except anger. Intense, justified anger.

"Maybe let the rest of us in on the secret?"

"I apologize, Lee." Kana inclined her head in my direction. At least one of them had manners. "There is a series of sandstone caves in the foothills at the base of the mountain. DuShane had a tunnel built from the caves to the subbasement of the mansion."

"That's right!" Shaina sat up despite the fact she still looked kinda green. "The smugglers' tunnel. He used it during Prohibition. The Silver Screamers had heard of it. They weren't sure where either end of the tunnel actually was, but they were positive it exists."

"Okay, we know there's another way onto the property, but we don't know where it is." I looked over at Cayden. "Any chance you can find it?"

"Given time, yeah," he replied, "but I don't think we have any to spare."

"Shaina?"

"It's somewhere at the base of the foothills, near the mansion, but that's all I know."

Like where I'd found Jada's Xterra. The shadowed slit in the sandstone I'd seen before Detective Fitzgerald and the Kolchak Squad had arrived.

"I think I know where the entrance is."

CHAPTER TWENTY-NINE

Seth and Sean set up wards in the barn and back area to help protect the wildlife that had come here for refuge, and so Shaina and Drift would be safe from DuShane's influence as well. So they stayed behind.

"So how do we sync up with you?" I asked. "I mean, we don't know how long it'll take for us to get into the mansion, find the wards, and remove them."

"We'll know," Sean assured me.

"*I'll* know." Cayden stared at Sean as if in challenge. If we survived, I was *so* going to get to the bottom of whatever was up between Cayden and everyone I knew.

"You should leave us at the back acre," Seth said.

"Good idea," Sean agreed. "We can create a distraction at the mansion's gates to draw attention away from you."

Cayden and I looked at each other. "Yeah," he said. "Let's do it."

Kana got to her feet. Cayden put a hand on her shoulder.

"You don't have to do this."

"I think you will need me," she said calmly, tucking a lone stray lock of hair behind her ear.

†

Tendrils of psychic poison began to spread, drifting outward from the mansion on invisible currents that had nothing to do with wind or weather. Most people were affected by it on a subconscious level. Many smiled as though they'd just heard a secret or received an unexpected gift.

Those who it couldn't touch felt a momentary revulsion, as if something like a slug or spider had brushed their skin. A tired young mother in Reseda struck her child after she'd asked one too many times for another cookie. Her six-year-old daughter responded by picking up a fork and stabbing her mother in the arm.

†

A teenage boy smoking a cigarette in a park playground in Camarillo looked around at the dry leaves scattered on the grass, tossed the still smoldering butt onto the ground, and watched as the leaves caught fire before walking quickly away. Luckily a passerby saw the flames and stomped them out before the fire could spread.

†

At a Trader Joe's parking lot in Encino, a woman in a BMW cut off another woman in a Mercedes in an attempt to snag the last parking spot. The Mercedes owner promptly smashed the front of her vehicle into the side of the BMW, killing the driver.

Then she parked her car, got out, and went inside the store to shop.

†

Choking, Ray spat out his half-chewed bite of cheeseburger. Framed by the chipped white plate, the food sitting in a spattered bed of meat juices and spittle made for a nasty bit of abstract art.

Hooking a finger in his mouth to fish out one last bit of gristle, the trucker glared at the wet clump as though it was alive and squirming. It looked like something a sick cat would hack up, a blood-tinged hairball, or the remains of a mouse.

"Shit-fuck!"

Shocked by his outburst, the diners at the neighboring tables froze, some of them mid-bite, and stared. Ray extricated himself from the booth with another rumble of muttered profanity. Embarrassed and angry now, he stormed over to the startled waitress at the counter.

"This a goddamned joke?" he barked.

"What's the matter, hon?" The waitress was well-practiced in dealing with rude customers, but today she was at the end of her rope. "There a problem with your meal?"

"You're fucking right there's a problem! Look at this!" He waved the uneaten half of his burger at her like a prosecuting attorney.

"Sugar, there's no need to be raisin' your voice. You give me just a minute, I'll have the cook fix you a new one."

"I'm not gonna eat another bite of that bastard's food. I'm going to kick his ass!"

That was it. She dropped her voice low and firm, the glare in her eyes all business.

"Look mister, you get that out of my face right now, or I swear I'm calling the cops."

"Call 'em! I'll sue all your asses!"

"Alrighty then." She abruptly turned her back on him and called into the window to the kitchen, "Carl! Get the sheriff here!"

"Carl, huh? That his name?" Ray made for the end of the counter. "Well, I'm just gonna have a little talk with Carl." Still clutching the burger, he shoved his way past the waitress and barged into the kitchen, advancing on the skinny fry cook at work on the grill. Carl was grinning.

"Hey! You think you're funny, you scrawny little—"

The trucker halted, struck by a horrible stench. The cook had been cleaning the grease trap, and had a dirty bucket filled with a congealed mess the color of rotting pumpkins. He was in the process of dipping in his spatula and carefully dolloping out globs of the rancid mixture, mixing it *into every sizzling meat patty he put on the grill. The toxic sludge was speckled with floor sweepings—dirt, hair, grime, and bits of unidentified crud —and smelled like raw sewage.*

The cook looked up at him and smiled.

"Flavor's in the fat," he said matter-of-factly. "You see? That's where the flavor is." He turned back to his work, humming a merry little tune.

The remains of the burger slipped from the trucker's numb fingers and dropped to the floor. The waitress continued to holler at him from the window. Dumbstruck, the trucker stood stock still for a long moment. Then he reached a decision.

Stepping up behind the cook, he grabbed him, yanking the apron and dirty T-shirt up around his neck to expose the little man's chest and belly. Overpowered, the man shrieked and squirmed, but the bigger trucker had no problem hoisting him up, and then pinning him firmly face-down on the hot, greasy grill.

The shrieks grew louder and louder... then stopped.

There. Now it smells better, *Ray thought.*

†

Emergency Room, Los Robles Hospital, Thousand Oaks. Afternoons were always bad, but this one was worse than usual. Every seat was filled, and it was standing room only. The packed waiting room felt like a Civil War field surgery, and smelled like a slaughterhouse.

Jesus, what's in the water today? *Cora wondered.* Folks out there losing their damn minds. *In the distance more ambulance sirens wailed like alley cats. The admissions nurse turned her attention back to the fretful mother at the front counter.*

"Ma'am, I'm sorry that you have to keep waiting, but we have to attend to the most serious cases first," Cora explained yet again.

"But my son's eye—"

"We're taking your son's injury very seriously, Mrs. McAdams, and I promise you we will get him stitched up just as soon as we can. But it's not a life-threatening injury. The doctors are back there working to save someone's life right now."

She fought to retain her composure, and kept her gaze carefully averted from the boy's face. Blunt force trauma orbital fracture. A teammate at his softball game had lost his grip during a wild swing, and the McAdams boy had been clipped by the pinwheeling bat. Now his left eye bulged ominously from the bruised and bloodied socket. He might even lose the eye, she knew—but he wasn't going to die. So, he would have to wait until the surgeons saved the stabbing victim—or lost him.

The boy's mother, however, refused to move from the counter. Mrs. McAdams opened her mouth to raise more objections, when a commotion came from down the corridor, loud voices in the operating room.

"My god, what's all that noise? Are they finished in there?"

Cora kept her expression impassive. The nurse had no idea know what the racket was, but she doubted it was good news for anyone.

She felt anger begin to blossom.

"Mrs. McAdams, I need both of you to please sit down. They'll tell us when they're ready for you."

"Well, can you check?"

Unleashing a shriek of rage, Cora shot out a hand to grab the woman by the neck, yanking her into the window and landing a fist squarely in her face. Cora hit her again, and again, and again—in her imagination.

In reality, she only frosted the woman with a death-stare.

"Sure. I'll do that," she said. "Just wait here, please."

Anything for a moment's break from these insane people. She rose and slipped out into the hallway that led to the surgery, shaking her head. At the threshold to the OR she paused and listened. There was a strange outburst coming from behind the double doors.

It was laughter.

Not just laughter. Howls *of laughter. What the hell?*

She hesitated, then dared to peek in. A piercing yet monotonous electronic drone issued from the EKG monitor, its screen nothing but a solid flatline trailing through blackness. But the surgeons weren't finished attending to their patient—they were bent over him, meticulously unspooling all of his intestines onto the floor of the operating room. The attending nurses and the anesthesiologist roared at the macabre scene.

A wave of vertigo and nausea shivered through her, and Cora nearly passed out. Then another sound rose. Screams suddenly echoed off the hospital walls, coming from the waiting room.

What the hell?

Turning, she stumbled back down the corridor. Mrs. McAdams and her boy stood there, blocking her way. The mother turned to her son.

"Show the nurse, honey."

He had pulled his bloodied eye from the socket. It dangled from the stretched-out optic nerve, lolling on his cheek.

"So now we're next, aren't we?" Mrs. McAdams smiled.

†

"There," Dr. Palmer said, slowly extracting the hypodermic syringe from Derek's mouth as muzak played in the background. "Now, that wasn't too bad, was it?"

Mouth full of cotton padding, Derek could only shake his head in response, unclenching his fingers from the armrests. The injection had been excruciating, but he could already feel the numbing agent at work.

"Alright then, we're going to give the shot a couple more minutes to work, and then I'll be back to fix you right up," the dentist said, giving him a friendly pat on the shoulder as he rose and left Derek to his own devices.

Should have brought a book, he thought glumly. He looked around for Jeannie, Dr. Palmer's cute dental hygienist, but she was *nowhere to be found. A shame—Derek liked flirting with Jeannie. She had a great smile and the prettiest long-lashed brown eyes. There was little else of interest in the suite, so he stared upward at the overhead light. It always reminded him uncomfortably of the head of a giant praying mantis bending over him.*

Going over the week's schedule in his head, Derek made a mental to-do list, then did the same for the grocery shopping. Looked around to see if there were any stray magazines. No dice.

What's taking Dr. P. so long?

A muffled thud, almost covered by the sound of the Muzak, came from somewhere in the office. Derek listened intently for a follow-up. Just the sound of Michael Jackson's "Beat It," reduced to elevator music.

Another soft thud.

Derek ignored it at first, but a combination of boredom and anxiety began to nag at him. Long minutes passed, until he lost track of time. Finally, losing his internal debate to stay where he was, he pulled himself out of the chair to investigate.

One of his legs had fallen asleep, so he stood for a moment, shaking it back to prickling, painful life. Then he heard a metallic clanging, and froze in panic, wondering if he could make it back into the chair before Dr. Palmer returned and caught him out of his seat.

No one came in. He opened his mouth to say something, but with all the cotton packed in there, he knew he'd sound like a feeb if he tried to call out for anyone. Besides, something about the tinny clattering had sounded accidental, like something had hit the floor. Maybe his dentist had passed out—had a heart attack or something.

Or what if Dr. P. and Jeannie were getting it on?

His mind shifted into overdrive. All the possibilities both titillated and terrified him. Made him feel light-headed. If Dr. Palmer had passed out or needed medical attention, he should call an ambulance. And if Dr. P and his hygienist were indulging in a little extracurricular activity… well, maybe he could catch them in the act. So to speak.

Shaking the last of the pins and needles from the leg, he crept as nonchalantly but stealthily as he could manage into the little hallway. It was freaky how quiet it was in the office. Putting his ear to the nearest door, Derek listened carefully, but there was no sound, so he risked a quick peek.

Nothing. Just a dental chair and the usual setup. Taking a step, his foot slipped on a damp spot on the floor and he lurched for the chair, grabbing the armrest to keep from doing a header. He didn't dare look down, and risk the cotton falling out.

"Derek!" The sound of Dr. Palmer's voice nearly made him faint dead away. He tried to explain, but was having enough trouble just trying to keep his footing. The doctor was swift to help steady him.

"Easy there, friend. Hey, if you wanted to be in this room instead, you should have said something," the dentist joked good-naturedly. "Here, take a seat. I'm almost done cleaning up. I'll be right back." Derek gratefully took him up on his offer and slipped into the new chair, trying to catch his breath. Sighing, he adjusted the hang of his bib, and tried to collect himself.

This room was much the same as the first. The same boring furnishings, same praying-mantis-light looking down on him. Same rollup tray next to the chair and little spit sink. The tray was neatly covered with a cloth.

Driven by morbid curiosity, Derek reached over and slowly lifted the corner for a look at the dental tools—the diabolical instruments about to be employed on him. There was a trio of slender silver picks, lined up perfectly, each hooked in a slightly different fashion. Next was a tiny mirror on a stick, and an elongated set of tweezers. Then an imposing pair of forceps. And another. And some hefty pliers. And a tooth.

And another tooth, blood still on the roots from where it had been *torn out. And another, and another, one after another down the line until he'd uncovered a good two dozen teeth placed on the tray. Going numb with terror but unable to stop himself, Derek continued to lift back the cloth until he came to the final tooth. And a pair of eyeballs.*

Jeannie?

He froze in shock, unable to drop the cloth, unable to look away.

"Hey now." *Dr. P was behind him.* "You went and spoiled the surprise. Shame on you."

CHAPTER THIRTY

Cayden, Kana, and I approached the foothills, about a half-hour hike from the Ranch. I had a small bag slung across my chest containing a Maglite and a Spydeco knife. I'd clipped a sheath containing a seven-inch KA-BAR to my belt. I was ready to stab things.

We'd made our way to the back fence and climbed through the rails while a ruckus rose up behind us, as the crazies hollered at the gates. Not sure what Sean and Seth did to distract their attention, but whatever it was, it had worked.

"It's up here." I led the way to the gully where I'd found Jada's car, and then across to the place where I'd seen the shadowed opening in the rocks.

There it was. A small slit at first glance, covered with old branches that looked like a deliberate camouflage, now that we knew. When those were tossed aside, a much larger opening was revealed. Not big enough to walk through, but large enough to gain entrance by crawling, even for Cayden with his broad shoulders.

"I will go first," Kana said. "I am quite comfortable in small spaces." I started to ask if she was sure, then stopped. The woman knew her own mind.

"We'll follow you," Cayden said.

I offered Kana the Maglite but she shook her head, then

slipped easily into the opening, her body seeming to conform to the available space. Later I'd ask her how she did that. For the moment I was too busy contorting my own limbs to fit through the opening, while trying to ignore the creepy feel of something brushing against my skin. There was a sort of feral, musky odor that became more sickly-sweet and corrupt the farther we went down the tunnel. My scar itched, and the amulet was hot.

More than one thing had died down here.

Knowing that Cayden was right behind helped keep me calm as we continued. The tunnel opened up relatively quickly, still pitch-black but no longer as claustrophobic. We could stand, I could move my arms around without hitting rock, and the air moved somewhat, although the odor was still rank. My Maglite provided illumination, as did whatever Cayden was carrying.

My toe hit something on the ground and I stumbled, throwing my hands out to catch myself. They hit something in front of me. Maybe a wall but soft, almost springy. Whatever it was clung to my hands when I pulled away.

This couldn't be good.

"What is it?" Cayden said from behind me.

"Webs."

They lined the tunnel walls. I looked up, shining the light on the ceiling. It too was covered with what looked like silvery-gray cotton candy.

Son of a bitch, I thought. *Nigri*.

The tunnel made a hard left a few feet ahead, webs dripping off the ceiling like lace stalactites. *Interior design by Shelob.* I glanced back at Cayden, seeing a marble of blueish light the size of a golf ball bobbing in front of him. A witch-light.

"I will stay in front," Kana said.

"Why?" I didn't mean my tone to be suspicious, but it was nonetheless.

"Because I can protect you both against what might lie ahead."

I cut a look at Cayden, who nodded. "Trust her," he said.

More than you, I thought. Even though I didn't say it aloud, a shadow passed over his face, visible in the dim illumination of his witch-light. I tried to ignore it, along with the sudden stab of guilt I felt.

Sometimes it sucked to be female. He hadn't exactly given me any reason to trust him, though. He'd withheld information that might have helped stop things from going this far. At the very least, he'd put the lives of everyone on the production in danger, all because of his arrogance. He'd assumed that if he'd put up a ward, nothing would disturb it. Pure arrogance. That was Cayden's Achilles heel.

I didn't want to think about what mine might be.

Kana moved quickly and quietly through the tunnel as if she weighed nothing. It was an odd alien grace, not entirely human.

Cayden and I followed close behind, using the Maglite to stay in the center of the tunnel, avoiding thick tangles of webbing, some of which had insects and larger things caught in them. I tried not to look.

The rich, loamy smell of damp earth was slowly overwhelmed by the thick, sickly odor of rot. Sweet and rank. Nothing else smelled like decay. I tried to breathe through my mouth and not think about the fact that smell was particulate.

The tunnel narrowed again, the ceiling dropping a few feet so that we had to walk in a sort of crab scuttle, hunched over to avoid whacking our heads on outcroppings. Cayden's shoulder knocked into one, causing dirt and rocks to rain down on us in a disturbingly steady shower. He and I froze, and he held his arm out like a bar in front of me. Finally the falling debris slowed, and then stopped.

I so did not want to be buried alive.

We kept following in Kana's wake.

After a few hundred feet, the tunnel opened up again ahead, dim light indicating some sort of opening in the ceiling. Any relief I felt at the thought of being able to stand up again was counteracted by the smell. If it had been unpleasant before, here it was like being thwacked in the face with a bag filled with rotting body parts. My gorge rose and I had to fight the urge to vomit—I didn't want to be vulnerable down here.

Then I shone the Maglite into the open space, and almost lost the battle.

CHAPTER THIRTY-ONE

We'd reached a cave, and it had been turned into a larder.

Cocooned corpses hung from webbing draping the ceiling and walls. They were desiccated, as if the liquid in their bodies had been sucked out. Some were missing chunks, portions of limbs, eyeballs, as if whatever had snacked on them couldn't decide which parts were the tastiest.

Despite the carnage, I thought I recognized the Ford family—Glenn, Rose, the twins—and their handyman, and a good dozen people I didn't know but suspected were among those who'd gone missing in the area over the last month.

Kana gave a hiss of indrawn breath, muttering something in Japanese while Cayden took a closer look at the bodies. If he felt any horror at the sight, he didn't show it. The only time he showed any sign of emotion was when he came to the hellions, faces open in silent screams. A muscle twitched in his jaw. That was it.

"Are any of them still alive?" I tried to breathe as shallowly as possible, wishing I had a scarf to tie around my nose and mouth.

Surprisingly it was Kana, not Cayden, who replied.

"While it is possible to keep prey alive for a certain length of time after they receive a *Jorōgumo's* venom, so that the meat and fluids stay fresh, these people are past that point.

"It is better this way," she added. "If they were still alive, their suffering would be unbearable."

I didn't ask her how she knew this.

"We have to keep going." Cayden crossed the cave to where the tunnel picked up on the other side, vanishing into the blackness, his witch-light bobbing in front of him. I started to follow when a low moan sounded in the darkness across the chamber. I spun on my heel, shone the beam of light, illuminating what looked like an alcove in the sandstone surface. Creeping forward, I tried not to touch any of the cocoons on either side, wincing when a limp arm fell out of one of them and a cold hand brushed against my shoulder. I looked up, recognized the sadly shrunken remains of the Lyft driver who'd ferried me home from LAX. Poor guy.

The moan sounded again, low and filled with pain.

Someone was alive back there.

"You go ahead," I told Kana. Without waiting to see if she did, I switched the Maglite to my left hand and pulled the knife out of its sheath with my right. I held it in a reverse grip, the tip of the blade angled toward my forearm, edge facing forward. Moved slowly, just in case whatever was making that noise was laying a trap.

Pushing my way past another cocoon, which contained the almost unrecognizable remains of a calf, I reached the alcove and shone the beam inside. It was deep enough to almost qualify as a small cave itself.

The alcove was filled with webbing, attached to the walls and ceiling, an opening in the center like a hollow wad of dirty gray cotton candy. In the middle of the hollow, arms and legs secured by strands to the sides of her prison, was a woman. She was naked, cuts and bruises up and down her face, neck, and body. She'd been used badly, by someone or something. It was easy to tell she wasn't meant to leave this chamber.

"Jada…?"

Her eyes fluttered open. Looked at me without recognition for a few seconds and then registered who I was.

"Lee…?" Her voice was barely audible. Rough, as though she'd been gargling acid. She must have screamed her throat raw since she'd been taken.

"Yeah, it's me," I replied softly. "I'm gonna get you out of here."

"He thought…" she swallowed. "He thought I was you…"

Nigri. He'd kidnapped Jada and then played nice with me while he was doing god-knows-what to her all this time.

I'd kill him.

"When he found out I wasn't you, he… he still wouldn't let me go." Tears leaked from the corners of her eyes. Her cheekbones were hollow, as if she hadn't eaten anything for days. She had to have had water, at least, or she wouldn't still be alive.

"I'm getting you out of here," I said, and started cutting through the sticky strands holding her to the web hammock. My amulet was burning hotter than ever, my scar itching like crazy, but ever since things had gone pear-shaped in the mansion, my early-warning system had been blaring its alert to me so non-stop it was essentially useless now. I tried to ignore them both, and focus on the task at hand.

"Even when… when he found out I wasn't you, he still wouldn't let me go. He wouldn't… he…" She started to thrash in the webs, making it difficult for me to cut her free without potentially slicing her flesh.

God, what did he do to her?

"Jada, you have to hold still, okay? I don't want to cut you by accident."

She looked up at me. Stilled for a second. Then her eyes flickered past me and she screamed, a primal shriek that sounded as if it ripped her throat raw.

"What?" Before I could react, something hit me from above, a solid impact that drove me to the ground under its weight. I lost my grip on the Maglite and it skittered away, bouncing against the webbing where it stuck, the beam of light shining back in my direction.

Whatever had driven me down grabbed my shoulders and flipped me over onto my back, holding me there with multiple limbs. My other hand, still clutching the knife, was pinned underneath me, and something settled on my hips. There was just enough light for me to see the features of the thing that held me—a spider walker somewhere partway between arachnid and human form.

Fangs dripped with foul-smelling venom, several droplets falling onto my upper chest, burning the flesh. Even worse was the smell of the breath wafting out from the mandibles that currently formed its mouth. Its eyes were brown with human irises and pupils, though, and I recognized the lascivious expression in all eight of them.

"Hey, Lee."

Fucking Skeet.

CHAPTER THIRTY-TWO

"Well hell," I said as calmly as one can when pinned to the ground by a man-sized spider. "And here I thought it was Nigri who'd done all this." The knife was digging into the middle of my back, though not cutting into me. I didn't try to do anything with it yet.

"Nigri?" Skeet spat on the ground next to my head. The sputum sizzled and stunk as bad as his breath. "That *pendejo* doesn't have the balls to hunt like I do."

"That's what this is? All the bodies? A fucking hunt?" I know I should have been afraid, but something about Skeet made fear almost impossible. Which could be a good or a bad thing. "Those were your neighbors, you sick fuck!"

"Nah. They're just food." His grin was a hideous thing. "Just like you're gonna be after I've had the chance to show you a thing or two." He rubbed his crotch against mine.

"Hope you brought a magnifying glass, 'cause I left mine at home." My voice dripped with contempt.

The grin vanished and he slapped me hard across the face, the blow smacking my head into the rock floor. It also released some of the weight pinning my right hand under my body, enabling me to yank the knife out and plunge it into the spider walker's side. He shrieked, the sound earsplitting, and I pulled the blade downward. It cut through both human flesh and spider skin as if it were melting butter, amulet flaring with heat. The Maglite gave off enough light for me to see the agony on Skeet's face.

Good.

He rolled off me, started to scramble back up the webbing from which he'd ambushed me. Two arms and legs, and four more appendages that weren't quite whole spider legs. Something— maybe pain—stopped him from being able to shift back fully into his spider form. Seizing him by an ankle, I hauled him back off the web-covered wall.

"I told you I'd rip your legs off one at a time if you fucked with me or mine," I growled. Grabbing one of his spider legs, I did just that, pulling and twisting it until it popped off with a wet *crack*. Skeet wailed in agony.

I wasn't done. The heat of my amulet was nothing compared to the rage I felt. Throwing the leg aside, I grabbed another and repeated the motion. He fell on his back, squealing as viscous fluid ran out of the sockets. I was reaching for a third leg when a hand fell on my shoulder. The crazy white-hot flare of amulet and scar cooled off as if someone had dipped them in ice.

"Lee," Kana said. "I will finish this. Take your friend now and follow Doran-san."

Abruptly I felt totally calm, almost detached from the pure rage that had possessed me less than a minute before. I didn't even think of questioning Kana, instead finishing with the webs, gently pulling Jada from her former prison, and supporting her nearly limp form as we moved back into the main cavern. I made it to the tunnel before she passed out. Luckily Cayden was waiting to take her from me, scooping her up in his arms as if she weighed less than a paper doll.

I started to follow him down the tunnel toward the mansion, then stopped. "Let me get my Maglite. We'll probably need it." Without waiting for an answer, I dashed back to retrieve the fallen light—then stopped dead in my tracks as I watched a huge white spider with a crimson red hourglass on its underbelly spinning a web around a now blubbering Skeet, using its legs to turn him round and round as it encased him in an inescapable cocoon.

"There now," the spider crooned in Kana's beautiful voice. "You should not have done what you did to these people. I tried to teach my children this lesson and they, too, would not listen. I want you to stay here and think about this… until it is time for supper."

As Skeet started to plead with her again, Kana spun webbing over his mouth, stopping his cries, and then secured him into the web where he'd kept Jada.

Quietly, I picked up the Maglite. The spider turned toward me. I managed not to flinch. Almost within a blink of an eye, the spider form faded, leaving in its place Kana, dressed in her leggings, white silk top, and black ballet slippers, chignon without a hair out of place.

"Shall we go?" She held out a hand to me.

I took it without a word, and we rejoined Cayden and Jada in the tunnel.

CHAPTER THIRTY-THREE

The tunnel ended at a brick wall. Someone—probably Skeet—had pulled bricks away from the crumbling mortar to create a hole not quite large enough for us to crawl through.

"How did Skeet get through here?" I wondered out loud.

"Spiders can fold their legs up to fit into spaces much smaller than they are," Kana replied.

Not creepy at all, I thought.

Setting Jada gently on the ground, Cayden grasped one of the bricks around the edge of the opening and pulled. It came away in his hands without any apparent effort on his part.

"I would be a liar if I said that wasn't impressive," I said, shining the beam so he could see what he was doing, and so I could watch. I was angry with him, but I wasn't dead.

"And I would be lying if I said that didn't make me happy," he replied, yanking out another brick with what might have been an extra flex of his biceps. Kana gave a soft harumph sound.

"More digging, less flirtation," she said.

Cayden obliged.

Within ten minutes, he'd pulled enough bricks away to allow him to go through with Jada in his arms, only having to duck his head slightly, and for me to stroll right on in. When I saw what was in that room, I had to fight the urge to turn right around and go back the way we'd come.

An oversized terracotta planter filled with cement, a skeletal head, mouth stuffed with a disintegrating rag. The energies in this room were overwhelming.

"DuShane," I said flatly.

Cayden nodded. "The very same." A ragged hole had been blown through the door, concrete and wood littering the hallway beyond. "Guess he was pissed off, too."

I get how that feels, I thought, but I held my tongue. We had bigger decaying fish to fry.

"What now?" I asked.

"You need to find the last ward and take it down, while I do what I can to prepare. Timing is everything here. If you take it down too soon, things are going to go south really quickly. Too late, and the spell might not work, and we're left with the same situation we're in now."

"No pressure, then. Any hints as to where I'll find it?"

"Each one is—was—hanging on a chain from one of the finials in the fence along the property—east, west, north, south. Pretty sure it's not the one on the east side, since none of the folks chasing us even hesitated when they went through the front gates. So save that one for last."

I nodded.

"Where are you going to be?"

He gestured around. "Hanging out here with my good buddy Ned Dushane. This is the center of his power, and if I'm going to reverse what he's done, I'll need access to it."

"Shall I go with Lee, Doran-san?" Kana asked.

"No," I said before Cayden could reply. "He'll need you

here to run interference. Pretty sure once DuShane realizes something's up, he'll be sending his rotting and/or crazy minions to try and stop it."

Neither of them argued.

In a movie this would have been the time for Cayden to take me in his brawny arms for a lip-scorching kiss. For the two of us to profess some sort of deeper feelings for each other.

Not gonna happen. Instead, I threw him a mock-salute. "How am I going to know when to take down the ward?"

"Just do it," he replied. "I'll know when you take it down."

Turning, I climbed through the gaping hole. The subbasement hallway was gloomy, but at least there were lightbulbs strung up along the ceiling that cast more illumination than either Cayden's witch-light or my Maglite. And so far, it was empty of people, spiders, and decades-old corpses. I didn't expect it to stay that way once DuShane got wind that Cayden was up to something in his tomb. Hopefully, I'd locate the ward before that happened.

Reaching the wooden stairs that led up to the pantry, I climbed them as quietly as possible. When I got to the top, I pressed an ear against the door, listening for sounds of movement or activity on the other side.

Nothing as far as I could tell, but the amulet and scar were still both working overtime. There was so much malignant intent out there, there was no way to sort it out.

Oh, for simpler times, like just hunting Ol' Nal.

Taking a deep breath, I turned the handle and pushed open the door separating basement and pantry, ghosting into the pantry as quietly as possible. Nothing jumped out and tried to kill me, so I shut the door behind me and paused, once again listening for any noise. The door leading from pantry to kitchen was closed.

Still nothing, so I ventured into the kitchen, and almost immediately regretted my decision.

Blood. Lots of blood. Bits and pieces of bodies. Some recognizable, some just chunks of meat. There was nothing alive, but that didn't mean there wasn't anything there that could hurt me. As if reading my mind, the upper half of a woman in a gore-covered T-shirt started quivering, the head turning in my direction. Dead eyes stared at me and it started pulling itself along with bloody fingers. I practically ran into the hallway, shutting the kitchen door behind me.

To the left were the dining room and Cayden's study, while the main hall and access to the Great Room lay to the right. Blood spattered the floors and walls of both corridors, but thankfully no corpses. I heard noises coming from the main hall, however, so I went to the left.

Walking as quietly as possible, I made my way to Cayden's study, figuring I could go out the window there and make my way undetected around to the back of the mansion. When I reached it, however, I found the door closed and locked.

"Shit." I muttered the word under my breath, but immediately regretted it—it sounded as loud as a shout to my ears.

"Lee?" A familiar voice came from behind the study door.

"Oh my god… Eden?"

A lock clicked and the knob turned, the door opening just wide enough to show part of Eden's face, blue eyes peering through the crack. When she saw it was me, she opened the door so I could come in, quickly shutting and locking it again before throwing her arms around me in a fierce hug.

"I'm so glad you're okay," I whispered, hugging her back. Then I noticed another person in the room, one of the gladiator-servers from the party scene, all muscles and body hair and—

"Nigri?"

The spider walker gave me a grim smile. I looked at him, then over at Eden, who had somehow escaped the carnage unscathed. Then I understood how, and turned back to him.

"So," I said. "You wanna help me save the world?"

A pause.

"*Sim.*"

CHAPTER THIRTY-FOUR

Voices raised in the invocation, the three chanted in a tongue meant for a different medium than the frail atmosphere of the Earth. The language would have ruptured human eardrums, had any been close enough to hear it. Every word etched bright flaming sigils into life, the otherworldly script dancing on the air, as if to create a kind of neon arch floating above the dusty road leading to the Ranch.

The air rippled, like the surface of a gently windswept pond. Then it began to distort and flow, spiraling as the power of their words twisted the fabric of reality, the way a glassblower worked molten glass. Ember-sparks and tiny ghost lights appeared from nowhere, and fleeting comet-streaks joined them in circling firefly waltzes. Together their dance made the currents grow ever and ever brighter, until their movements formed an incandescent whirlpool, thrumming with power, throwing off erratic sparks of lightning as it spun into a new form.

The first seal manifested. All the white-hot aerial streams solidified into spinning bands of an unearthly material the width of a hand, gleaming like translucent metal or a faceted golden gemstone. They nestled within one other, wheels within wheels, forming a whole circle some six feet across.

Off in the distance, the glow of five more seals flared up like shining beacons. Their ley lines of power now came into view, stretching between the six anchor-points to form a Star of David illuminating the whole of the valley, with the entire Ranch safely contained within the walls of its inner hexagon.

Their first feat accomplished, the three continued their incantations.

Next came a rushing, building sound, like the crashing of ocean waves on a rocky shore. The wind rose up around them as at the other six points of the star—each a whirlwind, raw and furious. The guardians of the seals were being summoned to parley.

Their leader, the first and closest seal's defender, appeared in a sudden burst, looking and sounding like a murder of crows all taking wing at once, but the fluttering never ceased. The creature didn't appear to be a single thing, but an ever-shifting multitude of things, a storm of chain lightning, multitudes of unblinking eyes and burning coals, radiant living bodies both animal and human, all superimposed and fluctuating between spirit and substance.

There was the hint of a dazzlingly brilliant humanoid form, of human limbs with something akin to hands and feet, but the face morphed continuously, shifting from human to aquiline, flickering between roaring lion and horned minotaur, a kaleidoscopic chimera. Its body—or rather, its presence—seemed to move without moving, sliding closer or farther, slanting in and out at strange angles, all while it seemed to remain perfectly still, hovering in place.

Across the valley, its fellow creatures took up their stations. There could be no doubt—these preternaturally spirit-beings, called down long ago and consecrated as guardians to the six seals, were warriors, created for battlefields and opponents wholly alien to those of earthbound mortals. And they were not unarmed.

A nimbus of blazing energy whirled before each of them, looking like twirling, fiery scimitars gripped in the effortless hands of sword masters. The streaks of flaming brightness burned the same elliptical patterns as *particles swirling around an atom at blistering speed, white-hot comets seized and harnessed into flailing nunchaku. Altogether, the crisscrossing intersections of unimaginable energy formed a halo surrounding each of them—both shield and deadly weapon.*

The invocation came to an end. Above the three, the sky over the valley was preternaturally still. Samuel stepped forward and spoke.

"Noble Lord Seraph Chalkydri, we ask you lay down your fiery ophanim, *you and your stalwart cherubim."*

Deep within the storm, the shimmering creature's limbs seemed to shift from human-shaped into the body of a crouching lion, and its deadly orbiting blaze of fire flared up in anger. The sphinx responded in a voice not just deafening, but somehow also blinding, at the same time indescribably beautiful and terrible.

"Who bids us thus? Thou hast the countenance of the mortal. None in the shape of man may command us to cast aside the burning Wheels of Galgallin, nor stray from our appointed task until the coming of the Day."

"Could mere mortals speak to you by name, in your own tongue?" Samuel shouted back, raising his voice to be heard. "Behold, we are of the Nephilim, and serve the same elohim as you." He raised his arms slightly, as did Sean and Seth. The three rose gently into the air. Chalkydri altered his inner form again, from leonine sphinx to a human-headed winged bull, and gave them a curt nod.

"I see thee, Sammu-El of the Nephilim, and thy kindred, Seanachán and Sheth-Enokhu, honored among men."

It was impossible to tell whether that least comment was meant as a mark of respect or disdain. Regardless, Samuel pressed on.

"Peace, Chief of Seraphs. Our request is urgent. You must release the seals upon this place, for a short while, less than an hour as time is measured by men."

"Art mad? Hath the Ancient of Days finished with this wearisome little world so soon?"

"The vortex is in danger of being overrun, and we must lend the power of our stronghold in its defense."

"Never."

"You must!" Samuel pressed, calmly but firmly. "If you do not, we fail, and the Earth is doomed." Unmoved, the cherub shrugged his winged shoulders.

"All flesh is grass. Not for great riches and reward would we abandon our sacred duty—less still for so trifling a sum."

"The Most High still rules the world of men and gives it to whom he will," Samuel continued. "If you do not obey, we can compel you, in the name of whom we both serve, and by the signs and words of authority granted to us."

"Hold. Who is this one of whom thou speaketh, that wouldst be lent such power? For who could wield it? Surely not She whom thou and thy kindred are charged to watch over?"

"Not her. The demi-mortal called Cayden, whom you know from of old."

"He cannot withstand so great a tumult—and were he able, what then would prevent him from seizing that power for himself?"

Samuel frowned. "What do you mean?"

"Thou wouldst allow the might of both the Fountain of the Great Deep and the power of thine own divine stronghold to fall into the hand of a mere Son of Adam? That wouldst surely destroy him…"

The creature's voice, made for divine proclamations and shouts of battle, dropped to the equivalent of a whisper.

"Yet if it did not, then might he be strong enough to think in his heart, 'Now may I overthrow the very Host of Heaven and become the Most High, the next El Elyon?'

"*Hear me, Nephilim—now is the Most High divided into many, and the elohim confused and besieged by the works and thoughts of man. Fewer now are the faithful than in the days of old, and all the gods suffer for it. The elohim must drink from the Fountain of the Great Deep for his mana, that he may remain now and forever, Amen.*

"*Therefore, we shall suffer none other to partake of its stream. Better we let this petty world perish instead.*"

"If it goes wrong," Samuel said, "then we will kill him ourselves."

"*If thou canst.*"

"Enough." Samuel raised a hand. "The elohim knows the task for which he appointed us, and has given us authority to enforce it. By this word of power and in his name, I so command you: release the seals." In a voice that reverberated across the valley, he spoke another flaming sigil into being, and from the six points of the star, each of the cherubim let out a shout and obeyed at once.

The seals separated into their ringed bands, their radiant jeweled translucence fading into more solid forms, like some precious metal more golden than gold.

"*Nehushtan, Melchizedek, Zorokthera, Sraosha, Tzadkiel! Come forth!*"

Chalkydri called out to the others by their names, and they flew swiftly to stand in formation around their leader. Samuel took note that they were shaking with terror.

"*The wrath of the Most High will be great—we shall be cast into outer darkness for eternity!*" one of the cherubim wailed in despair.

"*The Heavenly Host shall know of this betrayal!*" Chalkydri cried out to the three Nephilim. "*And then let us see who is to be judged!*"

With a final flurry of wings and wind, the cherubim vanished, departing across unimaginable gulfs of space and dimension. Samuel, Sean, and Seth softly touched down on the ground.

"Come," Samuel said. "It is time."

CHAPTER THIRTY-FIVE

The grounds were clear of crazies as I slipped out of the window of Cayden's study and dropped to the bushes below. I crouched down quick, watching to see if my fall had been spotted, as Nigri slipped down the wall, quickly and quietly. Eden waved to us both from the window of the study before shutting it again. Hopefully she'd be safe in there until we could get back.

We faced the northern wing of the estate gardens. Around the corner to our right was the east-facing front of the mansion. To our left stood the forested hill that butted up against the mansion from the west. Nigri pointed up into the trees.

"The last ward, it can only be up there."

No shit, I thought. We'd searched up and down all the other sides. I kept my editorial comment to myself and just nodded.

"It would be fastest if we climbed the hill directly from here," he continued. "Maybe better if you wait here for me to do it? I am the better climber." He said it so nonchalantly, I couldn't tell if he was deliberately being an asshole or just patronizing. Either way, there was no chance I was staying behind.

Making one last quick sweep for wandering maniacs, we hunkered down and ran for it. I don't know if either of us meant it to be a race, but it became one, and I won. At least until he reached the face of the hill and kept scrambling up its steep face as easily as if he was crawling across the floor. Damn him. He was waiting for me at the top, his hand extended. I pretended not to see it and pulled myself up.

We stood for a better look around. Nigri frowned. "No fence." I frowned too. Cayden had told us the wards were inobtrusive little amulets, hung like a necklace on the central finials of each wrought-iron fence. So where was the western fence?

"*Então...*" Nigri muttered to himself. "Okay. We split up. I go look this way, you that." With that, he shot off before I could even get out a word of protest. Damn him.

It was a bad idea to split up, but what to do? I could chase after him, or head off on my own, and I didn't love either option. At least on my own, though, I wouldn't have to worry about him bitching me out, so I headed off in the other direction.

What was the worst that could happen?

I stopped after a few yards and rethought my plan. If the other wards had been situated in nearly the dead center of each fence, then that meant this one should be...

Crap. Nigri was heading the right way. I made a mental note of how just far it should be from where I was, and headed off, keeping careful track of my paces.

When I reached what I thought was the exact spot, I stopped and scanned my surroundings, but couldn't find any sign of any finials, wards, or spider walkers. I double-checked, secretly hoping that he'd head back with prize in hand so we could get the hell out of here.

No such luck. Maybe there *was* a fence, I mused, but it was set farther back in the forest. We were well into twilight and the forest was growing darker every minute, but if we didn't find it soon, we'd just have to keep searching by night. Not liking that idea, I moved deeper into the tree line.

It was a bad idea. I was moving slowly, trying to keep the noise down and to make absolutely sure I still had my bearings. Just as my enthusiasm reached its lowest ebb, I caught a glimpse of metal ahead. Not a fence, just a single pole topped by a wrought-iron fleur-de-lis. Standing in the middle of the trees like a lost Narnian lamppost. The ward dangled from it, on its little chain.

I reached up to take it, then stopped. Had I heard something? No. Grabbing the ward, I pulled it down and quickly stuffed it in my pocket. Then I definitely heard the crunching of footsteps.

"Nigri?" I called out softly. The sound got louder, then began to multiply, until it was the crunching of *many* feet, crashing through the undergrowth. *Shit!* I ducked behind the nearest tree and listened intently.

The heavy footfalls came closer. Crouching down, I peered around my cover at my pursuers. To my surprise, it was just one— one giant tarantula, about thirty yards away, visible only as a dark shape in the underbrush. It came scuttling right toward me.

Fucking Brazilian Asshole.

I stood up, damned if I was going to let him know that he'd scared me. Held up the ward for him to see, grateful for the chance to lord *something* over his smug ass. He crawled on all eights, like a dog charging up to greet me.

And then he leapt to the attack.

If my arm hadn't already been up, he might have sunk one or both of those fat foot-long fangs into my chest. The impact still hit me like freight train, and I crashed backward to the ground. Instantly he was right on top of me, those incredibly ugly mouthparts chittering away, trying to chew me up or stab those venomous fangs into my flesh.

Pinned to the ground by his giant bulk, it was all I could do to keep his mandibles at bay. Big drops of poison dripped onto me—I shook my head to keep the venom out of my mouth and eyes. Just as the ache in my arms became excruciating, he slammed his monstrous body down on me again, crushing all the air from my lungs. As I gasped desperately, he reared back and gave out a piercing arachnid screech, fangs raised for another plunge.

It never came. The gigantic spider stretched out his legs to their full extension like some arachnid version of the Vitruvian Man and trembled, massive frame dwindling down to human form again as he died.

Eduardo.

Nigri, still in spider form, had sunk his fangs into his friend to save my life. He backed away and shifted back to human form, quickly gathering up his clothes.

With Eduardo off me, I could catch my breath again. Nigri came over helped me to my feet. He said nothing, looking down at the friend he had just killed, then turned to me. There was no recrimination in his eyes. I held up the ward. He nodded, and we got the hell out of there, preparing to fight our way through the mansion and into the subbasement.

CHAPTER THIRTY-SIX

As Nigri and I crept our way back down, snatches of dark whispers in a strange language echoed through the dank hall leading to DuShane's tomb. Even in the splinters of half-light coming from that room, we could make out the twisted bundles and dark pools littering the stone floor. I recognized them—members of the film crew, and members of the cast and extras, all still in their costumes, the corpses scattered all the way to the inner chamber.

Stepping carefully around and over body after torn and bloodied body, we entered the room. The only light came from the hallway, and it took a moment for our eyes to adjust.

There was no longer a floor, only ragged piles left from a bloody battle. Dozens of bodies, mortals and revenants alike, were strewn throughout the chamber, staining the floor and walls with red streaks and splatters. Here and there were twitches, or quiet groans from the wounded and the dying, but apart from the planter that held DuShane's mortal remains, only two shapes stood upright in their midst.

In the center of the room, on the only scrap of bare floor left, Cayden stood calmly with eyes closed, murmuring arcane formulae. By this time, I had expected to find him surrounded by glyphs and runes, or a hastily drawn arcane circle of protection, but there were no amulets or talismans, no wands or staves in hand. There was no sign that he had moved at all from within his island of tranquility in the churned-up sea of carnage surrounding him.

Nearby, the terrifying giant white spider that was Kana dropped her final victim to the floor. She raised her forelegs, smooth and white like fishbones, and made a sweeping gesture. The massive form contracted, those front legs shrinking down to four lithesome arms on a human torso. They waved like those of a dancing Kali for a moment, before becoming two. Meanwhile, the shiny black globes of her eight huge eyes softened into two rows of enormous but beautiful human eyes, then a quartet, then merely two again, framed by her serene face and long lustrous hair.

The rest of her remained in the form of a spider, and she had not come out of the fight unscathed. Claw-like hands had torn her flesh, and worse, she had suffered fresh stab wounds. Kana grasped at her side, bleeding from both her human torso and her spider body below, a wounded centaur of sorts.

I rushed to her, Nigri beside me.

"Stay still," I said, but Kana only shook her head.

"No. Protect him. More will come. DuShane will come. If Cayden-san cannot stop DuShane, we are all lost." A shudder went through her, and suddenly she grabbed my neck, pulling me close. "But… if he can…" she struggled to whisper in my ear, "… you may… have to kill him too." She abruptly went silent and slumped in my arms.

Nigri immediately knelt to check Kana's neck, then shook his head.

"She is not dead yet, but *San La Muerte* wants her…"

"*San La Muerte?*"

"Saint Death. He lingers so close I can smell him. Hold her for me." While I cradled her human half, Nigri ran his hand slowly along her wounds, leaving behind swathes of silk to bandage her. His gentleness was more surprising than his ferocity had been. He caught me looking up at him.

"Don't!" he snapped. "Keep watch for those bastards—they'll be coming back." So much for his bedside manner, but I did stay alert while he attended to her, my eyes peeled for any sign of revenants or human crazies.

During all this, Cayden still hadn't moved anything but his lips as he continued intoning his sorcerous preparations. In the chamber's silence, the echoes of those harsh whispered syllables reverberated eerily off the stone walls. So it startled me when I heard his voice.

Lee! I'm not ready yet…

I set Kana down carefully, and got back to my feet. Cayden stood there like a statue, eyes firmly closed, his lips still speaking the words of whatever spell he was weaving. He was speaking in my head.

I thought my reply back at him.

What do you need? I hoped he wasn't short on any magical ingredients at this point, because we didn't have time for a grocery run.

For now, just my abilities. Anything else would just be window dressing. But I need you to protect me long enough to enable me to cast the final magics.

We'll do everything we can, Cayden.

That would have to be enough. We had no backup plan if anything fell apart now.

How will you know when it's time?

Can't you feel it? he replied. *It's happening now.*

He was right. I *could* feel it, like a vibration deep in my bones, and the raising of my hackles. Something big had just changed outside, though I could only guess if it was good or bad.

Cayden raised his arms and drew air into his lungs. He continued to murmur the formulae. Nigri suddenly snapped his head toward the entrance of the room, quill-like bristles popping out of his skin.

"*Puxa vida!*" he said. "They're coming!" Then he shifted back into full spider form with a roar that began as a human shout and warped into an inhuman ear-piercing shriek.

Shadows moved on the walls of the outer hall, silent shapes creeping closer. Realizing they'd been spotted, DuShane's crazies gave up stealth and charged, their screaming like an eerie battle-cry. Nigri threw himself at the doorway, spraying webbing at the onrushing attackers and physically blocking the entrance with his bulk.

As I ran to join him, I realized I had no weapon at hand, but I still had the last ward in my pocket. It would have to do. I fished it out and felt the flow of my power go into it, infusing that delicate piece of jewelry with the destructive powers of a heavy medieval war-flail.

Spider-Nigri fought to hold back the mob with webs and his impressive strength, but the crazies were as fearless as berserkers, and clearly bent on getting past us to their real target, Cayden—still immobile and defenseless.

Crazies squirmed to get past Nigri's eight arms and through his thick, sticky barriers of silk, but there were just too many. For every struggling victim he ensnared, another one managed to slip past. That's where I came in. Swinging my new weapon in wide, deadly arcs, I cut down two or three at a time, or brought it down on another's head to send them crashing to the floor with a bashed-in skull.

I risked a look back at Cayden and Kana. She was lying completely still, either unconscious or close to it. A shrieking crazy came bounding past me. I plucked a jeweled Victorian comb from one of the costumed corpses, sent energy into it, and slashed out with it. Rippling with power, my makeshift *bagh nakh* raked him nearly in half as he crashed across the floor, joining the other torn remains.

"I'm sorry," I whispered, even as I turned to do battle with the next one.

Nigri had stopped trying to bite the heads off his opponents—there were just too many, and they were coming too fast. It was all he could do just to beat them away, or seize them up and toss them back over the heads of the mob. I struggled to hold a second line of defense, lashing out with my flail and tiger-claw, but both of us knew we weren't going to be able to keep Cayden safe much longer. The instant the lunatics got past us, they were going to tear him to pieces.

I swung my flail madly, cutting them down like a scythe through wheat, when in my peripheral vision I spied some slipping around me on both sides. I turned and stabbed out with the comb, catching the closest from behind, but the others rushed toward their objective.

Cayden's head jerked up, eyes wide.

"*NOW!*" he bellowed, and with that the shadowy room erupted into light. Torrents of radiant energy poured in from the walls, in flowing waves of blinding bright streams. They buffeted him like hurricane winds, and he fought to keep his footing.

His hands stretched out like claws, he crossed his arms together to hold back the onslaught. The rest of us, friend and foe alike, struggled against the incoming surge too. It plucked up the closest wave of charging crazies and hurled them through the air to smash against the unforgiving stone wall.

The intensity on Cayden's face was startling. I had never seen him fighting anything so fiercely. Sweat poured from his brow, mouth bracketed by lines of pain.

"Cayden! Hang on! You're doing it!"

What the...?

There was something more. On his forehead, a strange glow appeared, getting brighter with his exertions—a weird birthmark? Or a type of mystical symbol I hadn't seen before. Had he been concealing it with some kind of glamour spell all this time, or was it a side effect created by the overload of arcane energy? In any case, it seemed to help his control, and the mana-storm seemed to become less randomly destructive.

However, it was driving the crazies to a new level of frenzy, one they could barely endure. Their bodies contorted, hapless limbs flailing or twisting in agony. They were no longer trying to attack—they were dying. Nigri forced back a final press of the tormented mob, spraying webbing until the entrance was fully sealed. He had walled it off using their own helpless, grasping bodies as bricks. A living barrier that writhed with pain.

That unsettling job done, he reverted from monster-size back into human form, looking exhausted as he crossed the slaughterhouse floor toward where I stood watch over Kana and Cayden. His hairy body almost made him seem clothed. Almost. Even badly clawed up and bruised, he was still in better shape than Kana.

"Good job," I told him as he caught his breath, keeping my

gaze on his face. "Now let's let him finish what—"

The shock from a thundering explosion knocked us to the floor—even Cayden. A charnel house's worth of grisly remains filled the air, peppering us with blood and flesh. When the smoke and clattering rain of shrapnel cleared, there was nothing obstructing the entrance to the chamber anymore.

DuShane strode into his tomb, leading a bodyguard of revenant undead. Dozens of men, women, and children, some from across the decades, others from the production, staring at us with murderous intent.

"So *you're* the ones causing the ruckus," the dead man said. "How 'bout you knock it off."

Tentacles of control began to insinuate themselves into my mind, trying to sink mental hooks into the soft gray flesh of my brain. He was trying to make us the latest draftees in his army of the insane. Nigri clutched at his temples, and even Kana's unconscious body shook as if in the throes of a nightmare. She groaned, shaking her head, and her half-human, half-spider form changed back to a prone woman wrapped in a bloodstained white kimono.

Cayden staggered to his feet and opened his eyes.

He smiled.

"The man I would call master…" he sighed, "…could never be a pathetic soul like you." He took up his sorcerous chant again, and the torrents of power returned, flowing to his open arms.

"Nice try, DuShane," I said, gently swinging my weaponized little bauble of jewelry. "Get ready to die for good this time." I was talking tough, but hoped Nigri and Kana weren't vulnerable to his powers. I knew my limits, and fighting them all wasn't an option.

DuShane looked mildly annoyed.

"Aww, just kill 'em."

At that Nigri turned to me, an intense expression darkening his face. His grimace turned into an open-mouthed roar, and then his human face was lost under a blossoming of monstrous fangs and eyes as he hulked out into his spider form, and leapt to attack. I jumped as he flew past me…

…and into the charging revenants. I joined him in the fight.

The enormous spider walker tore into them like a pit bull fighting a swarm of rats, while I messily sliced away limbs or heads with every swing. Like the crazies, DuShane's undead minions were fearless, but being already dead gave them a big advantage—we couldn't kill them. The best we could do was render the bodies until the pieces were too small to continue the assault.

Easier said than done.

"Nigri!" I shouted. "Use your webs!" He shook off the revenants that were clinging to him, and sent blast after blast of silk across the room to entangle more. I killed my way to his side, keeping more off him so he could buy us time with his web-making.

Chopped-off arms still groped blindly for us, and decapitated heads bared their teeth to bite, but it was easy enough to toss or kick them into the nearest web. God knew where he was getting it all, but it had to be taking a toll.

Mentally I began gearing up, preparing for a second blast from DuShane, but Cayden's spell seemed to have done the trick. DuShane appeared to have reached his limits—yet he still had some tricks up his sleeve.

"Sing me a little torch song, girls," he said with a sickly grin. Three of his female revenants, beauties in their day, came to the fore and suddenly burst into flame, like human matchheads. Burning brightly, they continued to saunter toward us, and Nigri's webs were no match for their flames. The silk crackled and peeled away, the fire quickly spreading along the entire web.

Nigri shrank back, as well.

"Cool it, ladies." A pitiful attempt, I knew, but I couldn't resist. Running straight at them, I used the flail to cut them down in smoldering pieces. That just opened the way for a new wave of the undead, and the back-and-forth of the battle continued. There was no denying it—as hard as Nigri and I fought, DuShane's minions pushed us inexorably back until we had Cayden at our backs, with Kana's stricken form just beside him.

Then, despite all the noise caused by the carnage, something made me stop in fear. Not a sound, but rather the *absence* of a sound.

Cayden stopped chanting.

He bowed his head, then bent over as if in pain. When he rose again, it was with eyes blazing like white-hot coals and fingers locked in arcane gestures.

"*Begone!*" he bellowed.

Bolts of sorcerous lightning fanned out from his fingers, striking the frontline of undead soldiers, turning them into clouds of glittering diamond sparks. DuShane's eyes went wide, and it seemed to be that even for a dead man, his face paled.

It didn't last.

"Not so fast!" He lifted a hand and snapped his fingers. From the hallway, a pair of thuggy-looking revenants emerged, holding between them a struggling captive. "Bring her forward."

It was Eden.

CHAPTER THIRTY-SEVEN

"Alright, Mister Wizard." DuShane smiled, and it was a nasty, slimy look. "That was a glitzy performance, but I think we both know you just used up your flashiest gimmick. Otherwise, you wouldn't have stopped there—you'd have just fried *all* of us. Am I right?

"So it's time to cut a deal," he said, and the smile disappeared. "Unless you don't mind seeing this sweet little canary get torn to pieces before your eyes."

Cayden and I exchanged glances. It had been a good bluff, but the dead producer held all the cards. Somehow he'd seen what Eden meant to me.

We were screwed.

Nigri had reverted back to human form and was staring daggers at DuShane.

"Alright," I said. "What do you have in mind?"

"Simple. Houdini here stops with whatever he's trying to pull, and I give you Goldilocks. Get the hell out of my house and you get to go home safe and sound."

"Don't do it, Cayden," Eden said tersely.

"I wasn't going to," Cayden replied darkly, the look in his eyes as flat as his voice. "DuShane, you and I both know what's at stake here. What makes you think I'd give up all this power just to save a girl I barely know?" He gave a joyless laugh.

I'd never played poker with him, but something told me that his cold nonchalance masked a deeper connection than I had ever suspected. What *was* Eden to him? She kept her face stoic, tougher than I gave her credit for. She seemed to know she was going to die, no matter which way this played out. DuShane seemed to think so, too.

"You sure about that?" he said. "Awfully pretty gal. Oh well— hey, sport, I've got a math problem for you. How many of my soldiers do you think you can kill—well, you can't exactly *kill* them, can you?—before they kill all of yours, and then you too? Think about that while she's screaming, begging for death." He gestured to the two thugs. "Go ahead, boys."

"Wait!" I shouted.

"No," DuShane said. "No more waiting. He does what I say, *right now*, or she dies, you die, everybody dies. *Right now*."

I looked at Cayden. He didn't seem to care.

"Cayden?"

"I'm sorry, Lee," he said in a voice that made me doubt. "I *do* like Eden." He raised his voice. "*I do like you, Eden!*" he called out. She stared back at him, expressionless, and he laughed again, an ugly choking sound. "I promise there's going to be a happy ending."

DuShane scowled. "So we have a deal, then?" His revenant thugs, poised to tear Eden in half, looked confused.

"Oh, it won't be a happy ending for *all* of us," Cayden continued. "Probably not for Eden. Probably not for Lee and the bugs, either—and sure as hell not for you, DuShane."

"*Seu traidor de merda!*" Nigri spat, kneeling with a protective arm around Kana. He twitched as if he was ready to leap up and kill Cayden with his bare hands. As inconspicuously as I could, I passed the little hair comb from my left hand to my right, unsure who I needed to be ready to attack.

"That's it," DuShane declared. "Time's up!"

"It certainly is," Cayden said. "You see, until I got my hands on all this power, I didn't—*couldn't*—realize just how big a prize we've been juggling. So much more than you ever tapped into, you ridiculous two-bit poltergeist Svengali. Oh, I'm sorry, DuShane. Were you saying something? You wanted to kill Eden, I think? Please, go right ahead."

Enraged, DuShane stabbed a finger out at Cayden. "Think you're gonna play me, you goddamned wise guy? I'm *Ned DuShane*, you mortal fuck!" The finger stabbed out again. "*Tear every one of them apart!*"

But his goons did nothing.

"*Do it!*"

Instead, every last one of them trembled, the hate on their malevolent faces melting away as they moaned in fear.

What the hell? A sick hole opened up in my stomach.

"While we've been standing here talking," Cayden continued, "I've cut you off from all that delicious power… So intoxicating, so… so… *necessary*. You can feel it, can't you, DuShane? It's gone. Can I tell you how *I'm* feeling?"

"Oh, god…" DuShane's voice quavered as reality set in.

Cayden's eyes were iron and ice.

"Exactly."

The revenants were the first to go, sinking slowly to the stone floor like the clipped marionettes they were. DuShane watched in horror as they crumbled to dust before his eyes. In that instant, he realized there were worse things to be than dead. For one terrible moment, he looked as though he would try to plead with us, then, like an overheated frame of old film in a flickering projector. He flared out, and bubbled away into nothingness.

Eden scrambled to her feet and ran over, seizing me in a bear hug. I held her for a moment, then pulled away, turning to Cayden.

"It's not over, is it?"

He stared back at me with an unreadable look, while I fought off a familiar cold chill in my bones, and a looming sense of vertigo.

"You're not Cayden, are you?"

†

At the Ranch, the three Nephilim looked to the skies.

"Something's wrong," Samuel said, frowning.

Sean nodded. "Cayden has returned…"

"…but not alone." Seth finished the thought.

"Who is with him?" Samuel asked. Sean closed his eyes to see farther.

"Not one of ours… one of the high goetia, *and judging by the strength of its malevolence, at least a sub-prince."*

"Ashmodai!" Samuel spat the name. "Raise the Magen *now, and take back our power. Prepare to attack!"*

"No," Seth shouted. "He's already merged with the vortex. We can't abandon him now—even if it doesn't kill him, there's no guarantee we can channel the power back!"

"We have to!" Samuel shouted back. "We can't take the chance! Do it now!"

†

"You're not Cayden," I repeated.

His unsettling smile only confirmed what I knew in my bones—and heart.

"Not *just* Cayden, anyway," he replied. "What gave it away?"

"You make my skin crawl," I whispered, although that wasn't

the entire truth. "Who *are* you?"

"His name is Ashmodai," Eden said in low voice. Just the sound of it slipped a cold knife between my shoulder blades.

"Quiet, bitch," he growled at her before turning back to me. "How can you not remember *me*? I've burned for you for such a very long time." I flashed on red eyes wrapped in the blackest shadow, burning with hate and lust. His voice like rough velvet, whispering sweet poisonous lies in my nightmares... I shivered.

"Lee, you need to kill him, *now*," Kana urged.

"Do you really think she can?" Cayden turned to her, looking genuinely intrigued at the thought. He turned his gaze on the others. "Or *any* of you? I mean, of course you can kill *Cayden*, or at least die trying, but surely you're not mistaking *this*—" he patted his chest "—for *me*? Flesh is nothing but the boots I put on when I have to trudge through the muck."

"You killed DuShane," I said. "What more do you want?"

"DuShane?" He roared with laughter, and the sound conveyed terror. "DuShane was *nothing*, A fleeting shadow of a nothing that was never there."

He caught Eden staring at him with undisguised loathing, and his laughter shut off like the snap of a steel trap. "Oh, don't be jealous, sweet. I haven't forgotten about you. I'll deal with you soon enough."

I had to turn his attention away from Eden.

"Is it me, then?" I asked. "Is this why you've been creeping around my dreams?" My words gave him a moment of pause.

"Certainly I'm pleased to finally be this close," he said, a flash of red ember in his eyes, "but the truth is, it was higher stakes that lured me here. When our Cayden allowed me to hitch a ride with him, albeit inadvertently, I seized it. Then to find you here?

There are no coincidences, only elegant proofs of my destiny. After all," he continued, "it's one thing to serenade you from the barred windows of my prison, but to actually break free and encounter you in the flesh…"

Nausea threatened to rise as he hungrily looked me up and down.

"To touch you…" He offered me his hand. I still had the deadly little comb in mine. Slipping it into my back pocket, and against my better judgment, I took his hand.

"To smell you, and taste you…" He pulled me in to him, closing his eyes as he breathed in the scent of my hair, the nape of my neck. "Truly heaven in hell."

With my free hand, I pulled out the ward and threw the chain around his neck. He recoiled as if I had turned into a serpent, tugging desperately at the length of silver. When he clasped his hand around the ward itself, in an effort to pull it off, he shrieked in pain and let go as if it was a hot coal.

"*Bitch*," he bellowed. "Treacherous woman! What have you done? *What have you done?*"

"It's nothing," I breathed. "Just a ward to bind evil spirits. What's a cheap trinket to an aspiring god like you?"

"*I'll kill you!*"

"With what? Your bare hands?" I leaned in close to his face. "I'd love to see you try it. Or you could blast me with one of those spells? No? Nothing?" His rage drained away into a stunned silence. "That's what I thought. Now be quiet, I'm going to talk to Cayden."

At least, I hoped I could. As I spoke out loud, I also reached out with my mind, the way we had spoken together earlier.

Cayden, can you hear me? There was only silence. Then, as if from the bottom of a well, came his voice.

Lee? Lee, I'm here. How did you—?

It was easy. I bound him with one of your own wards.

His laughter rang out in my mind. It sounded beautiful.

I feel like a Russian doll—me locked up in here, him locked up in me. Mexican standoff.

"You have no idea the power with which you are toying," Ashmodai hissed, cutting in. "*I* can handle the power of the vortex—*he* cannot. First it will rend him apart, then burst free to lay waste to a wide portion of this world. And I will be there to laugh at your destruction."

"How do you know what Cayden can handle, and what he can't?"

"A father knows his own son."

I stared at him, and my surprise made him smile. There was something truly horrible about the demon's smile, overlaid on top of Cayden's face. I... I could see the resemblance.

"Liar," I said quietly.

"Am I?" He shut his eyes. "Here are some other truths, my son—you would be wise to listen."

Don't call me that. Especially not in front of her.

"Don't worry about her. Worry about yourself. Worry about your pain growing ever more unbearable, until you beg for death, a death that is approaching fast, but not fast enough. You know this is true. You will die—but you don't need to."

Nothing you say means shit to me, Cayden responded.

She will die along with you. Her, and the rest of these insignificant creatures—yet you can save them. We can accomplish so much. When you release the vortex over to me, we will have the strength of the Most High. El, that cruel, senile old bastard you hate so much, so befuddled and divided into ever-weaker versions of himself. He will be cast down, and all the Host of Heaven will hail us as the true lord of the elohim. And you, my only begotten son, with whom I am very well-pleased, will be seated at my right hand.

Don't listen to him, Cayden, I thought desperately. I grabbed his hands. He jerked away as if burned. No, not Cayden… Ashmodai. He didn't want me touching him. Touching *them.*

He didn't want an emotional connection tying Cayden to anything here.

Especially anything to do with me.

I knew what I had to do. If I was right, I ran the risk of giving Cayden a powerful weapon he could use against me if we made it out alive. If I was wrong… it wouldn't matter. We'd all be dead.

"Please, Cayden, don't let him win," I said. "Come back to us. Please come back to *me.* I…"

The words stuck in my throat. I forced them out.

"I love you."

"Lying bitch!" Ashmodai roared.

Did I mean it?

Again I tried the words on for size. "I love you."

Ah hell, yeah, I did.

Ashmodai regained his composure. "We both know this woman is exceptional, my son," he said. "If she pleases you, she will be the crown jewel of our harem, along with any other you desire."

During all this, Nigri stood protectively by Kana and Eden. Moving away from them, Eden came over to me and took my hand. I was struck by the outpouring of love I felt coming from her.

Come back to us, Cayden. She added her silent voice to mine.

My confidence boosted, I approached Ashmodai. He glared at me, but there was uncertainty in his gaze. *Good.* I ignored him and sent one last *Come back to me, Cayden,* before I kissed them, kissed them both, letting them feel the truth of my feelings.

Then I pulled the ward from around his neck.

He… they stepped back.

What makes you think I would share her with you? Cayden said with burning contempt. There was disbelief in Ashmodai's borrowed eyes in that split second, when Cayden released the vortex. Through Cayden I could feel the unleashed power of the cosmic deluge, like a metaphysical hurricane, as the torrent overwhelmed the demon, driving him back into the hell-dimension where he belonged.

Then the vortex settled back into its natural place again.

I love you, Lee.

Cayden collapsed to the floor, face-first in the gore.

CHAPTER THIRTY-EIGHT

Before we could react, there was a deep rumbling all around. The ceiling of DuShane's tomb began to collapse. The hallway was blocked by dozens of corpses—we would never get past them in time.

"The tunnel," I shouted. Scooping up Jada, Nigri grabbed Eden's arm and pulled her after him through the opening, while Kana and I hefted Cayden's limp figure between us. I tried not to think of the expression "dead weight" as we hefted him into the smugglers' tunnel. Cayden was heavy and solid, and I couldn't have done it without Kana's help. It reminded me of the ease with which she'd lifted Skeet's body as she wrapped him in webbing. He deserved it, mind you, but still... that sight would haunt my dreams for nights to come.

Even in the tunnel, the walls and roof shook as we stumbled through, dirt and rocks raining down on us. We may have escaped being killed in the rubble of the collapsing mansion, but we still stood a good chance of being buried alive under tons of sandstone.

As if reading my mind, Kana said, "The webs will help shore up the walls and roof for some time." Another tremor, and more rocks fell on our heads, one of them bouncing off of Kana. She gave it a displeased glare. "But we should still hurry."

As we reached Skeet's larder, Nigri swore, first in Portuguese, and then in whatever language the spider walkers used. He stared around the cave in disbelief and disgust.

"My cousin did this?"

"Yeah, he did," I said, omitting the part where I'd thought it was him. "Skeet might have been under DuShane's influence, but I think…" I paused, remembering how pleased with himself Skeet had been—before I'd ripped his legs off. "I think he enjoyed everything he did."

A muffled noise came from the alcove where Jada had been held captive. *Speak of the devil.* Kana paused mid-step, looked in that direction.

"I should deal with him now," she said. "If the tunnels collapse, he will most certainly die, but it will be far slower than a swift death from my venom." The cave shook again, the cocooned bodies swaying back and forth.

"I don't think I can get Cayden out of here without your help."

"Ah. Then that is what I must do." A sad expression flitted over her beautiful face. The earth shook. We continued into the tunnel leading out at the base of the mountain. When we reached the opening, Nigri insisted that Eden exit first. Then he climbed out with Jada, who was thankfully still unconscious. Kana and I muscled Cayden through, and Nigri grabbed him under the arms, dragging him clear so Kana and I could get out.

"You first," Kana insisted. Dust puffed through the air as the ceiling trembled. A rain of dirt spattering painfully off my forehead convinced me to climb through, Nigri and Eden both reaching out to help me climb down from the narrow opening. I turned to help Kana… but she didn't move. She smiled at me from the opening above. "Take care of Doran-san," she said, and then vanished back into the tunnel.

She's going back for Skeet.

I started to go after her, but Nigri grabbed me around my waist and hauled me back.

"She will not die," he said. "She is more than she seems."

That seemed to be the theme of the day. I collapsed onto the ground next to Cayden's prone form, exhausted. Felt for the rise and fall of his chest to reassure myself he was still alive.

"He'll be okay," Eden said softly, hunkering down next to me, "but we should get him to the Ranch."

"I'll call Sean and ask him to drive up here." Reaching into my jeans pocket, I groaned. "My phone's still at the mansion."

"We can go back for it later." That called up visions of having to wade through puddles of gore to find it.

"I'll get a new one," I said. "Meanwhile, we still have to get Cayden out of here. I can't manage it without Kana's help, and Nigri needs to carry Jada."

"I can help," Eden said simply. With that, she and I each put an arm under Cayden's shoulders, hauled him to his feet, and set off across the scrub brush toward the Ranch, Nigri striding ahead with Jada. I cut a sideways glace at Eden, at her torn satin gown and clunky heels.

"You're stronger than you look."

Eden flashed me an affectionate smile. "So are you."

CHAPTER THIRTY-NINE

When we reached the property line of the Ranch, Eden and I were both exhausted. Cayden was still pretty much out of it, so we'd been supporting his not insubstantial weight between us for the better part of a mile and a half over rough terrain. Nigri was carrying Jada, and even with his strength, he still looked knackered. Considering how many revenants he'd fought, not entirely surprising. Even shifters have their physical limits.

"Are you as tired as I am?" Eden asked as we limped our way slowly to the back gate.

"I could use a cold beer," I admitted.

"Or a glass of chardonnay," she said wistfully. Sweat dripped from her forehead, down into the neckline of her dress.

"You are a warrior, Eden," Nigri said with an intensity that gave truth to all the cliches about Latin lovers. I wondered how she felt about arachnids.

Animals were still hanging out within the Ranch's borders, like the most unlikely petting zoo. A half-grown mountain lion lay next to the fence, a bobcat and a few jackrabbits curled up against its back as it slept. There were also still more than the usual number of birds, rabbits, goats, and such, but some of them were wandering slowly toward the fence and gate. Most of the

335

crazies had vanished, although a few were still at the front gate, looking shellshocked.

I kicked the gate open with my left foot so I wouldn't accidentally kick Cayden. Not that I wasn't tempted, even after all we'd been through. No matter how I felt about him, he'd still lied to me. Kept information hidden that might have prevented things from becoming the nearly apocalyptic shitstorm they'd become.

"Lee!" Sean was heading toward us from the house, Seth close on his heels.

And Cayden wasn't the only one.

"Thank god you're safe!" Sean reached out as if to hug me, but luckily, I had Cayden to prop up.

"Yup, just peachy." My tone was flat. I didn't even look at Seth. "Maybe one of you two, or both, could take some weight off us?"

"Yeah, sure," Sean said, as off-balance as I'd ever seen him. He reached out to take Cayden's weight from Eden. His gaze brushed over her face, went to Cayden's, and then skittered back to Eden. "You…"

"Oh, don't tell me you're gonna ask for an autograph." Eden managed to make a laugh sound genuine. Mine would have been maniacal about now.

"What?" Sean looked genuinely confused. Seth, on the other hand, laughed.

"You'll have to excuse Dad," Seth said. "You look a lot like Dawn Jardine, one of his favorite actresses from the twenties." He stepped in and put an arm around Cayden's back, relieving me of the burden.

Sean, in the meantime, had recovered his composure. "Sorry," he said, relieving Eden of Cayden's weight. "My son is right— you really do look remarkably like her."

Eden gave a tired smile. "Which is why I was hired to play her in *Silver Scream*, I suppose."

I glanced sharply at all of them. Were there yet more secrets being kept from me? After all, Cayden and Eden had a past that she didn't want to go into. But... at least she'd admitted they had one, and I guess she didn't owe me an explanation, although I hoped she'd offer me one someday.

"Let's get Cayden and Jada into the house," I said.

Inside, Shaina and Drift were sitting in a corner of the living room, deep in conversation. They both looked better, as if they'd had some one-on-one time with hot water and washcloths.

Sam was there as well, sipping from a brandy snifter and looking as disapproving as he always did. I guess saving the world didn't cut me a pass in his eyes.

Asshole.

He glanced sharply at me. Not for the first time, I suspected he could read minds, or at least very loud thoughts. Big difference was that now I didn't care. I didn't need his approval or his affection.

Sean and Seth set Cayden down on half of the sectional couch, where he collapsed against the cushions and just breathed, deep rasping inhales and exhales that sounded like they hurt. I looked at him, that rough-hewn face for once lacking the expression of someone who'd flirted with madness more than once. Now he just looked exhausted.

"I'm gonna take a shower," I said to no one in particular.

Before anyone could respond, I headed off to my bedroom, grabbed clean clothes, and locked myself in the bathroom. I took my time, letting the hot water wash away dirt, blood, and stuff I'd rather not think about. It also gave me time to calm down enough to face my family. Putting on baggy sweatpants and an oversized black and red jersey advertising a bar called Devil's Brew, I returned to the living room.

Things didn't look like they'd changed all that much during the time I'd been in the shower—Cayden was still sprawled on the couch, and Eden and Nigri were sitting on the other section, next to Drift and Shaina. Sean, Seth, and Samuel were spread out across the rest of the living room, as if they wanted space from one another. I didn't know where Jada had ended up. When he saw me, Sean started to rise from his leather armchair. I waved him back and ripped the Band-Aid right off.

"I'm leaving the Ranch."

He smiled sadly as if he'd expected my announcement. "Lee, you don't have to do that."

"Yeah, I do." My voice was still flat, almost emotionless. "You've been lying to me for… well, I don't know for how long. And even if you've just been trying to protect me, I still don't know if I can ever trust you to be honest with me again."

"Trust?" Samuel suddenly loomed between us, his voice a basso profundo sonic weapon. "What would you know about trust?"

What the actual hell? I stared at him, too tired to tell him to fuck off.

"Fuck off, Sam." Or maybe not.

"You've always been a troublemaker." His voice dripped with venom. "The world would be a better place if you'd never—"

"That's enough, Samuel." Seth stepped in between us, forcing his uncle to back up.

At that moment I realized that Samuel didn't just dislike me— he actually *hated* me. Once upon a time the realization would have bothered me deeply. Now? I wouldn't lose any sleep over it.

"You always did take her side." The look Samuel cast toward Seth wasn't exactly warm and fuzzy.

That was news to me.

"She just helped save the world," Seth shot back.

"That she did." We all looked toward the couch, where Cayden was pushing himself slowly to a seated position. His voice was raw and ragged, as if he'd been gargling Drano. "I guarantee we'd all be up shit creek in hell without her."

Samuel wheeled on him. "And we wouldn't have been there at all if you hadn't shown your usual disregard for the rules."

Wait, they know each other too?

I'd had enough.

"Eden, you okay if I come over tonight?"

Her smile lit up the room. "I'd love it," she replied. "We can finish *The Witcher*."

I walked over to Sean, who sat silently in his armchair. He looked up at me.

"I love you," I said. "But I can't stay here."

"Hon, you don't need to leave." Rising to his feet, Sean put a hand on my shoulder. "We can talk this out. This is your home."

"And maybe it will be again, down the line," I replied, trying hard to keep my voice steady. "But not right now. Not until I know I can trust you again."

Samuel snorted in disgust. "You—"

"Shut up." Seth's tone was as cold as his stare as he faced down his uncle. "This has nothing to do with you." To my surprise, Samuel subsided.

"The cars," Nigri said. "They are all still at the mansion."

"Is it safe to go back there?" Shaina directed the question to Cayden, who nodded.

"If anyone's still alive, they'll be back to normal," he said. "More or less."

"Except they'll remember what they did," she whispered, "and they'll have to live with it."

After a brief hesitation, he nodded again.

"I can drive you all up there," Drift offered.

Sean heaved a huge sigh. "You can use the Xterra."

†

Going to my room, I packed an overnight bag—I'd come back for more stuff in a day or so, preferably when Sean wasn't home. Banjo followed me in there and lay smack in the middle of my bed, nose on paws, staring at me with sad dog eyes.

"I can't take you with me," I told him, "but I'll be back to visit."

"Promise?" Seth stood in the open doorway.

I walked over and hugged him. "Yeah, I promise. I'm totally spoiled by your cooking."

He snorted, hugging me back.

"Take care of Jada," I added.

Seth hesitated. "I'll do my best."

†

When I came out, Drift was waiting to drive me, Eden, Shaina, Nigri, and Cayden back to the mansion to retrieve our vehicles. Sean stayed in the house when we left.

As we walked over to the Xterra, Cayden leaned over and whispered, "Did you mean it?"

I knew what he was talking about. "Did you?"

He grinned. "Guess we'll find out."

EPILOGUE

Despite the lack of streetlights, the base of the hillside near the DuShane property was well illuminated by the moonlight, signs of the recent cave-in still visible if one knew what the topography had looked like before it had occurred. The entrance into the tunnel that led to the DuShane subcellars, small to begin with, was now a mere slit about an inch or so wide and maybe half a foot in length.

A half-grown coyote ambled along the chaparral at the base of the mountain, sniffing the ground for the scent of prey. This was the first time it had ventured off the mountain since the stench of danger and death had permeated the land below. Whatever had hunted it was no longer a threat.

When it reached the place where the opening had been, it paused. Looked up warily.

Then froze.

Something was wriggling through the crack. The clawed tip of a slender white stalk. Then another one. Impossibly, six more followed, and a bulbous body, somehow squeezing through the gap with the ease of toothpaste through a tube.

Trembling, the coyote lost control of its bladder, wanting to run but unable to make its limbs obey.

The jorōgumu *rose above it in spider form… then morphed into a woman in a white kimono with a red hourglass on the back.*

"Don't fear, little one," she said in a voice like silk. *"You are safe this night. I've already eaten."*

ACKNOWLEDGEMENTS

Writing a book during a major life move (relocating from San Francisco to Eureka in 2020) and then a pandemic was one of the most challenging things I've done in my life. I was pretty much burned out creatively, emotionally, and physically. Luckily, I had the support of my husband and sometimes writing partner, who spent many hours helping me brainstorm and put up with a lot of stress on my part. He also pitched in on a couple of scenes that needed a knowledge of linguistics that I do not have, and generously lent me his creativity when I needed it.

I also had the support of my incredibly patient and understanding Dark Editorial Overlord, Steve, who got me deadline extensions, worked with me through my burnout, and always made me feel that yes, I could finish this book.

As always, thank you to the rest of the marvelous Titan crew, and to my agent Jill Marsal.

Also, thank you to my sister Lisa, who also put up with me in full-on stress mode when I was writing *Hollywood Monsters*. I'm not very fun when I'm in full-on stress mode.

Thank you, Jonathan, for being an awesome and understanding boss who always encourages me to put my writing first, even when you have work you need me to do.

And a huge thank you to all my readers, who have been so patient waiting for this book to finally come out!

ABOUT THE AUTHOR

Dana Fredsti is an ex-B-movie actress with a background in theatrical combat (a skill she utilized in the film *Army of Darkness* as a sword-fighting Deadite and fight captain). Through seven-plus years of volunteering at EFBC/FCC, Dana's been kissed by tigers, and had her thumb sucked by an ocelot with nursing issues. She's addicted to bad movies and any book or film, good or bad, which includes zombies. She's the author of *The Spawn of Lilith*, *Blood Ink*, the *Ashley Parker* series (touted as *Buffy* meets *The Walking Dead*), the zombie noir novella *A Man's Gotta Eat What a Man's Gotta Eat*, and the cozy noir mystery *Murder for Hire: The Peruvian Pigeon*. With David Fitzgerald she is the co-author of *Time Shards*, *Shatter War*, and *Tempus Fury*, and she has stories in the *V-Wars: Shockwaves* and *Joe Ledger: Unstoppable* anthologies. She tweets at @zhadi1.

ALSO AVAILABLE FROM TITAN BOOKS

ANNO DRACULA
BY KIM NEWMAN

It is 1888 and Queen Victoria has remarried, taking as her new consort the Wallachian Prince infamously known as Count Dracula. His polluted bloodline spreads through London as its citizens increasingly choose to become vampires.

In the grim backstreets of Whitechapel, a killer known as 'Silver Knife' is cutting down vampire girls. The eternally young vampire Geneviere Dieudonne and Charles Beauregard of the Diogenes Club are drawn together as they both hunt the sadistic killer, bringing them ever closer to England's most bloodthirsty ruler yet.

"Compulsory reading... Glorious"
Neil Gaiman

TITANBOOKS.COM